WITH ALL MY HEART

ROMANCE COLLECTION

Five Nov...

Living Love t...

Love on the Mend • Karen Witemeyer
Out of the Storm • Jody Hedlund
Love by the Letter • Melissa Jagears
Gentleman of Her Dreams • Jen Turano
Appalachian Serenade • Sarah Loudin Thomas

BETHANYHOUSE

a division of Baker Publishing Group
Minneapolis, Minnesota

Published by Bethany House Publishers
11400 Hampshire Avenue South
Bloomington, Minnesota 55438
www.bethanyhouse.com

Bethany House Publishers is a division of
Baker Publishing Group, Grand Rapids, Michigan

Printed in the United States of America

ISBN 978-0-7642-1811-8

Library of Congress Control Number: 2016931074

The sonnet in Chapter Four of *Love by the Letter* is *Sonnet VI* from *Sonnets from the Portuguese* by Elizabeth Barrett Browning.

Scripture quotations in *Love on the Mend* and *Out of the Storm* are from the King James Version of the Bible. Scripture quotations in *Love By the Letter* are from Webster's Revision of the King James Version of the Bible.

These are works of fiction and/or historical reconstruction (*Out of the Storm*). In historical reconstruction, the appearances of certain historical figures are therefore inevitable; all other characters are products of the author's imagination, and any resemblance to actual events or persons, living or dead, is entirely coincidental. In works of fiction, the names, characters, incidents, and dialogues are products of the author's imagination and are not to be construed as real. Any resemblance to actual events or persons, living or dead, is entirely coincidental.

Cover design by Dan Thornberg, Design Source Creative Services

16 17 18 19 20 21 22   7 6 5 4 3 2 1

Contents

A FULL STEAM AHEAD NOVELLA

LOVE
ON THE
MEND

KAREN WITEMEYER

To all the medical professionals who minister to
our soldiers and to civilians ravaged by war:
May you never grow weary in doing good.
Thank you for your service,
and may God grant peace and rest to your souls.

Forbearing one another, and forgiving one another, if any man have a quarrel against any: even as Christ forgave you, so also do ye.

Colossians 3:13

1

COLD SPRING, TEXAS—1868

Peace and quiet. That's all he sought.

Dr. Jacob Sadler pulled his mount to a halt outside of town and braced himself against the tidal wave of memories cresting at the sight of the weathered wooden sign that announced he'd finally arrived home. He inhaled a deep breath and let it slip from between his lips on a slow, silent hiss.

Peace and quiet. After the horrors of the War Between the States—the endless barrage of wounded soldiers, amputated limbs, and death—they were the two commodities he most craved. The quiet he could have found in any small country practice, but finding peace required something more. Something it had taken him seventeen years to face. His past.

"Come on, Galen." Jacob nudged his buckskin into a walk. "No use putting it off any longer." He'd procrastinated enough, spending the past two years with Darius and Nicole Thornton down in Galveston.

He'd needed the time to recover from the war, and as always, the Thorntons had welcomed him with open arms. He owed them everything. They'd taken him in as a kid, sheltered him, loved him, and paid for his education. More than once, they'd asked to adopt him into their family, but he'd always refused. Seemed disloyal to his true parents. Better to simply earn his place in their household through work.

This last visit had been no different. He'd unloaded freight at the docks with Darius and helped Nicole in the evenings with the books, when he wasn't reading his medical journals. Though he'd been reluctant to set up a medical practice there, he had tended the sick and injured of the Renard Shipping crews and their families whenever the need arose and even delivered a baby when the local midwife had been occupied with another birthing.

It had been a satisfying two years, filled with joy and purpose. Yet beneath his surface contentment, a lingering turbulence roiled in his soul. A turbulence that wouldn't calm until he'd made peace with the past.

So when the town of Cold Spring advertised for a doctor in the Galveston paper, Jacob recognized the call for what it was—an invitation from the Lord to face his demons and finally put them to rest.

Jacob guided his mount to the west, along the fork that would take him by the churchyard instead of through the center of town. The churchyard . . . and the cemetery where his parents lay. Most likely his baby sister, too, though he'd not stayed long enough to discover if his drunk of an uncle had had the decency to see to her burial. The old reprobate was probably interred there himself by now. The biggest demon of them all.

A scream shattered the afternoon quiet, spooking Jacob's horse and chilling Jacob's blood. He scanned the roadside, then shifted his gaze farther afield, his knees tightening about

Galen's midsection. That had been no demon. The sound had been all too real. The cry of a woman or child.

The horse shied and pranced, tossing his head back and forth. "Be still, Galen," Jacob snapped as he took up the slack in the reins, his eyes still scouring the landscape for clues. Why did there have to be so many dad-blamed trees? He could barely make out the church through the loblolly pines. "Someone may be hurt."

Finally movement caught his eye. Well, more of a flash of color. Blue. There. At the church. Jacob kicked Galen into a canter, veering off the road in favor of a more direct route. The gelding surged through the trees as if sensing his master's urgency, finding his way over the choppy terrain and leaping over a fallen log before shuddering to a stop in the clearing outside the church.

Jacob slid off the horse's back and quickly moved to untie the doctoring bag he kept strapped to the saddle. "Hello!" he called as his fingers worked the leather strings free. "Is anyone hurt?"

A muffled shout came from inside the church. Jacob couldn't make out the words, but the words didn't matter. He had a direction.

Armed with his medical kit and his army revolver, he strode to the church entrance, taking the steps two at a time. A board groaned under his boot when he landed, and the banister wobbled, as if his nearness was enough to scare it out of its moorings. Jacob jerked his gaze upward, only then noting the shutters that hung askew and the whistle of wind blowing through the weather-warped wood. What had happened to the cheery whitewashed building where he had worshipped all those years ago?

Gone. Just like his family.

A second scream spurred Jacob into the building.

"No, Mollie. Stop! It hurts!"

Jacob rushed down the aisle, not waiting for his eyes to adjust to the dimmer light. Which explained why he tripped over the rope strung across the floor at ankle height. Tucking his medical bag into his midsection to protect the glass vials inside, he stumbled forward and jammed his shoulder against a pew.

A groan echoed in the rafters, but it wasn't his. The sound reverberated at a higher pitch.

"Mollie?" A panicked, weeping call.

"I'm fine, Adam. Don't worry. Some fella just tripped over the rope and gave my middle a bit of a squeeze." The tightness of her voice had Jacob immediately extricating himself from the rope. The poor girl sounded as if he'd inadvertently cut off her air supply.

Shadows began to take more distinct shape as his vision sharpened. Jacob followed the line of the rope. Knotted around the base of a pew, over the floor and . . . along a pair of prone legs draped in plain cotton petticoats and a blue-striped skirt. The rest of the young lady's form was not to be found, having disappeared into the hole gaping in the sanctuary's floor.

Not wanting his greater weight to strain the already weakened floorboards, Jacob hung back and lowered himself to the ground near the woman's feet, setting his doctor's bag on the nearest pew. "What can I do to help?"

"Man the rope." She lifted her upper half and scooted backward a bit on the floor, before twisting to get a look at him. Disheveled, dark blond hair spilling from a messy bun veiled her features before she blew the tresses aside with an impatient huff. Turning her gaze on him, she scanned him briefly, then nodded. "You'll do."

"Do for what?" he couldn't help asking, a little bemused.

He'd expected the woman to rush at him, pleading tearfully for him to rescue the boy who'd obviously fallen through the floor, but she apparently intended to remain in charge of the situation.

"Hoisting us back up, of course." Clasping the rope tied about her midsection, she pulled herself around to a sitting position. "I would be down there with Adam right now if I thought I'd be strong enough to climb back up with him, but I couldn't risk getting us both trapped down there. But now you're here, so there's no reason to delay." Like a rabbit slipping free of a snare, she wriggled the rope past her hips and down her legs until the loop pushed free of her feet. Then without so much as a word of warning, she flipped to her stomach, slid her legs over the edge, and disappeared into the hole.

Jacob lunged for her, but his hands grasped only air. Thankfully, the crazy woman had the sense to slow her descent by dangling from her fingertips a moment before dropping the rest of the way. Thrusting his head over the side, Jacob spotted her scurrying over to a boy who lay huddled on the dirt floor. He released a breath. She seemed hale and hearty. The boy, on the other hand, did not. Even with the heavy shadows, Jacob could see the unnatural angle of the boy's left leg. A break. Hopefully a clean one. If it was compound . . . Well, he prayed it wasn't.

"Toss me the rope," the little general commanded. "We need to get Adam out of here. He's looking awfully pale."

The kid was probably going into shock. "Are his eyes focused?"

"What does that matter? His leg's busted. We gotta get him out and take him to Doc Bradshaw's." She moved around behind the boy and anchored her arms beneath his. "Get me that rope, mister."

"Don't move him!"

Jacob's warning came too late. Mollie had already lifted Adam's arms and dragged him a few inches, when Adam's scream stopped her. The high-pitched shriek ricocheted through the abandoned church like a tortured soul seeking salvation.

Mollie's face tipped up to find Jacob. Tears rolled down her cheeks. "Please, mister." Her voice trembled. "I need the rope."

"I'll get it," Jacob promised, the dent in the young woman's composure softening his heart. Thankfully, his brain remained firm. No way would he be hoisting that kid up like a fish at the end of a line. Too many things could go wrong. Not to mention the excruciating pain it would cause him. He wouldn't bother telling Mollie that, though. She'd just argue about it and then try to manage things herself.

He knew the type. Doers. Impossible to ask them to sit back and wait. A good trait when it came to getting things done—a bad one when patience could mean the difference between saving a leg and amputating.

So he'd give her something to do.

"I need you to lay the boy down on his back. Gently," Jacob instructed in his best *doctor's orders* tone. "He's going into shock. We need to help his body relax. Be careful of his leg. If the movement pains him too much, sit behind him and lay his head across your lap. Loosen his collar. It'll make breathing easier. I'll need to splint that leg before we can move him."

"But you can't do that from up there."

Jacob smiled. "That's why I'm coming down."

Mollie shook her head so hard, what was left of her bun tumbled around her shoulders. "You can't! You have to pull us up!"

"Easy, Mollie." Jacob shushed her. "There's bound to be a cellar door outside somewhere. I'll come in through there. We can take Adam out the same way."

16

"Don't you think I already thought of that? It was the first thing I checked." She glared up at him. "That door is chained and locked. You can't get in that way."

"Oh, I'll get in. Don't worry."

She spun away from him then, muttering something that sounded remarkably like *arrogant toad* before returning to Adam's side and gently laying him on his back. The boy whimpered at the movement but didn't protest. Mollie stroked his brow and murmured soft, reassuring words. There was nothing soft about the glare she shot at Jacob, though.

"Don't just stand there." She shooed him with her free hand. "South side. Behind the parson's apartment. We'll be here when you get back."

Jacob grinned. He couldn't help it. He'd always loved fireworks. "I'll see you when I get *through*."

2

"Boneheaded stranger," Mollie grumbled under her breath when the man's face finally disappeared from above her.

Not that I'm complaining, Lord, she mentally amended. *I appreciate that you sent help. Truly. It just would have been nice if the fella weren't so all-fired sure he knew best. Adam ain't got the time to waste.*

Mollie sighed and turned her attention back to her charge. Poor kid. He was only ten, too young to know the risks of playing in an old building. She was nearly twice his age. Full-grown. Responsible. So why hadn't she made the church off-limits during their game of hide-and-seek? She'd known the place was run-down. Should have guessed it'd be dangerous, too. But she hadn't.

All he'd done was drop down from the rafters after she'd discovered his hiding place, and the floor had completely given way. She could still hear the crack of the wood ringing in her ears . . . and the crack of Adam's leg before his scream drowned out all other sound.

When she'd found the cellar door locked and chained, she'd

nearly panicked before finding that length of rope in the storage closet. She'd tied all her hopes on that rope and now that stubborn, know-it-all man wouldn't even toss the end down.

"I'm going to get you out of here, Adam." She smoothed the hair off his forehead, alarmed by how clammy his skin had become. "You'll be all right. I promise."

Please let him be all right.

Adam moaned but made no effort to speak. Was he losing consciousness? Mollie's heart thumped against her ribs. He had to be all right. He and Uncle Curtis were the closest thing she had to family. She'd never forgive herself if—

Bang!

Mollie jumped. *What on earth?* Had that been a gunshot? She swiveled to look behind her.

Something crashed. Then a shaft of light penetrated the darkness and illuminated the outline of a man climbing down the cellar stairs.

Her jaw slackened. The boneheaded fella had actually done it. He must've shot the lock clean off the chain.

He marched straight up to her and dropped a coil beside her hip. "Here's your rope." It hit the dirt with a thud. She expected a smirk or a gleam of gloating in his eyes, but he didn't even look at her. His attention zeroed in on Adam. "I'll need wood for a splint. All this is rotted," he said, scowling at the debris scattered around them. "See what loose boards you can find laying around. No nails."

Well, of course, no nails. She wasn't an idiot. Mollie pushed to her feet, a scowl scrunching her forehead. Just because he succeeded in breaking down the cellar door didn't mean he could come in and start taking over. Adam was *her* responsibility, and she wasn't about to let some stranger mess with his leg. She'd seen what could happen when a bone wasn't properly set. On the streets in Galveston, where she'd grown up, many of the beggars had been crippled by similar injuries that had healed poorly. She wouldn't risk the same thing happening to Adam.

Fisting her fingers in her skirt, she planted herself in front of the stranger. "We should wait for the doctor to tend his leg."

The man glared at her. "Lady, I *am* the doctor." He raised his hand and jiggled a black bag. A doctor's bag.

Mollie sucked in a breath. The Lord had not only sent her a man who could help get them out of the cellar, but he'd sent her a doctor. An honest-to-goodness doctor. One who wasn't ancient like Dr. Bradshaw but young and strong and . . . down-right handsome.

She glanced away before he caught her staring. Really, a man's eyes should not be that blue. Especially not when his hair was so dark. And here she'd been complaining.

"Hurry and fetch those boards," he repeated as he hunkered down next to Adam, *her* looks obviously not distracting him in the slightest. "I'll need your help setting the leg after I examine him."

At least he didn't expect her to stand around and wring her hands. That would save her from having to disabuse him of the notion later. After giving a quick nod to let him know she'd heard, Mollie turned and jogged toward the exit. She was at the top of the stairs when she heard him introduce himself to Adam as Dr. Jacob Somebody. His last name failed to carry to her, but she didn't let that slow her step. Adam needed her.

Sprinting around to the front of the building, she took stock of her choices. Should she rip out a stair? Pull down the shutters that were already unhinged? How would she remove the nails? She had no hammer. A rock, maybe?

She spun back toward the yard, scanning the ground. That's when she spotted the large fallen pine bough. It must have broken off during a storm. Dead and dry, it lay abandoned, just begging to be useful. Well, today was the day.

Not knowing for sure how long the splint would need to be, Mollie decided to break off several branches of varying lengths and thicknesses. She snapped them free with her foot, then stomped off the needle-bearing ends, doing her best to even out the jagged edges until only a smooth, straight piece remained. Once she'd collected five acceptable sticks, she grabbed them up and hurried back to the cellar.

"I've got the wood," she called as she trotted down the stairs. "Where do you . . ." Her mouth went completely dry at the sight that greeted her.

Dr. Jacob was tearing a piece of white cotton into strips. White cotton that must have belonged to his shirt at one time, for the man was bare to the waist. Well, not completely bare. He'd put his black vest back on. Not that it covered much. She still saw every play of his muscles as he tore the cotton. Very fine muscles, she couldn't help but notice.

"Bring it over here." He pointed to a spot on the floor beside his open medical bag.

Mollie swallowed hard, ordered her feet to move, and then complied. Forcing her gaze away from the fine pair of shoulders and biceps on display, she turned her attention to Adam. He lay still, appeared to be unconscious, but his chest continued to rise and fall. His left trouser leg had been cut from the hem to above the knee and spread wide. Blood stained his skin and a piece of white bone jabbed out of his flesh. Mollie dropped the wood and covered her mouth with her hand.

"You're not going to faint on me, are you? I thought you

were tougher than that." The doctor's disgruntled tone lit her temper.

She pulled her hand down and stiffened her spine. "Of course I'm not going to faint. I just didn't know the break was so bad. It caught me by surprise—that's all."

"Well, get over your surprise and help me." He gestured for her to station herself by Adam's head. "I administered chloroform, so he won't feel the pain, but I'll still need you to hold him steady. I'm going to have to tug firmly on this leg to get it back into place."

Mollie slid onto the floor and pressed her hands gently against Adam's slim shoulders. Then she nodded at the doctor. "I'm ready."

He met her gaze, his eyes hard and confident, though there seemed a touch of compassion there, too. As if he knew how difficult it was for her to see Adam in such circumstances.

"I've sprayed the bone and surrounding tissue with a carbolic acid solution that will reduce the risk of infection," he explained as he took hold of Adam's ankle, "but it's essential that we get him to the surgery so I can clean his wound more thoroughly and get it closed as soon as possible."

He glanced back up at her. "Are you ready?"

Mollie pressed firmly against Adam's shoulders, pinning him to the ground. "Yes."

Then, with a firm yank, he pulled Adam's lower leg and twisted. Once the bone edges were in place, he gently released the leg and immediately began splinting it. Seeing what he was about, Mollie moved to his side and handed him the strips he'd torn from his shirt. He accepted her help with a nod, and in a manner of minutes they had Adam's leg braced.

Doctor Jacob closed up his medical bag, shoved it into her

hands, and bent to gather a still-unconscious Adam into his arms. "My horse is out front. Tie my bag to the saddle and wait for me."

Mollie grabbed the doctor's bag and dashed off. If the doc thought time was the enemy, then she'd not waste a single moment. She found his horse munching on a bit of grass beneath a stand of pines and took charge of the reins. By the time she had the bag secured behind the cantle, Doctor Jacob had arrived.

"Do you think you can hold him for a moment?" He examined her slim stature with a doubtful look. "I can't mount with the boy, so I'll need you to hand him up to me."

Mollie straightened her shoulders. "I'm stronger than I look, Doc. I'll hold him as long as you need me to."

He raised a brow but offered no argument. After gesturing for her to come close to the horse's side, he handed Adam into her arms.

She'd often carried Adam around on her back when they'd played, and he'd never seemed very heavy. But his limp form dragged at her arms like solid lead. Not that she'd let the doctor know that. She braced her knees and leaned backward to take as much of his weight on her chest as possible. Thankfully, Doctor Jacob mounted swiftly and reached down for Adam in no more than a handful of heartbeats. Still, her arms burned something dreadful as she tried to lift him up. The doctor had no such issues. He bent sideways in the saddle and collected Adam from her as easily as if she were handing him a pair of saddlebags.

"Take the reins," the doc said once he was settled with Adam. "Lead Galen to town at a walk. We don't want to jostle this leg too much."

Mollie did as instructed, taking the most direct route to Dr.

Bradshaw's office. They reached the clinic less than ten minutes later. Mollie hurried to tie the new doc's horse to the hitching post, casting a worried glance over her shoulder at Adam's limp form.

Dr. Bradshaw stepped out onto the porch, drying his hands with a white towel. His smile of greeting faded as he caught sight of Adam.

"Mollie?" He tossed the towel over the porch railing and headed down the steps. "What happened?"

"I need to use your surgery," Doctor Jacob announced without so much as a *howdy*. He carefully slid from Galen's back, Adam still in his arms. "The boy's got a compound fracture of the tibia. Bone's been set, but I need to flush the wound and check for fragments before I suture him."

Dr. Bradshaw frowned. "You'd be better off just amputating. The boy's gonna lose that leg anyway. And he could lose his life if infection sets in, which it always does with this type of break."

Mollie's fingers froze on the saddle straps she'd been untying. Lose his leg? Adam? No! He was too young to face a life without being able to walk or run or ride a horse. But losing a leg was better than losing his life.

"I'm not amputating," Doctor Jacob growled, his face nearly savage in his denial. "I sawed off more limbs than I care to count during the war, and I'm not about to subject this child to that fate."

"Then I'm not letting you into my surgery." Dr. Bradshaw crossed his pudgy arms over his chest and glared mulishly, his cheeks reddening around his white sideburns. "I won't be a party to a procedure that will end up costing that boy his life just because the war left a bad taste in your mouth."

"Haven't you heard of Dr. Lister's advancements with carbolic acid? I've already started the treatment and have every confidence we can save the boy's leg. If infection does set in, there will be time to amputate later should it become necessary."

Dr. Bradshaw's face had progressed from red to an alarming shade of purple. "How dare you question my professional judgment? I've been a respected physician for thirty years. My experience is vastly superior to you and this Lister person. I've heard of his theories. Poppycock, every one of them. Infections are caused by miasma, and once the body is opened up to this bad air, infection is certain to follow. I suggest, sir, that you hand that boy into my care at once and go about your business."

"My business *is* this boy." The new doc shifted his hold on Adam and edged closer to the clinic steps. "I'd hoped we could work together for a week or so as a matter of professional courtesy as I got settled, but I see now that I'm just going to have to ask you to step aside. I'm relieving you of duty, Dr. Bradshaw."

Mollie's gaze bounced from one man to the other, her pulse throbbing as tensions escalated. Questions volleyed inside her as well. What treatment would be best for Adam? Was Dr. Bradshaw's suggestion the safest thing, or could new techniques spare Adam's leg?

"Who do think you are to order me about?" Dr. Bradshaw demanded.

"I'm Dr. Jacob Sadler, new town physician hired on by the Cold Spring city council. I'm your replacement. Now step aside. I have a patient to tend."

Sadler? Mollie's mind spun so fast she felt a little dizzy. Was his name some kind of crazy coincidence, or could he be—?

"Mollie?" The new doc turned to look at her. His face remained hard, but a touch of vulnerability softened the edges of his eyes. "I'm going to need your help."

"I'm right behind ya, Doc." She wasn't about to leave Adam. But even if Doc Sadler had been fixin' to treat a complete stranger, she'd still follow him up those stairs. The man oozed self-assurance, yet his eyes had pleaded for understanding. As if he needed her to believe in him. *Her.* Mollie Tate. As if her opinion mattered.

Dr. Bradshaw sputtered but sidled out of the way when the new doc climbed the steps with Adam in his arms. Mollie made to follow, but Dr. Bradshaw grasped her elbow as she passed.

"Don't be a party to this, Mollie Tate," he hissed. "He'll kill that boy. You mark my words."

She patted the old man's shoulder while she tugged her sleeve free of his hold. "I know you mean well, Dr. Bradshaw. But if there's a chance to save Adam's leg, we've got to try." She glanced through the clinic's open doorway. "I believe Doc Sadler can do it, and I aim to give him all the help I can."

"God have mercy on the lot of you, then," the old doc grumbled.

Mollie just smiled and nodded. "Yes, sir. I'll be praying that he does."

3

Mollie's quiet statement of confidence filled an empty place in Jacob he hadn't been aware existed. He'd paused only a moment in the entry to get his bearings, but it was long enough for her words to wash over him. And what a gift they had been. Buoyed by her faith, he strode through the parlor area and located the surgery in a back room. He laid Adam down on the table and proceeded to wash his hands with soap and water thanks to an ewer and basin left on the counter of a medical cabinet. Soft footsteps behind him announced Mollie's arrival.

"In my bag is an instrument kit," he stated. "Open it and set it on the counter while I cut away the rest of Adam's trouser leg."

The girl made a perfect nurse, following his instructions, anticipating his needs, all without gabbing his ear off with point-less questions. After scrubbing her own hands clean, she set out his instruments, sprayed them with the carbolic acid solution, and then handed them to him the moment he requested them. In short order, they had the wound clean and sutured.

"Look in the cabinets for some bandages." Jacob nodded

toward the glass-doored shelves along the wall as he washed the last of the blood from his hands.

"Linen or cotton?" Mollie asked. "I see both."

"Linen. The more porous the better."

She scrunched her nose as she compared two sets of linen bandages. "Does that mean you want bigger holes?"

Jacob hid his grin. "Yep."

It was so refreshing to deal with someone who cared more about getting things right than hiding a lack of knowledge. Maybe he should offer her a job working in the clinic. Heaven knew she had enough energy to keep the place going. And judging by the way she interacted with both Adam and the bristling Dr. Bradshaw, she had a nurturing temperament that would put folks at ease. Not to mention her lack of squeamishness. She hadn't faltered once during the surgery, had calmly kept pace with him. Yes, she'd definitely be an asset.

He glanced at her from the corner of his eye as he retrieved the gypsum powder from his bag. It wouldn't hurt matters any that she was nice to look at. Eyes that hinted at mischief when they weren't clouded with worry over the boy in her care, full lips that curved easily, and a slender figure bearing enough curves to turn a man's head. He should know. They'd turned his head often enough. Not that he'd allowed her to distract him. On the way to town, though, it'd been impossible not to notice the sway of her hips or her willowy waist as she led Galen down the path in front of him.

"Here you go, Doc." She set several rolls of linen bandages on the tray beside his elbow.

"Thanks." Jacob cleared his throat. All right, so maybe he'd allowed her to distract him just a touch. "We'll need a sponge and clean water as well."

While she dumped out the old water and poured new, Jacob unrolled the first bandage and began rubbing the gypsum powder into it.

"Is that some kind of medicine to keep the wound from getting infected?" Mollie leaned close, peering over his shoulder. Evidence of other curves made themselves known.

Jacob stepped closer to the table. "No. This will make a plaster. Once we get Adam's leg wrapped, we'll moisten the bandages and work the gypsum until it forms a thick casing. When it dries, it will harden and protect the leg, keeping the bones in place until they heal." He began working the powder into the second bandage. Mollie came around to his side and started in on a third, mimicking his technique.

"I suppose if it keeps the leg away from that bad air that Doc Bradshaw was talking about," she said, brushing his fingers as she reached for more gypsum, "it might help keep infection out as well as keeping the bones together."

He tilted his head to consider her more closely. "An intelligent observation, Miss Tate. Keeping the air out, as well as dirt and other impurities, can only help."

Pink tinged her cheeks, but it was the grin that blossomed across her face that stilled his heart. Their eyes met and held for a moment before she returned her attention to the bandages. "I'm glad Adam will have the extra protection."

"He'll still need to stay off the leg for at least six weeks, maybe longer, and he won't be able to get the plaster wet. However, as long as we don't find any sign of infection in the first few days, I expect he'll recover."

Her hands stilled, and her gaze once again found his. "Thank you, Dr. Sadler. For what you did at the church, for what you've done here, for . . . everything."

This time Jacob was the one to turn away first. "Yes, well, the true healing remains in God's hands."

"Of course." She laid her fingers atop his. His entire body stilled. "But God is the one who put you in the right place at the right time. He's working through you, and for that, I am grateful."

Mollie pulled back her hand and reached for another bandage. It took Jacob a moment to recover. Not just from her touch, but from her words. How often had he prayed for God to work through him to heal those who sought his care? Yet the flood of wounded during the war had drained the optimism from his soul. So much death. So many left maimed—by his hand. It had carved gouges of doubt into his faith, left him questioning his calling.

Hearing Mollie credit him as being a conduit for the Lord's healing bound up those still-oozing inner wounds in a way he'd been helpless to accomplish on his own during his two-year sabbatical from regular practice.

"Would you consider staying on as my nurse?" Keeping her near suddenly seemed of paramount importance. "You could organize the clinic inventory, assist me with patients, perhaps do some cleaning when things are slow. I'd pay you, of course."

Her eyes went wide, and she blinked several times before attempting to answer. "You don't even know me, Doc. Why would you—?"

"Can you read and write?" he interrupted, not wanting to answer her question.

"Y-yes."

"Then the offer stands. I know everything else that I need to know. You're good with people, you don't faint at the sight of blood, and you're a quick study." Jacob set to work wrapping the gypsum bandages around Adam's leg. "You don't have to answer right away. Just consider it. All right?"

Mollie stared at the new doc, too numb to do much more than nod and hand him another bandage. *Be his nurse?* Mercy, how she wanted to say yes. To work beside the man who'd rescued Adam, the man who actually saw qualities to admire when he looked at her. No fat pocket had ever tempted her more.

And that was the problem. Dr. Sadler didn't know her history, didn't know how her light fingers used to pick plump pockets along the docks of Galveston. She couldn't accept his offer without revealing the truth of her past, not with a clean conscience. Yet once he learned the truth, the light of respect glowing in his eyes would dull into pity or, worse, contempt.

Uncle Curtis had saved her from that life, had given her a home, had introduced her to Jesus and a forgiveness that could take a stained life and make it whiter than snow. She couldn't dishonor such a gift by burying the truth. Maybe she should just turn the offer down. Keep her distance. But in the past hour, she'd felt a part of something that mattered. Not that keeping house for Mrs. Peabody didn't matter. It was honorable work and provided her with a place to stay. But working in the clinic? She'd be helping to save lives, to ease pain and suffering. A chance to be a part of that . . . well, it might be worth the risk.

"Hand me that basin and sponge, will you?" Dr. Sadler tucked in the end of the last bandage, then tipped his head in the direction of the basin of clean water she'd prepared earlier. His hands were white from the plaster dust, as were hers.

31

Mollie grabbed a towel to wipe off the worst of the dust before handing him the basin, but she needn't have bothered. He plunged his hands into the water, dust and all, grabbed the sponge, and started moistening the bandages. A paste formed, and he molded and shaped it until it looked the way he wanted. Then he propped Adam's foot on a thick cushion so air could flow around all sides of the bandages.

"It will need to set and harden before he can be moved," the new doc said as he washed the white plaster from his hands and forearms. A dusting of white powder had even found his chest, standing out in stark contrast between the closures of his black vest and tempting her to brush at with her towel. Mollie gnawed on her bottom lip. She really needed to find the man a shirt.

Doc Bradshaw had already cleared out all his personal belongings from the clinic a week ago, so there wasn't much chance of finding anything in the bureau drawers. The new doc hadn't had a carpetbag or anything tied to his horse, so he must have arranged for his things to be transported from Liberty through one of the freighters. Which meant they likely wouldn't arrive until later tonight. Maybe Mrs. Peabody would let the doc borrow one of her late husband's shirts. Or Uncle Curtis . . .

"I take it you know the boy's family?" the new doc asked. "His parents will need to be informed of what happened. I'm sure they'll want to be by his side when he awakes."

"He doesn't have any parents," Mollie said absently, still preoccupied by the shirt issue. "He lives with Uncle Curtis just outside of town. I can—"

The sound of the front door flying open and banging against the wall cut off the rest of her sentence.

"Mollie? Where are you, girl? I just heard about Adam." Uncle Curtis's deep, gravelly voice echoed through the small house.

"Back here," she called, the panic in his tone urging her to rush to the surgery door and pull it open.

Uncle Curtis hated to see his kids hurt. Shoot, the man had cried when he'd had to pull a bee stinger from her shoulder when she'd been twelve. Every time she winced he'd apologized, as if it were somehow his fault that the critter had stung her. "Adam's fine," she assured him. "He busted his leg, but the new doc set it and has it all wrapped up tight."

Uncle Curtis lumbered forward, his stiff gait awkward as he maneuvered around the parlor furniture. Mollie took his arm to help him into the room, but he stiffened and halted in the doorway.

He swallowed slowly, his gaze glued to the new doc. A gaze shining with regret and a longing so stark it shocked her . . . and nearly broke her heart. "Hello, Jacob."

She swiveled her attention back to Dr. Sadler. His face had drained of color, and his hand grasped the cabinet behind him as if it were the only thing keeping him on his feet.

"I thought you'd be dead by now." The words emerged barely above a whisper, yet Uncle Curtis heard them.

The older man's lips curved slightly in a sad, lopsided smile. "I can't tell you how many times I wished I was."

Uncle Curtis? He was the most hope-filled man Mollie had ever met. What had happened between these two?

Neither spoke again. They just stared at each other, letting the silence grow so oppressive she could feel its weight bearing down upon her.

Enough. "Come this way, Uncle Curtis," Mollie said, tugging his arm. "I'm sure you're wanting to see Adam. He's resting now but should wake soon. Why don't I bring in a chair so you can sit with him?"

"No!" Dr. Sadler lunged away from the cabinet and blocked their path. "He's not getting anywhere near this child!"

Uncle Curtis stopped, not a hint of the shock reverberating through Mollie visible on his face. "Jacob, I'm his guardian. He lives at the farm with me."

"Yeah, well, we lived at the farm with you, too, *Uncle Curtis*, but you didn't give two figs for our well-being, did you?"

Mollie frowned at the snide tone. Where had her heroic, dedicated doctor gone?

"You *shot* Emma!" he shouted.

Mollie gasped. *No*. Uncle Curtis would never hurt anyone. Never!

"My baby sister died because of you." His hands fisted at his sides, and he took a single menacing step forward. "Get out of my clinic."

Uncle Curtis nodded but held his ground. "I've been waiting seventeen years for you to get that accusation off your chest, Jake. Maybe now that the boil's been lanced we can finally see about healing the wound."

Mollie's heart beat a painful rhythm against her ribs. Why wasn't he denying it? That poor little girl. Uncle Curtis couldn't be responsible for her death. Could he? The man had rescued her, raised her. She knew his character, his kind nature. There had to be more to the story. Some explanation. Maybe . . . maybe there'd been a horrible accident that couldn't have been helped. Yes, an accident. That must have been what happened. So why didn't Uncle Curtis just clear up the misunderstanding?

She silently begged him to explain, but the man she loved

like a father simply patted her hand and slipped his arm free of her hold. "Watch over Adam for me, my girl," he called over his shoulder as he limped back through the parlor. "I'll be back to try again later."

The clinic door closed softly behind him.

4

Jacob sagged against the far wall of the surgery for support as strength seeped from his body. His uncle was alive.

When he'd decided to return home to make peace with his past, he'd wanted to reclaim part of what he'd lost. His parents' old homestead had sat neglected for eighteen years. He wanted to restore it, bring back the cozy home he remembered— perhaps make it into a place where he could start a family of his own. Doctoring would require him to office in town, but he could work on the cabin in the evenings once he got his practice established.

And the graves of his family. They needed to be tended by someone who'd loved them, not strangers. He'd thought he was ready to face the memories, to let go of the bitterness he'd carried for so long. But then again, he'd also thought he'd only need to mumble a few words of forgiveness over Curtis Sadler's grave to be done with it. He never imagined coming face-to-face with the man.

Jacob rubbed a trembling hand over his face as he struggled

to regain his emotional footing. The eruption of rage had taken him by surprise.

So did the small fist that collided with his chest.

"You cold-hearted scoundrel." Another fist connected. "No one treats Uncle Curtis like that in my presence," Mollie stomped on his foot to punctuate her assertion. "Not even you. Tossing him out like someone's garbage, refusing to let him near Adam. It was disgraceful, and I won't stand for it. Curtis Sadler is the most decent, God-fearing man I know. He—"

"Curtis Sadler is a roaring drunk and a child killer!" Jacob shoved away from the wall and raised himself to his full height in order to glower Mollie into silence.

It didn't work.

"I've never seen Uncle Curtis drink so much as a drop of spirits." She glowered right back at him, apparently not caring a whit that she had to crane her neck to do so. "He won't even keep a bottle of whiskey in the kitchen cupboard for medicinal purposes."

That sounded nothing like the uncle he remembered. But what difference did it make if the man had sobered up? He'd still killed Emma.

"I don't know what happened to your sister, but I'm sure it had to be an accident." Her tone softened and for a moment he thought she might try to offer him comfort, but he shoved away from her before he could find out.

"Uncle Curtis loves children," she insisted, her voice following him, making his head pound with words he didn't want to hear. Jacob turned his back and braced his arms against the counter. "He would never intentionally harm a child," she said. "He saves them. He rescued me from Galveston when I was nine and brought me here. I was an orphan, living on the streets. He fed me, clothed me, took me to church every Sunday, saw to my schoolin'. Once I was old enough, he found me a job with Mrs. Peabody. I clean for her and fix her meals in exchange for room and board and a few coins at the end of each month. Don't you see? He's treated me like family. He does the same for Adam and the other kids out at the ranch."

"Well, then, he's been more family to you than he ever was to me." Jacob's muscles bunched so tightly, he feared they'd snap. The man she described sounded too much like the Thorntons. He refused to lump Darius and Nicole, the kindest people he'd ever known, into the same category as Curtis Sadler. The picture Mollie painted of him—all light and flowers and happiness—was wrong. It needed a slash of darkness, of reality.

"My mother and father contracted influenza the year I turned eight," he said without turning to look at her. "They died, leaving me and my sister to live with Uncle Curtis at his farm. He'd been close to my dad and took his death hard. Emma and I reminded him too much of our pa. To the point he could barely stand to look at us. So we learned to stay out of his way, especially when he turned to drink for comfort. Which happened more and more often as the weeks went by.

"The farm suffered from neglect. As did we. Uncle Curtis started spending his days at the saloon in town, leaving us to fend for ourselves. I did my best to look out for Emma, to take care of her, but one day Uncle Curtis came home earlier than expected. Drunk as usual, he slid off his horse and started hollering about a coyote that he'd heard was in the area and how we had to protect the stock. He staggered around the yard and pulled his gun, aiming at imaginary coyotes. He shot once in the air, and Toby, his old hound dog, loped out of the barn and started barking. Emma ran after the dog, trying to get him to hush."

Jacob closed his eyes. The scene emerged behind his lids as it had unfolded that day, every horrifying detail burned into his memory as if a hot iron had seared it there, leaving a permanent scar. Emma's dark hair blowing in the wind, her chubby little hands reaching desperately for Toby's neck, the tears running down her cheeks.

"Uncle never saw her. All his alcohol-laced mind could see was a wild coyote coming to kill his chickens. He shot at Toby and hit Emma. She died instantly. I left the same day and never looked back."

"How horrible." The shocked whisper brought Jacob's head around. "I can't even imagine . . ." She wiped a tear as it rolled down her cheek. "I'm so, so sorry." Mollie touched him then, her hand gentle and light on his arm. He flinched but didn't pull away. "For you *and* for him."

What? Jacob jerked away from her touch. The soft comfort of it had turned to scalding fire at her words. "Sorry for *him?*" How could she say that? He was the one responsible. He didn't deserve sympathy. He deserved punishment. "It's his fault Emma is dead!"

"Yes." Her eyes pled with him to understand. "Can't you imagine how much worse that must have made him feel? Not only did he lose his beloved brother's child, but he pulled the trigger. The guilt must have nearly killed him."

"I wish it had." The bitter words escaped before he could stop them, and the shock of hearing them aloud made him stagger back a step. He was a doctor, one who saved lives and fended off sickness. How could he wish death on someone? It violated everything he believed in. Yet, for one vile moment, he'd meant it. God forgive him.

He hung his head and covered his face with his hand, half

expecting his uncle's defender to start pummeling him again. Heaven knew he deserved it. But she didn't. No, she actually stepped closer and touched his arm again.

"Why'd you take the doctorin' job here in Cold Spring?"

He didn't answer, didn't trust himself to hold back from spewing more poison.

"You returned for a reason, didn't you?" she prodded, compassion lacing her voice. Yet there was a note of challenge there, as well. "To put your past to rest."

Again he held his tongue.

"God has blessed you with the chance not only to forgive the wrong done against you, but to mend what was broken." Her hand slipped from his arm. Soft footsteps echoed behind him as she moved toward the surgery table. "Just as you brought together the broken bones in Adam's leg, God has brought you and Uncle Curtis together. It will take time, but healing will come if you let it. If you keep your heart clean from the dirt of bitterness so that infection won't set in."

Ha! It was too late for that. Infection had festered in his heart for seventeen years.

"Jesus can heal any wound, redeem any past," she said as if she'd heard his thoughts. "That's what Uncle Curtis taught me." Her shoes clicked lightly against the floorboards again, this time heading for the door. "That's what Uncle Curtis *shows* me, every day. He's a changed man, Jacob. A godly man. A man consumed with doing good."

The door creaked on its hinges when she eased it open. Jacob waited for the sound of her footsteps walking through it, but it didn't come.

"You know," she said. "A sinful woman with an ugly past once anointed Jesus's feet in the house of a religious man, and when that man scolded the Teacher for allowing someone so sinful to touch him, Jesus told him that those who have been forgiven much, love much; and those who have been forgiven little, love little. Uncle Curtis loves much, and that includes you, Jacob Sadler. Don't amputate when a little carbolic acid solution has the power to preserve something precious."

And with that clever twist of his words, she left.

Mollie spied Uncle Curtis's wagon exactly where she expected it to be, in front of the Cold Spring church. Unlike the abandoned building outside of town that was falling apart, this red brick church with its gleaming white steps and modest steeple seemed to throw its arms wide in welcome to any who might pass by. Mollie opened the door and slipped inside. With it being a Monday, the place stood empty. Except for the man in the third pew on the right.

Making her way down the aisle, Mollie smiled at the circular hat mark creasing Uncle Curtis's salt-and-pepper hair. She'd always known something awful lurked in his past. He'd hinted at it but never told her the details. Now that she knew, she needed to show him that her affection for him hadn't changed—that he was still her Uncle Curtis and always would be.

Hesitating only a moment, she slid into the pew beside him. His head was bent, his eyes closed. She folded her hands in her lap and joined him in prayer—first for Adam's recovery, then for the more delicate mending of two men broken apart by tragedy.

Not wanting to disturb him, she held her tongue, choosing instead to reach between them and clasp his hand. His knuckles were rough and dry, his skin weathered from a lifetime of farm work, but when he squeezed her fingers, she couldn't think of anything that felt more wonderful.

"It's true, Moll," he murmured, his fingers tightening even more around hers. "I was a drunk, and I killed my own niece."

"On accident," she insisted.

He finally turned to look at her, his face more haggard than she could recall ever seeing it. "Don't let me off the hook so easily, gal. Emma died because of choices I made. Choices to drown my grief in whiskey instead of turning to God for comfort, choices to hide from my responsibilities instead of facing them like a man, choices to let two innocent children—my *brother's* children—pay the price for my weakness. I might have been crazy with drink when I pulled that trigger, but I was of sound enough mind when I made the choices that led up to that moment. Everything Jacob said about me was true."

He pulled his hand free of her and braced his forearms across his thighs. He hung his head low, reminding her of the way Jacob had acted after saying those horrible words she was sure he regretted.

"It might have been true then. But it's not any longer." Mollie turned sideways in the pew to face him more fully. "You aren't that man anymore, Uncle Curtis. You aren't the man who took Emma away. You're the man who gives lost children a home, the man who rescued me."

"Ah, Mollie. How did this worthless reprobate ever manage to find such a gift of sunshine as I found in you?"

She grinned and slid her fingers into his pocket. "I believe I found you—or your watch, anyway." Mollie deftly pulled his watch from his vest pocket and held it out in front of him.

Uncle Curtis laughed and leaned back against the bench. "That you did, you little scamp." He snatched the timepiece from her palm and shoved it back into his pocket. "One of the best things that ever happened to me."

Mollie smiled. One of the best things that ever happened to her, too.

"It had been nearly a year since Jacob left," Uncle Curtis recounted, "and I had finally started getting my life together. The first few weeks had been torture, trying to break myself free of the whiskey. Then without the drink to numb my mind, the guilt nearly did me in. I can't tell you how many times I thought about putting an end to my miserable existence."

Mollie closed her eyes and hugged hers arms around her middle, trying to ward off a sudden chill. She couldn't imagine her life without Curtis Sadler in it and thanked God he hadn't followed through on any of those grisly thoughts.

"But then I found that verse in Corinthians. Remember, the one I taught you about inheriting the kingdom?"

"'Know ye not that the unrighteous shall not inherit the kingdom of God?'" she quoted softly. "'Be not deceived: neither fornicators, nor idolaters . . .'"

Uncle Curtis joined his voice to hers as they continued to list the sins, each giving special emphasis to the ones that fit their experience. "'. . . Nor *thieves*, nor covetous, nor *drunkards*, nor revilers, nor extortioners, shall inherit the kingdom of God. And such were some of you: but ye are washed, but ye are sanctified, but ye are justified in the name of the Lord Jesus, and by the Spirit of our God.'"

The same awe that filled her the first time he shared those words with her flooded back into her soul. She was washed, sanctified, justified because of Jesus's love and sacrifice.

Uncle Curtis continued, "'For ye are bought with a price: therefore glorify God in your body, and in your spirit, which are God's.'" He shifted on the seat to face her. "That's when I realized my life wasn't my own to throw away. It belonged to God. Bought and paid for, despite my unworthiness. He didn't ask me to wallow in guilt and sadness over my past misdeeds and sins. He called me to repent, to change, and to spend the rest of my days glorifying him.

"I thought I was supposed to do that by finding Jacob and making things right. So I set out to look for him and found him in Galveston. He'd already been taken in by a wealthy couple. They cared for him, provided for him, and gave him a home free of all the bad memories that tied him to me. So I let him go, knowing it would be in his best interest. But that left me at a loss as to how to follow God's call on my life.

"Not knowing what direction to take, I went to work cleaning up the ranch. It took several years before the place turned a consistent profit, but during each of those rebuilding years, I made a trip to Galveston to check up on Jacob. And each time I stepped foot on that island, I asked God to show me what he wanted me to do for his glory. During my fifth visit, you picked my pocket, and everything became clear." He smiled, the same smile he'd given her the day they'd met, the one that instantly made her feel safe.

"I love you, Uncle Curtis."

He pulled her into a hug. "I love you, too, Moll."

She flung her arms around his neck and held on tight.

How much Jacob Sadler was missing! The love Uncle Curtis had to give was rich and deep and true. The new doc just needed someone to open his eyes, someone to help him see the man Uncle Curtis had become. The new doc needed someone like her.

5

If he had to shake the hand of one more enthusiastic towns-
person singing the praises of Curtis Sadler, Jacob thought he
might retch. Over the last ten days, he'd met nearly every citizen
of Cold Spring, and each one had felt the need to welcome him
to town by recounting some kind of personal anecdote about
how wonderful his uncle was. He'd been able to stomach the
first few but when the bombardment continued, the nausea had
built to dangerous levels.

He'd learned, for example, that his uncle sat on the school
board, was a deacon at the church, and singlehandedly orga-
nized the fund drive that paid for the new barn at the Wilcox
farm after the old one burned to the ground last summer, taking
a large portion of the family's winter hay stores with it. Fredda
Wilcox had chattered on about the good deed throughout her
entire examination. No wonder the woman complained of a
scratchy throat. She never ceased talking.

The most disturbing bit of news came over the dinner table,
when the head of the city council—Archie Larimore—revealed
that they had ultimately decided to accept his application for

town physician due to Curtis Sadler's glowing recommendation. The man had bragged about how Jacob had finished top of his class at Harvard and distinguished himself as an army surgeon during the war. Described his dedication to his patients and told the council straight out they'd be fools to let a man of his credentials and character get away.

How in the world had Uncle Curtis known all of those things? Jacob shoved the medical text he'd been reading aside and rubbed a hand over his face. Every bit of it had been accurate. Even the story he'd related about Mrs. McCurdy, one of the patients Jacob had seen in Galveston after the war. The woman had suffered extreme pain from gallstones. He'd performed a cholecystectomy based on Robert Graves's procedure and removed the stones. The first time he'd ever done so. It'd been touch-and-go for a while, but the woman had been young and pulled through.

Jacob had been rather proud of that success, yet he'd never spoken of it to anyone outside of the Thorntons. He supposed word could have spread through Mrs. McCurdy or her husband, who was quite a vocal fellow. But to have the news travel all the way to Cold Spring on its own? Highly unlikely.

So how had Uncle Curtis known?

The bell he'd installed above his front door rang, pushing the mystery to the back of his mind. Jacob rose from his kitchen table, shrugged on his coat, and started making his way to the parlor.

"It's just me, Doc," a feminine voice called.

Mollie. Another mystery he'd yet to decipher. How could a woman pummel his chest and call him a coldhearted scoundrel one day then show up the following afternoon to accept his job offer? And all without even a hint of a grudge. It was quite remarkable, really.

Then she'd gone and confessed her past to him, insisting he know her childhood secrets before allowing her to take the job. Guileless, straightforward honesty. She was like a fresh sea breeze that blew through him each afternoon, bringing a tang of salt with her no-nonsense manner and an invigorating coolness that lightened his heart. The woman was proving more addictive than morphine.

"Mrs. Peabody said the powders you gave her are helping," Mollie said, entering the surgery from the parlor at the same time he did through the short hall that connected the front rooms to the rear of the house. She beamed a smile at him, then bustled over to collect her apron from the hook on the wall behind his desk. "She's sleeping much better, and her joints don't seem to ache as much."

"I'm glad." For more reasons than Mrs. Peabody's health. If Mollie's landlady slept better, Mollie slept better. Heaven knew his new assistant could use the extra rest. The woman worked longer hours than a cowhand on a cattle drive. She agreed to help out at the clinic in the afternoons while still cooking and cleaning for Mrs. Peabody in the mornings and evenings, leaving her little or no time to herself. Not that she ever complained.

Which was why he'd be stuffing his own preferences into a deep pocket that afternoon and taking her on a house call.

"Who does that horse outside belong to?" Mollie asked as she reached behind her back to tie the apron strings. "I expected to see a patient in here when I came in."

Jacob snapped the clasp closed on his medical bag. "He's yours. For the afternoon, anyway." He avoided looking directly at her, his pulse jumping in a ridiculously erratic pattern. *Good grief.* It wasn't as if he were asking the woman on a courting expedition. It was strictly professional.

So why did he hope so badly that his gesture pleased her?

He cleared his throat and forced himself to meet her widened eyes. "I thought you could come with me to check on Adam. It's been a week since Curtis took him back to the farm. I'm not worried about infection, that would have set in the first day or two, but I need to make sure the—"

"Yes!" Mollie bounced in front of him, her grin so bright he had to blink several times just to bring her back into focus. "When can we leave?"

Jacob shrugged, pretending every nerve ending in his body wasn't tingling in delight. "I suppose we can go as soon as we deal with the long line of patients waiting to be seen."

Mollie played along, giving a cursory look into the empty parlor. "Done. Race you to the horses!" She bounded away, leaving Jacob free to release the smile that had been demanding freedom.

For the first time in years, he felt young and alive. And competitive. Jacob dashed out the back to where Galen waited and leapt into the saddle. Not taking the time to tie down his bag, he simply gripped it in one hand and the reins in the other as he nudged Galen into a trot and then a lope.

"Come on, slowpoke," he called to a waiting Mollie as he rounded the corner. He didn't slow as he reached the road, somehow sure his assistant would rise to the bait.

She did. Admirably.

Light as she was, she flew down the road, leaning over her mount's neck and urging him to greater speed. Galen surged in response, despite carrying a load nearly eighty pounds heavier. Jacob grinned into the wind, twisting his head to the side to gauge Mollie's progress. She was gaining on him.

"To the fallen tree," he yelled, signaling a log beside the road about a hundred yards out that would serve as a finish line.

Mollie nodded, her eyes narrowing in concentration even as her smile grew wider. It was such a captivating sight, he forgot to race until she was nearly abreast of him.

Turning his attention back to his horse, Jacob leaned forward. "Come on, Galen, you can't let a rented nag best you." As if he'd heard, Galen found a burst of speed and pulled ahead, crossing the imaginary line with a full-length lead. Jacob reined him in and patted his neck. "Good job, old man. I knew you had it in you."

"We might have taken you if you hadn't cheated at the beginning." Mollie's laughter nullified her accusation as she steered her gray alongside his buckskin.

"It's not our fault you were slow getting out of the gate," Jacob teased.

Mollie pushed at his shoulder. Jacob pretended to slide off the far side of the saddle. They both laughed.

While the horses walked off their exertion, Jacob analyzed his riding partner. Mollie had a zest for life that he craved. A zest he hadn't felt since before the war. No, since before medical school. Maybe even before that. He'd had plenty of opportunities for fun and games growing up with the Thorntons—sailing adventures, pirate tales, and more chances to build and explode things than any young boy could wish for. Yet even then, he'd held a part of himself back. A part he'd hidden away when his parents died. One he'd buried even deeper after Emma's life was taken.

One that was perilously close to being exposed the more time he spent in Mollie Tate's exuberant company.

"I wanted to thank you for not taking back your job offer after you found out about my past." Mollie's earnest face turned toward him as she spoke, but then her gaze dipped toward the ground. "Not many people would trust a former thief with the keys to their business or home."

Jacob missed those greenish-brown eyes the moment her lashes covered them. "You were a child, doing what was necessary to survive. I can't blame you for that. Besides, Mrs. Peabody trusts you with her keys," he said in a light tone, hoping to recapture their earlier playfulness. "I figured if she could trust you, I could, too."

"Actually, she doesn't." Mollie slowly raised her head.

Jacob frowned. "Doesn't what?"

"Trust me with her keys. She gives me a curfew to make sure I'll be home before she locks up at night and keeps the key to her jewelry box on a chain around her neck at all times." Mollie shrugged as if such behavior were to be expected, which only intensified Jacob's outrage.

The woman had employed Mollie for three years. How could she not trust her? From the little bit he'd been able to piece together from neighbors and Mrs. Peabody herself, Mollie was basically the woman's personal servant—cooking, cleaning, running errands. And knowing Mollie as he did, she wouldn't do anything half measure. She probably brought more sunshine into that crabby old lady's house than ten plate-glass windows.

"She does trust me with money when it's time to restock the pantry," Mollie said, a bit of her usual gumption returning. "Though, after the time the grocer raised the price of coffee and left me with less change than Mrs. Peabody expected, I now make sure to ask for a detailed receipt. Makes things easier. Anyway, I just wanted to thank you for the job. I know I still have a lot to learn, but I really feel like this might be something I can be good at. A way to help people."

"You're a natural." Jacob squashed his boiling rage at the

image of Mrs. Peabody raking Mollie over the coals for a missing nickel of coffee money and smiled. "I've never had a better assistant. Before long, you'll probably be able to run the clinic yourself when I'm out on a call, at least for minor ailments."

Her eyes glowed at the compliment, and her smile brightened, all trace of what he'd diagnosed as Peabody syndrome gone. In that moment, Jacob wanted nothing more than to keep Mollie by his side for always, to stave off any future flare-ups of nasty Peabodyitis. Someone so lovely should never fall prey to such a depressing illness.

"Did I ever tell you how I met the Thorntons, the family who raised me?"

"No." She turned in the saddle to face him more fully, her face pleading for the story.

"They caught me climbing out a window after stealing as much food as I could carry."

A gasp echoed over the steady clop of horses' hooves. "You didn't!"

He nodded. "Yep. Tried to outrun them, but they were fast for a couple of grown-ups." His lips curved at the memory. "I expected them to drag me off to the local law, but Mr. Thornton offered me work and a place to sleep in his barn instead. Raised me like a son." An urge to steer his mount closer and reach out to cup her cheek punched a hole in his gut, but somehow he managed to resist. Instead he focused his attention on the road ahead. "So you see," he ground out, "we're not so different after all."

He sensed her nearness a split second before he saw her. She'd brought her horse close enough that Jacob's boot brushed the animal's flank. Then she placed her hand on his forearm. "God brought the people we needed into our lives at just the right moment. We're both blessed."

God brought you *into my life at just the right moment.* His need for her suddenly obliterated common sense. Tugging Galen to a stop, he gave in to the urge he'd been fighting. He cupped her cheek in his palm, pulled her face to his, and let his lips discover just how blessed a man could be.

Mollie's knees weakened in an instant. If Dr. Sadler hadn't been holding her, she would have surely tumbled right off her mount. But then it wasn't really Dr. Sadler who was holding her up, was it? No. It was Jacob. Handsome, capable, brusque Jacob, the take-charge man who'd been taking charge of her dreams far too often of late. And heavens, how he was taking charge now.

His lips, warm and firm, pressed insistently against hers. His fingers stroked the line of her cheek. She quivered at the onslaught. So impulsive, so inappropriate, so wonderful.

So . . . over.

A coolness met her overheated face as Jacob yanked his mouth from hers. In a swift motion, he set her solidly upon her saddle and reined his horse back into motion.

"I'm sorry," he muttered. "I shouldn't have done that. Forgive me."

Her horse followed without any prompting from her, which was a good thing, since in her dazed state she was liable to sit in the middle of the road for hours before recalling how to nudge the beast into motion.

Of course, she was also too dazed to come up with any kind of response to his apology. What could she say? *You're right. You shouldn't have kissed me, but I'm oh, so glad you did. Do you think we might try it again sometime? I rather liked it.*

Mollie bit back a groan. She couldn't say *that*, even if it was the God's honest truth. So she simply said nothing until Uncle Curtis's farmhouse came into view.

Jacob reined in before they reached the yard. He scanned the property like a shopkeeper taking inventory. Lines furrowed his forehead as his gaze traced the frame of the house, lit briefly on the pig and chicken enclosures, and then paused over the garden where Mrs. Grady, the housekeeper, was showing the Dunster siblings how to weed.

Victor, the oldest, worked the hoe while his little sisters, Bessy and Mable, squatted in the dirt and pulled at the small weeds growing close to the vegetables. The Dunsters had only been at the ranch a few months. Their father had dumped them on Uncle Curtis's doorstep after his wife died birthing a stillborn son and then ran off to places unknown. He'd never been fully right in the head after returning from the war, but Curtis hoped that if the man got himself together, he'd come back for his kids one day. He'd probably avoid trying to find them another home for just that reason.

Many of the children that came to the Sadler ranch ended up being adopted by families in the surrounding counties, but a few, like her, ended up staying around long term.

"I imagine it's changed a bit since you saw it last," she finally ventured.

"Everything's repaired, cleaner, painted over." His gaze zeroed in on the barn. "As if that day never occurred."

How could she be so dull? She'd been eager for him to recognize the improvements Uncle Curtis had made, to see a reflection of how he'd turned his life around in the way he'd turned his farm around and made it a home to needy children. How could she not have understood the agony such a sight would inspire? Jacob had watched his sister die in this very yard.

"I'm so sorry, I didn't think . . ."

He glanced her way, his brows raised. "Why are you apologizing? It was my idea to come here, not yours." He straightened his shoulders and turned his attention to the house. "I'm Adam's physician. A few old ghosts won't keep me from checking on the boy." He urged his horse forward. "Let's get going."

Mollie followed, somewhat subdued. She recalled the whispers of the townspeople when she first came to live with Uncle Curtis. The scornful looks. The pitying glances sent her way. She hadn't understood them then, but she'd felt their impact. It had taken years for Curtis Sadler to earn back the respect of his neighbors. To earn their forgiveness. How could she expect Jacob to give his after mere days, when his wounds went so much deeper?

"With men this is impossible," a familiar verse whispered through her memory, *"but with God all things are possible."*

Mollie's lips quirked, her natural optimism returning with a vengeance. She had nothing to mope about. God was at work and in control. Surely between the two of them, they'd have the Sadler menfolk acting like family in no time.

Twenty minutes later, a bit of the shine had worn off her rose-colored glasses. Jacob had grunted more than spoken to Uncle Curtis and had gone so far as to give her instructions to relay instead of addressing his uncle directly. He'd been friendly with Adam and had even smiled at the boy a time or two, but she could tell it'd been forced. Tension radiated from him in waves, a tension that hadn't lessened even though they were back on their horses heading for town.

Not only would the man not talk to his uncle, but apparently he'd given up talking to her as well. That would never do. Mollie squared her shoulders. "He's kept up with you through the years, you know."

She threw the statement into the silence, hoping to shatter his reticence, but Jacob's lips did nothing more than tighten into a thinner line.

"He has a box under his bed filled with letters and newspaper clippings, all about you."

Still nothing.

Well, fine. The Grumpy Gus could just sit there and listen, then. "A friend of his down in Galveston wrote to him regularly," she informed him, "and the letters were always full of news about you. You should have seen how Uncle Curtis's face lit up whenever one of those letters arrived. He'd read it to me the moment he got home."

Those had been treasured times. Times when her imagination would run wild about a boy she'd never met. A boy who, according to the letters, got to ride ships on the ocean and scamper on the beach. Who won the school footrace five years in a row. Who excelled in every academic subject except for spelling. A boy, if she were to be completely honest with herself, she'd always been just the slightest bit jealous of—for holding such a place of honor in Uncle Curtis's heart.

"Did you know that he found me only because he was keeping an eye on you?" Mollie pressed.

The block of stone riding the horse beside her cracked just a bit. He actually turned and met her eyes with a disbelieving scowl before jerking his attention forward again. A little surge of triumph shot through her. He might not want to admit it, but he was interested.

"After the accident, Uncle Curtis made it his mission to clean himself up and make himself a proper guardian, to find you and bring you back home. By the time he tracked you down, though, you were already living with the Thorntons. He saw how kind they were to you, how they took you in and provided for you as if you were their own child. Most of all, he saw that with them you would be free from the constant reminders of all you had lost. He wanted that for you, for you to grow up with love and happy memories. So he never pushed himself back into your life, but he did return to Galveston every year to check up on you. And on one of those visits he found me."

The outskirts of town grew visible up ahead, and Mollie fell silent. The horses' hooves thudded abnormally loud into the packed dirt of the road. The call of a jay echoed like a cannon blast.

"Who wrote the letters?"

Mollie started, her gaze swinging around faster than a gate on a well-oiled hinge. "What?"

He turned, his jaw still as stony as ever, yet his eyes . . . his eyes seemed almost vulnerable. "Who wrote the letters to my uncle about me?"

"A Mr. Alfred Yates." She smiled slightly at the name. "He would sign his letters *Alfie*, which always made me giggle. But then, he and Uncle Curtis had known each other since they were boys."

Jacob lifted his chin in a slow, exaggerated motion. "Ah, yes. I remember Mr. Yates and his wife from church. They were good friends of my . . . of Mr. and Mrs. Thornton."

Why did he speak of them so formally? Mollie's brow

57

furrowed. It had sounded like he'd been about to call them his parents but stopped himself. Why?

"I had wondered how Curtis knew enough about me to make his recommendation to the council." Jacob nudged his horse into a trot. "Now I know. He had a spy." At the word *spy*, he kicked Galen into a canter, veering off the road and into the woods.

Where was he going? Mollie nibbled her bottom lip, unsure if she should follow or give him privacy to deal with his demons on his own. Jacob was intelligent enough to recognize the difference between a concerned friend and a spy. That's not what worried her. What made her want to give chase was the fact that he seemed determined to erect barriers around himself, keeping people out. Uncle Curtis. The Thorntons. *Her*. If he kept pushing people away, he'd end up alone. She knew what being alone felt like, and she wasn't about to let him fall prey to that miserable fate.

Decision made, she steered her gray in the direction Jacob had headed but held the horse to a walk. Only one place to the south made any sense as a destination. The graveyard at the old church. He'd want to see his family. Be close to them as he tried to find his way through the tangle he found himself in. She'd give him time to think things through before she intruded. Besides she had some thinking of her own to do.

Specifically about that kiss.

Dr. Jacob Sadler had kissed her. Ardently. And on horseback. She wasn't sure why that last detail gave her such a thrill, but it did. It hinted at something unplanned and unrestrained. Something inspired by passion. True, he had apologized for it afterward, but an apology couldn't undo the kiss. Couldn't steal the memory of the way his lips felt pressed against hers or the way his hand had cupped her face and locked her in his embrace. For one blissful moment, she'd felt like she belonged, truly belonged, to another person.

Uncle Curtis had given her a home. He loved her and watched out for her, yet she didn't feel as if she belonged to him. He had other family, or at least memories of other family. And Jacob. Whether the new doc wanted to admit to the relation or not, it existed.

She had none of that. All she had were vague memories of prim ladies in black dresses and white aprons who would slap her knuckles with a ruler if she misbehaved. No mother or father. No brother or sister. Just an orphanage, and then a group of street thieves who taught her how to pick pockets in order to line their own, and finally a kind man desperate to atone for his mistakes.

Oh, she didn't doubt Uncle Curtis's sincerity. He loved her. Just as she loved him. Yet that deep sense of belonging she craved always lingered barely out of reach.

Until Jacob kissed her.

She couldn't let him push her away, not if there was a chance that he'd felt that belonging, too. Such a gift was too precious to toss aside just because things got a little difficult.

When the old church came into view, Mollie scoured the yard for sign of Jacob. His horse stood tethered near the large pine where she'd found the branches for Adam's splint on the day of the accident, the doc's coat draped over the saddle. She pulled her gray alongside Galen and dismounted. Making her way on foot, she circled to the rear of the church. Expecting to find Jacob at his family's gravesite, her eyes immediately sought the marble angel Uncle Curtis had erected at his niece's grave. It stood next to the tombstone marking Jacob's mother's final resting place, with his father's stone on the opposite side. But no Jacob. The graves had been swept clean of debris, proof that he had been there recently, yet the man himself was not in evidence. Mollie scanned the entire graveyard to no avail. Then a dull *thwack* echoed from around the side of the church.

Jacob?

Mollie moved cautiously, not wanting to startle him—or draw attention to herself if whoever was making that noise turned out to *not* be Jacob. A second thud sounded as she made a wide arc around the corner of the building. She kept to the trees, using them to camouflage her approach.

A relieved breath escaped her as she recognized the new doc's tall frame, wide shoulders, and the black leather vest he always wore. His back was to her as he strode up to the wall of the church and pulled something free from the old boards. A knife. She'd seen the sheath he wore on his belt but had never thought much about it. All men in these parts carried either guns or knives or both. Too many dangerous critters roaming about not to. Still, it seemed out of character somehow for an educated man, a doctor, to be wielding one—against a church, of all things.

Jacob tugged the blade free, then strode back to where he'd been standing several yards away. He turned, lifted his arm, and with only the slightest hesitation, flung the blade again. *Merciful heavens!* He'd nearly hit the exact same spot. She watched in awe as he repeated the procedure again and again. Each throw hit the same board in the old church wall, but some of the time the blade landed vertically, sometimes horizontally, and sometimes on a diagonal. And nearly every time, the blade landed farther to the right than the previous shot. At first she'd assumed the variation was due to natural error, but as she watched him, realization dawned. He knew precisely where each shot would land.

Mollie finally left the shelter of the trees, her curiosity luring her in. She'd nearly reached Jacob's throwing spot when he yanked his blade free of the wall and turned. He froze, his gaze locking on her.

"What are you doing here?"

Mollie ignored the churning in her stomach, praying she hadn't made a mistake by following him. "I didn't want you to be alone."

He lifted a brow and continued toward her. "I'm a big boy, Mollie. I can take care of myself."

"Can you?" she challenged.

In answer he spun on the balls of his feet and flung his knife in a sharp, fluid motion. It landed diagonally, the blade piercing the same board all his other throws had hit, the slash it would leave behind closing off the letter *A*. Mollie stepped closer to the church, not quite believing what she saw. There in the wood stood four nearly perfect letters. *E M M A*. He'd spelled out his sister's name.

Mollie followed him to the wall and ran her fingers over each of the letters as he pulled his knife from the wood and thrust it into the sheath at his waist.

"I've never seen such skill," she said, pivoting to look at him.

A hint of a grin played at his mouth. "My m— er, Miss Nicole taught me. Darius calls her his pirate. Can't say that I'd disagree, though she's as good with numbers as she is with knives."

"Why do you do that?"

His brow crinkled. "What?"

"Stop yourself from calling the Thorntons your parents? They raised you. Do you not think them worthy of the title?"

Fire sparked in Jacob's blue eyes. "Darius and Nicole Thornton are worthy of any parental honor ever bestowed. They loved me like a son, and even after they had children of their own, they never once made me feel any less a part of the family. Any distance in our relationship was at my instigation, not theirs."

His spirited defense shouted his love for them, his respect, his loyalty. So why would he feel the need to keep himself distant from them?

He must have read the question in her eyes, for he let out a heavy sigh and leaned his back against the church wall. "They wanted to adopt me," he said at last. "Asked me every year on my birthday, in fact. But I always refused. Deep down, I think I was afraid that if I accepted their offer, I would forget the family I'd left behind. My mother. My father. Emma." His voice cracked a bit on his sister's name.

He turned his gaze aside and cleared his throat before continuing. "I didn't want to forget them. They were my reason for living. My reason for becoming a doctor. Everything I became, I did to honor them. Their memories." He grew silent for a minute, until at last he brought his eyes back to meet hers. "The Thorntons understood. They knew even before I figured it out that my keeping things separate was just semantics. I didn't call them *Mom* and *Dad*, but I loved them like they were. I insisted upon earning my way with them, and Darius always found a job for me to do, paying me a wage to salvage my pride even as he and Nicole made room for me in their home as a son."

A small ironic laugh erupted then, surprising Mollie, and perhaps Jacob as well. "You know, as soon as their other kids were old enough to start doing chores around the house, Darius started paying them a wage, too. Nicole said that it was a good way for them to learn how to be responsible with money and to reinforce the value of honest labor, but I think what they really wanted was to make it clear to me that I was no less a son to them than any of their natural children."

Mollie blinked at the moisture that had gathered across her eyes. "They sound like lovely people."

"They are."

He held her gaze for a long moment, and Mollie felt it again. That connection. Belonging. As if they were kindred spirits, after a fashion. And why not? The new doc had said it himself earlier. They weren't so different. Both orphans, both rescued, both . . . thieves.

Jacob pushed away from the wall, and Mollie glanced aside, hoping he hadn't read her thoughts as clearly as he had last time.

"Come on," he said, trudging off in the direction of the horses. "I'll see you back to town."

Mollie followed, though at a slower pace. *Both thieves.* The stubborn idea refused to release its hold on her mind. What if . . . ? She glanced at the man in front of her, then slipped her fingers into her pocket as if pinching a watch. Maybe, if she were exceedingly clever, she'd find a way to steal the new doc's heart. It'd be risky. She'd have to use her own heart as bait, but the poor thing was half gone already, so she might as well give it a go. The fact that Jacob preferred to keep his emotions firmly locked away simply added another layer to the challenge.

Mollie quirked a grin as she watched Jacob ready their mounts. Guess it was a good thing she'd learned to pick locks as well as pockets during her days on the streets.

7

That night, Jacob lay in his bed and stared at the rafters. She'd worried about him, followed him, had not wanted him to be alone. Even after he'd been daft enough to kiss her. What madness had possessed him? He was her employer, for heaven's sake. Such an impulse would only serve to impair their working relationship and create awkwardness between them. It had been a stupid move on his part.

Yet he couldn't dredge up a single ounce of regret over it. Shoot, he could still taste her. Spicy. Sweet. Everything that was Mollie Tate. Jacob let out a groan and rolled over.

But he couldn't escape the memories of that moment. Sensations so vivid they were nearly real. The compassion in her gaze as she reached out to him, the lightning that passed through him at her touch, the softness of her skin as he palmed her cheek and pulled her to him. The perfect way her lips fit against his. The shiver that coursed through her the instant before she began to kiss him back.

No, he couldn't regret it. Not when that kiss had filled every abandoned, lonely place inside him that he'd thought impenetrable. Something more than lips had met when he'd kissed Mollie. Something more profound had linked them. Something that urged him to return again and again until the ties running between them were so reinforced that nothing would be able to tear them apart.

But how could he tie himself to a woman whose loyalty lay with his uncle? He hadn't missed the censorious looks she'd cast his way when he avoided speaking directly to Curtis while they'd been at the farm. She expected him to mend fences, to forgive and forget. Jacob grabbed a fistful of sheet and twisted it into a painful band around his wrist. How did one go about forgiving the man who'd killed his sister?

As he lay there, a new image flashed before him—bloody and dark and full of death. Faces of the soldiers he'd been unable to save. Battle-weary eyes that had pleaded for relief, voices that begged for healing, hands that grabbed at his coat as he'd left them behind to tend the ones who had a better chance at survival. What would their families say if they knew he had ignored the pleas and let their sons, their husbands, their fathers die? Would they understand the horror of the situation, the impossibility of tending so many with such limited resources? Or would they simply hang on to the pain of their grief and cast their blame and bitterness upon him?

It took a strong man to step out of his own pain to see a situation from another's perspective. Jacob slowly loosed his arm from the cotton manacle he'd fashioned from the sheet and closed his eyes against the realization he'd fought for so long. He'd believed himself strong because he was a survivor, but in truth he was weak. Too weak to forgive his uncle because the man had the audacity to still be alive. He'd been prepared to face his past as long as it was easy. Deep down, he'd hoped to find a grave, to discover that Curtis Sadler had paid the ultimate price for his crime. That would have made Jacob's token forgiveness a simple matter of words. Instead he'd found the man very much alive, and worse—changed. Godly. Kind. A good neighbor. A man who saved children from the streets. A man he would respect under other circumstances.

A few mumbled words wouldn't be sufficient. He'd have to live out his forgiveness day after day. Anything but simple. It would require strength of character, a strength he feared he might lack. Holding on to his pain, his anger, would be easier, but if he wished for the parents of the soldiers he'd been unable to save to forgive him, he needed to find the strength within his soul to forgive the one who had wronged him.

Help me, Lord. I can't do this on my own.

How had Jesus been able to forgive his crucifiers as he hung dying on the cross? Jacob draped his arm over his eyes and pressed away the dampness. If he could find even a fraction of that nobility, perhaps he could—

A pounding from the front of the house interrupted his thoughts.

"Doc Sadler!" The pounding intensified. "Doc, come quick! Somethin's awful wrong with Amy and the babe. Please, Doc. You gotta come."

Jacob jumped from the bed, his own difficulties forgotten. He turned up the lamp and tugged on the pair of trousers he always kept on the chair by his bedside, a trick he'd learned during the war. Since he slept in a regular shirt, he could be dressed in under a minute.

He did up the buttons at his neck as he made his way to the front of the house, where the pounding continued. New fathers tended to be nervous, but Trent Walters already had three youngsters at home, and when Jacob had spoken to Mrs. Walters at church last Sunday, she'd assured him that she had no need of an examination. All her births had been straightforward, and she preferred to have the midwife attend her. Many women were more comfortable with other women at such a delicate time. Besides, Mrs. Horeb had delivered each of her other children. The woman was quite capable.

Something must have gone wrong for Walters to be banging on his door.

Jacob grabbed the knob and swung the door inward. "Come in," he said, narrowly dodging the man's fist as it descended for another pound. "I just need to collect my boots and bag."

"Hurry, Doc." Walters lunged across the threshold and immediately started pacing the length of the parlor. "She's been laboring for hours. Mrs. Horeb's done all she can, but the babe won't turn."

A breech. Jacob hid his concern from the worried father. If the babe was trapped high in the pelvis, two lives could be in jeopardy, not just one.

"Amy's slipping away, Doc." The anguish in the man's voice tore at Jacob's heart as he stamped his feet into his boots. "She ain't got nothin' left to give." Walters's hand latched on to Jacob's arm. "You got to save her, Doc. Please. Even if it means sacrificing the baby."

Jacob straightened, meeting Trent Walters's red-rimmed eyes.

The man swallowed and grimaced as if something sour had just been poured down his throat. "The midwife . . . she took me aside and told me that doctors have ways of taking the babe out. It . . . kills the child, but sometimes the mother is spared."

A craniotomy. A vile procedure. One of the few that succeeded in turning his stomach when he'd studied it in school.

Though it would only work if the babe presented head first and was simply too large to pass through the birth canal. With a breech . . . Well, that was even more gruesome.

Jacob clapped a hand to the man's shoulder and gave it a firm squeeze. "Let's not get ahead of ourselves. I haven't even examined her yet."

Walters nodded, his jaw stiffening.

Jacob ducked into the surgery to collect his bag. He always kept it stocked for any emergency, but he took an extra moment to retrieve a small spool of fine silver wire from the locked medical cabinet. Something told him he'd be needing it.

A light tapping tugged Mollie into wakefulness. Frowning into the darkness, she tilted her head. The tapping came again, a little louder this time. The back door?

She pushed the covers aside and hurriedly donned her wrapper. Only bad news came calling in the dark of night. Lighting a candle, she left the tiny room that served as her chamber and wove her way through the kitchen, past the stove and cabinets, to the back door. She unlatched it and opened it a crack, just enough to peer out.

"Mrs. Horeb? What are you doing here?"

The older woman's haggard features sent a pang through Mollie's chest. "Doc Sadler needs you at the Walters place. He sent me to fetch you."

"The babe?"

Mrs. Horeb nodded. "It don't look good for neither of 'em. I didn't want to bother you with this, told the doc it weren't fitting for an unmarried woman to attend a birthin'. But he insisted he needed you for the surgery." Her head wagged slowly as her shoulders drooped. "Amy and that babe of hers are as good as dead. It's cruel for the doc to offer false hope, if you ask me."

Mollie curled her arms around her middle. "I've seen Doc Sadler accomplish the impossible before," she said, thinking of Adam's leg and the lack of infection. "Perhaps the hope is not as false as you fear." She swung the door wide and gestured for Mrs. Horeb to enter the kitchen. "Come in and sit. I'll just need a minute to change."

After rushing back to her room, Mollie grabbed the first dress she laid hands on. Not bothering to take the time with under-garments, she pulled it on over her nightdress and fastened the buttons. She left her hair in the long braid that hung down past her waist and slipped her feet into her shoes. At the last min-ute, she remembered Mrs. Peabody and scribbled her landlady a quick note explaining where she'd gone and why. Then she dashed back out to the kitchen, collected Mrs. Horeb, and left the note on the table.

As she climbed into the midwife's small cart, prayers for Amy Walters and her babe spun through her mind along with one other significant thought—Jacob needed her.

8

Mrs. Horeb pointed Mollie toward the front of a small farm-house. "Go on in. He's waitin' on ya."

Mollie climbed down then glanced back at the midwife. "Aren't you coming?"

"No. Doc Sadler's in charge now. He don't need me gettin' in the way." She tightened her grip on the reins and glanced up at the nearly full moon that offered just enough light to make slow travel safe. "Amy's young'uns are over at her sister's place," she said, still not looking at Mollie. "Think I'll go offer to tend them so Alice can come back here in case Amy don't make it through. Poor gal has no idea how serious it is."

When the older woman finally turned toward Mollie, moon-light glistened on the wetness that had gathered in her eyes. She gave a little sniff, then jerked her chin a final time toward the house. "Quit dallyin', missy. Whichever way things go, they're gonna need your help."

Galvanized, Mollie spun around and hurried to the house as the cart behind her pulled away. A lamp glowing in the parlor window guided her to the door. She raised her hand to knock but then realized how foolish that would be and simply let herself in. A trail of quiet moans led her to a bedroom at the back of the house.

Amy Walters lay on the bed, her blond hair matted to her head with sweat. Skin pale. Eyes closed. Little lines scrunched her forehead each time she moaned, but even they looked dangerously lifeless. Trent sat in a chair by her side, holding her hand, smoothing her hair from her brow, whispering words of love that sounded suspiciously like good-byes. Tears rose to Mollie's eyes, but she ruthlessly blinked them back. Tears wouldn't help Amy and her babe. This room had enough sorrow already. What it needed was someone who knew how to fight the odds and survive.

Lifting her chin, Mollie marched over to where Jacob stood with his back to her, his head bent over the instruments he'd arranged on the dresser top. She recognized the scalpel as well as the atomizer filled with carbolic acid solution. A little shiver traveled through her at the thought of him cutting Amy open, but she trusted his judgment.

"I'm here, Doc," she whispered, laying a hand on his shoulder as she approached from behind.

His head jerked up, his eyes flying open. Had he been praying? Mollie retracted her hand. "I'm sorry. I didn't mean to interrupt."

"I'm glad you did." Jacob's voice was quiet, his face grim. "Mrs. Walters doesn't have much time." He grabbed a cloth and a small bottle. "Come." He signaled her to follow with a flick of his chin as he strode to the bedside.

Trent Walters's gaze lifted to follow his approach. "Is it time, then?"

"Yes." Jacob gave a single, curt nod.

"And you swear she won't feel anything?"

Jacob met the man's eyes without wavering. "She'll be unconscious. She won't feel a thing."

Trent nodded and lifted his wife's hand to his lips. "I love you, Amy. I always will."

Amy struggled to open her eyes and look at her husband. "Love . . . you. Take care of . . . our babies."

He squeezed her hand tightly against his face and nodded as tears ran down his cheeks. "I will. But I want you to come back, Amy. Come back to me."

Her eyes slid closed as she rolled her head toward Jacob. "I'm ready, Doc." Her voice was barely audible, yet it carried a thread of steely determination that gave Mollie a surge of hope. Amy was fighting for her child.

Jacob dosed the cloth with chloroform and held it gently to Amy's face, encouraging her to inhale the thick, sweet vapors until she lost consciousness.

"Wash at the basin," Jacob instructed Mollie in low tones. "Then hold the tray of instruments where I can reach them. When I get the babe out, you'll have to clean the mucus from its nose and mouth and get it to cry while I tend to the mother. I want to have her sutures done before the chloroform wears off."

Mollie immediately rolled up her sleeves and scrubbed her arms and hands, doing her best to mask the panic swelling inside her. God help her, she'd never even *held* a newborn before, and now she was expected to save one's life? She prayed that every maternal instinct bred into her gender would somehow manifest itself when the time came.

"Trent." Jacob waited for the man to look up at him before continuing. "I know you don't want to leave her, but I can't afford to have you in the room during the surgery. Miss Tate or I will come get you the moment we're finished."

The anguish on Mr. Walters's face cut through Mollie's heart as sharply as any scalpel. She crossed the room to him and took his arm. "She's in good hands, Mr. Walters. I've seen the new doc in action, and he knows what he's about." She steered the reluctant husband toward the door. "Why don't you make a fresh pot of coffee? Mrs. Horeb mentioned spelling your sister-in-law so she could come join you. Alice will probably be chilled by the time she arrives. She'd appreciate a hot drink, I'm sure."

Mollie saw the man to the kitchen, then bustled back to the bedroom. Jacob had already prepared Amy for the procedure. Her nightgown had been folded high upon her chest and her legs lay covered by the sheet, leaving only her middle exposed. He was spraying the carbolic acid solution over her belly when Mollie returned to his side.

She took up the tray of instruments and held it at the ready. "Have you ever done this before?"

He lifted the scalpel from the tray, his face set in hard lines. "No, but Caesarian sections have been performed since ancient times. And I have read papers by Dr. James Sims, a well-known physician specializing in female disorders, who claims that when silver wire is used for internal sutures, the wounds heal properly, without putrefaction. It is the best chance we have to save both the mother and the babe."

His voice carried authority and confidence, yet Mollie sensed the touch of uncertainty that lingered beneath it all.

"I believe in you, Jacob," she said softly. "And I will pray for God to guide your hands."

His blue eyes met hers. "Thank you." All hint of doubt vanished as he held the scalpel over Mrs. Walters's abdomen. His hand completely steady, he made the incision.

After that, everything moved so fast, Mollie could barely

wrap her mind around what was happening. The blood made her uneasy at first, and she turned her head, but then Jacob dropped his scalpel onto the tray with a clank and dug both hands into the opening he'd made.

"There you are, little one," he murmured, and Mollie couldn't help but watch as he pulled the tiny being out from the depths of his mother's womb. "Put the tray on the bed and grab a towel," Jacob ordered.

Mollie obeyed. She opened the towel over her hands, knowing she'd be taking the babe from him. Jacob placed the newest Walters child in her hands, blood and fluid coating the boy's skin. She wrapped the towel about his tiny body, snuggling him close to her breast. Her heart softened in an instant, then raced in fear as she realized that he wasn't moving.

"Clean out his mouth with your finger and clear his nose as best you can. Then swat his backside. He needs to cry in order to breathe." Jacob's eyes met hers, challenge rife in his gaze. "Do whatever it takes, Mollie."

Stiffening her spine, Mollie nodded and carried the babe over to the dresser. "Come on, sweetheart. You're gonna have to help me." Alarmed by the slight bluish tint to the boy's skin, Mollie rubbed him vigorously with the towel, hoping to pinken him up. She tried to hold him with one arm so she could work her finger into his mouth, but he nearly slipped from her grasp. Needing more leverage, she laid him on a folded towel on the dresser top and pressed her stomach flush against the bureau to eliminate any chance of him falling.

"Let me help you, baby. Please." Rolling him onto his side, she swiped out his mouth with her finger, then scraped the mucus off on the far edge of the towel. Using a fresh cloth, she rubbed at his nose, cleaning it as best she could. He still made no effort to draw breath. Mollie's stomach lurched. She rubbed his skin again, desperate to gain a response.

Please, God. Please help him breathe.

Remembering Jacob's instructions, she picked the boy up, draped his chest over her arm, and gave his bottom a quick swat. No cry. Her pulse throbbed, despair rising in her throat. She hit him again, harder. Nothing.

"Come on, baby. Your mama needs you. Just take a breath. Please?" She swatted again.

Nothing.

Tears blurred Mollie's vision. She couldn't let this babe die. Not after all Amy had gone through to bring him into the world. *Whatever it takes.* That's what Jacob had said. But spanking the child hadn't made him cry. She had to try something else. What?

An image of Adam sputtering and coughing after he fell in the pond one summer before Uncle Curtis had taught him to swim flashed through her mind. Uncle Curtis had slapped his back to clear out his lungs. Plopping the limp babe with his bottom on the towel, she leaned him against her arm and supported his chin with the curve of her fingers. She pounded against his back, three firm thumps, then reached into his mouth and cleared out another fingerful of mucus.

Why wouldn't he breathe? Hands shaking, Mollie laid him down again. If only she could breathe for him. If only . . . Her gaze snapped to the babe's mouth. What if she could? What if she could breathe for him? Bending over him, she pried his mouth open with her fingers and fit her lips around his. She blew a tiny puff of air into him. His chest lifted! She did it again and again. When she raised her head to take a new breath, she paused to give his face a quick examination. Had his eyes flickered?

Please, Lord. Please.

Lifting the boy back into her arms, Mollie turned him over and swatted his bottom with a sharp sting of her palm.

A small, mewling cry broke the silence. The sound was weak, but it was the most beautiful music Mollie had ever heard.

"Praise God," she whispered as she wrapped the baby in a clean towel. "Praise God." Tears ran unchecked down her cheeks, and suddenly, standing required too much effort. Cuddling the baby close to her chest, Mollie slid gently to the floor and leaned her shoulders against the dresser. Her head fell back against the wooden support as she listened to the evidence of life. The babe's cry grew stronger. A tiny arm flailed beneath her chin, the little fist at the end bumping into her jaw. A knee poked her ribs. A foot pressed against her arm.

She reveled in each movement, her lips curling into a smile that stretched all the way into her soul.

"You did good, Mollie."

She glanced over to the bed. Jacob stood bent over Amy Walters, a needle poised between his bloodied fingers. His nod of approval sent waves of pride rioting through her chest.

"Finish cleaning the boy off, and then take him out to his father. I imagine Trent is climbing the walls about now." Jacob's gaze locked with hers for a moment, and in that moment, Mollie swore she felt his emotions. Gratitude for the babe, concern for the mother, determination to save the life in his care, and just a touch of fear that he might fail. It was that last that gave Mollie the strength to rise from the floor.

"I'll see to the babe and Mr. Walters. You tend Amy." She smiled, full of faith in him and in the one who worked through his hands. "It will all come out right. You'll see."

9

Jacob turned his attention back to his sutures. *"It will all come out right,"* she'd said. He shook his head as he tied off another stitch. He'd seen firsthand how often things didn't come out right. Yet her simple words buoyed him anyway. Perhaps because he'd seen in her eyes that she actually believed them. She wasn't spouting platitudes or trying to make him feel better with false assurances. No, this woman had just experienced one of God's greatest miracles—not only in the birth of a baby but in bringing him back from the brink of death. Relief and joy radiated from her until he swore he could taste them in the air.

Finished with the internal sutures, he traded the silver wire for the softer catgut that had recently come into favor among top physicians. He sprayed the sealed incision line with carbolic acid, then closed up the outer wound.

Jacob moved to the dresser to clean the blood from his hands. He stretched the crick from his neck, twisting it back and forth, up and down. The bed's height had been too low for him to operate comfortably, but there had been no time to move Mrs. Walters.

He was a little surprised she was still breathing. He'd seen the dull look of death in her eyes—a look with which he was far too familiar. She'd spent every ounce of her energy during the hours of unproductive labor that had preceded the surgery. She'd torn some places inside from her efforts and hemorrhaged slightly. Thankfully, the blood loss had not been too severe. If it had, she would have been gone before he'd even arrived.

Jacob dried his hands then ran them through his hair as he exhaled a heavy breath. He'd done all he could. Sewn up her tears as well as his incisions. Now all he could do was wait on God to stave off infection and bring about the healing necessary for recovery. He prayed the Lord would prove merciful.

Amy began to stir, her hand instinctively reaching for the newly stitched wound. Jacob strode to her side and stopped her before she could touch it.

"Mollie," he called, loud enough for the sound to carry through the door but not so loud as to cause undo alarm. He hoped.

In an instant, Mollie pushed open the door and stood in the opening.

"Help me apply a dressing. Then we'll need to get her into a clean nightdress."

A second woman came up behind Mollie in the doorway. "I can help with that."

The sister.

Jacob shrugged and waved them both in. He didn't know Alice well, but she seemed a sturdy sort, not the type to fall into a fit of hysterics at the first sign of adversity. He supposed he could allow her to assist.

"I told Trent to keep the babe close to the stove to ward off any chance of a chill and promised to fetch him when Amy began to wake." She shot him a meaningful look. "He won't be interfering."

Thank the Lord for sensible women. Jacob nodded his appreciation.

The three of them worked in tandem and had the incision dressed, nightclothes changed, and even bed linens switched out in short order. Mrs. Walters remained groggy and limp through the entire episode, though her awareness gradually improved. By the time they were done jostling her about, her eyelids were fluttering.

Alice took her sister's hand and slapped the back of it softly. "Amy? Can you hear me?"

Mrs. Walters stirred, turning her head toward the sound of her sister's voice. "Alice?" she croaked in a barely audible whisper.

The sensible Alice sniffed a bit, then patted her sister's hand again. "Time to wake up, sister. You have a new babe to feed."

"Babe?" The lines around Mrs. Walters's mouth tightened as if she were physically battling her way out of the chloroform haze. Her eyes finally cracked open. Her gaze fixed on Alice, then scanned the room. "Where?"

"Your husband has him in the other room," Mollie explained from her position at the end of the bed. "I'll go fetch them for you."

Jacob stood at her side, his hand wrapped around the bedpost. Mollie turned to him and smiled, the beauty of the expression stealing his breath. It wasn't simply a smile of joy or relief but one that radiated pride—pride in *him*. A man could run for days, weeks even, with a smile like that fueling him. What he wouldn't give to have such a blessing in his life permanently.

The thought so startled him, he jumped when she touched

his arm. Her brows drew together, but when he nodded to her, they smoothed out again.

"A . . . a boy?" Mrs. Walters murmured, her gaze following Mollie out the bedroom door.

"Yep," Alice answered. "Trent finally got his son. If he wasn't so worried about you, he'd be burstin' his buttons about now."

Amy's eyes slid closed as a small smile curved her lips. "A son."

Jacob thought she might have fallen asleep, understandable given the ordeal she'd been through, but when her husband rushed into the room, her eyelids propped themselves up once again.

"Amy?" Trent Walters slowed as he reached the bed, almost as if he were afraid to have his hopes dashed. Alice released her sister's hand and stepped aside to give the man better access to his wife.

He came closer, the babe cradled in his arms.

"Let me see him, Trent." Amy tried to lift her arms, but the effort seemed too much for her.

Her husband closed the distance between them in a single step and sat on the edge of the bed in order to hold the child out for her inspection.

"Alice." A desperate tone edged Amy's voice. "Help me sit up a little."

Her sister rushed to her side and began shoving pillows behind her back. Mollie came around to the opposite side to assist. When the women stepped back, Trent Walters placed the babe in his wife's lap and helped her wrap her arms around the sleeping bundle.

"He was worth it." The whispered words rang loud in the room and even louder in Jacob's ears. The pain, the exhaustion, the very real chance that she might still die echoed in the weariness of her voice, yet her conviction drowned out all else. No matter what the sacrifice she was called to make, her love for her child made him worthy. "William," she announced, her eyes again growing heavy. "For your father."

"William," Trent repeated. "It's a fine name." He leaned forward and brushed a kiss across his wife's forehead.

Jacob knew what he would be wanting to do if it had been his wife who had barely survived the night. And he certainly wouldn't be wanting a roomful of company looking on while he climbed into bed beside his woman and held her and the babe she had blessed him with. He caught Mollie's eye and signaled for her to gather his instruments while he pulled Alice into the front room in order to give her further instructions about caring for her sister and little William.

"She'll need lots of rest. Tell Trent not to let her out of bed for at least a week. I'll stop by every day to check for infection and to be sure the child is getting enough nourishment. She'll need to feed the babe regular, even if her own strength is flagging. You can help her set the child to her breast if need be."

"I'll plan to move in for the week, Doc." Alice crossed her arms over her chest and gave him such a fierce look, Jacob was sure neither Trent nor Amy Walters would be able to dissuade her should they try. "I'll keep my nieces busy, take care of the cookin' and cleanin', and see that Amy gets the rest she needs."

Jacob was nodding his agreement when Mollie slipped out of the bedroom and handed him his doctor's bag.

"Alice," she said softly. "Mr. Walters asked to see you."

The other woman scuttled off without another word. Jacob had just placed his hand at the small of Mollie's back to lead her toward the door when Trent rushed out of the bedroom.

"Wait, Doc." The urgency in his voice had Jacob turning and walking back toward him in a flash.

"Has something happened to your wife? The babe?" His grip on the doctor's bag grew painful. Could he have missed something, some symptom hidden beneath the mother's fatigue?

Trent Walters shook his head. "No, Doc. They're both sleeping. I just . . . I wanted to thank you." The liquid glimmer in the man's eyes made Jacob's throat constrict. "I thought I was gonna lose them both. Mrs. Horeb said as much. You saved my family, Doc." He reached out and clasped Jacob's free hand in a firm grip. "Thank you."

Never much good at accepting thanks, Jacob turned his gaze away and cleared his throat. "Yes, well . . . you should be thanking Miss Tate as well. If it weren't for her quick thinking, your babe would surely have perished."

Mollie blushed as Mr. Walters released his hold on Jacob in order to embrace her in an enthusiastic hug. Jacob frowned at the sight of another man's arms around his woman, but it was only right that she receive credit for the part she'd played.

His woman. Had he really just labeled her as such? It seemed odd yet so very, very right. What also felt very, very right was getting Trent Walters's arms away from Mollie.

Jacob clasped the man's shoulder. "Your wife's not out of danger yet. Neither is William. I'll be stopping by regularly to check on their progress." Trent stepped away from Mollie to regard Jacob with solemn eyes. "I left instructions with your sister-in-law. Be sure to follow them."

The man vowed to follow each instruction to the letter, then showed Jacob and Mollie out. Jacob took Mollie up in front of him on his horse and kept Galen to a walk as they rode back to town. Dawn had begun to lighten the sky, but

Jacob didn't want to risk his mount tripping over an unseen obstacle.

Who was he kidding? He held Galen to a walk because Mollie felt too good leaning against his chest. He wrapped one arm about her waist and drew her even closer. She tipped her face back to look at him.

"We made a good team tonight, didn't we?"

He thought they'd make a good team every night. If she would consent to a different type of partnership. He squeezed her a little tighter. "We made an excellent team. Thank you for coming."

"I'll come whenever you need me, Jacob." Her face looked so earnest. It seemed only natural to bend down and touch his lips to hers.

"I fear I'll always need you, Mollie." He whispered the words in her ear, low and gruff. Then he kissed her again. Urgent. Breathless. A kiss that conveyed all his words could not. Her lips responded, softening under his onslaught. Her fingers tangled in the hair at his nape as she turned to accept his kiss more fully. A warmth that defied the predawn coolness suffused him. This *was* his woman.

Galen meandered to a halt at his master's lack of attention, then shifted restlessly. The sideways motion brought Jacob back to his senses. He eased his lips away from Mollie's and stroked his hand over her hair. Her dazed expression made him smile. One of these days, he really ought to try kissing her when their feet were on the ground.

"I need to get you back to Mrs. Peabody's," he said, as much a reminder to himself as an explanation to her. He took the reins more firmly in hand and nudged Galen into a trot.

Once outside her back door, he held out his arm and helped

Mollie slide down. He instantly missed her warmth and her gentle weight pressed against his chest.

"Take the afternoon off and get some rest, Mollie. You deserve it after your hard work tonight."

"I don't mind coming to the clinic," she said, even as a yawn snuck up on her and stretched her mouth wide before she could hide it with her hand. "Mrs. Peabody doesn't take kindly to idlers who take to their beds when the sun is shining."

"Then go visit Adam. I'm sure Curtis would let you make use of a spare bedroom for a couple hours."

Mollie stepped close to his horse and placed her hand on his knee. His blood pumped at the contact, but it was the happy glimmer in her eyes that captivated him. "You know," she said, "I think that's the first time I've heard you speak of him with no trace of bitterness in your voice. I like it."

She turned away then and disappeared into the house, leaving Jacob to stare after her. How had she snuck past his defenses so completely that he found himself wanting to please her more than he wanted to hold on to the grudge that had fueled him for so long?

An irrational urge to follow her into the house and hold her close nearly took him off his horse. The last time he'd felt love this strong was when his parents and sister were alive. Could he risk opening himself to that kind of pain again?

He had to. Because the pain of seeing her share her life with another man would be immeasurably worse.

10

Early the following afternoon, Jacob stepped out of the Cold Spring Café after treating himself to a slab of beefsteak, roasted carrots, mashed potatoes, and a slice of blackberry pie made from local berries that had just come into season. The sweet tang of the syrupy berry filling lingered deliciously on his tongue. Could this day get any better? Two lives spared in the dark of night, a soul-searing kiss with the woman he loved as dawn broke, and a string of satisfied customers that morning with minor ailments that could easily be remedied. Life was sweet.

"Dr. Sadler." The tart, pinched voice matched the puckered, disapproving face of the woman marching with military precision toward him. The click of her heels on the boardwalk tapped out a cadence as tight as any drummer's on the battlefield. "I'd like a word with you, sir."

The flavors he'd just been savoring soured in Jacob's mouth. "Mrs. Peabody." He dipped his chin and touched the brim of his hat. "What can I do for you, ma'am?"

The silver-haired woman glared at him from beneath a straw bonnet that sported so many feathers he marveled that the thing hadn't taken flight. "What you can do is cease encouraging my boarder to engage in improper behavior."

The humor he'd found in Mrs. Peabody's hat vanished. Jacob clenched his jaw as he fought to maintain a polite expression. Had the woman been awake before the sun that morning? Had she somehow witnessed the kiss he and Mollie had shared? But no, she couldn't have. They'd still been on the outskirts of town. Even if Mollie's landlady had the eyes of a hawk, she wouldn't have been able to see. But what if someone else had seen and had spread the tale?

"To what, precisely, are you referring, madam?" Jacob adopted his best elitist airs. One couldn't spend holidays in New York and Boston attending parties with the Thorntons of King Star Shipping without learning how to put an upstart in their place with a downcast glance, superior tone, and a sniff of disapproval. He'd been on the receiving end of such tactics often enough to mimic them with frightening accuracy.

Mrs. Peabody retreated a step and blinked. But he had to hand it to her, she didn't stay cowed for long. "I'm referring, of course, to the fact that you sent for her in the dead of night to attend a birthing." She gave a fairly credible sniff of disdain of her own as she eyed him. "Everyone knows it's indecent for an unmarried lady to attend such an event. It's far too indelicate for an innocent. Besides, she has absolutely no experience that would make her an asset in such a situation, which means the only thing your little stunt accomplished was to expose Mollie's reputation to further censure."

Jacob tightened his hands into fists in order to keep them from wrapping themselves around the prudish woman's neck. He glared a warning at her, but Mrs. Peabody's righteous indignation would not be stifled.

"It's bad enough the girl has thievery in her past, but now every decent man in town will worry that her nightly escapades have irreparably tarnished her virtue as well. No one will have her."

"That's enough," Jacob ground out through his clenched jaw. A quick glance told him no one had yet taken notice of them. He needed to keep it that way, so he kept his outer demeanor polite even as his voice lowered to a dangerous growl that did nothing to mask his fury.

"The only one impugning Miss Tate's reputation is you, madam. While it is true that Miss Tate is not yet married, she is an excellent nurse. If it weren't for her intervention last night, Trent Walters would be burying a son today, and possibly a wife as well. I won't apologize for calling her to that birthing, nor will I allow you to cast suspicion upon her character in my presence."

Mrs. Peabody's eyes widened, as did her nostrils, as if she'd finally caught scent of the predator stalking her.

"And if I hear any disparaging remarks about Miss Tate's reputation, I will place the blame firmly at your feet. I'm sure the Walters family would be glad to champion her. As would my uncle. It would be a shame for someone as socially prominent as yourself to lose her standing in the community because you could not refrain from wagging your tongue."

The woman reared back and sputtered. Jacob took that as his cue to leave. He tipped his hat and strode away from her. He needed to get Mollie out from under that woman's roof as soon as possible. The most desirable option being moving her into the clinic as his wife. But she deserved a proper courtship, not some rushed affair that would lend itself to whispers behind closed doors. Of course, if he were openly courting her, the hours they spent together in the clinic or on house calls could raise eyebrows as well. Jacob smacked the trunk of one of the young pines that stood outside his clinic with enough force to shake needles loose. Shoot, maybe he should just abduct her and elope. A smile finally curved his lips as he imagined Mollie's response to that idea. She'd probably dose his coffee with castor oil for a week if he suggested such a thing.

He was still smiling when he entered the clinic's parlor and found Curtis waiting for him. Oddly enough, he didn't immediately frown at the older man's presence. The usual tightness still gripped his chest, but the pressure had lessened. Perhaps the healing between them had truly begun.

"Curtis." Jacob nodded politely to his uncle as he moved across the room. "What can I do for you? Is Adam's leg paining him?"

"No. The boy's fine. I was looking for Mollie." The worry lines cutting into the man's forehead set off a twinge of unease in Jacob's gut.

"She assisted me with a birthing last night. I gave her the afternoon off. Hopefully she's resting somewhere." Jacob kept his tone light even as a growing sense of dread dug claws into him.

Curtis gave no sign of relief at the news, which only intensified Jacob's trepidation.

"I know all about the Walters baby. Mollie told me herself this morning when she came out to the house. Even asked if she could use the spare room for a nap later this afternoon. Then she spent a good thirty minutes chatting with Adam before heading back to town to prepare lunch for Mrs. Peabody. She promised to return with a surprise for Adam. We expected her an hour ago. The boy's sure she's delaying just to torture him, but something inside me warns that it's more serious. I came to town to search her out. Checked with Mrs. Peabody first. Caught her as she was headed out for some shopping. She informed me that Mollie had left nearly an hour past, right after cleaning up the luncheon dishes. Now I learn that she's not here, either."

Curtis shifted from one booted foot to the other, then finally looked Jacob square in the eye. "I think something's happened to her, Jacob. I can't explain it, but I can't shake the feeling, either. Will you . . . will you help me look for her?"

The man swallowed hard but held Jacob's gaze. Between the bitterness Jacob had spewed at him the first time they'd met followed by the cold silence he'd doled out when he'd made that house call yesterday, it must have taken a lot of fortitude, not to mention desperation, for his uncle to ask such a favor of him. It was the desperation that spurred Jacob to agree.

"I will."

Curtis nodded, his relief palpable. Jacob felt no such consolation. Acres of forest lay between Cold Spring and Curtis's farm. Too many places for an injured person to lay undiscovered.

"Saddle my horse," Jacob said as he strode toward the back of the house. "I'll be ready as soon as I grab my gun and medical kit."

He'd search every inch of land between here and the farm until he found her. He'd not allow another loved one to be taken from him without a fight.

11

"There was no sign of her along the road when I came to town," Curtis relayed as the two men set off on horseback. "She likes to cut through the countryside when she's on foot, though, so I thought we could split up and search the wooded area between here and the farm."

Jacob gazed into the trees. He scanned left, then right, desperate for some indication of where they should start, but the pines gave away no secrets. "Are there certain paths she would follow?"

Curtis shrugged. "Probably. But there aren't any worn trails, so I can only guess which way she might have gone. If Adam was up and about, he could probably lead us, but he's not, so . . ." His words died away, but Jacob's mind filled in what his uncle didn't say. Their chances of finding Mollie before nightfall were slim.

"Let's pray she hears us and can call out if we get close." *And that she's alive and that we can find her before darkness sets in.* Darkness wouldn't stop him from looking, but it would be one more impediment standing between him and Mollie. There were enough of those already.

Curtis circled his mount in front of Jacob's and pulled his gelding to a halt. Jacob reined Galen in with a frown. He'd just opened his mouth to ask why they were wasting time, when his uncle bowed his head.

"Lord, you know where Mollie is. Lead us to her, and protect her from harm while we search. In Jesus's name, amen."

Jacob bent his head. Since walking into the clinic, he'd been so focused on getting to Mollie that he hadn't taken the time to tune his mind to the Spirit. He'd been determined to find her—vowed never to give up. Yet in the face of his uncle's prayer it became instantly clear that he'd been relying on his own strength without more than a cursory thought of the one who could see all.

When his uncle met his gaze, Jacob nodded to him. "Thanks for that."

Curtis nodded back. "You take the northern side. I'll search to the south. Fire two shots if you find her. If we both make it to the farm without seeing her, we'll regroup and start again."

"Right." Surrendering to both his uncle's greater knowledge of the land and to the Lord's greater knowledge of everything, Jacob did as instructed and steered Galen into the trees.

He rode in a slow zigzag pattern, calling Mollie's name until his voice became a hoarse rasp. He crawled through ravines, scoured the pines for broken branches, and even tore apart a scrawny lean-to some squatter had set up, then abandoned years ago.

Not a sign of her anywhere.

Jacob prayed for a pair of pistol shots to shatter the quiet of the forest and announce that Curtis had found what he had not, but nothing beyond an occasional birdcall met his ears. By the time he made it to the farm, Curtis was already there waiting for him. Without Mollie.

After dismounting, Jacob led Galen to the trough for a much deserved drink, all while doing his best to subdue his rising panic. He couldn't lose her. Not when he'd just given his heart to her. *Please, God. Don't take her from me.* He had to look harder. Longer. She was out there somewhere.

"I spoke to the boy while I was waiting for you to come in," Curtis said, striding forward to meet him. "I hoped he could help us narrow the search."

"And?"

"Well . . ." Curtis scratched at his beard. "All he could tell me was that Mollie was planning on making him a treat. Usually that means baking something. The boy has a powerful sweet tooth. But I don't think that is going to help us. The only kitchens she might use are mine and Mrs. Peabody's. She's in neither."

Jacob paced along the corral fence, staring down at the dirt without really seeing it. "Maybe she needed something special for the treat. Something she had to retrieve before she could make it." He swiveled to face Curtis. "Could she have gone to the grocers or the restaurant?"

"Possibly, but that would have taken less than an hour." He glanced up at the sun's sinking position in the afternoon sky. "I guess it's been closer to three hours now."

"Did you check the bed in the spare room, just in case she came back while we were gone and cozied down for that nap?" Jacob knew he was grasping at straws, but he needed so badly for her to be safe.

Curtis held his gaze, understanding and shared concern connecting them in a way Jacob could not dismiss. "I checked. Checked every room in the place. Even the cellar. Mrs. Grady hasn't seen her. The other kids haven't seen her. Mollie's not here." He pulled off his hat and scrubbed at his short, graying hair. "We could go back to town and ask after her there, but my gut tells me that would be a waste of time." He plopped his hat back on his head. "Mollie has never broken a promise. If she told Adam she'd bring him a surprise, something would have had to physically hold her back to keep her from following through."

That was his Mollie. Impetuous. Self-sacrificing. Loyal to the bone. Jacob closed his eyes and saw again how she had dropped through the busted church floor to get to Adam the day he'd met her. No hesitation. No caution. No care to her own well-being.

Ah, Mollie. What scrape have you gotten yourself into this time?

"So what kind of treat would she make?" Jacob asked his uncle, determined to work the problem instead of getting hung up on worrying over possible outcomes. "Cake? Cookies?"

Curtis looked back toward the house, a thoughtful look on his face. "The boy loves pound cake, but none of those ingredients require any special effort."

"What about pie? I had a slice of fresh blackberry pie at lunch today. Would Adam—"

"Blackberries! Of course. I should have thought of that hours ago." Curtis's face split into a grin as he staggered excitedly over to his horse and started pulling himself into the saddle. "Mollie makes blackberry cobbler every year when the berries ripen."

Jacob snagged Galen's reins and mounted in a single motion.

"Where are we headed?" Not that it mattered. He was just thankful to have a direction. Any direction.

Curtis jerked his head toward the east. "The creek."

Something nudged Mollie's shoulder. With the nudge came a reminder of the pain. She tried to snuggle back down into the darkness that had cushioned her from the agony in her head, but then someone called her name. Someone she knew. *Jacob.* He sounded far away. Surely he wouldn't mind if she just slipped back into the warm darkness for a little while.

"Mollie Tate. Don't you dare leave me."

Goodness, he sounded demanding. And worried. And perhaps just a tad panicked. Mollie frowned at that. Or she would have if she could've remembered how. The darkness made everything fuzzy. But one thing she did remember—Jacob never panicked. She'd never met a man so calm in a crisis. So what had him rattled?

Hands roamed over her arms and legs. They prodded and probed and seemed to jab every sore spot on her body. She wanted to scream at them to stop, but she only managed a pitiful little whining sound that barely even vibrated her throat. The hands must have heard it, though, for they stilled.

"Mollie? Can you hear me?"

Jacob. Heavens, how she loved that man. She'd gladly be his nurse for the rest of her days just to be close to him.

"Curtis, hand her up to me after I mount."

Uncle Curtis was here, too? They were working *together*? The thought made her want to smile, but some kind of heavy blanket hung over her, weighing down all her muscles.

"She's hasn't broken any bones, just a bunch of small lacerations from the blackberry thorns. It's the injury to her head that has me concerned. I need to get her back to the house to examine her more carefully."

Arms slid under her back and beneath her knees. Agony shot through her skull. She fought the pain, needing to remember something. Something important.

The arms lifted her high and jostled her.

Oh, yes! The blackberries. They had to take the blackberries with them. She couldn't disappoint Adam.

Just as the thought materialized, a new set of arms claimed her, and the motion of the transfer shook the well-fought-for memory right out of her head. Thinking hurt too much.

"Hang in there, Mollie." Jacob's voice rumbled just beneath her ear. She tried to pick out his words as the darkness rose to claim her. "I'll patch you up, I swear it. Don't leave me, sweetheart. Please. I love you too much to lose you."

She reached through the pain to grab on to that last statement, then tucked it against her heart before the darkness could steal it from her. Once she was sure the treasured words were safe, she surrendered to the black oblivion.

The next time awareness stirred, the pain wasn't quite as piercing. And when she heard Jacob's voice mumbling something, she strained to push through the fog to listen. Would he tell her he loved her again? Or had she just imagined those words?

"Go get some sleep, Curtis. I'm going to try to get another cup of willow bark tea into her. I can't risk morphine or laudanum in her condition. I need her to wake up." His voice cracked as he spoke, and Mollie's heart thumped.

He needed her.

She had to crawl out of this wretched darkness and get back to Jacob. It would hurt more, but since when had she ever taken the easy road? She had to assure him that she wasn't going to leave.

"It's been hours, son." Footsteps echoed in the room. "Let me sit with her for a few minutes while you go—"

"I'm staying. I have to. I love her, Uncle Curtis."

There were the words again. Only this time instead sounding like a promise, they sounded like torture.

"I want to have a family. With Mollie." He paused. "With you, too."

"Jacob." It seemed to be all Uncle Curtis could say.

Mollie couldn't blame him. It was the only word she wanted to say, too. "Jacob."

He was at her side in a flash, taking her hand in his. "Mollie?"

She focused all her energy on lifting her eyelids. They cracked just a bit, enough to let a sliver of lamplight in. Slowly, her lashes parted and she saw him. Red-rimmed eyes, stubbly jaw, hair a wreck. Her man.

"I won't leave you." She gave him her promise before exhaustion once again overtook her and dragged her back into unconsciousness.

Jacob remained by Mollie's side throughout the night, clinging to her hand as well as to her vow. She wasn't going to leave him. She'd given her word, and Mollie never broke a promise.

He prayed. He tended the cuts she'd suffered from the blackberry brambles when she'd fallen. The vines had grown entangled within a cedar's branches, and as best he could tell, she'd climbed the tree in order to reach the ripe berries that other pickers had left behind. Unfortunately, the limb she'd shimmied out on had been weak and had broken beneath her weight.

"You know, this tree climbing and dropping through busted church floors is going to have to stop after we're married. My heart won't be able to take the stress." He smiled and ran the back of his finger down the smooth line of her cheek. "Not that I expect any dictate I give you to have much effect. My only hope is that you'll grow to care enough about me that you'll take pity on me and cease taking unnecessary risks with your life."

He gently ran his hand over the lump at the back of the far side of her skull. The swelling had gone down a little. A good sign. He knew he just had to be patient and let God heal any swelling on the inside that he couldn't see, but he longed to have her open her eyes again and renew her vow not to leave him.

Leaning forward, he brushed his lips over her forehead. "I love you, Mollie." He closed his eyes and breathed in the scent of her hair, her skin.

"I love you, too."

Jacob started. His eyes flew open. Mollie blinked at him, her beautiful dark hazel eyes glowing with a clarity that sent relief surging through his chest. She was going to recover.

"I love you, Jacob Sadler," she repeated. Then her lips curved into a smile so sweet it made his teeth ache. "And if you promise to help me pick blackberries for Adam once my head stops pounding, I'll promise not to climb any more trees once we're married."

Jacob grinned. "Deal." He bent down and touched his lips to hers to seal their pledge. The gentle contact sent waves of triumph gushing through his veins.

She loved him, and she'd just vowed to be his wife. True, it had been a rather unorthodox proposal, since he'd thought her unconscious at the time. But she'd agreed, and he aimed to hold her to it.

As he dropped tender kisses on her eyebrows and forehead and drew a line of them down to her jaw, he silently made vows of his own. Vows to protect her, to cherish her, to give her the family she'd never had: in-laws who would adore her—Darius and Nicole Thornton would welcome Mollie with open arms, of that he had no doubt; children of their own to nurture and love; and an uncle they would share a life with, free of bitterness or grudges. He owed that much to Mollie. Shoot, he owed it to himself. But perhaps most of all, he owed it to God who'd found a way to mend the broken pieces of his life and taught him to love again.

OUT OF THE STORM

JODY HEDLUND

1

PRESQUE ISLE LIGHTHOUSE, MICHIGAN
OCTOBER 1854

"Everyone's dead."

Isabelle Thornton shuddered at her father's words.

Facedown in the cold water near her feet, a sailor bobbed up and down in the never-ending waves of Lake Huron that had pushed him to the rocky shore.

Carefully her father flipped over the body to reveal a translucent face and blue lips. The man's unseeing eyes stared up at the dark gray clouds covering the early morning sky, a reminder of the passing storm's fury.

Isabelle swallowed the revulsion rising in her throat.

Flotsam littered the beach around them, the remains of a steamer that had been ripped apart by the thrashing squall. Her father had warned her against coming outside. But she'd wanted to help, hoping and praying there would be survivors she could comfort.

"Go back inside, Isabelle" came her father's gentle reprimand. "There's nothing here for you to do."

He hauled the waterlogged sailor out of the foamy water and into the rusty-colored sea grass. Her father's broad shoulders slumped, and his old captain's coat stretched at the seams. Underneath the brim of his cap, his eyes radiated sadness and frustration.

"I don't want you seeing this," he said. His British accent came out stronger whenever he was distressed. "Besides, you'll catch a chill."

Isabelle hugged her mittened hands against her heavy wool coat. It was too early for the winter gale that had swept through last night. But she'd lived on the Great Lakes long enough to know the lakes had a personality all their own. They were temperamental and refused to be tamed.

"There was nothing you could have done to save the ship, Father," she said, trying to hold back the shivers that fought for release in her petite body.

He straightened to his full, imposing height and glanced to the now-darkened lantern room of the lighthouse behind them. The whitewashed conical tower wasn't tall, but on the elevated corner of the isthmus it rose high enough to light the surrounding bay and enormous lake beyond.

Yet even though her father had kept the lantern burning tirelessly all night long—in the howling wind that threatened to blow the tower over into the storm-tossed lake below—the steamer had wrecked anyway. The bright beam hadn't been enough to save the ship from the whipping that had beat against her like a cat-o'-nine-tails.

Her father released a sigh and bent over another lifeless body that had washed up on shore.

Isabelle frowned at the thunderous waves and wanted to rebuke them for their callousness toward her father and the ships he was devoted to protecting. The biting cold wind lashed at her and tugged at her knitted wool cap, blowing back her dark curls from a hastily tied ribbon.

A flat piece of wreckage rose up, then fell on the waves. Two men clung to it, even as a large wave crashed over them and attempted to wrestle them off.

"Father," she said, pointing to the makeshift raft. "Look!"

Though the men couldn't hear her over the roar of the lake, one of them raised his head and looked toward the shore.

At the sight of the survivors, her father let go of the lifeless body he was hauling and hurried across the rocks, his narrow face lighting with hope beneath the dark whiskers on his cheeks.

He plunged into the water, the waves instantly reaching above his knee-length leather boots. Soon he was up to his waist in the churning water. If any man could combat the stormy waves, her burly father could do it. And yet her breath caught as he pushed deeper into the lake.

While he strained to grasp the piece of wreckage the waves pushed nearer, it kept slipping out of his reach. A whitecap surged against him, but he lunged toward the survivors regardless. Her father was too strong, too determined, too fearless to let the lake overpower him.

She wasn't surprised when a couple of moments later he caught hold and began pulling the survivors steadily back to shore, making it look as if it were the easiest thing in the world to haul the waterlogged wreckage loaded with two men out of the lake.

Yet he was breathing heavily when he finally stumbled onto the beach, dragging the mass of broken boards and men over the rocks to the safety of dry land. The piece of wreckage was the size of a twin bed, likely from the deck of the foundered steamer. The young man who'd lifted his head earlier now clung to the edge of it with one gloved hand, also clutching the arm of the older companion sprawled next to him.

Isabelle dropped to her knees. From the blackened singes in their clothing, she could see they'd both suffered burns. And from the time spent in the frigid water, she had no doubt they were in danger of freezing to death.

Her father lowered himself more slowly, his big-boned body already stiff from the cold. "Son, you're safe now."

The younger one stirred, but didn't make a move to release his grip on the side of the plank or the man lying near him. His face was pale and icy, his lips and ears blue like the first dead sailor they came upon. He was soaked, and his blond hair stuck to his head. In spite of being half drowned, there was no concealing the fact that he was a very handsome man, with a strong jaw and chin, and muscular overall.

Her father yanked off one of his wet gloves and pressed his fingers against the other man's neck. He was as rigid as a frozen sturgeon. There was no rise and fall of his chest.

Her father pulled his hand away and sat back with a shake of his head. "He's gone."

Isabelle swallowed the disappointment she felt and reached for the younger man. "Let's get this one to the house before we lose him too."

Her father nodded.

She grasped the wool of the man's coat sleeve and tugged. But he only tightened his grip on his companion. "Just hang on, Charlie," he mumbled. "I won't let go of you."

"He's delirious," she said.

Her father pulled at the man's arm, attempting to pry his

grip loose. Again he resisted, crying out, "No! I promise I'll save you!"

A gust of wind blew off the lake, bringing with it a spray of icy rain. Her father couldn't contain a shudder. She had to get the survivor and her father inside right away.

Bending over the young man, she took off her mitten and pressed her warm hand against his cold cheek. "Charlie is going to be just fine," she said, praying he was in heaven now, warm and safe.

The man stirred again, this time shivering uncontrollably.

"You'll be fine too. But you need to let go so that we can carry you up to the cottage."

His eyes flew open, he gave a heaving gasp, and then he twisted his head until she found herself looking straight into the man's striking blue eyes.

She offered him a smile. "It's all right. You're on land now."

"Are you certain?" he croaked through chattering teeth.

She nodded. "You're safe, but we need to get you inside where it's warm."

He studied her face and then smiled lazily. "Are you sure I haven't died and gone to heaven?"

"No. You're still alive." Although she couldn't be sure for how much longer if she didn't act quickly.

"You're the most beautiful woman I've ever seen," he said. "You must be an angel." His gaze traveled around her face with an intimacy that made her squirm and glance at her father.

He was too busy to notice as he attempted to pry the survivor's fingers off his companion.

"It's okay to let go of Charlie now," she said, hoping to keep her voice calm and soothing.

His grin cocked up higher on one side. "Will you marry me?"

He really *was* delirious.

She ducked her head to hide her embarrassment, even though she knew she should feel none. "I'll only marry you," she said, "if you promise to let go of Charlie." She knew she was spouting as much nonsense as the young man, but at this point she had to do whatever it took to save him.

His eyes flickered shut, and his smile turned serene. "You drive a hard bargain." His voice grew faint. "But I accept . . ."

Finally his hand slipped away from Charlie. His eyes closed, and his head lolled as he drifted into unconsciousness.

Her father carried the young man up the rocky beach, past the weathered lighthouse, and into the keeper's one-story cottage.

They settled him into the bigger of the two bedrooms, the one her father used, considering Isabelle's room was nothing more than a closet off the kitchen.

"I'll doctor his wounds, Father," she insisted when he started to wave her out of the room. "You need to get out of your wet clothes and warm yourself."

He draped a bearskin over the man, heedless of the lake water dripping from his own coat. Worry creased his face. "I don't like the idea of you being alone with a complete stranger."

"I'll be fine." She tugged at the shoulders of her father's coat. "You can't take care of me if you become ill."

At that line of reasoning, her father let her help him out of his coat. And he didn't protest when she shoved dry garments into his arms.

"Besides, the man's weak and unconscious. He has burns and bruises and is half frozen." She shepherded her father toward the door. "I'll see to the man's wounds while you get out of your wet clothes."

He paused in the hallway with an anxious frown. "I'll let you tend him, but only until I can take over his care."

She nodded. Her father was too conscientious not to return to the wreckage and check for more survivors. He would also have to bury the dead bodies that had washed ashore before the wolves and bears made a meal of them.

The job of caring for their guest had to fall on Isabelle's shoulders whether her father liked it or not. And they both knew it. Nevertheless, she could understand his concern. If there was one thing certain in her uncertain life, it was her father's love. She'd never once doubted how much he loved her. She knew he'd do anything for her.

She also knew why he treated her so carefully, why he did everything within his power to protect her. He only wanted to make her life as pleasant as possible while she still had the chance to enjoy it.

She wasted no time warming water and gathering the scant medical supplies in the medicine chest her father had kept from his days of serving as a ship captain for the British navy.

By the time she returned to her patient, her father had already changed and gone back outside, but not before admonishing her to keep his hunting rifle nearby.

She flipped back the bearskin and examined the survivor quickly. His face was even paler than before, showing the blue veins that were sluggish from being drenched in the frigid lake water. His cold, soggy garments clung to him like leeches, drawing the life from him.

She darted to the end of the bed and began unlacing his shoes—shoes that were made of the finest kid leather and polished black without a scuff. His socks were silk. And as she worked his arms out of his coat, she could see that it too was of the best quality wool and matched his double vest and checked trousers. The triple-strand watch chain attached to his vest appeared to be gold, as were his shirt studs and cuff links.

"He must be a fancy gentleman," she whispered, placing all his accessories on top of the chest of drawers where they would be safe.

She stepped back to the bed and undid several buttons of his dress shirt, which had pleats and decorative needlework near the collar.

The man expelled a soft breath that brushed her arm.

She paused and glanced at his face, at the smooth angular lines and the high cheekbones that gave him an aristocratic look. A well-muscled chest showed above his undershirt. He wasn't nearly as stocky as her father, but he was chiseled and bronzed.

For an instant, she was tempted to step away and let her father take care of the patient after all. Surely it would be scandalous for her, a young innocent woman, to unclothe him any further.

He winced and gave a low moan, the lines in his face tightening. Obviously the man was in a lot of pain.

"Isabelle Thornton," she scolded herself, "this is no time to be a prude." Not when this man's life depended on her speed and nursing skills.

She finished unbuttoning his shirt and worked him out of it, taking note of the severe burns on his arms. An oiled leather pouch was strapped across his chest, and she gently removed it, hoping it contained identity papers should he not make it.

And as she tugged off his trousers, revealing his long sturdy legs, she refused to look at his underdrawers.

She could feel the heat rising to her cheeks. In the five years she and her father had lived at the remote northern Presque Isle Lighthouse, she rarely had the chance to interact with men, except for the occasional fisherman from the settlements in the Thunder Bay Island area to their south.

"That's perfectly fine with me," she whispered to herself, reaching for the jar of elderberry salve. "I don't want to meet any men."

At least that was what she'd been telling herself over the past year whenever she had the strange desire to experience love. At nineteen, she was of the age when thoughts of marriage were bound to come from time to time. But for her, that was all they would remain—thoughts.

She screwed the lid off the salve and dipped two fingers in the thick mixture. The scent of shaved elder mingled with the greasiness of the unsalted lard.

She'd resigned herself to the fact that no man would ever want her . . . not when he learned she didn't have a future. And she was content with the idea that she would spend the rest of her life with her father. Well, she was content most of the time anyway.

And just because this man had landed on the beach and was half naked in the bed didn't mean she had to turn into a flushed mess.

"He's only a patient." She took a deep breath and then boldly applied the salve to a swollen red area below his knee. "A wounded man, a soul in need of help." She was the doctor. That was all. And doctors had to touch their patients.

A spot of crimson seeped onto the sheet near his outer

thigh. She squinted and bent closer. The stain seemed to be spreading.

Without any more thought to modesty, she rolled him onto his side and slid up his drawers until the linen reached the rounded flesh of his backside. She gasped at the sight that met her.

A bullet lodged firmly in his thigh.

2

The only practice she'd had with removing bullets was from the carcasses of the deer, rabbits, and other game her father brought home. After positioning the stranger on his stomach, she fished out the bullet as carefully as she could. Thankfully it was near the surface and not too difficult to extract. As far as she could tell, the bullet had nicked neither bone nor artery.

She was glad the man was unconscious during the removal of the bullet and the stitching she had to do afterward. When she finally finished bandaging the wound, as well as the assortment of burns he'd suffered, she'd forgotten all about the fact that he was a man and she a woman. He'd simply become a survivor in dire need of her care.

Later, when her father stumbled into the cottage, he told her the count of the dead that washed ashore had reached twenty. After burying them all, he'd been too weary and heartsick to protest Isabelle's continued doctoring of their lone survivor. Instead, he'd collapsed onto the bed in Isabelle's room and attempted to get a couple of hours' sleep before having to head up to the lantern room of the lighthouse and begin his nightly routine of tending the light.

Isabelle slept in the chair beside the patient, waking several times during the night when the patient stirred or when her father came down to check on her. She fumbled in the darkness to reheat the warming stones and make the stranger more comfortable.

Even though unconscious, he grew increasingly agitated. She had no choice but to give him some laudanum, upset that in her bumbling efforts she spilled precious drops of the pain-killer.

As usual she was relieved when the first rays of light slanted through the window, casting a glow over the bedroom.

"Charlie?" the patient mumbled. "Charlie, are you all right?"

Isabelle rose from her chair and moved to the edge of the bed. She pressed a hand to the man's forehead. He'd finally warmed up. And from what she could surmise, he didn't have a fever. Yet. Time would tell if his bullet wound would fester or not.

Soft strands of his hair tickled her fingers. She brushed them back.

"Mother?" His voice was muffled, his eyes still closed.

"No," she said. "I'm Isabelle."

"Izzy?" He reached for her hand that was still on his forehead and captured it in a grip that was surprisingly strong. "I've missed you."

Before she could react, he pulled her down and wrapped both arms around her in a hug. For a moment, she was too startled to resist. She could only think about his cheek pressed against hers, the day-old whiskers scraping her skin. His breath was warm, his arms thick and comforting, and his chest solid beneath her.

His nearly bare chest . . .

Heat flamed through her. She squirmed to free herself from his hold.

He immediately released her.

She took a step away from the bed at the same time his eyes flew open. He looked at her through long eyelashes, confusion rippling across his face.

"You're not my sister," he said.

"No, I'm not," she replied, fighting the embarrassment that flooded her. "I'm Isabelle Thornton. And I'm sorry for . . . for . . ."

Hugging him? Unclothing him? Removing the bullet from his bare thigh? She clasped her hands together and stared at them.

"Don't be sorry," he said with a weak laugh. "I'm the one who hugged you. I only hope I managed to kiss you at some point too."

"Kiss?" The word was laced with scandal.

His laughter grew louder.

What kind of man was this? Not only had he asked her to marry him but now he was wishing he'd kissed her?

"I'm Henry," he offered, grinning up at her. "And I'm *very* pleased to meet you."

She was taken aback by his emphasis on the word *very*. The man's forwardness had rendered her speechless.

"And to what occasion do I owe the pleasure of our meeting?"

Was he delirious? After a brief moment, she found her voice again. "I wouldn't exactly call what happened pleasurable."

He blinked, then looked around the room, as if taking in his surroundings for the first time—the unadorned walls, the simple bedstead and hand-hewn bedside table, and the wooden chair she'd brought in from the sitting room. He glanced down at his prostrate body covered with heaps of blankets. Frowning, he asked, "Where am I?"

"Presque Isle Lighthouse."

He shifted and then winced again as his tender backside made contact with the bed.

"I removed a bullet," she said. She paused then, hoping he'd give her an explanation as to how he'd been shot.

He remained silent, staring past the calico curtains in the direction of the lake. The color that had returned to his face drained away. "The storm," he whispered.

"Yes. It was a terrible storm." Outside, the sky was finally clearing. After several days of wintry weather, the gale had blown itself out at last.

Henry closed his eyes, and his Adam's apple moved up and down. Was he reliving the nightmare of all he'd gone through in the storm?

"Providence was watching over you," she offered. "You apparently dragged yourself aboard a piece of wreckage."

He nodded, the muscles in his face twitching.

"You hung on so tightly we had to pry your fingers loose when we found you."

"And my companion?" When his dark blue eyes met hers, there was a desperation in them that made her wish she could tell him everything would be all right.

"You held on to him and kept him from drowning." Her shoulders sank, and she blew out a breath. "But he didn't make it. I'm sorry."

"No . . ." Henry's cry was anguished. He shook his head and shoved back the covers with his feet. "Not Charlie!" He rolled over with a groan and slung his legs out of the bed.

"You can't get up." She grabbed his arm to push him back against the mattress. "Please, you're too injured—"

With another cry of despair, he shrugged out of her hold, stood to his feet, and stumbled forward.

She reached for him, to keep him from falling, but he staggered away, taking unsteady steps like those of a drunken man. His bare feet slapped against the floor as he moved down the hallway, bumping into the walls. He was heading for the front door.

"Henry, you're not well!" She hurried after him. "You need to stay in bed."

He wrenched open the door and stepped outside.

Sunshine poured down on them, yet the wind was rough and cold and contained the sting left over from the storm. Regardless of his injuries and that he was dressed only in undergarments, Henry careened across the yard, past the whitewashed lighthouse, and down the knoll that led to a stretch of rocky beach and the lake.

"Henry, please come back to the house," she pleaded. Her father peered down from the round tower room through the pristine glass, his tired face lined with sudden concern at the sight of their runaway patient.

Henry didn't stop until he reached the water's edge, where foaming waves crashed against the rocks. He stared wildly out at the lake, and she was afraid he would do something foolish in his grief, like plunge into the cold water and drown himself.

But after a moment, the wildness dissipated and he collapsed to his knees. "It should have been me." He buried his face in his hands. "If anyone had to die, it should have been me."

She crouched next to him and hesitated only a second before

laying a hand on his back. There were no words to ease the pain of his loss. Even so, she felt she must try.

"God is the giver of life. And He's also the taker. If He spared your life, then He must have something left for you to do."

A fresh spot of bright red showed through the back of his drawers. She had no doubt that with all the movement he'd ripped open his stitches.

"Charlie was a good man," he said. "A much better man than me."

"Isabelle!" Her father's shout came from the beach behind them.

Henry struggled to his feet. His stricken eyes met Isabelle's. The blue in them drew her in like the tide, magnetically, irresistibly. She could feel her heart breaking with his pain.

Then he crumpled to the ground, unconscious.

Isabelle stuck the pencil behind her ear and examined her sketch. The sunlight streaming through the bedroom window lit up the jagged edges and intricate veins of the red-maple leaf she'd drawn. She'd shaded every shadow, every slight change in the coloring, wanting to imprint the image in her mind for the future.

Satisfied with the outcome, she flipped her sketchbook to the next blank page. She picked up a pinecone from her collection and placed it in the spot of sunshine that lit her drawing board, eager to examine the pinecone and memorize every tiny detail.

At a soft moan from the bed, she stood and set her sketchbook on the chair.

Henry's eyes flickered open, and he stared at the ceiling for a moment. Then his eyelids fell again as if reality were too much to bear.

She needed to wake her father. After carrying the unconscious stranger back from the beach, her father had given her explicit instructions to call him the second Henry regained consciousness.

She went to her patient's side and touched his arm. "Henry?"

His long lashes lifted, and slowly he found her face.

"How are you?" she asked.

His lips cracked into a half smile. "I've been better."

She gave his arm a brief squeeze and hoped he could sense her understanding.

He shifted, but the slight movement caused him to grimace.

"You ripped your wound open," she said. "I had to patch you up again."

"Ah, I see. I meet a beautiful woman here in the wilderness and my introduction to her is by way of a bullet hole in my leg."

Though she'd tried to ignore his bare thigh when she cleaned and then stitched the wound, it was difficult not to notice. She ducked her head so that he wouldn't see the revelation in her eyes. Her father was appalled when he'd discovered the extent of her ministrations toward the patient, even while they both realized it had been unavoidable.

"I hope you know this isn't the usual way I acquaint myself with pretty ladies," he said. "I'd much prefer you fall in love with my face first."

Fall in love?

"You have nothing to worry about," she said, striding to the window. She supposed a wealthy, handsome man like him was used to having *pretty ladies* falling all over him. "I doubt I'm like the other ladies you've known."

"I can see that." His voice turned playful.

She tugged the curtains open wider, letting the sunlight flood the room. The bedroom window overlooked the grassy yard next to the tower.

"It's quaint," Henry said, straining to see out the window toward the lighthouse. "And short." The lift of his brows told her he wasn't impressed by the structure.

At forty feet high, it was one of the shortest lighthouses of the Great Lakes. Built fifteen years ago, it was already in need of repair. The harsh Michigan weather had been brutal on the stone-and-brick tower. Even so, its Lewis lamp did a more than adequate job of illuminating the dangerous rocky shoreline, serving as a guide to the many passing vessels.

"It must be difficult for your father, not having the lighthouse and cottage attached."

"He's a tough man and doesn't mind," she said, turning away from the window, remembering she must do as her father had bid. As much as she wouldn't mind staying and talking with Henry, she needed to wake Father and let him speak to the patient.

Her father may have been strict, but he was always good and fair toward her. Having served as a sea captain and civil magistrate for many years, once married he'd chosen to remain at home with his family and so had become a keeper. It was the only life she'd ever known, and she had no doubt it was the only life she'd ever have. Reluctantly, Isabelle left the bedroom and went to retrieve her father.

Minutes later, she moved as silently as she could in the kitchen as her father sat down next to Henry and questioned him in his usual no-nonsense manner.

She learned that Charlie had been Henry's assistant in business, that they'd been traveling together around the Great Lakes, visiting the lumber camps and mines his father owned.

"So your father is Ethan Cole?" Her father's voice rose with a note of surprise.

Isabelle stirred the pot of turkey broth slowly, curious about the young man in the other room.

"Yes," Henry replied. "Ethan Cole, of Cole Enterprises."

Given her father's silence, she had the feeling the news was somehow significant, though she wasn't sure in what way.

"I told my dad not to send me to the Midwest," Henry said with a trace of humor. "But he insisted I go. He thought the trip would help me grow up, become more responsible, and ready to step into my role as his business partner."

"And did it?"

Henry laughed. "Let's put it this way—it's given me a new appreciation for civilization. I'm ready to get back home to New York and to real life."

Her father didn't laugh. "Tell me how you got shot."

"I was being robbed at the time." Any hint of humor soon faded. "I probably would have been killed if the storm hadn't hit when it did."

Isabelle let the spoon grow idle in the steaming pot.

"Why was someone trying to rob and kill you?" Her father asked the question on the tip of her tongue.

"I suspect the thief was hired by our biggest competitor, Big Al Rainer," Henry answered. "I'd just acquired a large tract of prime timberland near Cheboygan. And my guess is that Big Al wanted to destroy all proof of the claim so that he could make the purchase for himself."

"You believe he sent out men to kill you?"

"Absolutely. White pine is green gold, Captain Thornton."

"And Cole Enterprises has decided to capitalize on this 'green gold'?"

"Not decided. We already have. My father has timber cruisers all over northern Michigan and Wisconsin, locating tracts of superior cork pine."

"So having millions isn't enough? You need more?"

Henry laughed. "Why not?"

Her father didn't say anything. Isabelle had the feeling he was doing his best to digest Henry's situation, just as she was.

"Tell me more about the steamer and the wreck," her father finally said.

As Isabelle put together a tray of broth and coffee for Henry, he relayed how the storm had hit them without warning. He'd been asleep in his berth and was abruptly awakened when the ship pitched in the storm. The thief was in their cabin, and the sharp motion threw him to the floor, which was when both he and Charlie saw him there.

Henry had wrestled with the thief, but he wasn't able to get ahold of the man's pistol. The storm then swept down on them with such ferocity that within minutes the steamer was torn apart beam by beam until she began to take on water. He'd gotten himself shot in the scuffle before jumping ship with Charlie.

"So when Big Al learns you're still alive, he'll send men after you again," her father said after Henry finished his tale.

"Don't worry," Henry said. "By then I'll be gone."

"Let's hope so," her father said, his chair scraping across the floor. "Let's pray that by some miracle you're gone before you bring danger to my doorstep."

"My father will send someone for me soon enough."

"Not if he thinks you're dead."

120

"Then I'll simply post a letter to him."

"Even if your letter reaches him, we'll be lucky if he can come for you before the lake freezes and commerce halts for the winter. And if this past storm was any indication, then it would seem we're in for an early winter."

"Fine. I'll leave on the next steamer," Henry said.

"There aren't any steamers that stop here. They refuel down at Thunder Bay Island. And even if you were in any condition to travel, there won't be many boats passing through now, not after the recent storm."

"Are you saying I'm stuck here?"

Isabelle didn't like the desperation in Henry's voice. Presque Isle might be a remote post, but it was the most beautiful place on earth—at least she thought so.

Or maybe he was so wealthy that he was repulsed by the idea of living in their tiny home without the comforts he was used to. Though her father claimed that a new settler by the name of Burnham had purchased land in the harbor and was developing a fishery, there was nothing else within miles of the lighthouse.

They were about as isolated as anyone could possibly get.

"Young man," her father said in his most severe tone, the one she imagined he'd used back when he commanded his own ship. "I don't like that you're here any more than you do."

"You'll be compensated for any inconvenience—"

"I don't care about your money," her father said, a bit too loudly.

Isabelle cringed.

"I want you to keep to yourself while you're here," her father continued, his voice cold. "Stay away from my daughter."

She was glad when Henry didn't respond. While she told

herself she didn't care what the man thought of her, there was something within her that longed for companionship with someone her age.

She loved her father dearly, yet she couldn't deny the strange feelings Henry had elicited, feelings she wanted to explore and savor just once in her life.

3

Henry gritted his teeth and stifled a moan into the sagging mattress. Every part of his body ached. His skin was on fire in a dozen spots where he'd sustained burns. But it was his thigh that was bringing him the most agony. It was as if someone were stabbing him with a knife, twisting and digging it into his flesh.

The padding of Isabelle's footsteps sounded in the hallway outside his room. After Captain Thornton had interrogated him earlier, he'd overheard the man warn his daughter not to linger in his room but to only tend him if he needed something.

Henry had been disappointed when she so readily complied. She hadn't come into his room for several hours. Instead, the captain had been the one to change his dressings and bring him lunch. The captain hadn't smiled once, but instead he'd been brusque and grouchy.

Henry's mind had strayed all too often to the nightmare he'd lived through during the storm, the near fatal escape from the would-be assassin. To escape the murderer, he and Charlie had hidden aboard the sinking vessel as long as possible before the exploding furnaces and rapidly spreading fire had forced them to jump, like all the other passengers had done earlier. Fortunately, with the explosion they'd been able to find a piece of wreckage large enough for both of them to climb aboard.

The challenge had been to stay on the wreckage with the wind and waves threatening to drown them in the icy water. Charlie had given up at least a dozen times, pleading with Henry to let him go, to allow him to find oblivion in a watery grave. Henry hadn't been able to release his friend to death but was determined to save him.

Except he'd failed.

"Father's sleeping," Isabelle said from the doorway. "If you need anything, I can help you while he's resting."

"I'm in great need," he said.

"What's wrong?" Her light, elegant steps drew nearer.

He waited until she was next to the bed and then turned his head so he could look up at her. She wasn't tall like her father. In fact, where the captain was powerfully built, she was delicate, thin-boned, almost petite. Her father was tanned and weather-roughened, while she was pale-skinned as if she rarely went outdoors.

Her features, as he'd noticed before, were exquisitely beautiful and angelic.

"What do you need?" Her thin brows furrowed with concern.

"I need to see your pretty face." He flashed his most charming grin, the one that melted the hearts of most women. "I was about to die for want of seeing it."

A faint flush rose into her cheeks. Her eyes widened, and for the first time he noticed the color. They were light brown and glossy, like tea with honey. The color was in contrast to the rich ebony of her hair.

"Ah, that's much better," he said, feasting upon her beauty. If he had to be stranded in the vast wilderness of Michigan, then at least he'd have a pleasant diversion in Isabelle.

"Mr. Cole," she chastised, glancing toward the door as if expecting her father to come charging in.

"I insist you call me Henry. Mr. Cole is my father's name. And besides, don't you think we've already moved past formalities?" He cocked his head toward his thigh and winked at her.

She took a quick step back, but not before he caught sight of the embarrassment in her expression. He laughed, but the movement jarred his body and a fresh wave of pain choked him.

"Since you seem to be doing just fine," she said with censure in her voice, "I'll come back later." She spun and started across the room.

"No!" he said, the word coming out weaker than he wanted. Thankfully it was enough to stop her. "Don't leave me, Isabelle." He didn't want to be alone. Even with the recent dose of laudanum the captain had given him, the pain was too intense. He needed something—or someone—to take his mind off his predicament.

He'd already thought about Charlie too much. And every time he did, guilt overwhelmed him. It was his fault Charlie was dead. His faithful assistant hadn't wanted to leave the Keweenaw Peninsula, but had insisted on staying for several more days to finish taking stock of the mine in Eagle Harbor, one of the many copper holdings they had in Copper Country.

But of course, Charlie hadn't been able to withstand Henry's plea to move on. After being away all summer and fall, Henry had grown impatient to return to the social life he'd missed, the rounds of dining and visiting, the parties and dancing. Even though he'd be too late in the season for yachting and racing, he was eager to resume his life of ease and fun.

He'd made a pretense of working long enough. Hopefully, his father would be pleased with his efforts, even though technically Charlie had done most of the management of affairs over the past months. Charlie had preferred it that way, and Henry hadn't complained. It allowed him more time to locate nightclubs and dancing and card playing as often as the circumstances would allow.

If only he'd listened to Charlie and stayed a few more days in Eagle Harbor. Henry exhaled a pained sigh. Now Charlie was gone, and it was all his fault.

"Please stay," he said again.

Isabelle hesitated.

"I promise I'll be good." He wasn't used to pleading with women to be with him. Even over the past months sailing around the Great Lakes from Chicago to Grand Rapids to Marquette, he'd never had any trouble attracting attention.

Isabelle finally turned. Her eyes narrowed on him.

"Okay, maybe I won't be good," he confessed with a smile. "But I promise I won't try to seduce you."

Again a rosy flush spread over her cheeks, making her all the more appealing.

"You're so beautiful that looking at you is enough to take my mind off my pain."

She rolled her eyes and started to retreat again.

"Please, Isabelle." He didn't care that he was begging her. The truth was he couldn't bear the thought of being left alone any longer. "Really. I need a distraction."

The compassion in her eyes told him she could sense the

depth of his discomfort. "All right," she said. "I'll stay for a few minutes."

He hadn't realized his muscles had tensed until she slid the chair closer to the bed. He allowed his body to relax again—or at least as much as the pain would allow.

"I can't stay long, since Father wouldn't approve." She positioned the chair at least an arm's length away from him.

"What your father doesn't know won't have to hurt him, right?"

"I'm not planning to deceive my father." She picked up the big Bible on top of the dresser before settling herself into the chair. "But he surely won't disapprove of me reading the Bible to you."

"Surely not." Henry couldn't stop himself from grinning. She didn't return his smile.

He wished he could sit up and make himself more presentable. He guessed he was quite the sight—unwashed, unshaven, and uncombed. Maybe if he'd had the chance to groom himself, Isabelle would find him more attractive.

She fished a pair of spectacles from her apron pocket and perched them on her nose before reverently opening the Bible. The yellowed pages crinkled as she carefully turned them.

"Might I suggest Song of Solomon?" he said with as much seriousness as he could muster.

Her fingers stalled, and she frowned at him over the rim of her glasses. "Are you ever serious about anything?"

"I try not to be."

"Well, try now." Her expression contained a mild rebuke.

He had to work hard to force his grin into a somber line, and even then his lips quirked with the need to smile.

She focused on the page in front of her, smoothing it with

long fingers. "I'll read from Proverbs. Chapter fifteen, verse twenty-one says, 'Folly is joy to him that is destitute of wisdom; but a man of understanding walketh uprightly.'"

Laughter welled up and burst out before Henry could stop it.

Her lips twitched into a smile that she couldn't hide. She flipped ahead a page. "And chapter seventeen, verse sixteen says, 'Wherefore is there a price in the hand of a fool to get wisdom, seeing he hath no heart to it?'"

He laughed again, his heart warmed by her bantering. "So I'm a fool, am I?"

She pursed her lips, clearly trying not to smile.

"I think you need to read down a couple of verses," he teased. "Doesn't chapter seventeen, verse twenty-two say, 'A merry heart doeth good like a medicine: but a broken spirit drieth the bones'?"

This time her smile broke free and lit her face and eyes.

Something warm and satisfying spread through him. It was a strange feeling, not one he'd experienced before but one he wanted to have again. He wanted to make her smile, even make her laugh. But not because of himself or for his own selfish need.

No, he wanted her to smile because he could see that she needed it, that she'd had too little merriment in her short life.

Maybe he was stranded in the middle of nowhere with nothing to do, away from the pleasures of his life, but he'd never been one to let anything stand in the way of having fun.

He'd have to make the most of his situation. And part of that—a large part—would include teaching Isabelle Thornton to have fun. It would be a challenge he'd relish.

4

"Isabelle," called Henry from the bedroom. "I need you!"

Isabelle finished pouring the steaming mug of coffee, set it on the tray next to the toast, and then counted to ten. Slowly.

After several days, she was learning that when Henry *needed* something, he usually only *wanted* her attention. Maybe hordes of adoring ladies came running whenever he spoke or batted his long eyelashes, but she wasn't going to fall prey to his wiles.

"I want to show you something," he said.

She picked up the tray and forced herself to walk with measured steps. She didn't want to appear too eager to see him, even if she was.

She peeked over her shoulder toward the back door. Her father hadn't been gone hunting for more than ten minutes, and she was embarrassed to admit she'd already plotted an excuse to go visit Henry.

Her father had taken over most of the care and forbade her from stepping into the bedroom when he was there. As a result, she found herself counting down the minutes until he would sleep, ascend the tower, or go check his traps as he was doing now.

She enjoyed being with Henry much more than she wanted to acknowledge and certainly more than she ever wanted him to know. He was already proud enough and didn't need to realize his effect on her.

"Will you please come, Isabelle?" His voice turned soft and plaintive.

She forced down a smile, tried to conjure her most severe expression, and then entered the room.

He was lying on his side, propped up on one elbow. On the edge of the bed next to him was a board covered with rocks. At the sight of her, his grin took wings with enough power to take her breath away. "I've been waiting all day to see you."

She'd been waiting all day to see him too, but she absolutely would never tell him that.

"If I'd had to wait another minute, I was planning to get up and kick the captain out of the house."

"And I'm sure that would have worked well." She set the tray down next to the bed.

"What?" His eyes winked with teasing. "You don't think I'm a match to fight your father?"

"Perhaps you are, if you want a broken arm and leg to go with your other wounds."

He chuckled. "You don't have much faith in my abilities, Isabelle."

She handed him the mug of coffee. "I know the abilities of my father when he's provoked."

"He reminds me of a big black bear standing on his back two feet, ready to roar."

She smiled at the image, knowing it was true.

Henry took a sip of coffee. "He's overprotective of you."

"He loves me."

"He can't keep you away from everyone and everything forever."

"He's not."

"Then why is he working so hard to keep you away from me?"

She took the mug back from him and replaced it on the tray. Then she handed him the piece of toast. "Maybe he's not keeping me away. Maybe I'm just not interested in spending my every waking moment in your company."

He locked eyes with her, probing, searching, seeing past her words to her heart. Taking a bite of the toast, he grinned through his mouthful. "You like me," he said. "I can tell."

She quickly spun away, afraid she'd blush or smile or do something that would give away her curiosity. She busied herself folding a blanket that had slipped onto the floor. All the while she could feel his attention upon her.

"Now that the bear is out of the way," he said after swallowing the last bite of bread, "I want to teach you how to play a game."

The board next to him had light-colored rocks on one end and darker ones on the other. She'd collected them for him earlier at his request. "I don't play games."

"You'll like this one." He brushed the toast crumbs from the sheet and nodded to the chair. "If you don't like the game, then I'll let you kiss me. For as long as you want."

Her mouth dropped open before she could stop it.

He laughed. "I'm just joking." But when his gaze dropped to her lips, she wasn't so sure he was teasing.

She couldn't stop herself from glancing at his lips, at the playful curve that was also strong and inviting. She'd never kissed a man before. In fact, she'd never desired to and never imagined she would. But at his suggestion, suddenly all she could think about was what it would be like to touch his lips with hers, to experience just one kiss in her life.

As if reading her thoughts, his grin inched up. "Then again, if you want to make a bargain, I'm willing. If I win, you kiss me. If you win, I kiss you."

She shook her head to free herself from the snare he caught her in every time she came near him. "Stop flattering yourself. I don't want to kiss you. And I won't."

"Well, at least play the game with me." The plea in his eyes was irresistible.

Heaving an exasperated sigh, she went to the chair and plopped down.

"This game is called checkers," he said. "You'll have the light pieces and I'll have the dark."

After the first few awkward moments, she began to relax as he showed her what to do. And after some time, she actually found herself enjoying it. She caught on quickly, and she beat him in the fourth game.

"You owe me three kisses, and now I owe you one," he said as he moved the stones back into place for a rematch.

"I don't owe you anything." She put her stones into position too, eager for another game.

"You at least owe me the chance to teach you another game later."

He stared at her with such hopefulness that she didn't have the heart to tell him no. "Maybe after Father goes up to the light."

With a pounding heart, Isabelle crept into Henry's room after her father had heated the sperm-whale oil and carried it to the tower through the cold evening in order to light the lantern. As the October days grew shorter and darkness arrived earlier, her father had to spend longer periods in the lighthouse.

She told herself she wouldn't play games with Henry for long. But after countless rounds of checkers, he taught her to play fox and geese, which she enjoyed just as much. She was surprised when the glowing light from the oil lantern began to flicker.

She'd stayed up far too late and now the lantern needed refilling.

"Time for bed," she said, rising and stifling a yawn. Then the lantern fluttered out completely and plunged the room into darkness.

She grabbed the back of the chair to steady herself. She knew what was coming and she dreaded it, since it occurred most nights. But she didn't want it to happen in front of Henry.

She blinked, trying to focus, trying to see past the dimness. But the room was completely black. It was almost as if someone had blindfolded her and blocked out any trace of light that came from the tower beam and the moon.

"Is everything okay?" Henry asked.

She tried looking at him, in the direction where she'd heard his voice. She wanted to pretend everything was normal. That *she* was normal.

But the world around her was gone.

"I need to get to bed," she said, pivoting away from him. "That's all."

But as she took several steps from the chair, she felt lost. The opposite side of the room stretched out as though miles away instead of eight paces.

"Something's wrong," Henry stated quietly, without any of his usual humor.

She didn't answer. All she knew was that she had to make it out of the room and away from him before she tripped over something. Her foot snagged against the chair and she stumbled. She resisted putting out her hands to help feel her way across the room, because in the faint light coming through the window, he'd be able to see her fumbling.

The mattress squeaked as if he was trying to push himself up. "Are you ill?"

"I'm fine, Henry. Just stay in bed." She managed several more steps and had the sense she was almost there. This time she held out her hand, and it brushed against the wall. She skimmed her fingers in the direction she thought might be the door until she made contact with the doorframe.

She fumbled into the hallway, growing more embarrassed with every step. Once out of Henry's sight, she stopped and leaned against the wall. She pressed her cheek against its coolness and had to gulp down her mortification.

How had she let it happen? She hadn't wanted Henry to see her in her weakest moment. She didn't want him to pity her or to treat her differently. For once in her life, she wanted to be able to forget about the darkness of the future, to pretend it wasn't coming.

She'd been able to do that when spending time with Henry. He made her smile, and he took her mind off the morbid.

Yet if he knew her true condition, all that would change. Maybe he wouldn't want to be around her at all.

Her throat tightened. She would have to be more careful and make sure that didn't happen.

5

The back door in the kitchen banged open. Isabelle jumped out of the bedside chair. "Father!" She grabbed the tray containing the empty breakfast plate and a half-filled mug of lukewarm coffee. "He's down from the tower early."

Henry was counting his winnings. "Or maybe you were having so much fun that you forgot about the time."

Her father's footsteps thudded heavily in the opposite room.

"Quick. Hide the game," she whispered over her shoulder as she started toward the door.

But of course Henry only grinned and continued counting his stones. "I have nothing to hide. We have every right to play a game of checkers together."

She wanted to argue with him and demand that he cover the board with his blanket, but she only shook her head and picked up her pace.

When she'd taken Henry his breakfast earlier, she wasn't able to resist when he pulled out the checkerboard again. He hadn't said anything about her hasty departure of the previous night. And even though she'd seen him studying her more

135

intently during their game, she was grateful he hadn't spoken of the incident.

She entered the kitchen to see her father sitting in a chair, unlacing his boots. He glanced up with wariness in his face, searching her as if he expected that Henry had mauled her during his absence. "Is everything all right?"

"Everything's just fine, Father. There's no need to worry." She didn't dare look at him for fear he'd see her guilt. Instead, she busied herself cleaning off the tray. "Henry's a nice man."

"That's what I'm afraid of," Father said with a growl. "He's *too* nice."

If he agreed that Henry was nice, why was he opposed to her spending time with him?

"It looks like we're in for a fair-weather day today," he said in a more controlled tone. "Warm and sunny."

"It's about time." Winter was already long enough in Michigan without it starting in October.

"I've been putting off rowing down to Thunder Bay Island. I was praying by some miracle that Henry would recover quickly enough to come along." Father shrugged out of his coat. "But I think I better take that trip today while the lake is calm. I need to file a report regarding the shipwreck and send a letter to Henry's family, letting them know he's alive."

"I'm sure they'll be worried."

"They probably think he's dead."

"Then we should get them word as soon as possible." She could only imagine how devastated Henry's mother and sister were at this moment. They likely already received the news by telegram that Henry's steamer had gone down.

Her father nodded gravely. "Yes, his family deserves to know Henry is still alive. But once they learn of it, his competitor will too. I've heard Big Al Rainer is ruthless. And I don't want to take the risk that he'll come after Henry and put you in danger."

Isabelle poured her father a mug of coffee and handed it to him. He took a noisy slurp, then scooted his chair up to the small kitchen table.

"I don't want his family to suffer needlessly on account of my safety," she said, scooping a bowl of porridge from the pot and adding a spoonful of sugar just the way he liked it. As she placed it on the table, he touched her arm gently.

"I want you to be careful today around Henry."

His warning had a tone she didn't understand but that filled her with strange embarrassment. "I'm always careful. You can trust me."

"I trust you," he replied as he stirred his porridge. "I just don't trust *him*."

She turned away, ignoring the feeling that maybe she wasn't as trustworthy as either of them believed.

"Now that the big grouchy bear is gone, you get to stay by my side all day."

"Get to?" She threw open the curtains and let the sunshine pour into the bedroom. "I hate to break the news to you, Henry, but not everyone wants to spend an entire day at your beck and call."

The bright light revealed the paleness of his face beneath the unshaven layer of whiskers. He blinked hard to adjust to the light.

"And just why wouldn't you want to spend an entire day with me?" he asked. "Especially with me looking like a skeleton dragged up from the bottom of the lake."

"I won't argue with you there." She certainly wasn't going to tell him the truth—that from the moment her father had rowed out of sight, she'd thought of nothing else but spending time with him. Though he may have been a bit scraggly looking, he was still the handsomest man she'd ever seen.

"I don't have time to sit around and play all day," she said, even if the idea of playing games with him was more than a little enticing. "I have work to do. The washing and baking and cleaning won't wait."

"Find someone else to do it and stay here with me."

"Maybe in your world you can call a servant to come do your work so that you can play." She snatched up several towels and rags she'd discarded on the floor at the foot of his bed. "But out here, I have to do the work or it doesn't get done."

"Then leave it for another day." He was already setting up the game board as if he expected her to do his bidding.

"I have work *every* day," she said. He was obviously used to a pampered way of life and had no idea what her day-to-day existence was like. "But apparently you don't know what it means to work hard to survive."

"True. I'm often allergic to work." He glanced up at her, and his dark eyes were altogether too warm and inviting.

Even when she wanted to be angry with him, she couldn't. She walked swiftly to the door, her arms full of laundry. She had to make her escape now before she gave in to him, which was all too easy to do.

"Please, Isabelle." His soft appeal followed her.

"I'll be outside if you need me." She planned to take advantage of the rare warm, sunny day and do as much of her work outside as she could.

"If you must go out, then take me with you." The desperation in his voice stopped her in the hallway.

She debated for a long moment. There wasn't anything wrong with assisting him outside into the sunshine, was there? He could lie on a blanket. The fresh air might actually be good for him.

Father had forbidden her to spend unnecessary time in Henry's room with him. But he hadn't said anything about being with him outside.

She retraced her steps, and when she peeked in the bedroom, Henry was plucking at the sheet, his face a mask of disappointment. Then he caught sight of her, and his eyes lit up as a genuine smile broadened his face.

"All right. You can come with me," she conceded, "but only if you promise to stay out of trouble."

"That's asking a great deal from a man like me," he said. "But if you insist . . ."

As she gathered the rest of her washing supplies, she could hear him gasping and grunting with the effort to dress himself. She transferred the supplies to the backyard and then returned to the bedroom door. Standing in the hallway, she could hear him struggling still.

"Would you like any help?" she asked, praying he would say no, that she wouldn't have to put herself in an embarrassing predicament.

"I'd love it," he called back, his voice strained.

She stepped into the room, but at the sight of him sitting on the edge of the bed with bare legs, she almost fell backward. He'd managed to pull up his trousers to his knees, but his unclothed thighs gleamed at her.

"Oh, dear," she said, averting her eyes.

He was panting and sweating. Seeing his pinched expression, she pushed aside her discomfort and moved to his side.

"Hold on to me and stand up," she instructed.

He placed his hands around her waist and hoisted himself up, making a pained groan at the back of his throat. When he was finally standing, his fingers spanned her hips and seared through her skirt.

He was so near she could almost brush her head against him if she leaned in just slightly. His chest expanded and contracted in rapid succession, and his quick breaths fanned her forehead. She needed to move away from him, but at the same time she knew she had to help him get his trousers on.

Don't think about him, she told herself as she slipped her arms around him and reached for the back of his trousers. *Just pretend he's not there.*

His fingers tightened on her hips. The length of each hand wrapped around to her back, and she almost gasped. It was too difficult to pretend he wasn't there. She would just need to move quickly.

With a burst of fresh mortification, she yanked at his trousers, shimmying them up until she reached his wound.

"Be careful, Isabelle." His voice was near her ear and took her by surprise.

She paused when she realized they were nearly in each other's arms. What would her father think if he could see her now? Perhaps his warning had merit after all.

"Hold on to me with one hand," she said, "and then help me get your trousers up with the other."

Working together, they were able to clothe him finally. He leaned against her, and they managed to shuffle outside. She led him to a sunny spot near her washing. Once he was settled on a quilt, she tried to ignore his presence a mere dozen feet away.

He lay quietly, his eyes closed, the muscles in his face taut. He was battling pain from the jarring of his wound.

"I should have insisted you stay in bed." She dipped her father's shirt into the large tin washtub.

He tried to smile, but it was more of a grimace. "And miss out on watching you scrub clothes? You'd be cruel to deprive me of such lovely entertainment."

She rubbed the bar of lye soap over the front of the shirt. "You don't have to be cheerful or jovial around me all the time. I won't think less of you if you have to be serious, especially now when you're in the throes of pain."

As tempting as it was to peek at him and gauge his reaction to her words, she resisted. She focused instead on the shirt and rubbed it up and down the corrugated washboard. When she finished all sides, rinsed it, wrung it, and hung it to dry, she allowed herself a sideways glance.

His eyes were closed, his face pointed at the sun. He wasn't smiling, but the tightness in his jaw was gone and a peacefulness hovered over his features.

He cracked open one eye and caught her staring.

She ducked her head and reached for the next shirt.

He still didn't say anything. And the next time she chanced a glance at him, he had a half smile on his face, though his eyes were closed. His chest rose and fell with the rhythm of slumber.

Henry watched her through heavy lids. He didn't know how long he'd slept, except that Isabelle had obviously finished the laundry.

Now she sat nearby on the overturned washtub with her

sketchbook in her lap. Although he couldn't see the page, he'd surmised from the way she studied a fuzzy black caterpillar inching across the paper that she was drawing it.

Clean laundry flapped from the clothesline, the fresh soapy scent wafting in the breeze. With the clear blue sky overhead and the sun bathing him, he could almost be content for the moment. Almost . . .

A quick glance around gave him his bearings again: the little whitewashed keeper's cottage, a garden that was already harvested, and a hen house with a few chickens inside. The squat lighthouse sat a short distance away, with a black lantern room on top surrounded by a gallery. Through the tall windows he could see a birdcage-style lantern. He didn't know much about lanterns, but he could see that it was the old style. Many of the lighthouses around New York had already been updated with the superior French Fresnel lenses.

Beyond the lighthouse was a rocky beach filled with boulders and dotted with clumps of tall, dry weeds. The turbulent waters of Lake Huron spread out endlessly, although the lake appeared much tamer today than the last time he'd seen it.

The remains of the steamer littered the shore, wreckage that had drifted in, telling the awful tale of the disaster he'd somehow survived but that Charlie hadn't.

He shuddered, and the movement, though slight, was enough to draw Isabelle's attention. She looked up from her sketch and eyed him over the rim of her spectacles.

"I see you're not *always* working," he said.

"I'm not entirely boring."

"And I'm not entirely jovial." Yet he couldn't deny that most of his friends expected him to be. The women liked him for his playfulness. But he had to admit, he'd appreciated when Isabelle told him he didn't need to be cheerful all the time. It was almost as if she'd given him permission to be himself.

"Let me see what you're drawing," he said, reaching out a hand toward the sketchbook.

"It's private."

"Come on," he urged. "Or are you too embarrassed to let me see it?"

She gently placed the caterpillar in the grass, watched it a moment, then stood and snapped the book closed. "There's nothing in it that will interest you."

"How do you know unless I see it?"

"I have a feeling you're the kind of man who likes big fancy things."

"Perhaps." He did sorely miss all the glamour of his life back East. What he wouldn't give to soak in a hot bath and have a massage afterward.

"My drawings aren't fancy, and I do them just for me." She walked over to the clothesline and ran a hand over the nearest shirt to feel whether it was dry or not.

"Then tell me, what else do you do for fun out here?" He took in the thick stand of pines that stood to the west of the cottage. There was obviously nothing else in this remote spot of Michigan except the lighthouse. There were no yacht clubs, no ballrooms, no mansions, no parks.

"I don't need anything fancy to have fun," she said. "I find plenty of enjoyment in the simple things, like watching a sunset, reading, or drawing." She stared into the distance, and sadness draped a veil over her glossy brown eyes for the briefest instant.

What did a young woman like Isabelle have to be sad about? Maybe she wasn't happy with her situation living here after all. How could anyone be satisfied for long out in the wilderness?

He sighed at the thought of the long, boring days ahead of him, especially if he found himself stranded at Presque Isle for the winter. He knew the captain was hoping he'd be gone before the lake froze. Maybe if he started working on regaining his strength . . .

"Do me a favor, would you, please?" He pushed himself up onto one elbow. "Bring me some pieces of wood from the wreckage."

"Are you planning to take a piece as a souvenir home with you?"

"I'd like to fashion a crutch," he said, "to start getting around."

She frowned at him. "Your wound isn't ready for that kind of strain."

"Please, Isabelle," he pleaded, using the voice he knew was irresistible.

And just as he predicted, she nodded, but not without giving an exasperated sigh. "Very well. But don't say I didn't warn you."

He watched as she headed down the beach. Her sway was graceful and resolute, unlike last night when she'd stumbled across the room until she bumped into the wall. Something had been wrong, and she was clearly embarrassed about it and had wanted to leave as quickly as possible.

Now, though, the sunlight reflected off the lake and created a halo around her. She'd tied her long, dark hair back into a girlish ribbon. Wisps had come loose and blew in the breeze against her rosy cheeks.

Not only was she one of the prettiest women he'd ever seen, but she was also one of the most unusual. She was kind and compassionate. She'd gone out of her way to care for his needs, and yet she wasn't enamored with him the way most women were. While he was doing his best to charm her, she wasn't making his job easy.

He continued watching her as she reached a pile of the wreckage. As she picked up a piece of dark wood, he smiled.

Who said he didn't like to work? He was working hard at making her like him. And he would continue to do so because he wasn't one to shy away from a challenge.

6

Henry spent the next couple of hours making a crutch for himself while Isabelle beat and aired the rugs. She'd needed to show him how to whittle and shape the wood, until he'd caught on how to use her father's tools.

When he'd finished with the crutch, he used the leftover wood to fashion a cross. He held it up for Isabelle's inspection as she came out of the cottage carrying a tray of lunch.

"What do you think?"

She put down the tray, took the cross from him, and examined it. "I think it's beautiful in a rustic sort of way."

The dark wood cross was uneven and a little jagged, but it had a simple beauty nonetheless.

"What will you do with it?"

"I wanted to mark Charlie's grave."

She nodded and handed it back to him. "When you're able to make the trip, I'll take you to where Father buried him."

Henry twirled the cross in his hands. "In the meantime, it'll be my reminder to pray that my father will be able to send someone to rescue me before I'm snowed in for the winter."

"Rescue you?" She knelt and began to place the meal before him: a wedge of cheese, dried beef, a thick slice of bread, and an apple. "Are we so cruel that you must be rescued from us?"

"It's not you I need rescuing from." He reached for the apple and took a bite. It was wrinkled and soft but still sweet. "It's this godforsaken wilderness."

"Well, then I'll be praying for your rescue too. Put the cross where we can both be reminded to pray without ceasing."

With a stormy expression, she started to rise. He grasped her arm. "I'm sorry, Isabelle." His glib words had obviously offended her. He didn't like the thought that he might have hurt her. "I'm not used to thinking before speaking."

"If you truly hate being here, why pretend otherwise?" She tugged to loosen herself, but he didn't let go.

"I don't *hate* it." He scrambled to find a way to make up for his thoughtlessness. "How could anyone hate being here with you around?"

"You're full of too much flattery." Again she tried to rise.

"I mean it," he said, holding her down. "I really like you."

Her eyes widened and flashed with worry.

Not only was he angering her, now he was scaring her. "I think we could be good friends, you and I."

She searched his face, her eyes weighing his words. After a moment, her shoulders relaxed and she sat back on her heels, no longer straining to move away from him. "Friends?" The word came off her tongue as if she were tasting it.

"*Good* friends." He smiled. "Maybe even *very* good friends."

"All right." There was a measure of relief to her response. "I don't think Father would disapprove of our just being friends."

A sliver of guilt pierced his heart and reminded him he'd never *just* been friends with any woman. But as quickly as the guilt came, he ignored it. If his statement made Isabelle more comfortable, then so be it.

"Now sit with me," he said, "and let's have a picnic."

"A picnic?"

"You've never eaten a meal outside for the pure pleasure of it?"

"Meals are a necessity. We eat to live—"

He held up a hand to stop her. "Isabelle, my dear, that's not true. Meals are a time to talk, a time to rest, and a time to savor one another's company as much as we savor the food."

Her eyes rounded, filling them with light, making them clearer and more beautiful.

"What do you say?" he asked. "Will you join me for a picnic?"

She smiled. "Very well. Let's have a picnic."

He made room on the blanket for her next to him. As they ate, he found she was easy to talk to. She answered his questions freely about her life on Presque Isle and in turn asked him about his family, his father's business, and what life was like back home in the East.

He lost track of time as they talked. And he even forgot to flirt and add his customary wit to the conversation. He found himself relaxing and taking his own advice to heart by savoring her company.

"First thing I'm going to do when I can walk again is go up into that tower." He peered up at the glass windows at the top of the lighthouse. "I bet the view is spectacular."

She sighed softly. "I wouldn't know."

He tilted his head to look at her. "Do you mean to tell me you've never been up there?"

"Not once."

"Why on earth not?"

She hesitated as she picked at a loose thread on the blanket. "My father doesn't want me to."

"Sounds to me like he doesn't want you to do much of anything."

"He has a good reason for keeping me out of the tower."

"And what could that possibly be?" Henry couldn't keep the sarcasm from his voice.

She worked at the thread on the quilt, unraveling it, making it even longer. For a moment he didn't think she would answer him, that perhaps he'd made her angry for being too blunt about her father.

But then she let go of the thread and looked at him. "Before we moved here, when my father was a keeper in Rhode Island, my mother slipped and fell from the tower."

He pushed himself up to his elbows, a boulder lodging itself in his gut.

"When she hit the ground, she broke her neck and died instantly."

"I'm so sorry, Isabelle." He reached for her hand and laced his fingers through hers. The motion was instinctive, and he didn't even realize he'd done it until she stared at their intertwined hands with surprise. It was too late to pull back now, even if he'd wanted to—which he didn't.

"So the captain fears the same will happen to you?" he asked.

"He only wants to keep me safe."

"Maybe he's trying too hard."

She shrugged. "I don't mind. Most of the time."

He gave her hand a squeeze. "He might think he's loving you, but when fear is involved, it often has a way of taking over and running things."

She opened her mouth as if she would say more, then clamped her lips shut.

He had the feeling he was pushing her too far, and he didn't want to lose the connection he'd built with her. "I'm saying too much again, Isabelle. Forgive me."

"He worries too much about me," she admitted. "But I can't blame him."

He expected her to explain why. Instead, she stared down at their fingers mingled together, her delicate ones fitting so perfectly within his hold.

He had the urge to lift her hand to his lips and press a kiss there. In fact, he started to, but then stopped. She wasn't a plaything like so many of the other women he'd met over the years.

She had a sweet innocence about her that made him want to cherish her like the rare jewel she was. He could understand why the captain was so protective of his daughter, even if it did put a damper on his fun.

She released his hand. He didn't want to let go, but he did anyway because he knew a friend would. A friend would only hold hands to offer comfort, not merely for the pleasure of making contact with her.

"I may not be allowed to enter the tower," she said, tucking her hand into her lap, "but I've found a way to see out over the lake."

"Really? How?"

She stood and went into the house, returning a few minutes later with a dark walnut box. She opened it, and there sat a polished brass nautical spyglass in a cushion of felt. It had a black leather trim grip and was compacted to only seven inches.

"That's a beauty." He rubbed the rim reverently.

"It belonged to my father when he was a British captain."

She took it out of the box and twisted it open five folds until it lengthened to a full sixteen inches or more. "I use it to look out over the lake."

"And your father doesn't mind?"

She closed one eye and peered through the lens. "On a clear day I can see ships passing."

"Apparently the captain doesn't know you're helping yourself to his spyglass."

Her lips curved up slightly. "Here. You take a look."

He sat up as best he could without putting weight on his injury and then took the instrument from her. It was of the finest quality, and he doubted her father knew she used it as a plaything or he probably would have given her another more serviceable one.

Nevertheless he couldn't resist the urge to look through it to the distant waves and unending horizon of the lake. After getting his fill of the magnificent scenery, he made up a guessing game where they took turns finding something through the spyglass and the other had to figure out what it was by process of elimination.

When he tired of that, he managed to convince her to play other games with him throughout the afternoon. Soon she gave up all pretense of returning to her work. And he realized for the first time since he'd left home that he wasn't homesick.

"So we secretly exchanged the apple cider for vinegar," Henry said as they reclined side by side on the blanket later. "And my grandpa drank it with a straight face."

She laughed again, her belly aching from all the laughing she'd done.

"He never told Izzy and me if he knew what we'd done," Henry finished, regaling her with another of his childhood antics. "But I think he'd figured it out even before he took the first sip. So really I think the joke was on us."

She closed her eyes and relished the sweetness of the day. She'd talked and laughed and played more in one afternoon than she could remember in a long time—well, since before her mother had died.

"I had fun today," Henry said, turning serious.

She tilted her head sideways and found that he'd done the same. They were at least a foot apart, but together on the blanket, their eyes locked and she felt as though they were mere inches away.

"I had fun too."

His fingers fumbled against hers, and he wove their hands together, as if doing so was the most natural thing in the world. He'd said they were just friends, but she couldn't stop the warm feeling within when he touched her. She'd experienced that same warmth when he touched her hand earlier.

His eyes held hers, and she couldn't make herself look away. All she could think about was how she wanted to memorize his face. She wanted to sear it into her mind forever.

"Have I thanked you yet for saving my life and nursing me?" he whispered.

"You're welcome."

"Are you glad I didn't die?"

"Maybe." She smiled.

A breeze ruffled his blond hair, taunting her to reach up and touch it.

The wind teased her hair too, drawing his attention to a strand on her cheek. But of course he was bolder than her, and he didn't hesitate to graze it with his free hand and in the process skim her cheek.

At the touch, her breath hitched. Her slight gasp drew his eyes to her mouth.

"If your father wasn't on the verge of arriving home, I'd be tempted to tell you another story."

Father? Arriving home?

This time her gasp was loud, and she sat up straight. She stared south across the bay and saw a small boat on the horizon. Scrambling to her feet, she brushed off her skirt and began gathering the dishes and other items she'd brought outside throughout the day.

"Hurry," she said, starting toward the cottage. "I need to get you back inside before he sees you out here."

"We haven't done anything wrong," Henry called after her, "except maybe for using his special spyglass." He chuckled, and the sound calmed her racing pulse.

Henry was right. She'd done nothing to be ashamed about. Henry was the nicest man she'd ever met—besides her father, of course. And they were simply friends.

Even so, she felt it best to hide the evidence of her day of fun, though she wasn't sure why.

By the time she'd picked up, helped Henry back inside, and started a pot of coffee boiling, her father was clomping through the front door, his arms loaded with supplies.

As she rushed to help him, lines creased his forehead and framed his worried eyes. "How are you?"

She smiled, hoping to assure him she'd suffered no ill effects from being left home alone with Henry. In fact, it was quite the opposite. She felt strangely alive, almost as if she'd been slumbering and Henry had awoken her.

But she had the feeling that admitting the truth to her father would only worry him more and perhaps even hurt him. She chose her words carefully when she replied, "I'm fine. Henry behaved like a gentleman."

The creases in his face smoothed only a little.

She took several packages from him and started to retrace her steps to the kitchen. She could feel his questioning gaze following her, but she didn't turn to let him study her.

And when he didn't say anything more, she whispered a grateful prayer of relief.

7

Henry started to use his crutch to get around. At first he could only stand for a few minutes before sweat broke out on his forehead. He didn't complain, but the tightening of his jaw and the creases in his forehead testified that every movement was excruciating.

Isabelle frequently caught him staring at the cross he'd placed on the bedside table, and she knew he was hoping the letter her father had posted to his family would reach them in time.

She often saw her father peering to the south, searching for a lone steamer. He made no pretense of fervently praying that once Henry's family learned he was alive, they would send a ship out of Detroit to pick him up. She knew she should join them both in praying for Henry's rescue, yet for some reason she couldn't muster the words, especially as she spent more time with Henry.

Though her father continued to set boundaries for how much time she could spend with Henry, she found excuses to linger in his room to play games or to read with him.

The last days of October turned into the colder days of November, and Henry began to stand for longer periods, until finally he followed her around, talking with her as she did the baking, entertaining her with stories as she worked, and watching her as she sketched.

Her father walked into the kitchen one afternoon, after returning from checking his traps, to find Henry standing in the middle of the room, reciting Shakespeare at the top of his lungs. Isabelle had abandoned oiling her father's boots and was watching Henry with rapt attention.

At her father's scowl, she'd snatched the large boot from the table and quickly located the greasy rag.

After that, her father put Henry to work. He'd told Henry none too gently that if he was well enough to put on a theater production in the kitchen, he was well enough to earn his keep.

Her father showed Henry how to patch and paint the tower. He only had two barrels of lime, not nearly enough to repair all the leaks, but it was enough to keep Henry busy.

She peeked at Henry out the window more times than she should have. And she made up excuses to work outside so she could talk to him, even though the weather had steadily grown colder. At first Henry bumbled through his efforts to patch the leaky spots, but eventually he was high on the ladder and working with a proficiency that made her smile.

Wearing one of her father's heavy coats and hats, and with the growing whiskers on his face, he had a new ruggedness about him. If she didn't know better, she could almost imagine him living there. She was surprised by how much she wished he would stay and make Presque Isle his home.

"What are you sketching today?" His question caught her off guard.

Her pencil slipped, making an unnecessary line, and her heart gave a funny flip.

From where she sat at the kitchen table, the coldness radiating from his coat and face told her the day was another chilly one. She'd been too engrossed with the details of her sketch to hear him slip into the house. And now the warmth of his breath caressed her neck in the place where she'd pulled her hair aside into a ribbon. His gloved fingers lightly grazed the bare spot of her neck.

She resisted the desire to melt into his hand. Instead, she adjusted her spectacles and focused again on the half-drawn picture. "It's a spruce branch," she answered.

"The likeness is amazing." His words of praise tickled her ear. She'd finally grown accustomed to letting him see her drawings, and she coveted his compliments. "You've drawn each needle so perfectly."

"Thank you." She erased the smudge and then smoothed a hand over the picture. It was another of her attempts to memorize the world around her before its beauty and color disappeared from her life forever.

"Your father just left," he said softly.

Something in his tone sent a pleasant shiver through her. And when his gloved hand touched her neck again, she almost jumped up.

"Come with me," he said. "I want to show you something."

"What?" She closed her sketchbook.

"It's a surprise." When she stood and faced him, his eyes sparkled with the merriment she was growing to love.

"I don't like surprises."

He grinned and limped back to the door, which was still open a crack. "You'll like this one."

Weak sunlight streamed in. How could she resist going outside on a rare sunny day? "You're sure my father's gone?"

"I saw him head into the woods with an armful of his traps."

That meant he would be away for an hour or more—an entire hour she could spend with Henry. She didn't want to waste a single second of their time together.

"Get bundled up and meet me outside," he said, hobbling outside with his crutch. As he closed the door behind him, she hugged her arms to her chest at the blast of cold air that entered the room and took his place.

Was it wrong to pray that the ice would come soon and that the lake would freeze, trapping him there all winter? She was ashamed to admit that this had been her prayer lately. In fact, even though her prayers were in direct opposition to her father's and Henry's, they'd become more frequent.

The longer Henry was there, the more she couldn't imagine life without him.

Henry stowed the last of the tools inside the wooden chest in the shed. Hearing the creak of the cottage's back door, his heart began to race. He reached for his crutch and hurried as fast as his wound would allow. He was finally healing. The pain was less frequent. And now he wasn't quite sure how to feel about it.

He'd wanted to recover quickly with the hope that the captain would perhaps indulge in one more trip to Thunder Bay Island, this time taking Henry with him. Once there, he'd have a better chance of catching a ride on a passing steamer.

But he'd found himself moving slower on purpose around the captain. He didn't understand why he did it, except that lately he wasn't ready to leave. Not even the heavy labor the captain expected from him on a daily basis was enough to scare him away. In fact, once he'd bumbled through his initial attempts at the repair work, he discovered he rather liked the challenge of doing something useful.

"Are you finally ready?" he asked, stepping out of the shed into the sunshine.

Isabelle stood by the back door in her heavy wool coat, hat, and mittens. Her breath showed white in the afternoon air, and her cheeks were already pink.

"What exactly are you up to now?" she asked with a smile.

The curve of her lips was like an invitation, one he'd had to resist over and over during the past several weeks. He started across the yard toward her. "You'll have to wait and see." He stopped in front of her.

When she lifted her face, he had the almost overwhelming urge to drop a kiss onto the tip of her nose. Of course, there had been plenty of times since he met her that he'd wanted to kiss her. Any man would desire her. As beautiful and sweet as she was, that was only natural.

But he'd done his best to protect the boundary of friendship between them in a way he'd never done before. He'd surprised himself by resisting the challenge to woo and win her. He'd kept his hands off her—mostly. And he'd held back the longings that only kept growing stronger with each passing day.

"I need to blindfold you," he said.

She recoiled, bumping into the back door, almost as if he'd struck her. She was reaching for the knob when he seized her arm, preventing her from running away. "What is it? What did I say wrong?"

Her face went pale, and her lips trembled. "I don't want to be blindfolded. Now, or ever."

"Okay," he said, hoping to soothe her. "I won't. Forget I ever said it."

After a minute he was able to coax a smile from her and get her to agree to hold his arm while he led her to the tower.

She stopped at the door.

"Come on," he insisted, pulling her through. The light coming in the lower tower window illuminated the stone stairway leading up. "You won't deny me the pleasure of showing off all my hard work, will you?"

Her steps slowed.

"Please?" he begged softly. "This is the first time in my entire life I've done manual labor. Don't I have a right to be proud of my accomplishment?"

She nodded. "I'm proud of you too."

Her words warmed him. "Then let me show you what I've done."

She glanced behind her to the open door before giving a nervous nod and letting him lead her up the steps. He stopped every few bends to show her the painting he'd done.

"I didn't realize you were whitewashing the inside as well," she said when they reached the top of the stairway. Only the distance up the ladder remained, and it poked through the open hatch that led into the lantern room.

He grinned, not caring that his chest was swelling with pride. "After this, the lighthouse board will want to hire me to join one of their tender crews."

She laughed, the sound echoing in the narrow chamber.

It was warmer inside, especially standing close to her. She was breathless from the steep climb up the winding stairs, and all he could think about was the way her womanly form had moved as she climbed, so graceful and enchanting.

He had to step away from her before he did something rash. He started up the ladder. "Let's go all the way up."

She shrank back. "I can't."

"As long as we've gone this far, we might as well take a peek." He wanted to, even if she wouldn't. He hadn't had the chance to ascend to the top, since the captain was always there watching him.

But now . . . he couldn't resist the opportunity.

"You wouldn't want to go your whole life and never look out of the tower, would you? You'd always wonder what you missed."

As he clambered through the hatch, the ladder creaked behind him. Isabelle climbed the first couple of rungs. Fear warred across her features, but curiosity was winning the battle.

"Don't worry," he said, knowing she was remembering her mother's accident. "You'll be safe. Think about how many times your father has been up here and nothing has happened to him."

She nodded, took a gulp of air, and ascended the rest of the way. When he helped her to her feet, she collapsed against him.

He slipped his arms around her waist. "You'll be fine, Isabelle. You'll see."

She didn't say anything, yet her searching eyes moved to the oil-burning lantern at the center of the room. Sunshine poured through the window, glistening off the prisms that made up the lantern and diffusing the metallic scent of oil and gears.

With his own curiosity of the cramped lantern room quickly satisfied, he glanced out the window toward the lake. "Wow."

She followed his line of vision. "It's stunning."

For a long moment, they stood silently and stared over the rocky beach that ended at the foaming waves, which seemed to spread out forever.

"I'm glad we get to see this for the first time together," he whispered.

"Me too." And as she turned with him in a circle to take in the view, her eyes rounded with wonder. To the north and west, the thick forest of birch, balsam, cedar, and pine spread out endlessly. To the south was Presque Isle Bay. And then Lake Huron filled the eastern horizon as far as they could see.

"There are no words to do the scene justice," he said.

"I agree."

"Then you don't hate me for dragging you up here?"

"Of course not. I could never hate you."

They were facing the lake again. "So does that mean you like me?"

"A little." Her crooked smile teased him.

More than anything, he wanted to capture that smile into a kiss. Here, at the top of the world, with such natural beauty all around them, he couldn't think of a more special place to kiss her for the first time.

As if reading his thoughts, she dropped her gaze.

"Well, you already know that I like you." He couldn't stop from sounding out of breath. "I think you know you've got my heart in your hands."

"I don't know about that." Her breath came unevenly too.

"You own my heart, Isabelle." He had to kiss her. He bent and pressed his lips against her temple.

She trembled slightly.

His entire body ached with the need to kiss her with all the passion that had been building inside since he'd first laid eyes on her. But he had to resist. He'd promised her friendship.

His grip tightened in an effort to hold himself back. He pushed his lips harder against her forehead, closing his eyes.

"Henry?" Her voice was taut with a longing that set him on fire. "Please . . ."

Was she giving him permission to kiss her more?

He didn't know. Maybe in her innocence she didn't know what she wanted. Yet he didn't need any further invitation.

When she tilted back a little, it was enough that he could slide his mouth down from her temple to her cheek. Her lips parted with a tiny gasp. Then he let his mouth fall against hers with an explosion that rocked him.

The softness of her skin and the sweetness of her mouth made him lose all reason. Before he knew what he was doing, he had both arms around her. He removed her hat and untied her ribbon, desperate to release her hair and tangle his fingers in it.

Her lips mingled with his. She seemed to need him as much as he needed her.

One of his hands delved deep into her hair while the other spread against the small of her back. Instead of the shyness or reproach he'd expected, she wound her hands around his neck, pressing against him and drawing him even nearer.

When he released her mouth to drag in a breath, she gave a soft cry of protest and chased after him.

"Isabelle," he whispered against her lips, growing hungrier for her with each passing second. "Isabelle, I'll devour you if you let me."

"I'll let you." Her voice was thick with passion.

He pulled back enough to see the wildness in her shining eyes. He knew she was too innocent to realize what she was saying, and he was determined to protect her innocence. "We have to be careful."

Her lips were parted again, ready for more of him. This time she didn't wait but leaned in, cutting off his words with an unabashed kiss—one that told him she was offering herself to him.

With a burst of self-restraint he didn't know he had, he released his hold on her and broke the kiss, leaving his body tight with longing.

"Isabelle, I love you." The words came out hoarse. But once they were said, he'd never been more certain of anything in his life.

Her eyes widened, and she took her time studying his face, as if wondering what he meant.

"I've never said those words before," he said, "because I've never felt this way about anyone else."

"You're just caught up in the moment," she said.

"No. It's not just that, although I have to say, kissing you is burning me up."

She blushed prettily. He lifted a hand and touched her cheek, relishing the smoothness of her skin beneath his thumb. "I've been falling in love with you all along. And I'm just now finally admitting it to myself."

"You don't know me well enough—"

"I know you better than anyone else."

She lowered her lashes as if to hide something.

"Isabelle . . . could you ever return my love?"

She was silent for an eternal moment. His stomach began to ache, and his lungs hurt from the effort of not breathing.

At last she lifted her chin and looked him in the eyes. Hers glistened with both love and sadness. "I love you already. With all my heart."

He released the pent-up breath and allowed himself a grin.

164

She had no right to love him, none at all. But Isabelle couldn't stop herself, even though she knew she should. For just this one time in her life, she wanted to experience love.

He drew her back into his arms, into a crushing hug. And she didn't resist. She pressed her face into his chest and told herself to forget about the future, to live in the moment.

After all, he would leave. If not before the lake froze over, then certainly in the spring. He'd go back to his life, to the massive wealth and empire he would inherit.

She'd stay with her father in the life she'd always known. And Henry would never have to know what her future held.

Couldn't she enjoy this moment while it lasted? This love with him was a gift. It was more than she'd ever expected to experience.

His lips pressed against the top of her head, and his fingers combed through the long waves of her hair that spilled down her back.

Yes, she loved him. And for however long it lasted she would relish every second of her time with him.

She tilted her head back so she could see his face. She tugged off her mittens and then lifted her fingers to his face. With both hands she traced his cheeks, his jaw, his chin, and then his nose and eyes.

Even though she'd already tried to memorize his face, she wanted to make sure she knew every detail, every curve, every dip. Then she could store the memories like treasures to keep forever . . . after he was gone.

His hands moved up until one encircled the back of her neck. His blue eyes fastened upon her lips. He gently maneuvered her head so that her mouth was his for the taking. The firm pressure of his lips demanded that she respond.

She rose on her tiptoes. With her hands still on his face, she lifted into him, kissing him with all her strength.

"I knew it!" came a shout from behind them.

She released Henry and pushed away in time to see her father climbing through the hatch. His leathery face was contorted into a fierceness that made her quiver. His eyes were large with rage.

"You lousy scoundrel!" Her father stood, and his presence filled the small lantern room. "I knew you were the lowest kind of vermin, that you'd do everything you could to take advantage of my daughter."

"Captain," Henry said, tensing his shoulders. His expression was grave, his fists balled, as if preparing to do battle. "I can explain—"

"I don't need an explanation. I saw you from down below. I saw what you were doing to my daughter!"

"He wasn't doing anything I didn't want," she said.

Her father was focused on Henry. It was almost as if she wasn't even there. "And now I know what you've been doing every time I leave!"

"This is the first time I've kissed her," Henry said. "I swear it."

Her father straightened to his fullest, which was a head above Henry. He pulled one thick arm back. The seams of his coat strained, ready to split.

"No, Father!" she said. She slid in front of Henry and stretched out her arms. "Don't hurt him."

"Get out of my way, Isabelle. I should have let him die on the beach."

"Please, we didn't do anything wrong." She kept her arms raised, even as Henry struggled to get around her.

Her father shook his head. "I forbade you to come up here and you disobeyed me."

He'd only wanted to protect her, to keep her safe and prevent what had happened to her mother. She knew that. But now that she was here, she couldn't keep from wondering if Henry had been right. Was her father overprotecting her?

"I'm going to teach this man a lesson." Her father glared past her toward Henry. "When I'm done with him, he'll wish he'd drowned."

Henry tucked her behind him with more strength than she realized he had. "I would never dishonor Isabelle. I love her too much to ever hurt her."

"Love?" Her father barked a laugh. "You don't love her. You don't even know her."

"I know that she's an incredible woman," Henry said. "She's compassionate, kind, easy to talk to, and has a beautiful heart."

Her father only growled. And then before she could stop him, he swung at Henry, punching him in the gut first with one fist and then with the other.

Henry grunted and doubled over.

She cried out in protest. "Father, stop!"

But her father's fury had already boiled over. He shoved Henry against the glass with a force that shook the lantern room. "I'll make sure you never touch my daughter again." He slammed a fist into Henry's nose, and blood spurted on her father, the floor, and even splattered on the pristine windows.

She screamed past the sobs rising in her chest. "I said *stop*!"

Her father spun Henry around, grabbing his arm and yanking it behind his back. At the same time, he lifted a knee and rammed it into Henry's wound.

Henry cried out and dropped to his knees, only to cry out again as her father stretched his arm farther up his back.

In desperation, Isabelle flew at her father and began to pound on him. "Please, Father. Please. *I love him!*"

Those three words seemed to pierce her father. He froze. Slowly he pivoted to look at her.

"I love him," she said again, this time softer.

Hurt flashed in her father's eyes. He glanced down at Henry, who was arched in an effort to ease the agony of the brutal hold.

"You know you can't," her father said. "It's futile."

She nodded, heedless of the tears streaking her cheeks. "I know."

"It's not futile," Henry said through gritted teeth. "I want to marry you, Isabelle."

Her father yanked him again, and Henry's face stretched taut in pain.

"Father, you're hurting him!" She wiped at her cheeks, at the fresh tears trickling down.

"You *can't* marry Isabelle," her father shouted at Henry.

"If she agrees to it, then what could stop us?"

"She knows she can't marry you."

"Will you marry me, Isabelle?" Henry twisted, and his eyes implored her. His hair was in disarray. Blood dribbled from his nose, over his lips, and onto his teeth.

How could she say no?

"I love you." His voice cracked with emotion. "And I want you to know I've never said those words to another woman. Not once. I've never even come close. I've never asked a woman to marry me. I've never even considered it."

Her heart constricted, as though someone had coiled a rope around it and wrenched it from her chest.

"You're the only woman I've ever loved, Isabelle. I want to spend the rest of my life showing you how much I love you."

She believed him. She sensed the sincerity in his every word. And that made what she had to do all the harder.

"Are you going to tell him," her father said, his voice suddenly sad, "or do I need to?"

She shook her head and took a step toward the hatch. "I love you, Henry," she said, squeezing the words out as she climbed onto the ladder. "But Father's right. I can't marry you. As much as I want to, I can't—"

She choked back a sob, ducked her head, and hurried down the ladder, needing to get away—needing to find a place where she could bury her face and cry out the agony within that was tearing her apart.

She'd fallen in love with Henry, had wanted to experience the joys of love, even if only for a short time. But she'd never expected that amidst the overwhelming beauty that came with love, there would be so much pain too.

8

Henry hung his head. The blood had long since stopped flowing from his nose and now had dried on his lips and chin. His gunshot wound throbbed, and his arm ached from where the captain had dislocated his shoulder. Thankfully, when tying him up, the captain had yanked the joint back into place.

But none of the pain in his body compared to the agony in his heart.

Isabelle had rejected him.

He let his head slump against his knees. With his hands tied securely behind his back, and his feet fastened at the ankles, Henry's body had gone numb hours ago when the captain had tossed him onto the bedroom floor and then slammed the door closed behind him.

The house had been strangely silent for the rest of the afternoon. He didn't know where Isabelle had run off to when she'd disappeared from the tower. But from the murmuring coming from the kitchen, he had the feeling she'd closeted herself away in her bedroom and that the captain's attempts to coax her out had been unsuccessful.

At least Henry could draw some measure of satisfaction that Isabelle wasn't particularly happy with her father at the moment.

His heart throbbed again, however, at her bold declaration of love for him. And he asked himself again, as he had already a hundred times, why she wouldn't marry him if she loved him. Was she unwilling to leave Presque Isle to come live with him in New York? Perhaps she didn't want to leave her father alone.

It was the only barrier he could imagine that might stand between them. He wished he'd thought to reassure her that they could live wherever she wanted, that he didn't care, so long as they were together.

Heavy footsteps thudded in the hallway and came nearer to his room. As the door swung open, he didn't bother lifting his head. It was the captain, and Henry wouldn't give the man the pleasure of seeing the misery that was sure to be on his face.

The captain crossed the room with his long strides until he stood directly in front of him. The late afternoon sunlight coming from the window lit up the man's enormous, scuffed boots. He stood silently for a moment as if waiting for Henry to speak.

Henry clamped his jaw shut.

Finally the captain exhaled a sigh. "Weather permitting, I'm taking you down to Thunder Bay Island tomorrow."

The words didn't surprise Henry.

"I should have taken you last time, no matter how much pain it caused you to travel."

Henry didn't respond.

Another long silence passed before the man spoke again.

"Why did you have to make her fall in love with you?" he asked hoarsely. "Why couldn't you have just left things the way they were?"

This time Henry couldn't resist answering. "I didn't *make* her love me, Captain. She chose to of her own will."

The man wiped a burly hand across his eyes.

"Since when is falling in love a crime?" Henry asked.

"Because you're going to end up hurting her!" the captain cried out in whispered anguish.

"I won't hurt her—"

"You don't understand," he said louder, his face contorted with frustration. "She can't ever have a normal future or a normal life."

Something in the captain's tone stopped Henry cold. He waited for the man to explain himself.

"Isabelle's mother had a rare condition," the captain finally said. "We didn't realize it until after Isabelle was born. But after a while it became apparent that my wife was losing her vision."

A sick hollowness formed in the pit of Henry's stomach.

"At first she lost the ability to see at night," he continued. "And we prayed that was all she'd lose. But eventually the amount she could see out of each eye became less and less, even during the day."

Henry lifted his head and met the captain's dark gaze.

"Finally she went blind."

Blind. The word pierced Henry so sharply his chest hurt. He grasped to find a reply. "That doesn't mean Isabelle will go blind—"

"I prayed she would be spared," the captain said in a harsh whisper, "but she's already losing her night vision."

Desperation pushed into Henry. It cut off his words and thoughts so that all he could think about was Isabelle, his sweet Isabelle living without the ability to see the beauty she adored in the world around her. The very thought was enough to make him cry. She'd never be able to sketch again.

Maybe that was why she spent so much time on her drawings in the first place, because she was soaking everything in while she still could.

"Now you can understand why Isabelle can't get married," the captain said.

"No," Henry said. "I *don't* understand. There's no reason why she can't get married just because she's going blind."

The captain's features hardened. "What man would want a blind wife?"

"Did you love your wife any less because she went blind, Captain?"

"Of course not. I loved her more for facing the disease with such courage."

"Then what makes you think I'll stop loving Isabelle once she loses her vision?"

"She'll need constant care and supervision the rest of her life."

"And why wouldn't I be able to care for her?"

"Why would you want to?"

Henry strained against the rope binding his hands. "Because I love her more than I love my own life."

He hadn't realized their voices had risen, that they were shouting at each other, until silence descended over the bedroom again.

It was the captain's turn to hang his head. For a long moment, he let his head droop. Then he shook it. "I can't ask another man to take on the task. It's too much to bear."

"Maybe it's not your choice to make."

"It *is* my choice. She's my daughter." He spun away from

173

Henry as if the matter were settled. "And I'll be the one taking care of her when she goes blind."

As he exited the room, his boots struck the floor in finality. Each step stomped Henry's heart until it was broken into a thousand shards.

9

The next day, at a knock on the front door of the cottage, Isabelle shifted under the covers. She didn't want to get up, didn't want to face the light of day, didn't want to breathe. Though she should have been up hours ago, she hadn't moved, not even when her father had come in and pleaded with her to get out of bed. He'd returned one last time to tell her he would be leaving for Thunder Bay Island and would be taking Henry with him.

She shuddered. Henry was leaving. She'd never see him again.

She wasn't blind yet, but darkness had fallen over her all the same.

The knock sounded again, this time louder and more insistent. She sat up and listened, her hair tumbling over her face.

Visitors were so rare at Presque Isle that to have one knocking on their door was not something she could ignore, no matter how black her world had grown.

After several moments, she heard her father talking with someone outside the house. She couldn't make out the words, but when her father came back inside a short while later and spoke with Henry, every word was clear. Henry's family had received their letter and sent two men up from Detroit to fetch him. They'd arrived on a steamer that was now docked at Thunder Bay Island. And after rowing up that morning, they planned to take Henry home.

"Well, this saves me a trip," her father said from the hallway.

"Can I at least say good-bye to Isabelle?" Henry asked her father.

"You've hurt her enough as it is. Don't make this any harder on her."

She could almost see Henry nod in agreement. She wished she could reassure him that he hadn't hurt her, that their time together had been a beautiful glimmer of light that she would never forget.

Isabelle longed to see him one last time, to wrap her arms around him and tell him she loved him and always would. But she knew if she saw him, she'd only cling to him and cry and make the parting worse for both of them.

The best course was to let her good-bye from yesterday remain her final good-bye.

"Then would you give her this cross?" Henry said. "Tell her to never give up hope."

Was he giving her the wooden cross he'd made? She hugged her arms across her chest and fought back tears. He'd recently fashioned another cross for Charlie's grave and had kept the first one on the bedstead. He'd touched it often, almost reverently. She hadn't expected that he'd want to part with it.

When the door had closed and silence descended over the house, a sob burst out of the dark prison of her soul. "Henry," she whispered.

Desperate, she stood, flung open her door, and ran through

the house. She needed one last glimpse of him, one final image to imprint in her mind.

With heaving breaths, she pressed her face against the sitting room window and peered outside. She strained to glimpse past the brush and tall pine trees that stood in front of the house, shielding the path that led down to the dock. All she could see was the checkered coat of one of the men disappearing toward the shore.

She gave a cry of frustration, grabbed her father's spyglass, and rushed outside. The cold November air slapped her, as if rebuking her for letting Henry go. Ignoring her flyaway hair and the wrinkled skirt she'd slept in, she ran down the sloping knoll. Rocks and twigs poked the sensitive skin of her feet, clad only in her stockings.

Rounding the brush, she caught sight of Henry's hatless blond head. She was surprised that the two men had stopped Henry and were in the process of tying his hands behind his back. She couldn't see his face, but it was obvious from the way he was struggling that he didn't want to be bound.

Why were they tying him up?

One of the men cast a glance in her direction, and she quickly crouched out of sight behind a nearby tree. Her heart thudded with panic. Something wasn't right.

She lengthened the spyglass and stared through it. The man in the checkered coat pulled out a knife and pressed the blade into Henry's back, forcing him to cease his struggle.

Isabelle tried to understand what was happening. None of this made sense. If this was his family's way of rescuing him, then she didn't want them to take him. But how could she stop them?

The glint of the knife in the sunlight reflected blood. With a pounding heart, she scrambled backward, tripping over her skirt in her haste.

She had to find her father. He'd know what to do.

She ran the short distance to the tower and barged through the door. She stopped short at the sight of her father sitting on the bottom stone step, his face in his hands.

He glanced up, giving her a clear view of the utter despair clouding his features before he could hide it from her. His skin was drawn and wrinkled, his eyes drooping amidst dark circles.

"Isabelle . . ." He forced a smile and started to rise.

"Those men have tied Henry up, and one of them pulled a knife on him."

Her father's brow shot up. "What do you mean?"

"They're hurting him."

Her father stood and looked out the open door toward the dock. His muscles flexed as if he might charge forward to the rescue. But then he spun back around as hesitation flitted across his face. "He's not our concern anymore, Isabelle."

Fear for Henry ravaged her insides. She didn't know what else to do. So she fell on her knees before her father and reached for his hands. "Please help Henry. Please. I don't want him to come to any harm."

"Maybe it would be for the best if Henry were dead. Then he'll never be able to come back here and hurt you again."

She dropped his hands and reeled back. "Father, how could you wish that?"

His shoulders sank. "I hate seeing you in such pain."

"But you'll bring me even greater pain if you allow Henry to die."

After a long pause, her father nodded. "Very well, Isabelle. I'll help Henry. But for your sake, not his."

He left the tower and strode down toward the dock. She followed him but couldn't keep up with his pace. By the time she reached the beach, he was already approaching the strangers. The man with the checkered coat was sitting behind Henry in the boat, and the other was kneeling on the dock.

At first glance, nothing looked amiss. The knife was out of sight now, and Henry sat stiffly without moving. His face was pale with streaks of black and purple forming a crescent beneath one of his eyes, the aftermath of her father's beating.

Seeing her father, Henry started to say something. Then he winced, clamped his mouth shut, and sat up straighter.

"You forgot something," her father called.

The man on the dock stood. He tipped the brim of his hat up, revealing narrowed eyes. "No. We've got everything we came for."

Her father didn't slow down. He charged onto the dock, lowered a shoulder, and plowed into the first man.

The man didn't have time to react. He flew off the dock and splashed into the lake with his arms and legs flailing.

The one with the checkered coat behind Henry jumped up and waved the knife toward her father. But without the pressure of the weapon against his back, Henry sprang forward and aimed a swift kick into the man so that he toppled over the boat into the water.

"These men haven't been sent by my family," Henry shouted. He wobbled in the boat, swaying close to the edge. "They've been hired by Big Al Rainer to make sure I don't make it out of here alive."

The two men were splashing and spluttering, obviously unable to swim very well.

Her father reached into the boat and hauled Henry up onto

179

the dock. With his hunting knife, her father cut Henry's hands free. Afterward he grabbed a rope from the boat and tossed it out over the water to the first man, who latched on to it. The man with the checkered coat had already reached the dock and was climbing onto it, spitting water.

"Put down your knife," her father ordered, "or I'll send you right back in the lake."

Shaking his head, the man lunged at her father, the blade pointed directly at his belly.

"Father!" Isabelle screamed.

Her father quickly sidestepped and then shoved the man off the end of the dock, and again he splashed into the lake.

Within minutes, Henry and her father had towed both men onto the dock and tied them up tightly.

Isabelle stood motionless on the rocky beach, the cold wind whipping her disheveled hair and skirt. She watched Henry with a swell of relief so intense it immobilized her.

When Henry finally turned and acknowledged her, he didn't make a move toward her. Instead, he regarded her with sorrowful eyes, as if the sight of her was too much for him to bear.

The ache in her chest deepened further. Without Henry in her life, she'd be stuck in a dark prison worse than blindness.

She loved him more than she ever dreamed it was possible to love any man. Part of her argued that if she truly loved him, she'd free him from any obligation he might feel toward her. It wasn't fair to ask him to take on her burden. Maybe it didn't seem like a hardship now, but would he grow to resent her later after she'd lost all sight and needed assistance?

On the other hand, if the roles were reversed and Henry was the one going blind, she wouldn't have let that stop her from loving him. She would have wanted to be with him anyway

180

because she loved him for who he was, not for what he could or couldn't do.

The blue of Henry's eyes had darkened to the color of a stormy night sky. He took a halting step forward, then stopped, his hands fisted, his jaw clenched.

What did Henry need? Maybe it was time to stop thinking just about herself and listen to him. She'd let him make the final decision.

Exhaling a breath, she held one hand toward him. It was an invitation. He could take it or leave it. She'd live with his choice, yet she couldn't move forward without at least giving him the chance to make it.

He glanced at her hand, and hope sprang to his face. He didn't hesitate another moment but bolted toward her, limping along as fast as his injury allowed.

Her heart wavered with uncertainty. Still, she kept her fingers outstretched.

His determined steps didn't falter. He reached her and, ignoring her hand, slid his arm around her waist and dragged her against him. In one swift motion he lowered his head and captured her lips. His mouth was firm and unyielding, telling her without words that he was choosing her, that he wanted her, and that he couldn't live without her.

She sagged against him, her knees giving way.

Both of his arms were around her then, and he broke his kiss, pressing his lips near her ear. "I love you, Isabelle. And I refuse to leave you."

She started to whisper something, but he only pressed harder against her ear. "You can protest all you want," he continued, "but I'm never going to leave you, no matter what the future brings."

Light flooded her soul, a light she hadn't known before. It filled her with warmth and a sweet breath of freedom. She couldn't speak past the tightness of her throat, but she slipped her arms around him and nuzzled against his chest, breathing deeply of him.

"Say your good-bye quickly," her father said from behind them, "and then get your hands off my daughter."

Henry stiffened and started to pull away.

She clung to him as she turned to face her father.

He towered above them, his face dark and foreboding. "Looks like I'll be taking you to Thunder Bay Island today after all, along with the two of them." He cocked his head toward the men trussed up on the dock, drenched and shivering.

She dug her fingers into Henry and then straightened her shoulders. She didn't want to hurt her father. But Henry had chosen to love her. How could she throw that away again? "If you force Henry to leave, then I'm going with him."

Her voice faltered, but she kept her focus on her father's face. She needed him to know she'd never been more serious about anything in her life.

He swayed as if she'd struck him.

A chilled breeze swept off the bay and rent through the linen of her shirt. The cold rocks dug into her frozen feet. Her body gave an involuntary shudder.

Henry drew her into the crook of his arm, his solidness and strength giving her renewed courage. If Henry loved her enough to face all the challenges the future held with her blindness, then surely she could face her father.

"I love Henry." With one hand already behind Henry's back, she reached the other across his chest so that her palm rested on the steady thumping of his heart.

"Love's not enough, Isabelle," her father said. "There are more practical matters to consider, like the fact that you won't have children. A man in Henry's position will want an heir—"

"I don't care about that," Henry said.

"And why can't I give Henry a child?" Isabelle asked. "The disease affects my eyesight, not my ability to bear children."

"How can you take care of your children if you're blind?" Her father's voice took on a pleading quality. "And what about the fact that you'll pass along the disease to your children? That you'll force them into a blindness not of their own choosing? Can you willfully relegate someone to such a life as that?"

"You make it sound like blindness is a curse," Henry said, "the worst illness that could ever befall a person."

"You don't know the first thing about it," her father said.

"You're right. I don't wish to diminish the impact it will have upon Isabelle, but whatever our lot in life, whether blindness or some other problem, we can't just give up and stop living."

Isabelle nodded. She'd let fear of the future control her for far too long. At some point in her past, she'd concluded that when she went blind, her life would be over. But maybe Henry was right. A handicap in one area of her life didn't have to stop her from enjoying the beauty of the rest of it.

"Blind or not, Isabelle has so much of life yet to experience," Henry said passionately. "Give her the chance to live her life."

"I know firsthand what the blindness is like," her father countered, "the care involved, the hours of sacrifice—"

"Who better than me to help her?" Henry asked her father. "I have unlimited resources. I'll make sure Isabelle has the best doctors and care that money can buy."

Her father pressed his lips tightly together. The crash of the waves against the shore filled the silence between them.

When he started to shake his head, Isabelle spoke up. "I long for your blessing, Father. But whether you give it or not, I love Henry. I want to be with him."

She turned then and buried her face into Henry's side. He responded by wrapping his arms around her and pressing a kiss against the top of her head.

She was trembling. She'd defied and hurt her father, and it pained her that she'd had to do so. But she couldn't turn back now.

For an endless moment, she stood in Henry's embrace with her father looking on. His sorrow was tangible.

Why did love and heartache have to walk in such close companionship?

"You really love him?" Her father's gruff statement was more of an admission than a question.

"I do," she said.

Her father sighed, and his shoulders slumped. "If you'll be happy with him, then that's all I want for you—to be happy."

"Really?"

He nodded. "That's all I've ever wanted for you, Isabelle. But I never believed it to be possible, not with blindness ahead of you."

"But it *is* possible. Henry's shown me that."

Henry smiled, his bruises and scruffiness making him look more like a rugged backwoodsman than a gentleman. "You know I'll do my best to make her happy every day of her life."

"You'd better," her father said with a scowl. "If you hurt her in any way, I'll find you and rip you apart limb by limb—"

"Father," Isabelle chided softly.

Henry's grin cocked higher. "Sounds like we have a bargain."

Her father crossed his thick arms over his chest and

harrumphed. At the call of one of the men tied up on the dock, her father started back toward the boat. "Henry, you're still coming with me to Thunder Bay Island today."

Isabelle latched on to Henry's arm. "But Father, you said—"

"I won't be leaving Henry home alone with you again," Father said over his shoulder. "Not until you're married."

Married? Was it possible that Father would give his blessing on her marrying Henry? A wave of joy swept over her. Maybe there was hope after all.

"Since you have the legal authority as a civil magistrate, you can marry us tonight, Captain," Henry called after her father. "When we get back from Thunder Bay Island."

Her father threw up his arms as if disgusted with Henry's declaration. "An evening wedding? No. My daughter will have a proper daytime wedding or none at all."

Henry nodded. "Tomorrow then?"

Her father kept walking. "Fine. Tomorrow."

Isabelle didn't realize she was holding her breath until Henry faced her. His smile dimmed, and his eyes filled with worry. "You *will* marry me, won't you, Isabelle?"

She exhaled. "Of course I will. Just promise me you'll come back from Thunder Bay Island tonight."

"I have a feeling I'll be swimming well ahead of your father's boat in my hurry to get back to you."

She smiled but couldn't keep anxiety from pricking the back of her neck.

"We don't have all day, Henry," her father yelled from the dock. "Kiss her good-bye and get over here."

"Well, since your father insists . . ." Henry's grin turned devilish. He tilted his head and let his lips descend upon hers gently.

The tenderness of his touch once again took her breath away.

But at the back of her mind, a warning whispered that it was his good-bye, that as earnest as Henry was about marrying her, it was all too good to be true.

When he finally broke the kiss and limped off toward her father, her heart squeezed with every step he took away from her.

10

"You know I meant every word I said back there," the captain said without breaking the rhythm of his rowing.

"I meant every word I said too." Henry rested the oars to wipe the sweat from his brow. Even on a cold November day, the rigors of rowing were causing him to sweat.

The day was clear, with a strong northwest wind whipping the waves into whitecaps. The occasional spray of water into Henry's face made him flinch, reminding him of that fateful night of the shipwreck.

The captain's sharp eyes kept constant watch on the lake, sky, and shoreline. He steered the boat on a steady course southward, staying close enough to the shore that Henry could marvel at the thick forest of white pine that were ripe for the cutting.

Charlie would have been proud of him, because he'd been busy calculating the profit of the land and had even considered whether there were any tracts in the area available for purchase. It was what Charlie had urged him to do all along during their trip around the Great Lakes, only at the time Henry had been too lazy and irresponsible to take his friend's advice to heart.

It had taken nearly dying, losing Charlie, and being forced off his feet before he'd finally thought about how he'd been squandering his life, how he hadn't done anything to make a difference, not even the smallest one.

Living in the simplicity of Presque Isle, working hard for the first time in his life, and spending time with Isabelle had changed him—or at least made him want to be a better man.

Henry plunged his oars back into the churning water and tried to shrug off the burning sensation that shot through his thigh and aching backside. Their two captives sat silently in the hull, huddled in woolen blankets the captain had been kind enough to offer them.

The leather strap of Henry's pouch chafed the flesh of his shoulder with each turn of the oars, making it harder for him to ignore the pressure that was gaining strength with each passing minute. If Big Al could send these two after him, what would stop the man from sending more?

The captain's eyes met his above the heads of the men, and Henry saw there a worry that mirrored his own. It would only be a matter of time before someone attacked again. So long as he had the proof of purchase, he would bring danger to Presque Isle and to Isabelle.

The truth of what he needed to do hit him full in the face like the splash of a wave. He had to take the papers down to the land office in Detroit and file them once and for all, to make the sale official by obtaining the deed. He needed to personally deliver those papers. There would be too much risk to send them via the post.

Seeing the task to completion was the responsible thing for him to do for the sake of Cole Enterprises, as well as the safest course of action for Isabelle. And only after he'd done his duty and eliminated the danger could he return with a clear conscience to Presque Isle and marry Isabelle.

With the end of November fast approaching, there was the very real possibility that he might not be able to make it back until spring.

He shook his head. He'd promised Isabelle he would return today. They were to be married tomorrow. The mere idea of being away from her for one day was difficult enough to bear. But weeks? Maybe even months?

He couldn't do it.

Lowering his head, he pulled on the oars, letting the day's pain ripple through his body. Yet even as the excuses began to roll over him one after the other, he lifted his head and again looked the captain in the eye. "I'm not returning with you tonight, Captain."

The older man nodded gravely. "I understand. And I respect you for your decision."

The captain's rare praise would have warmed Henry on any other occasion. But he was already too miserable thinking about how much his absence would hurt Isabelle.

"Isabelle will be all right," the captain said.

Henry pushed down the lump in his throat at the thought of her reaction tonight when her father returned without him. She would feel betrayed.

The captain stopped his rowing. "Henry," he said calmly, "you just return as quickly as you can. She'll be waiting. We'll both be waiting."

Henry nodded. Maybe the captain hadn't given his explicit

blessing over their union, but somehow in urging him to return, Henry knew the man was accepting him. Finally.

At the sight of a small, dark shape on the opposite side of the bay and the glint of metal oarlocks, Isabelle rushed out of the cottage and down to the dock.

She clutched her cloak closed with one hand and held her father's spyglass with the other. The cold wind slapped at her, taunting her that Henry's love and his proposal were only a dream.

All day long, as she'd baked and sewn and decorated for her wedding, she told herself over and over that he loved her, that he'd chosen to be with her of his own accord, and that he wanted to marry her even though he knew the truth about her.

She'd seen the desire in his eyes. She'd felt it in his kisses and heard it in his promises.

He'd come back.

With a trembling arm, she raised the spyglass. But her hand froze halfway to her face. What if he'd changed his mind? What if the sight and lure of town life—albeit only a fishing village—made him realize all that he'd missed?

The boat moved painfully slow against the wind and waves. She couldn't wait a minute longer. She lifted the spyglass to her eye and peered out over Presque Isle Bay, finally catching the boat in her line of vision.

It rose and then fell, but not before she saw her father straining wearily at the oars.

A sense of panic clutched her. She fitted the rim of the spyglass more carefully against her eye and stared again. The vessel rode high and was taking a beating from the waves.

She wanted to deny what that meant—that the boat was light and empty of all but her father. But as she brought the boat into her line of vision again, she saw only one form, only one set of shoulders, only one head.

Her father's.

Agony erupted in her chest.

"No!" The word came out as a strangled cry. "Henry, no!"

She crumpled to her knees and screamed into the wind. Then sobs choked off her voice, and she buried her face in her hands and wept.

11

"Henry loves you. He'll come back to you." Her father had told her the same thing countless times since his return, but it hadn't eased the terrible ache in Isabelle's heart. Neither had her father's explanation for Henry's trip to Detroit, which he claimed was to keep her safe from the dangerous enemies of Cole Enterprises.

"He did the right thing, Isabelle," her father had said. "As hard as it was, he did what he needed to do. And for that I can respect him."

In spite of her father's assurances, Isabelle didn't have the same confidence. Henry was tied to his life back East. He'd missed it. Even if he loved her and had every intention of coming back, once he reached Detroit and experienced all the comforts there, he wouldn't want to go without such things ever again.

No matter the doubts nagging her, she couldn't stop herself from going down to the beach every day and watching the southern horizon for the sight of a boat. Yet as one week turned into two, a quiet desperation plagued Isabelle so that she could hardly eat or sleep. With the first of December and the dropping temperatures, she knew it was only a matter of days before the lake became impassable. And when it did, that would be the end of all hope.

Bundled underneath a bearskin, Isabelle released a long sigh at the empty horizon. Snowflakes swirled in a playful dance around her, unwilling to settle on the ground just yet.

"Come inside, Isabelle," her father called from the cottage. "It's too cold for you to be out today."

"I'll be right there," she called back. She glanced down at the wooden cross held between her mittens, the one Henry had made. She wished she could let the cross go, that she could toss it back into the lake and release him to the life he deserved. She'd been clinging to it every day. Despite herself, she let his words repeat themselves endlessly in her mind.

"Tell her to never give up hope."

Maybe Henry wouldn't come back, but would that truly be the end of hope? He'd made her feel things she'd never known were possible. He'd taught her how to laugh, and love, and live life to the fullest. Did that have to end just because he wasn't a part of her world anymore? Did hope have to die along with her dream of sharing a life with him?

She studied the coarse dark wood, uneven and crudely fashioned.

"Tell her to never give up hope."

She could still have a beautiful future, starting now. She didn't have to cower in fear again at the thought of going blind. The joy of life didn't have to cease just because she lacked sight or because Henry wasn't with her.

"Never give up hope. . . ."

She pressed the cross to her chest and held it there. She would always be grateful to Henry for helping her break free of her darkness. She would always love him. And with that love she would always carry a sense of loss.

But it was time to let go of him, to stop putting her hope in a person or in her ability to see or not. Instead, it was time to put her hope in the giver of life.

She raised her arm to throw the cross into the lake, but then stopped with a sudden resolution. She would write out her tale, she would share about the hope she'd found, and leave the note with the cross. And maybe someday it would bring hope to someone else who needed it.

With firm steps, she returned to the cottage, sat down at her father's desk, and wrote out everything that had happened. When she was done and the ink had dried, she folded the papers, sealed them, and tucked the cross and story safely in the bottom drawer of the desk.

Her fingers stung from the cold. She started to cross the sitting room to add more wood to the fire when a light tap sounded at the front door, followed by a creak as it slowly opened.

She'd thought her father asleep in bed for the afternoon. When had he gone out, and why?

"Father? Is everything all right?" she said, moving to the hallway. At the sight that met her, she sucked in a sharp breath.

Standing before her was Henry. He was bundled in multiple layers of woolen jerseys beneath a loose-fitting slop jacket, heavy gauntlet gloves, and an oilskin sou'wester with its flaps covering his ears. His cheeks and nose were red and frozen, strands of his hair poked out from his hat, and his arms were loaded with packages of all shapes and sizes.

At the sight of her in the sitting room doorway, he smiled. "There's still enough daylight left for a wedding today, isn't there?"

"Henry . . ." she stuttered, gripping the doorframe to keep from collapsing. "How did you get here? When? What happened?"

"I paid a schooner captain handsomely to drop me off here at Presque Isle."

"But I thought you were in Detroit."

"I was on my way there, but at a stopover to buy fuel at Port Huron, I met up with my father."

"Your father is here too?"

Henry shook his head. "We spent several days together in Port Huron, but then we parted ways."

Though a hundred more questions burned for release, she bit them back. She drank him in—his powerful presence, his achingly beautiful smile, his dark blue eyes—all of him.

Henry's smile faded into a straight line. He dropped the packages, stepped over them, and clomped in his heavy, wet boots, closing the distance between them.

Her legs grew weak as he came nearer.

He yanked off his hat and then his gloves, leaving a trail in his wake. When he stopped in front of her, his smile was gone altogether. His eyes held an apology. "Can you forgive me for having to leave the way I did?"

She glanced back into the sitting room, to the desk that contained her story and cross, and then she smiled up at him. "There isn't anything to forgive, Henry. You did what you needed to do. I understand."

He studied her face. "Are you sure?"

She nodded.

He lifted his hand as if wanting to touch her cheek, but then he crossed his arms over his chest. "I missed you so much," he whispered. "So much I thought I would go crazy if I had to wait one more day to see you."

"I didn't think you would come back," she confessed.

"There's nothing that could have kept me away," he said with a soft chuckle. "As my father quickly discovered."

"He's angry with you for returning?"

"No. Not really. Especially when he learned that you're the one who made me into a better man, the kind of son he could be proud of."

"I wish I could meet him and tell him the truth—that you *are* a better man."

"You will eventually. He's anxious to meet his new daughter-in-law."

Isabelle was afraid to ask him if he'd told his father everything about her, including that she would be blind one day.

"He doesn't care about your blindness any more than I do," Henry said, as if she'd spoken the question aloud. "He wanted to accompany me, but I told him that having one father here during our six-month honeymoon would be challenging enough and that we didn't need two."

"A six-month honeymoon?" She blushed at the very thought.

Again he raised his hand to touch her, only this time he didn't hesitate. He trailed his fingers down her cheek to her chin and then to her lips. "The one consolation for being frozen here all winter is that it will give us plenty of excuses to snuggle up together . . . in bed."

Sparks flickered in his eyes. She knew she ought to be mortified by his boldness, but she found she was growing accustomed to his flirting and rather liked it.

"Of course, I'm going to take you on another honeymoon, a much warmer and relaxing one. In the spring, once everything thaws." He slid his fingers up her jaw to her ear.

"Where will we go?" she asked, hardly able to think.

"Maybe to Europe. To Italy." He leaned in and nibbled at her earlobe. "Wherever you want to go, Isabelle."

She sighed at the softness of his breath brushing her neck. "I don't care where we live or where we go. All that matters is that we're together."

He pulled back and smiled. "Does this mean you're still willing to marry me? Today?"

"Maybe."

"What can I do to convince you?" He motioned toward the packages on the floor. "New books? New games? New clothes? Chocolates?"

She shook her head as she brought her hands up to his neck. "There's only one thing I want."

He quirked a brow.

"You. Just promise me we'll never have to be apart ever again."

"I promise," he said, "because that's exactly what I want too."

"I wouldn't mind one other thing," she whispered, staring at his lips.

His grin inched higher. "You're in luck because that's the one thing I have in endless supply."

She tugged his head lower. "Show me."

He bent in and took possession of her lips, kissing her with the promise of love and a lifetime of hope.

AN UNEXPECTED BRIDES NOVELLA

LOVE
BY THE
LETTER

MELISSA JAGEARS

MISSOURI
1858

An envelope with bright blue ink stamps landed in Dex's lap, a startlingly bright white against the faded tan of his trousers. He brushed the wood shavings off his legs and fingered the embossment around the edge of the envelope. Was it for him? He squinted at the loopy handwriting. Sure enough, his name, Dex Stanton, wandered under the upper left-hand stamp that said Independence, Missouri. He'd given up on receiving any replies a month ago. But this had to be it. He didn't know anyone who lived in Independence, though it was only a day's ride away.

"Since when did you start writing letters?" His brother, Grant, pushed up his bowler to scratch his hairline. With the sun's fiery shade of orange behind him, his younger brother was little more than a silhouette standing on the porch steps.

Dex wriggled on the hard bench. Only one letter . . . two months ago.

"Why didn't you ask me for help?"

"Not for this." He'd never ask anybody for help with this.

He set his carving knife and a half-formed miniature bear on the stump that served as his outdoor table.

No, Grant and Lily's table now. Everything that didn't fit into his nice, new covered wagon was no longer his. He glanced around the porch he'd added onto the farm house when he was fourteen. He'd soon be building his own place on land that didn't hold sour memories.

"It's from someone named Fannie." Grant walked up the stairs and took a seat on the railing. "You wrote a woman?"

Fannie. Her name was frilly, not a name he liked at all. He flipped the envelope over, and indeed, *Fannie Elaine Pratt* was scrawled across the back. "I didn't exactly write to Miss Pratt."

Grant's face contorted. "How can you not *exactly* write to somebody?"

Couldn't they talk about something else? Wheat and barley prices, fence mending, the weather? But Grant's firm jaw and pointed stare didn't invite meaningless conversation. Dex rubbed the back of his neck. "I wrote a company."

"For what?"

He kept from squirming; he wasn't ashamed. "It's a mail-order bride company."

"Seriously?"

Did he think men wrote to *The Marital News* on a lark?

Grant let out a long whistle that descended an octave. "But you're leaving for Kansas in a week."

"I didn't expect a reply to take this long." He'd have to speak plain before Grant started interrogating. "But if it hadn't been for Ma taking care of the house, God rest her soul, I couldn't have saved the farm. And if I'm going to succeed in western Kansas Territory, a woman will be important."

Grant leaned forward, his hands anchoring him to the railing. "Ain't there a girl in town you could ask after?"

"Nope." Dex ripped open the flap of his letter. When Grant didn't leave, he gave him the eye, indicating the conversation was over.

"Look, I understand the want of a wife."

Dex sighed. His brother had never been good at taking hints.

"God has blessed me with a wife and a son out of nowhere, but a stranger? I'd never thought you'd do something so . . . so . . ."

"Stupid, desperate . . . mad?" He crossed his arms, tucking the letter away from sight. Maybe his brother would enlighten him. "What young lady would marry me and pack herself up for a grueling walk across the plains before next Sunday?"

Grant sat beside him and spread his hulking arms across the back of the porch bench. "What about Emma Newsome?"

"No." She laughed like a monkey and never, ever stopped talking. His younger brother's advice was always so . . . horrible. "Would you marry her?"

Grant pulled a face. "All right, so she wasn't a good suggestion." He tipped his head back and stared at the porch ceiling, his mouth bunching in thought. "What about that redhead you used to walk home a few months back?"

"Engaged to Ralph." He'd already considered the few possibilities many times over. Unless he wanted to fight a handful of men more charming than he ever hoped to be for one of the Conner twins or marry a woman who'd need a very understanding man to live with her for the rest of her days—

"What about Rachel Oliver? She might go, seeing how her brother and sister are. Even if she's always got her nose stuck in a—"

"Don't bother rattling off a list." And that was the one woman he'd hoped his brother wouldn't light upon. He didn't want to have to spell out why Rachel wouldn't have him, though Grant should have realized. She was indeed available and quite attractive, but a man had to be realistic. "I know who's available and who isn't. And now, I have mail to read."

Grant smiled wickedly and grabbed for the letter. "Guess I could read it for you."

"Go bother your wife instead of me." Dex pushed against him.

Grant's thick body didn't even budge, but he chuckled, then stood. A glance through the window put a telltale gleam in his eye.

Evidently Lily was in the kitchen.

"Hmm, pestering the wife's a good idea." He slapped Dex's shoulder in passing and hollered at Lily before the screen door shut behind him.

Heaven help any passersby who glanced through the window. Those two were harder to pull apart than taffy. Dex rolled his eyes. The newlyweds made him squirm even in his own house. Well . . . not his house any longer since he was leaving in about a week.

He propped his feet on the porch railing, leaned against the bench seat, then pulled out the letter. After weighing down the empty envelope with his carving knife, he unfolded the expensively thin paper covered with the inky flourishes of a woman who liked to write fancy. He suppressed a groan. It was hard enough to read print.

The familiar pain behind his eyes crept in as he stared at the words, focusing on keeping the letters still. If only they wouldn't flicker around, reading would be painless. But no, they were up to their old tricks.

204

Dear Mr. Stanton, I have to say, I haven't had as much pleasure in a letter as I had in yours.

He read that twice to get all the words. So far, so good.

I do so love to laugh.

He liked to tell jokes, but he didn't recall writing any. That would have taken too much effort. His letter had been short and businesslike—at least, he'd meant it to be.

"Feoncay" was quite the puzzle! None of us could decipher it.

He read the sentence.
Then reread it.
Rubbing his forehead, he read it again.
Oh, *decipher.* He read it over again now that he'd figured out all the words.

The third man I asked at the post office finally figured you meant fiancée.

Fiancée. F-i-a-n-c-é-e. How did two *e*'s say *a*? And what on earth was the mark on top of the first *e* for? His headache intensified.

He's from France, so I'm certain only he could at the post office finally figured you meant fiancée.

Wait. He'd skipped up a line in the middle somewhere. He found the beginning of the sentence again.

He's from France, so I'm certain only he could have deciphered it since it was so horribly misspelled.

205

The spaces between the words fluctuated, and the words ran together. He pinched the bridge of his nose and took a long, deep breath. He could do this.

Which, given the rest of the letter . . . Did you even go to school?

And then he quit. He stared at the blue-gray cloud steadily crawling across the path of the sun, cutting off the light. He shook his head, which didn't help his headache.

He'd thought to try with the mail-order bride advertisements again when he got settled in Kansas, but should he even bother? Was his poor writing the reason he hadn't received a reply until this one? His fingers crinkled the edges of the paper, but rather than crumpling the letter and throwing it in the puddle off the porch, he folded it and folded it until the letter was nothing more than a tiny rectangular wad. He gritted his teeth against the woman's voice taunting him from the compacted paper.

He'd nearly written the word *betrothed* in his original letter, but he'd spent too long reasoning out the correct spelling and still hadn't been sure he was right. So he'd gone with *fiancée*. How dumb could he be, thinking a fancy foreign word would be easier to spell than an English one?

Why not toss the letter in the mud? This woman would never have him, nor take him seriously. With a hard flick, he sent the letter flying over the railing. The chunk of paper missed the puddle by an inch and lay as bright as a new stick of chalk on the heavily trod dirt.

Intended. He smacked his forehead and winced. Why hadn't he thought of the word *intended*? That would be spelled *i-n-t-e-d . . . e* or *e-a*? He ran his hands through his hair, then squeezed against the pounding between his temples.

Grant was right. Maybe he should consider one of the few unattached women here over the age of fifteen instead of a stranger. A few of the girls were . . . nice. Maybe he could look past the personality defects, inane chattering, the one with the blackened teeth . . .

But how could he court any of them when Rachel Oliver was in town?

Not that a brainy woman would give a man who could read about as well as a drunk horse a second glance.

But evidently, only a really desperate mail-order bride would overlook a man's inability to spell. Who was he kidding? He'd have to wait until families started settling in middle-of-nowhere Kansas to find a wife. But then, any woman making the trek was likely already promised or married.

A mail-order bride was his best chance to find someone who could make him forget about Rachel's engaging smile and her ability to do everything perfectly. Maybe he should pray that God would plunk a poor lost beauty who couldn't spell to save a kitten on his soddy's doorstep.

"Uncle Dex?" Allen's sweet voice grated against the ringing in his skull. Not in the mood to play sword fight or practice roping like he'd done every day this past week, he kept his eyes closed for a few seconds longer. He'd only gotten a nephew a few months ago and now, in a week and a half, he might not ever see the lad again.

He opened one eye and peered at his ten-year-old step-nephew, the boy's hair probably as mussed as his own. Smoothing back a lock, he stopped at the sight of the slightly unfurled chunk of a letter sitting in Allen's outstretched hand.

"Why'd you toss this in the mud, Uncle Dex? You don't ever get mail. Don't you want to keep it? Momma rereads her letters all the time."

"This coming from a boy who hates to read as much as I do." He snatched the fat wad of paper from the boy's hand lest he attempt to read it himself.

"Miss Oliver tells me I just have to practice reading more." Miss Oliver? "Rachel?"

"Yep, the older one, not the pretty one."

Dex bit the inside of his cheek. Rachel was pretty enough in her own right and much more mature than her younger sister. Besides, he'd hardly call nineteen old. "She's helping you read?"

Allen's head dipped emphatically. "And write better too."

"Why isn't your teacher doing that?"

"Miss Zuckerman says she don't have the time to help me. She told Momma I need extra help if I want to pass, but Momma grinds her teeth when I take too long, so she can't do it either. But Miss Oliver don't ever get frustrated with me. And she's helping me more than Miss Zuckerman ever did. Like having me figure out pictures for my words."

"Pictures?"

Allen leaned against the railing, grabbed the pole, and swung around. "I told her I couldn't see some words, so she helped me figure out a picture. Now I don't skip over the word *the* when I'm reading . . . well, most the time."

Pictures. Where'd she come up with that? "Does she have you make pictures for other words?"

"Some."

The porch floor creaked behind them.

"She's done wonders for him." Lily's hands were on her hips as she surveyed her freckle-faced boy, but her lips bunched into a half smile and pride flickered in her eyes. "Not that you don't have lots of room for improvement, young man. But I'm right proud you got a sixty on your spelling test today."

Dex sucked in a breath and held it. His father would have beaten him for a sixty. Not that he'd gotten many sixties. His grades hovered more in the thirty to forty range—that is, when he'd bothered to hand something in.

Dex ruffled Allen's hair. "Good job, keep at it."

Allen ducked his head and beamed. "Thanks, Uncle Dex."

"No thanks needed. If you work hard, we ought to be proud of you." It sure beat being forced to drill the same words over and over and getting a kick in the pants for good measure.

"Time to come in and wash." Lily flicked her dish towel at Dex. "You too." She turned and scurried into the house.

Allen stared at him.

Dex lowered his brows. "What? Didn't your mother tell you to go inside?"

"Pa told me you can't read none too good either."

Dex swallowed and waved a hand at Allen as if being unable to read well was nothing shameful—as if the flaw didn't matter. "All of us got our problems."

"Maybe you could ask Miss Oliver to help you like she's helping me."

Yeah, letting Rachel, the town genius, know he couldn't spell *genius* if his life depended on it wouldn't hurt his pride one whit. "Can you really read better?"

"Not as good as any of the girls in school." He scowled. *Overachieving girls.* Some things never changed.

"But I can read better . . . for me anyway."

"Allen Richard Carson the fourth!" Lily hollered out the window.

Dex cringed, giving his nephew a sympathetic look. "I don't envy you being 'the fourth.' Having my Ma use my middle name was bad enough."

209

"Don't I know it."

"Allen!"

The screen door flew open and slammed shut behind the boy.

Standing, Dex stretched and surveyed the fenced pastures, the repaired barn, the cellar he'd dug, and the hay fields he'd tended since quitting school twelve years ago. He was probably the only twelve-year-old boy in the world who was relieved when his father abandoned him. How could he complain since the beatings for every misspelled word had stopped, the one man God commanded him to respect never again told him he was worthless, and little girls in pinafores and braids could no longer outshine him on every test?

Like Rachel Oliver. The then six-year-old aced the spelling tests he flunked. He hadn't yet finished the second grade primer to his teacher's satisfaction, and Rachel had skipped through the first spelling book within a matter of weeks.

Good thing he left school a month later.

Or was it? Because now, if he wanted a wife, he'd have to write another letter—a better letter. One with all the words spelled right.

Maybe Rachel Oliver could help, but was it worth her finding out how stupid he really was? He'd worked hard to keep his secret from her. Anytime she'd joined his Bible study class, he'd find a need to attend another lest she wonder why he never volunteered to read. And the one time she had asked him to help with the children's nativity, he'd thought he'd been safe volunteering to build the set—until she'd wandered into the freezing barn to ask him to work with one of the struggling wise men to learn his lines. The poor boy was confused about why they practiced in the basement, far away from the others.

Could he stand Rachel knowing he was dumber than dirt?

A thick, official-looking letter dropped in front of Rachel Oliver's sheet music, and she fumbled the chord she was playing, the notes clashing together as if her family's fat tabby had decided to walk across the ivories.

"Did you really have to do that?" She swiped the letter out of the way, but her eyes caught on the stamped return address. No need to finish practicing Beethoven's Sonatina in G that she'd planned to play for Papa tonight. "Where'd you get this?"

"From the post office. Where else?" Her sister Patricia rolled her eyes.

"But I went to the post office with mother."

"Not before eight this morning."

Rachel hiked an eyebrow. Had her parents known her indolent sister had been dressed and traipsing about town that early? Nothing piqued Patricia's interest . . . except flirting. "Were you with Everett?" If she had indeed been flirting, she better not answer with anyone else's name.

Patricia's normally striking smile turned glorious. What Rachel wouldn't give for those perfectly straight teeth or the blond hair or—

"I spent all day with him." She clasped her hands in front of her flounced skirt and twirled as if she'd been rescued by some knight instead of visiting the man who'd courted her the last few months. "We went to the mercantile so I could suggest some things to take with us to Kansas, ate at Calico Café, and then he took me to the confectioners' for strawberries and cream." She sighed. "A perfect morning."

"Did you finish baking the bread?"

Her sister scowled in the most becoming way a person could

possibly scowl. Rachel scowled back so the girl would know how to do it properly.

Patricia stuck out her tongue. "You always pooh-pooh everything."

"Momma asked you to, and it'd be nice for her to remember you as an obedient daughter." Plus, she didn't want to get stuck with the baking. "I don't want to do it for you." Again.

"You talk as if I were dying instead of going with Neil to . . ." She fluttered her hand at the front wall of the parlor, which faced southeast—nowhere close to west. ". . . wherever it is we're going."

The door creaked open, and Neil's dark, stocky form stepped through the doorway.

Patricia sidled over to their brother. "You don't think my walking out with Everett today was wasted time, do you?" She laced her arm through his and looked at her sister smugly. "I learned all about wagon stuff. I could advise you on what you need for our trip."

"No need." He patted her arm with little enthusiasm.

"Oh, so you've already done that?" She batted her big blue eyes.

He nodded at their sister, but Rachel saw the slight shake of his head after Patricia looked away.

"See?" She leaned her head against his shoulder. "Neil doesn't fault me for not making bread."

He rubbed his stubbly chin. "I *am* hungry."

Patricia frowned. "You could have let me know." She pranced out of the parlor and turned in the direction of the kitchen.

Like a specter, Neil glided over to the settee and noiselessly dropped upon it. He leaned back and crossed an ankle over his knee.

Rachel glanced at her unopened letter, but Neil rarely remained in the room with her—or any female besides Patricia for that matter. "You must be anxious about leaving." She moved to the settee. "We'll miss you."

"You'll hardly know I'm gone." His smile was self-abasing. His hazel eyes and heavy jaw matched hers, and yet he was rather handsome for a brother.

"You might not say much, but your presence is soothing—especially when Patricia's in the room and I want to tear my hair out, or hers. I'm not picky which." She smiled." But I'll miss her too, of course."

"You can still come with us. It'd be better than New York."

She snagged her letter. "This one's thick. I might be going to Tennessee instead."

"Ma know?"

She slid the envelope around in her hands. Mary Sharp College in Winchester would not appeal to her mother's fancy ideals like Elmira Female College in New York. But she'd be more comfortable in Tennessee, and she'd still be going to one of those newfangled colleges that awarded women degrees equal to men's. Momma would just have to content herself with Tennessee.

Neil tipped her chin up, and the probing look in his eye and the uncharacteristic physical contact squeezed her heart.

She slipped across the seat and folded him in her arms. "I'll miss you."

He slowly wrapped his arms around her and awkwardly patted her back, then bussed the top of her head. "You'll do well at either school."

She held onto her brother, memorizing the feel of his firm chest and the smell of musk and wool. But within seconds, he started fidgeting, so she gave him a little girl grin and returned to sitting more ladylike. "Thank you, but your job will be harder than mine. You'll have Patricia."

He shrugged.

She'd never understood how her parents had produced a child as different as Patricia, but perhaps being the baby and spoiled was not a good thing. And for some reason, even Neil seemed to give in to her. "What are you going to do when she marries Everett? There won't be a word spoken in your little hovel for months on end."

His smile lit with genuine amusement, but then drooped.

"You'll miss her."

He breathed in sharply through his nose and scratched behind his ear, his fingers disappearing in his thick dark locks.

"How far will you travel before you settle? Do you think Patricia can handle all that walking?"

Neil shrugged. "As close to the Sixth Principal Meridian as we can get, I imagine." He re-situated himself and looked in the direction of the kitchen. "And she'll manage. She'd follow Everett anywhere."

Rachel clucked. "She'd follow any pretty boy anywhere." Though she couldn't imagine dainty little Patricia walking her way to Kansas without any fuss.

Neil frowned.

"Sorry, I know she says she's serious this time." Rachel fought not to roll her eyes. Patricia would probably start whining the first day. But their brother thought the sun rose and set on their sister for some reason. And he defended her mightily . . . using as few words as possible. But then, Patricia jabbered enough excuses for herself that he hardly had a need. "And you wouldn't take her unless you were sure she was committed since Everett hasn't proposed."

"Yet." Patricia sashayed back into the room, her hands on her hips. She stopped at Rachel's side but remained standing, the better to peer down at her, she supposed. "He'll ask me when he gets settled, when he's ready."

Yes, Everett would commit, but would Patricia? Neil, Papa, and Momma believed he could hold the seventeen-year-old's attention for the rest of her days. But if he didn't? Patricia would have far fewer men to flirt with on the prairie. Then again, maybe the isolation would get her focus off impressing others with her hair and dress and onto good, honest work.

Rachel stole a glance back at her letter. She needed to stop wasting her time and start school. She should have already been a junior. If only she hadn't wasted two years waiting for . . . well, never mind. That flimsy excuse would leave along with her siblings.

Sighing, she reached for the letter opener. She had absolutely no reason, or rather, no man to entice her into going to western Kansas Territory with her siblings, so hopefully she'd be headed to Tennessee over New York.

"Hello? Is anyone home?"

She froze at the sound of the warm, rumbling voice. Certainly he wouldn't be at her door now. Not after she'd given up waiting.

The visitor knocked. "Hello?"

But it was him. No one else's voice was that smooth and buttery. She dropped the letter, adjusted her skirt, and glanced toward the rippled windowpane to check her reflection.

Patricia sat on a nearby chair and picked up the tatting she'd left there earlier. "It's for you, Neil."

Her brother pushed himself off the settee and strolled out the door. "Dex."

"Neil, nice to see you."

215

Hinges whined, followed by the slapping of hands on backs.

Swallowing to wet her abnormally dry mouth, Rachel forced herself to retrieve her acceptance letter. Since Dex was going with her siblings on the wagon train, he must be there to talk over plans with them. Nothing more. If he'd never visited her in the years she'd hung around waiting for him to notice her, he wasn't there to see her today.

Dex and Neil tromped into the parlor, and Patricia slapped on her prettiest smile.

But Rachel didn't smile. If she did, Dex would have no choice but to compare her sister's flawless smile with her own gapped-tooth, flat one.

Without asking permission, Dex plopped beside her, making gooseflesh ripple up her arms. She scooted to give him more room, and Neil dropped onto the piano bench across from them.

Her hands fluttered conspicuously, so she slid her letter onto the end table and rammed her hands under her legs.

Dex inclined his head toward her. She pasted on a grin.

After no one spoke for a spell, Patricia narrowed an eye at her before clearing her throat. "Can I get you tea, Mr. Stanton?"

Rachel looked away, feeling the pink in her cheeks for not even seeing to their guest's comfort. But Patricia needed the practice anyway. She'd have to be a hospitable hostess for the lodging and trading post Neil intended to run—and later as Everett's wife.

"That'd be mighty nice, thank you."

"Rachel? Neil?" Patricia turned to her siblings for answers. Neil nodded, and Rachel whispered, "Yes."

Oh, why did Dex have to sit right next to her? The tremors of his jostling leg shook the seat, making her want to put a hand on his knee to stop the quaking. A rush of heat swooped up behind her ears the second she let her imaginary hand feel his knee beneath her fingertips. She turned toward her brother. Maybe he'd start a conversation for once.

He only eyed her.

Dex cleared his throat. "Since we're planning on leaving next Sunday after services, I'm going around and making sure everyone is set." He squirmed, and her skirt pulled.

She looked down to find him grinding a corner of her green and tan plaid gingham under the heel of his boot.

"You all have everything you need?"

Neil nodded, and Patricia returned with four cups of tea. She handed one to everyone and sat. The mantle clock's ticking seemed to slow. Dex stared at his lap as if he found his knees highly captivating.

Was he all right? He looked a little sweaty.

She took a drink to moisten her mouth. She was going to have to say something before the silence got out of hand.

"Is the sale of your farm final?" Neil's bass voice startled her. They must all be out of sorts if he was the sociable one.

"Yes, Grant and Lily are moved in and comfortable. I'm sending Luther and his wife their part of the money for the farm, so I'm squared away." He glanced down at his nervous footwork, then jerked his foot off her dress, tearing a bit of the ruffle with the action.

"Sorry."

"Nothing to worry about." She stared at the ripped fabric. Nothing for him to worry about anyway. But maybe instead of mending it, she's snip it off and make a bookmark. She shook her head at herself. Stupid thought. Her college roommates would question her ability to add two and two let alone excel in trigonometry if they discovered the reason behind her scrap memento.

Dex just needed to leave town. The man had never given her two thoughts, was always finding a reason to leave the room when she appeared, and so it was time to put away her Patricia-like obsession over him.

But the fixation wasn't Patricia-like at all. The men her sister fancied followed her around like bawling calves.

Dex had never looked her way. She bit her lip and squeezed her eyes shut. *I'm pitiful.*

A throat cleared. Then a second time. Opening her eyes, she found everyone staring at her.

"What did you say?" Patricia looked bewildered, though still cute.

"Um . . ." Had she said that out loud? Oh no. What rhymed with *pitiful*? *Visible, predictable, laughable*? Yes, *laughable* would work. "Nothing."

She evidently needed further education. Her brain must be going soft if her mouth ran off like that.

"I'm actually here to see Rachel." Dex turned his soft green eyes on her. "I, um, need to ask you a question. But I don't have much time before the wedding ceremony this afternoon. Are you going?"

"Maybe," she whispered. She could hardly hear herself over the heartbeat in her ears.

"We'll excuse ourselves." Patricia stood and beckoned at Neil before throwing her sister a wink. Romantic, silly girl. Dex wasn't here to propose or anything. But then, why else would he be squirming so much?

And all of a sudden, it was hard to breathe.

Neil glanced over his shoulder from the doorway and made a point to swing the parlor door wide open.

The second her brother's back disappeared, Dex stood,

walked a pace, then pivoted toward her. His chin jutted, and he put his hands behind his back and splayed his legs wide.

She sat up straighter.

He closed his eyes and sucked in his lips. As if he were about to bow his knee and declare himself her subject.

Should she stand? She rubbed her sweaty palms on her skirt.

"This is a rather hard thing for me to ask, but I don't have any other choice." He cleared his throat. "Or rather, you're my only choice."

Well, if this was a marriage proposal, Dex was about to give Mr. Darcy a lesson on how to thoroughly offend and insult a woman while asking for her hand.

"So I'm going to ask before I change my mind." Dex finally focused on her. "I need help—reading help—like Allen does. Would you mind giving me a few writing lessons before I leave?"

2

Dex's hands were frigid, so he stuck one of his big mitts against his blazing hot neck. He'd expected a look of derision, pity . . . something when he'd divulged his big secret, but Rachel only blinked.

Had she heard him? She appeared a bit ill actually.

Maybe she figured he was too old to learn to read. Perhaps she was scrambling in her brain for a polite way to decline. His gut quivered, but he dropped his hand and straightened as if he hadn't just forced himself to expose the one secret he'd hoped she'd never discover . . . and the one secret he wished she'd already known.

Maybe she wouldn't care. Maybe she could look past his inability to read and . . . no, better not think any more in that vein. She wouldn't want to marry a man who probably couldn't spell her name.

Rachel's face cleared with a little shake of her head, and her lips bunched in thought. She pushed herself off the settee, walked over, and tipped her head back a little to see him.

He should make sure to inquire about any potential brides'

heights. He'd need a tall woman like Rachel since he'd only have to lean a little to kiss—

"What are you looking at?" She swiped her thumb across her lower lip.

He snapped his eyes up to hers. "Nothing, ma'am." He needed to get a hold of himself. He'd done it for years, he could do it now.

"Ma'am?" Her face scrunched like Lily's did when Grant brought up her cooking failures.

"I mean Miss Oliver."

She folded her arms across her ample chest. Shucks, why were his eyes betraying him? He forced his focus back up on her face.

"I won't teach you anything if you treat me like a school-marm. You're older than me and more than my equal."

Not equally smart, she'd find that out sure enough.

"Rachel, then." He drug up a smile. Even if she skittered off like a barn cat when she heard him read, he could try to summon some charm to make up for his stupidity. "So that means you've got time for me?"

She frowned. "You're leaving Sunday. That doesn't give us much time."

"I've got the wagon packed already, so I've got nothing pressing for awhile."

"Then come over here." She skirted around the couch and opened the shutters. The afternoon sunlight shot through the floating dust. "Sit down, and I'll tell Papa what we're doing."

"What, you mean . . . now?" He ran a finger along the opening at the top of his shirt. Maybe this wasn't a good idea after all. If she asked him to read something right now, he'd stumble all over himself. He needed time to practice.

"Did you have something in particular you needed to read?"

He took a step back toward the door. "Not exactly, it's just that . . . I—" He fumbled to catch the fancy lamp that careened to the edge of the table. He was going to have a bruise on the back of his leg from banging the table corner, but he wouldn't rub it.

She smiled so wide, he lost his breath. She'd never smiled at him like that before.

"There's no need to run away from me." The lilt in her voice suddenly died.

He glanced over his shoulder to see if her father or Neil were scowling at them or something. Neil would notice right away he wasn't acting right. And he didn't want anyone to realize how much he'd fallen for a girl who'd never have him.

But the hallway was silent and empty.

Frowning, she waved him toward a chair at a small table. "I won't make this harder than it is, I promise. Allen comes home every night in one piece, doesn't he?"

If he continued to act like a pup afraid of his own shadow, she'd have plenty more to laugh at than how thoroughly he was about to murder the English language. "If this is the time you've got, I guess I'll take it."

"Good." She turned and shuffled out the door.

He sat and focused on breathing.

Come on, Dex, you know why you're doing this—it needs to be done. Though you should've gotten help earlier . . . much earlier.

Rachel and Neil's voices mingled in a far corner of the house over the clatter of dishes. He glanced at the papers strewn on the table. Letters mixed in with numbers and math symbols were written in neat rows. Allen had said she did math with the alphabet, but he hadn't actually believed him. Math with the alphabet? Who'd heard of such tripe?

What did those letters do anyway? Rachel's fancy math didn't make a lick of sense, so he looked around the room. Her father evidently made enough money in all his business ventures to do quite well. A fine piano, frilly doilies, fancy lamp shades. He turned to stare out the window, only able to see the brick wall of the house next door.

He could provide Rachel with much prettier vistas in Kansas, but a woman who lived in a house like this wouldn't be content with a hovel that might not even have a window, let alone a glass one.

Did Patricia know what kind of house Everett intended to build? He couldn't imagine that blond bundle of giggles in a soddy. He'd have to question the next lady he wrote about her living condition expectations.

Rachel glided back in and grabbed two books off the shelf. They were thick, too thick. "Would you prefer a seafaring adventure or a haunted house? Or rather, what the heroine imagines is a haunted house."

Couldn't he start with a much smaller book? He glanced around the shelves but they all seemed bulky. "Ah . . . the sea."

"*Robinson Crusoe* it is." Did she actually skip a little on the way back to the shelf? She put away the thinner book, twirled, and slid the larger one across the table before sitting. "Go ahead and read the first page."

He clamped his hand over the book to hide his shaking and dragged it toward him. Curse the courage that had prodded him to come today. He flipped past the exorbitant amount of fine blank pages to get to chapter one, then pressed the book flat. He grimaced at his sweaty hands and stopped to wipe his palms on his pant legs.

Why did it have to be such fine print? The lines wouldn't

stop congealing, and concentrating harder wasn't keeping the words still.

This would be more taxing than the time Miss Christmore threatened him with a ruler if he didn't come to the front of the class to read. He hadn't been able to squirm his way out of every fix back then, and it didn't look like he could now—and this time, he'd asked for it.

"Read aloud, so I can hear you."

He cleared his throat to keep from laughing. Did she think he'd been reading in his head? He hadn't even pinned down the first word.

"Don't be afraid to be wrong; I can't help unless I can discover a pattern to what you're misreading, so don't try too hard."

Easy for her to say. Hard was the only way he got any reading done. "All right." He focused on the first page and tried to breathe calmly. The first line proved no trouble. He wiped his brow. But the second?

". . . my Father being a foree—foray . . ." How was he supposed to say that? He had no hope of getting through this book with any pride.

"It's all right if you get the word wrong. But on this one, it might be better to guess at what you think it might be. Use the other words in the sentence to help you."

He was supposed to guess? How was that reading? Her warm fingers settled on his, and his jitters jumped double time.

She smiled. "I need to hear what's giving you trouble."

He had trouble with everything, especially the feel of her silky skin against his calloused knuckles.

With a start, she snatched her hand back and stuffed it below the table with her other. "And I won't correct you since that'd make it harder for you to concentrate."

That she sat close enough to hold his hand was enough to mess with his focus. If he didn't stop looking at her, he'd get no reading done. He pulled the book closer and stared harder.

". . . my Father being a foregg—foreggner." That wasn't even a word. He looked again.

"No need to fix anything, I'd rather you not think too hard and just read." She scooted closer and peered at the page over his arm.

The floral scent of her hair was making a muddle of his brain. He could barely think at all. How did she expect him to read this way? "I'm sorry, but I can't keep going until I figure it out. It might be important."

"Then go ahead." Rachel bit her tongue and moved her eyes off the page to keep from saying the word for him.

For a second, their eyes locked, but he returned his focus to the book, folding back the front cover as if strangling *Robinson Crusoe* with his giant hands would wrestle the story into submission. "Just tell me what the word is if I'm supposed to guess."

"Foreigner."

". . . foreigner of Brem . . . en?" He looked up at her.

She nodded. "Keep going."

After he started reading fairly fluidly, she noted he omitted or misread simple words like *a* and *the,* and apparently his brain skipped the middle letters in some words and substituted another word with the same beginning and ending sounds, like *ramping* instead of *rambling,* even if it didn't quite make sense. Just like Allen.

She stared at his profile. His jaw was awfully tense for reading aloud. The slight crick in his nose she'd never noticed before didn't detract from his overall handsomeness, but rather added to it.

He stumbled on a word and cut his eyes toward her. A blush crawled up her neck. She quickly located his place on the page and pointed to it, hoping to distract him from her heightened color. "That would be *competent*."

So much for promising not to correct him.

"Competent." He growled. "Now I've lost my place." His finger started at the top of the page and slid down each line until he found *competent*, then he started reading again.

Each word hummed in his low bass voice, and she couldn't help but smile at some of his mistakes. Oh, why hadn't he come to her earlier when she might have had time to help?

And maybe catch his eye.

What other man in town was as responsible and hardworking as Dex? Livelier girls might have been turned off by how mellow and relaxed he was, but he was the most mature man around by far. And his handsome face wasn't in the least disappointing.

She shook her head; she was more enamored than ever. This spur-of-the-moment decision to tutor him would only end in heartache—hers.

"So it's not *strongly*?" His Adam's apple bobbed as he squinted at the page and pulled the book closer.

"I'm sorry. I wasn't shaking my head at you. It is *strongly*, as you said." She reached out a reassuring hand but stopped herself. She'd never touched a man outside of her family— well, except for occasionally being helped down stairs or onto a buggy seat—yet she'd almost laid a hand on him a second time. Clenching her fingers, she blew out a breath.

He shut the book. "I'm sorry I'm doing so poorly. This was a bad idea."

"Oh no." And her hand was on his again. But if she snatched it back, she'd draw undo attention to where her hand ought not to be—again.

Surely her touch reassured him, though the opposite sensation coursed through her skin: a warm, prickling awareness mixed with cold shivers. "I'm afraid my mind wandered. I was only reprimanding myself."

"And what were you reprimanding yourself for?"

"Is it hot in here?" She jumped from her seat and went to the window. "Spring seems a bit muggy this year, don't you think?" She lifted the sash and let the entirely too cold air in. Suppressing a shiver, she ignored the impulse to slide the window back down.

"Do all women have malfunctioning furnaces under their skin?" He chuckled, the sound drawing out the gooseflesh already decorating her arms. "Mother often fought me over leaving windows open and then got mad at me later for shutting them."

Cupping the side of her neck, Rachel looked askance at the man driving her internal furnace up a notch past normal. Or maybe five notches. "Your mother was a lovely woman. I don't think I ever gave you my condolences."

"That's all right." He abruptly stood and rambled over. "You do look flushed. I should head home so you can lie down."

She took a step back. She'd seen his tricks before. The few times Miss Christmore had asked him to read in front of the class, he distracted the teacher with some outlandish behavior that earned him a spell in the corner or made everyone laugh so the teacher forgot she'd called him forward as she tried to regain control.

Miss Christmore hadn't seen through his tactics, but Rachel had. However, with his deep green eyes only a foot away and that strand of brown hair falling across his forehead, she understood how easily a woman could be distracted.

Dex reached up and tugged the mischievous strand back into place. "I think I've lost you."

No, Dex. You can't lose what you never wanted. Pushing away from the windowsill, she returned to the table. "Sorry. I wasn't thinking clearly." And it was time to do so. If Dex hadn't wanted anything to do with her before, he didn't now. She was still, maddeningly, under the spell of his handsome face.

But it was time to put away childhood fantasies—a man with homesteading dreams would never consider marrying a girl who'd spent more time translating Latin than learning how to bake a variety of breads.

She sat and pointed at the book. "You can't get out of reading that easily, Dex." His name felt better on her lips than she imagined.

She grimaced. *Get yourself together; you're supposed to be helping, not entertaining the daydreams you've given up.* "I want you to read another page before you go."

He dragged himself away from the wall and sat as if his seat were a pin cushion. "How is this doing any good? You're not teaching me anything."

"I'm assessing your needs."

"My needs?"

Why did his question sound so breathy? "Yes, how you read lets me understand what might help you." Though if he read and wrote like Allen, a handful of lessons wouldn't do much good.

"You make me sound like a science experiment."

"More like a puzzle."

"You like puzzles, do you?"

She stopped rubbing her hands together. "Yes, and research is awfully fun too."

"You're too smart for this town." He frowned. "Too smart."

He picked up the book as if she'd asked him to eat a cow patty, then abruptly put it down. "I should save us the time and call this what it is: a dumb plan. I haven't even finished one page."

"No, don't give up." Maybe it was a dumb plan. It was certainly dumb for her heart to pine . . . but he needed her. "I'll help as much as I can."

Hours later, Dex tugged on his sleeves as he stepped onto the church lawn where tables of food and a small dance floor were set up for the wedding's reception. He'd looked all over the sanctuary for Rachel's family while the mayor's daughter married a friend of his, but he hadn't seen any of them. Surely they'd attend since Mr. Oliver supported Mayor Isaacs's reelection campaign.

He jammed his hands in his pockets, scrunching the sleeves to the middle of his forearms where they always crept up anyway. He needed a suit with longer sleeves, but what was the point? Soon he'd be more worried about his shirts holding together until his crops turned a profit than whether his sleeves fit.

A fiddle sounded and another out-of-tune one joined in. The fiddlers were huddled together, tuning and checking the sound against Everett's guitar.

Everett. His eyes were always glued to Patricia, and Rachel couldn't be far behind her sister.

What would he say to her if he found her anyway? Would

she turn pretty pink like she had this afternoon? She'd blushed a lot even after the open window had sucked out all the warm air and he'd butchered two paragraphs of *Robinson Crusoe*. Or had she really been overheated?

Dex stopped next to his friend and turned to scan the crowd. "Where's your girl?"

Everett had won Patricia with very little effort. And they made a pretty pair—the two blond, blue-eyed angels belonged together. Whereas a girl genius like Rachel needed someone who could read more than seed catalogs that had pictures and do fancier math than count the skimmed gallons of milk every day.

Everett adjusted his guitar to match the fiddles. "Haven't seen her yet."

"I know this is a strange question, but how long did it take you to win over Patricia?" Dex kept his eyes pinned on the people spilling out of the church.

The silence grew so long, he looked down at Everett, whose foot was hooked on his knee as he rested his arms atop his guitar. "I'll tell you when you tell me why you're bothering with a mail-order bride service."

He dropped his hands from his hips. "Who told you that?"

"You're avoiding my question."

Grant. He'd have to strangle his thick-necked brother when he got home. "I'm twenty-four. You no more than turn eighteen and Patricia is ready to follow you to the middle of nowhere on nothing but a promise."

"I can't give her anything until I have something." He turned a peg on the head of his guitar and strummed.

He didn't have much either, and yet Rachel hadn't snubbed him even after listening to him trip over every other word on an entire page. Maybe she might consider a man who couldn't pass a test to get into college—not even a ladies' college. He touched the back of his hand where hers had landed not twice but almost three times.

He was letting a little hand touching get the best of him. A girl as smart as Rachel wouldn't throw away school to turn over Kansas dirt even if she did like him a little. But maybe after she had her degree, and he'd built a home . . .

"I don't get why you'd try to write for a girl though. Any woman agreeing to marry through the post has something wrong with her." Everett's eyes wandered to the left of the dance floor.

Dex followed his gaze and found Patricia, swathed in flounces of white with pink ribbons strung along every conceivable edge. Flushed with youth, she waved exuberantly when she saw Everett.

Dex sighed. His friend wouldn't be able to do much beyond strum and stare now. "I'm going to find Neil. He can't be far behind his sister."

"Sure." Everett made an effort to sort of glance at him before fastening his gaze on Patricia and flashing her a silly grin.

Dex walked up to her and she frowned, as if his obstructing her view of Everett would make him disappear in a puff of smoke.

"You look lovely, Miss Oliver. Where's your brother?"

"There." She didn't even look, just pointed behind her at the food-laden tables where Neil stacked a plate while juggling punch cups.

No Rachel. "And your sister?"

Patricia cocked her head to the side, causing a ringlet to slide off her neck. "You need to talk to her?"

More than he'd admit. He rubbed the slight stubble on his upper lip. "Not really."

231

"Well then, I suppose it won't make any difference if I say she's not coming?"

Why was she looking at him like that? He ran his tongue over his teeth. "I thought she said she was."

Neil sidled up beside his sister and held out a glass of punch.

"She doesn't dance anymore. Said if she isn't getting married, there isn't any point in dancing and she'd rather study." Patricia rolled her eyes and took the drink. "Which she finds fun for some odd reason."

Never marry? He'd known she'd go to school, but he hadn't thought she was that dedicated. For a second he'd thought maybe he could write her, but she'd evidently perused all the bachelors around town and found them wanting—including him. And that was before she knew he couldn't read or write for nothing. "Of course she wouldn't marry someone from around here. She's too good for any of us." Oh, how he wished the woman's standards weren't so high. But what had he expected?

Neil took a sip of red liquid from an etched-glass punch cup, his eyes pinning Dex to an invisible wall.

He needed to excuse himself before Neil figured out what he'd been thinking. "Too bad she isn't here. I wouldn't have minded a dance about the floor with her. Save me a dance if you would, Miss Oliver."

"Of course. I have plenty free since Everett's stuck in the band." She sighed.

He'd stay long enough to dance a jig with Patricia and then go home and make sure his wagon was ready for the long, lonely drive over the Kansas plains.

3

"I thought you and Allen said turning small words into pictures would help." Dex growled, fidgeting in the straight-back chair.

"It's not magic." Only his fourth lesson and he wanted her to conjure a miracle. Rachel clamped her hands under the little table, almost afraid to look at him. He turned downright trying with a book in his hand.

"But I still missed the word." He slapped the book down and glared at her as if she were a five-year-old questioning his authority. "And I know what the word *from* is. I use it all the time."

"Of course you do." She hadn't said anything to produce this testiness. Should she growl back at him? The mirth fighting to upturn her lips and the chuckle stuck in her throat were not helping the situation. "How about we move to the settee? Maybe if you were more comfortable—"

"You think I'm stupid." He raked a hand through his hair and winced when a split fingernail stuck in a strand. He grumbled while disentangling himself.

"No, I don't." Her lips fought against her determination not to smile. She wouldn't let them get the best of her, not if she

233

wanted to suppress the laughter. She pressed her lips together hard. Really hard.

"How can I not be?" By the way his hands snatched up the book, he was a second or two away from throwing *Robinson Crusoe* across the room.

"Shh." He needed to be gathered up and held tight. Like she'd do for a frightened little kitten. Three feet taller than his nephew, Dex seemed a hundred times more vulnerable. The laugh choking the back of her throat faded.

She couldn't imagine not being able to learn whatever she wanted to with ease. Her mother's book collection, her father's willingness to answer her every question, and her ability to soak it all in came without effort. What if her mind hadn't been so quick? "We just have to find something that works for you. Maybe the picture thing only works for Allen."

"But it makes sense." He grumbled and grabbed a cookie.

She set another cookie on his plate and took two for herself. "Well then, maybe you need more practice. I certainly didn't learn to read in a day."

"Are you sure about that?"

She stilled. She couldn't remember not reading.

He huffed and glanced at the mantle clock. "It's been four days."

"You sure don't give yourself much time to do things."

He tore apart his cookie in chunks but didn't eat the pieces. "Nothing else is this hard."

"But see? If you naturally excel at everything else, you can't be stupid."

"Even little kids read better than me." He shoved his plate away.

She reached toward him but let her hand fall beside him

before making contact. If she started touching his hand again today she wouldn't stop. "But you dropped out of school when you were twelve."

"My pa dropped out at eight, and he could read better than this." He shook his head. "And you were six then and read circles around the reading I'm doing now."

"So you have a problem we didn't." One that had caused him years of suffering she'd never known about. "Doesn't mean you can't overcome it. With enough practice, you could even go to college one day."

He snorted. "Not unless I packed you in my suitcase and hid you under my desk to do the work for me." He colored for some reason and turned to look out the window. "My ma handled all the farm's bookwork."

"Who's handling that now?"

"Grant."

"Who'll handle that in Kansas?"

He fidgeted in his chair.

He'd need somebody to do that for him. She scooted closer but bit back the idea, curling her tongue. Too forward. Unasked-for. Foolish.

But what if she was in love with the man?

She'd been trying hard lately not to offer people advice or help unless they asked. Most men thought her ideas weren't worth much because she was female. Did Dex feel threatened by her superior academic skills?

He shouldn't. He may not be able to parse *ambulo*, but he'd saved his mother from financial ruin at the age of twelve, worked every day from dawn to dusk so his brothers could finish school, and now ran the best little dairy in town. She'd follow him anywhere without an ounce of worry that he could provide.

But was she crazy enough to propose a convenient marriage when he'd never shown interest in her? She could do his paperwork, and surely he'd come to love her, right? Her shaky hand pressed against the jitters in her stomach. If anyone needed her, Dex did. People married for convenience all the time, in fact for lesser—

"That's the beauty of a homestead: no need to write or read anything to succeed at farming." Dex stared at the pen in his hand as if it were his nemesis.

The air left her lungs, sagging her shoulders. How dumb to jump back so quickly into her schoolgirl dreams. She stared at her twiddling thumbs. As if academic abilities were reason enough to push herself onto Dex when her skills mattered little to a farmer.

"And it doesn't matter how poorly I write my grocery list if I'm the only one reading it."

Right. What farmer needed to know Cicero? Or algebra? Well, some algebra would come in handy—

"Where's the cookies?" Patricia swooped in from the hall, and Rachel scowled. The door had to be open for propriety, but her sister didn't need cookies enough to interrupt.

Rachel held up the plate and didn't even look at her sister. "Here, take one."

"Hello, Dex."

Dex draped his arm over the back of the settee and hitched his ankle up onto his knee. "You look lovely today, Patricia."

And when didn't her little sister look stunning? Rachel put the plate of cookies back down with a thump and stuffed half of one in her mouth to keep her from grinding her teeth uselessly.

Her sister twirled, the rose-sprigged calico flaring about her feet and letting white cotton eyelets peek out from underneath her skirt. "I had a trunk full of practical dresses made, but sensible doesn't have to mean ugly."

Rachel humphed. Patricia's lace collar added considerable cost to the dress when the money could have been used for useful supplies instead.

"Rachel disapproves." Patricia's mouth scrunched to the side in a sorry attempt to look chastened. "But then, if she'd ordered my dresses, they'd all be brown, black, or gray. And you can't catch a man's eye in those."

Was her sister already feeling restless? Rachel narrowed her eyes. "If you've a need to catch a man's eye other than Everett's, you ought to stay in town and let Neil go alone."

Patricia slapped a hand to her heart. "I can't believe you'd think such a thing." She dropped in the chair on the other side of Dex. "Now tell me, what married man ain't gonna want his wife to look a vision?"

"*Isn't*," Rachel said through clenched teeth. More because of how much Patricia's eyelashes fluttered at Dex than her poor grammar.

"*Ain't* works perfectly fine. You know what I meant." Patricia turned her big eyes back on Dex. "And *she* calls *me* insensible. Why fight over words when they don't hurt nobody? School ain't going to make you a better person."

Dex folded his arms over his chest. "I agree, it won't."

Rachel caught the quick glance he threw her way before he angled his body to face her little sister. She tried to smile but couldn't keep her lips from trembling, so she let the frown have its reign. Surely some man in her future would want a woman of an improved mind.

"Rachel says people who don't go to school are doomed to

have closed minds. Says how else are people going to improve themselves?"

And with that, her little sister took away the teeny tiniest hope Dex might have wanted a woman like her. The little vixen. Rachel pressed her finger into her cookie until she poked a hole clean through.

Dex glanced at her from the corner of his eye. "School won't improve your sister any—"

"I just don't get why she wants a silly degree anyway." Patricia didn't even flinch at the scowl Rachel sent her way. "They won't give you a man's job unless they're trying to save money. And they'd still have to be desperate."

Patricia turned back to Dex. "I think she ought to come with us. She could do Neil's books or keep me company or teach school. No one would think she was uppity for those things."

He rubbed at the back of his neck. "She'd certainly be a help—"

"And you're right about no one around here wanting to marry her since she acts so snooty about things—"

"Yoo-hoo, Patsy!" A melodic voice belonging to one of the myriad girls her sister giggled with in the afternoons called from the front entrance.

Swiping the cookie plate, Patricia left without a wave of good-bye.

No one wanted to marry her? Was she that haughty?

Rachel bowed her head, staring down at the crumbs on the table as though a dunce cap pressed against her brow. She couldn't deny what Patricia had accused her of saying.

But she hadn't known how hard school was for some people until she'd started working with Allen.

The silence Patricia left in her wake grew long. Should she apologize?

Dex's hand ran agitatedly over the tablecloth. "Um, that's not what I said exactly, and I need to apologize for my earlier attitude."

Rachel frowned. "No, I'm the one that said those things, but—"

"But those of us without schooling are in a world of hurt." He dropped his leg with a thump onto the floor and leaned forward on both elbows, his hands clasped between his knees. "I didn't mean to get so fired up earlier. I was angry at me, not you. I thought I could pick up on this reading and writing thing quicker. And we haven't even started working on my spelling, which is what I really need fixed."

She tilted her head. "I've been working with Allen for months now and his reading isn't close to stellar. You can only learn so much in a few days."

"But I'm older. I should take to instruction better."

"I don't think it's a matter of instruction, per se." She ran her finger along the lamp shade's fringe. "I have a feeling there's something in your brain that makes reading difficult."

"Great. Then I'm hopeless." He sat back and crossed his arms.

Why was he so down on himself? He could learn to read better, maybe not in a week, but surely with help. "I didn't say that."

Dex sighed and took the book from her. "I guess we might as well continue."

Maybe she should stop these lessons. He needed more help than she could provide. But if he didn't think he benefited from the brief effort, he might never try again. Neil could help him in Kansas, surely. "You've done fine until now, and as you've said, reading won't affect running a homestead much. Plus Neil and Patricia will be nearby, they could—"

"No, I need to write better."

"But again, Neil and—"

"They can't write what I need written." He jabbed her pen into one of her equations, poking a hole through the paper.

"Sure they can. You could always ask them how to spell things if you want to write in your own hand."

His Adam's apple bobbed. With his eyes fixed on the pen and paper in front of him, he mumbled something.

"I'm sorry?"

"They can't help me write to my future bride."

Her heart froze. "Bride?" she sputtered. "I'm sorry, I didn't know."

"I've got to be able to write letters she can understand."

No wonder he'd never given her a second glance. A woman she didn't know had won him.

Oh! This tutoring had to end. Now.

Lord, get me out of this, please.

"I think perhaps a dictionary would be a wise purchase. Then you could forget these lessons and spend more time with your family and prepare for your trip." She lowered her eyes. Had this woman sat across from him in church and every community dance for years hoping to catch his eye? Had she dreamed about Dex for more than a decade?

But it didn't matter what the woman had or had not given up. Dex had chosen her.

"I've borrowed Lily's dictionary, but it doesn't help if you don't know how to spell in the first place." He flicked his hand as if he'd been holding all his confidence in his grasp and flung it away. "Maybe I just have to get over myself. Patricia would probably find the letter writing thing romantic, but I couldn't have her write down the personal stuff."

Personal words and feelings that would never be written to her. What would Dex write the woman he loved? Probably the same things she couldn't say to him. But it wasn't her inability to spell that had kept her quiet—a very good thing she'd stayed quiet.

Rachel's eyes grew warm, but she wouldn't blink lest she loose a tear over something that had never been hers anyway. "A woman in love would overlook your misspellings or your need for someone's help."

He paled. "A woman in love, perhaps, but not a mail-order bride."

Her lungs squeezed, and her hands sought one another to wring out the tension.

He'd not just chosen another woman. He'd chosen any woman but her.

The silence in the room weighed upon Dex's shoulders. Rachel's eyes had turned cloudy, and she'd grown pale though she hadn't said anything more. Probably because she hadn't anything nice to say about his mail-order bride decision. Everett and Grant hadn't either.

"Did I hear Patsy say cookies earlier?" Rachel's father poked his balding head through the door and smiled. "Good afternoon, Dex."

Dex tried not to sigh with relief at the interruption. "I'm sorry, Mr. Oliver, but the snickerdoodles Rachel baked are gone."

Rachel shook her head as if to clear it. "Sorry, Papa. Patricia ran off with them."

"You made the cookies?" Mr. Oliver's smile disappeared, and a bushy eyebrow popped up.

"Yes." Why did she look so sheepish?

"But you never make cookies." Rachel's father put his hands behind his back and shifted his bulky weight to one foot. "You never bake for that matter."

She shrugged. Her eyes followed her fingers playing with the lampshade fringe again. "Allen ate my lemon drops."

"What happened to the horehound I gave you yesterday? Don't tell me you ate all of them without sharing."

"No, I just felt like . . . having something different."

Mr. Oliver turned his way. "So she gave you snickerdoodles? Fresh baked?"

Dex cleared his throat and looked at Rachel, who'd turned several shades of pink. "Yes, sir."

"I see." And then he smiled. "You don't happen to have any more in the kitchen?"

Rachel shook her head. "No, Neil grabbed two handfuls the moment they came out of the oven. It's like he'd never eaten a cookie before."

"Well, my women aren't known for their baking skills."

Rachel slunk lower in her chair.

"Unless they've got a special reason to fire up the oven."

And she turned red again.

"No reason. I . . . uh . . . didn't want to share my candy is all. Well, besides with you, Papa." She clamped her lips tight and looked to the ceiling. "I'll make another batch tonight."

"Ah, no need. No need." He scanned the table littered with closed books with a smile. "How are the lessons going?"

Dex clamped down on the inside of his cheek and stared at Rachel. What would her answer be? Any sane person would have given up on him already, but she'd defended his intelligence. Had he been wrong about her this whole time? Could he fail academically, yet still be competent in her eyes?

"As well as can be expected. I won't be able to help him improve much before he leaves, but then . . ." She lifted a shoulder. "His life doesn't depend on it either."

Dex swept back the infernal lock of hair that always fell in his eyes. Maybe his life didn't depend on him writing a decent letter, and maybe some woman could look past his spelling . . . but a woman who'd never met him?

"Huh." Mr. Oliver peered at him over his spectacles. "So you're still leaving?"

Dex frowned. "Is there a reason I shouldn't be?"

Mr. Oliver gave a pointed look at Rachel, then at him, wrinkling his forehead by raising both eyebrows. "Oh, I don't know." He placed a hand on Rachel's shoulder. "I'm going up to your room for a handful of your horehound."

"Sure, Papa." Once he exited, Rachel leaned toward him, but didn't meet his eyes. "We don't bake sweets because Papa won't stay out of them."

Dex kept his gaze on her until she looked up. And when she did, her normally rosy cheeks colored a bit more.

Could a smart girl like her really have feelings for a man like him?

No, Mr. Oliver's crazy questions and her blushes didn't mean what his brain was trying to twist them to mean. Patricia had said Rachel didn't intend to marry. But why? Didn't all women want to? Of course, not many men wanted to marry someone smarter than the whole town put together. A woman like that would be rather independent, not to mention downright intimidating.

But what if Rachel had made him cookies for some reason other than hospitality?

When she glanced back at him, he loosed the slow smile he plied on little girls to make them giggle.

Rachel ducked her head and grabbed the book in front of her as if it was a life line. "Perhaps we should quit these lessons entirely. Neil would tutor you in Kansas, I'm sure."

"No." He let his tongue slide across his teeth. Maybe he couldn't improve in a week, but he could see if Rachel fancied him. "I mean, I'd like to continue. To learn as much from you as I can. I really don't know why this is so hard for me, but you're my best chance at learning." And spending time with her would help him decipher her feelings for him.

She didn't say anything.

Maybe he was misreading this whole situation. "Since I've never had the nerve to admit my problems to anyone besides family, I think I should try to see how this goes. I'll work hard every night."

"If that would make you happy." She didn't look thrilled.

He glanced at the algebra book, then the letters and symbols scrawled on the papers poking out from underneath the heavy textbook. He'd interrupted her math studies earlier, though she claimed she was solving the equations for fun. *Fun.*

If she did feel something for him, would it be right to hold such an intelligent woman captive on the prairie, keeping her from ever going to school?

Maybe Rachel would be willing to correspond with him while in college. If she could handle years of his atrocious spelling, then she could handle anything. He could put off writing a mail-order bride again if she—

Mail-order bride. He rubbed his hand down his face. Her

tense posture and firm pout as she studied the bookshelf across from her made him grit his teeth.

If her father's hinting and her fidgeting indicated she liked him, he'd ruined any chance he had by telling her the real reason he'd wanted these lessons.

How stupid could he be?

4

Rachel slid the last hot snickerdoodle onto a plate, then poured coffee in her father's favorite mug. The fading beams of the setting sun lit her way to the parlor where her mother always played their favorite songs every evening.

Patricia tatted by the light of the brightest lantern, her shuttle racing with quick second-nature movements. Neil sat with his feet propped on the hassock, their tabby curled on his out-stretched legs, and Papa rested his head against his chair, soaking in the familiar runs of Mozart.

The plunk of the plate on the side table stirred Papa from his reverie. He turned and smiled at the pile of fresh-baked dessert. "For me?"

Neil straightened in his chair, his eyes locking on the cookies.

"Yes, but you're going to have to eat fast before Neil gets them."

Her brother shoved the cat off his lap, hopped out of his chair, and grabbed a handful of cookies. "Night."

Her father chuckled. "Night, son."

Patricia sighed and put her work in a basket. "I can't do any more, so I'll turn in too. But I won't steal any of your cookies, Papa." She kissed his receding hairline, then shuffled out of the room with an exaggerated yawn. "Good night."

Rachel picked up the cat and took Neil's chair beside her father.

"Something must be wrong if you've made cookies a second time in twenty-four hours."

She gave her father an obligatory grin. "I suppose it's silly of me to wish to be a plain ol' housewife when I'm averse to cooking."

Papa leaned over the arm of his chair and twisted up the wick of the lamp glowing dull beside him. "Now hold on a minute. You've got too good a head on your shoulders to be a regular housewife."

"But what if that's all I want to do?"

The strain of Mozart abruptly stopped. "What did you say, honey?"

Rachel took in a deep breath. Momma wouldn't want to hear this, but since Papa would inform her later, she might as well air every doubt now. "I'm not certain I want to go to school. If I want to marry, then—"

"That's ridiculous. You've been studying languages, mathematics, and literature since you could read and write, and Elmira accepted you two years ago. We could have used the money we set aside for your tuition to buy a bigger printing press and probably earned enough by now to cover your expenses twice over."

"Now, Ava. Don't blame her. I could have bought some more property or expanded my inventories as well, but we decided together to save it for Rachel. We didn't know how well my paper would grow then."

Momma slid to the end of the piano bench, her ramrod spine held up by a corset cinched as tightly as Patricia could ratchet. "I haven't insisted before, but it's time for you to go. You can find someone to marry when you finish."

"I'll be an old maid in four years."

"Do you have a beau, love?" Papa asked whisper-soft.

Rachel sniffed. "No, Papa."

Momma crossed her arms. "You can find a beau in New York, a better man than any around here."

"At a woman's boarding school?" Rachel couldn't look at Momma. "Just because a man lives in New York, it doesn't mean he's better than . . . anyone around here. Papa never lived in New York, and you married him before he had money."

"Papa's an exception. He's a hard worker with a good head on his shoulders."

"Exactly." Rachel smirked, just a little. She wouldn't point out the flaw in Momma's argument. "But if I do go, I want to attend Mary Sharp's in Tennessee."

Momma's mouth closed and opened. Then she shrugged. "We'll think about it."

"But I'm not sure I should go at all." She turned to Papa. "You should buy your printing press."

"I want what's best for you, love. But what do you want? You've only ever talked about school."

"Of course school would be stimulating, but I didn't realize how many men would dislike me for going. I'm too smart for some of them already. If I add a degree declared to be equivalent to any male's . . ."

"Degree or not, love, you'll have to find a man who recognizes your intelligence and believes it's an asset. Like that Dex Stanton fellow, he's—"

"I'm sorry, Papa, but I haven't found a man who thinks my mind's an asset." Especially not Dex, who'd rather marry a stranger over her. But she couldn't think about that without tearing up. She could cry later, after Patricia fell asleep. "And if you had that press, you could put out more weeklies—"

"I didn't say I couldn't use the press but that I love you more than a brand-spanking new typeset."

"You must go, Rachel." Momma strode over and sat on the arm of her chair. "When I was your age, I would have given my left foot to go to college instead of a finishing school. Then maybe I could have been your literature professor. But the only true foundation for the social elevation of women is honorable employment and an independent livelihood. If no women earn degrees, they'll stop offering them. If you don't attend school for yourself, then do it for the women who wished they could."

Momma smiled over at Papa. "Most fathers would be pushing you to marry, obliging someone else to support you, but we want you to find pure affection, not a marriage of pity or necessity."

Momma pushed away the cat that insisted on a petting from the one person in the house who didn't like her. She pierced Papa with a glare. "Right, Marion?"

Her father, who'd taken a cookie to nibble during the lecture, quickly brushed crumbs off his chest. He'd clearly not anticipated the sermon running short. "There are pros and cons to both choices, my dear. If Rachel wants to hide her intelligence from potential suitors, a college degree will not help."

"No, Papa. I don't want to do that." She took her mother's hand and gazed up into her glinting eyes. "I won't play dumb to catch a beau. If I wanted to do that, I could have married Jedidiah Langston. He said he'd marry me if I stopped reading books that crowded my brain, blathering on about how a wife couldn't properly take care of a house and children if she read too much."

Rachel couldn't help but snort. Jedidiah hadn't ever realized he'd insulted her mother. Besides the library, mother's literature collection was the best in town. "But just because I don't attend school doesn't mean my intellect will disappear. I can still study whatever I get my hands on."

"It's not the same, Rachel." Momma extracted her hands and placed them on her hips. "But I don't understand why we're arguing this. Are you seeing someone in secret?"

"No."

"Has a man of good breeding and wealth caught your fancy?"

Rachel swallowed and tried not to envision Dex's rakish smile and thick ash-brown hair. He wouldn't pass any of Momma's criteria. "No."

"Then what will attending school hurt?"

"But what will it help? I'd be taking money from father's dream to pay for your dream." Rachel scooted against the opposite edge of the chair, putting space between them. "It's been your dream, Momma, not mine."

Momma's eyebrows descended as she glared. "Of course it's your dream. What have you been studying for?"

Rachel shrugged. "I like studying."

"Who likes studying and doesn't want to go to school?" Her mother scratched her head, messing up her coiffure, though she didn't seem to notice. "Help me, Marion."

"Well, we're letting Neil and Patsy go off to the wilderness though I have my doubts it's the best thing for them. Why can't we accommodate Rachel even if it's not our preference? She's old enough to make her own decisions."

Momma angled her chin at Papa. "You're not helping."

Rachel smiled. "Thank you, Papa."

"But love," Papa grabbed her hand between both of his. "A man who won't offer his hand because you have a degree isn't worth remaining degree-less for."

"Absolutely." Momma slapped the back of the chair with her open palm. "Sorry, I didn't mean to do that, but you've got me so flustered." She re-situated the doily neatly across the headrest. "You could accomplish so much more for yourself and women everywhere if you embrace the intellect, finances, and college acceptance God's given you. How can you ignore the doors He's opened?"

Rachel sighed. She had no marriage prospects, and she would enjoy school. This whole business with Dex was wreaking havoc with her decision-making. "You're right, Momma. If God has a man out there for me, it doesn't matter where I am or what I do. I'll pray about it some more."

With a paper bag in one hand and a book in the other, Dex stood in front of the Olivers' front door. He closed his eyes and took in a few cleansing breaths. But the longer he stood there, the more his insides quaked.

He quit trying to gather the nerve to knock and turned to pace. If his plan failed, he'd only have to suffer one day in the same town with a woman who'd rejected his court.

But if he went through with this, he had to do it well. Not slapdash or tripping-over-himself nervous.

The creak of the front door spun him around.

Neil eyed him from head to toe. "You going in?"

He tried to make his voice work, but nothing came out, so he blinked his acknowledgment.

"Good luck." And then Neil tromped down the stairs and walked toward town.

Dex swallowed, his necktie suddenly tight about his neck. He needed more than luck. Looking at his hands full of stuff, he could hide the items under the bench and endure his fifth lesson—trying hard to read, trying hard not to stare at his teacher like a lovesick schoolboy—or he could storm the castle with his weapons of choice. The damsel may not be in distress, but it'd sure feel nice to carry her away in his arms.

He rubbed the cover of Lily's book. His sister-in-law had helped him riffle through her shelves yesterday looking for just the right one. She'd thought his plan would work. Now all he needed was courage on the eve of battle. He'd been brave enough to write a mail-order bride company in anticipation of pledging himself to a stranger, so showing Rachel a little of what he felt shouldn't be making him sweat.

He dragged a sleeve across his perspiring forehead. How could he not try? Did Jesus not say one should seek in order to find, knock so the door would be opened? He'd pined after Rachel from afar, as if she were a palace door unworthy of being knocked upon by a lowly beggar. But isn't that what God asked everyone to do? Knock, and knock constantly on the Creator and Ruler of the World's door, though man was sinful and unworthy to touch it?

And those who delighted themselves in the Lord got the desire of their heart.

He would be happy with however God blessed him, and he had been content in the past, but he shouldn't just wait for things to fall in his lap, right? Not if being ashamed of how God made him caused his hesitation.

God, I've never asked, because I've been afraid You'd give

*me that snake instead of a fish when the Bible clearly states
You're a Good Father and would never do that. But even if You
don't help me win Rachel, I know it's not that You're giving
me a snake, You're just . . . Well, I don't know what, but You
obviously can't give me anything if I don't hold out my hand.*

All right then. He cleared his throat and strode toward the
door Neil hadn't quite shut. He wasn't doing anything drastic,
not really, only letting Rachel know he cared and asking if she'd
write to him from school. He wouldn't even demand she think
of him as often as he would her—since that would be thirty
times an hour. Or more.

Without knocking, Dex let himself in. He took a look around
the foyer and glanced into the sitting room. No one. He let
out his breath, shuffled to the parlor, leaned against the door
jamb, and took his fill of her. The weight of those dark brown
curls piled upon her head didn't bend her creamy, long neck
a fraction. Her tongue moved about her lips as they formed
half-spoken words as she read, the pages turning faster than
should be humanly possible.

At the turn of her sixth page, she stretched and startled.
"Dex!" She folded the book in her lap. "How long have you
been there?"

"A bit."

"Spying's not very gentlemanlike."

"No, but I'm all right with that."

Her forehead scrunched, and she glanced at the things in his
hands. "What do you have?" Her eyes roamed, taking in the
length of him. "And what are you wearing?"

"I'm dressed for the Founder's Day activities this evening.
And I've got candy and a book." He took a glass bowl with a
bit of ribbon candy left in the bottom off the shelf and dumped

his assortment on top, then shrugged. "I didn't know what kind you liked though."

"So you bought several pieces of everything?" She pulled the bowl toward her and sifted through the candy with her fingers.

"Yep." He twirled a chair across the floor and parked next to her. Sitting astride, he set down the book, crossed his arms atop the chair's back, and gave her the smile that'd made her blush yesterday.

She dropped her eyes from his and flipped the book to look at the spine. "*Sonnets from the Portuguese?*"

"I like number six. Let's read that one."

"If you thought *Robinson Crusoe* was difficult, why would you attempt poetry?"

"Well, Lily said they'd be good." And she'd read countless poems to him until number six caught his attention. But he wasn't going to admit his sister-in-law read to him like a boy unless he had to.

"Good for what?"

"You'll have to teach me to read number six and see for yourself."

She took her hand off the book and backed away from the table. "But these are love sonnets."

"Yep."

She swallowed hard and took a butterscotch from his bowl.

"So butterscotches are your favorite?"

She pointed at her mouth as if the obstruction of one bright yellow disk was reason enough not to attempt speaking. "Read," she slurred around her candy.

He pulled the slim volume closer and flattened the page he'd bookmarked. The familiar mind blurriness came over him, and he rubbed his eyes. Now was not the time to panic. He'd read the sonnet thirty times this morning, so he'd need to trust the words to work even if he messed up the cadence and rhythm.

"Go on." Rachel laid a hand on his tense arm, but he couldn't make head or tail of the first word.

She chomped on her butterscotch and swallowed, her lips slightly shinier than normal with a sweet candy glaze—

"Dex?"

His eyes jolted up to hers. Her cheeks were pink again.

"You need to relax. I'm not going to make fun of you. Tell me if you want me to help while you're reading or after you've finished."

"Definitely after." That is, if he could start. He pulled the volume closer and forced his lips to move.

> Go from me. Yet I feel that I shall stand
> Henceforward in thy shadow. Nevermore
> Alone upon the threshold of my door
> Of individual life, I shall command
> The uses of my soul, nor lift my hand
> Serenely in the sunshine as before,
> Without the sense of that which I forbore—
> Thy touch upon the palm. The widest land
> Doom takes to part us, leaves thy heart in mine
> With pulses that beat double. What I do
> And what I dream include thee, as the wine
> Must taste of its own grapes. And when I sue
> God for myself, He hears that name of thine,
> And sees within my eyes the tears of two.

He blew out a breath, fairly certain the afternoon he'd spent memorizing had made his reading fairly decent. "So what do you think?"

She looked at the words on the page, but not at him. "Excellent job. Maybe these lessons have helped."

"Not that you aren't helpful, but I think the hours of memorizing had a lot to do with it."

"Yes, you read so smoothly, it sounded as if you were reciting by heart."

"I was." His mouth dried before she looked up at him. "You know, I'd thought you'd think terribly of me a few days back after you heard me read."

She shook her head slowly. "If people can look down on someone for being smart, I suppose people could look down on others for anything. But no, I don't."

"And do you think a smart woman could endure reading letter upon letter of my terrible spelling if she felt something for me?"

"I, uh . . . I'm sure she could." Her eyes darted everywhere but at him.

"When are you leaving for college?"

She frowned. "I'm not sure I am anymore."

Wait. That poem couldn't have changed her plans, even if she'd guessed he meant those words specifically for her.

He scooted closer. "Why wouldn't you?"

She sighed and ran a leather bookmark through her hand. "I'd be wasting my time. No man seems to want a woman smarter than him. I mean, not that college would turn me into a genius, but the degree—well, what good is it if I don't intend to fight a man for his job or . . ."

So she did want to get married. He relaxed in his chair. But the twaddle about a man thinking college would ruin her needed to stop. "Don't give up your dream, Rachel, no matter who tries to change your mind." Though he wanted to give her every reason

256

to stay like the poet had, she needed to take advantage of the opportunity.

"If I go to school, I'm essentially making myself a spinster."

"You're only nineteen."

"And the earliest I'd get out would be twenty-three."

Dex winced. That would be bordering on old maid, but if he was waiting for her, she wasn't doomed. "But you have to go now. When you get married, it'd be too late."

"Or it'll keep me from getting married. Jedidiah asked me to marry him only if I'd forget about school."

"Well, that means he's a fool. And you wouldn't marry a fool." But with that reasoning, she shouldn't consider him either.

He'd never stepped out to court her, giving other men time to win her affections. If she'd said yes to Jedidiah . . . what a fool he'd been. And he'd thought candy and a poem could win her last minute. But even now she'd be gone for four years with hardly a notion of how he felt.

Dex shook his head.

He had to do something, but what could he do now? More sophisticated, intelligent men lived in the big city and were bound to notice the jewel she was. And they'd not shy away from selling everything to gain a treasure like her.

Her frown pulled at his heart—stupid men shouldn't make her second guess her dreams though. She encouraged every man, woman, and child in town to succeed; he could do no less for her.

He dared to put his hand on top of hers. "Whether you want to be a fancy professor or a mother, don't let anybody discourage you from school. Being smart and having a diploma won't make any difference to a man who loves you."

She blinked those big golden-hazel eyes at him, and with each downward flutter, he took in her pert nose, her warmed cheeks, her slightly parted lips.

"He would wait years for you." The whisper of his words seemed to make her hold her breath.

He'd never kissed a woman, not even the ones he'd walked home more than once. But the exposed flesh between her neck and shoulder called to his hand, and he leaned a fraction closer.

He shouldn't kiss her now. Not even a good-bye kiss. But her lips were too close, her breath too sweet, and the urge to kiss her powerful bad. He leaned forward another inch.

Her tender lips against his revived the words of the love sonnet he'd recited, except he'd leave the sensation of his mouth upon hers instead of a touch upon the palm and gain the flavor of butterscotch on his lips to haunt his dreams rather than the taste of wine.

A moment passed before her lips softened against his. He sank deeper and wound his fingers in her hair.

She inhaled sharply and broke away. "Your lesson is over."

He dropped his hand and blinked. "Because I kissed you?"

"No." She stood, her chair banging against the sofa, and she reached to steady herself. "I mean, yes. I shouldn't have done that. Not at all."

This was going wrong, terribly wrong. "I'm sorry. I shouldn't have done that either. I didn't mean to kiss you—"

"So you accidently kissed me?" She clenched her fists at her side. Her face was red again, but definitely not from a blush. "Your bride might not appreciate you kissing other girls for no reason."

He stood and reached out to her. "But I don't accidentally kiss other girls—"

"Oh? I never would've believed Dex Stanton would cheat on a woman." Before he could grab her, she'd disappeared into the hall.

"I'm not cheating."

"I doubt your wife would think so." Her slippered feet made swift work of the stairs.

He slid after her into the foyer. "Wait, Rachel. You're not listening. This is just a big mistake—"

She slammed a door.

He stood, shaking as hard as if he'd been forced to publicly read an unfamiliar passage. His chest rose and fell fitfully. The feel of her lips against his had twisted up everything inside him.

"Rachel! I've kissed no one but you. There is no one but you." Hoping to hear the quiet opening of a door, he waited until his breathing evened out. But only the mantle clock ticked and ticked and ticked. . . . What had he done wrong?

He went back to grab his sister-in-law's poems and trudged back into the foyer, taking one last hopeless glimpse upstairs. He'd used his lips upon hers to show her everything he'd bottled up inside, but it hadn't been enough to win the battle. That's what he got for doing nothing to win her until now.

For the rest of his life he'd have to be content spending his pennies on butterscotch.

5

The front door shut with a faint click.

Rachel wilted against her bedroom door. She pressed a hand against her lips still abuzz from Dex's kiss. She should have gone back downstairs and asked him what he meant by there being no one but her. Did that mean he didn't have a bride already? But he'd written one, so he must have considered all the girls in town and found her wanting. So why kiss her the day before he left?

Did it mean anything? The racing of her pulse and the long-ings of her heart were pushing her to read into things when his words had been clear: *A mistake.* An accident. If he'd had any desire to make her his only girl, he wouldn't have told her to go to school.

She needed time to think without his nearness clouding her judgment, so she shuffled over to her bed and sank onto the mattress.

Tucked up in a ball, she lay facing the window, a finger against her lips. The starlings in the catalpa tree twittered a sweet song, and the sun's lemony rays burst through its fat, velvety leaves.

The Founder's Day celebrators would have a beautiful spring evening for dancing.

Did Dex really think she should go to school or was he only saying what he thought she wanted to hear? If she didn't go, would he think less of her or more?

Open doors. Open doors. Would God really guide her through open doors? Momma acted as if disregarding her opportunity to attend school would be a sin.

She grabbed her Bible and ran her fingers down pages and columns and more pages in the New Testament looking for the word *door*. After flipping through several books, she scanned faster. She should memorize more.

The first passage she stumbled upon was in Acts. Paul and Silas stayed in jail despite the Lord opening the door with an earthquake. He'd even supernaturally unlocked their chains. And yet they didn't leave, saving the lives of the soldiers who would have been punished for their escape.

No one's life was in peril if she went to school or not.

But Paul and Silas had still ignored a door. So where did people get the idea that if God opened a door, they must go through?

She kept her finger moving over the columns until she hit upon another door in Corinthians this time. God opened a door for Paul to work in Ephesus, so he chose to stay and work though he wanted to visit the Corinthians again. So that fit her situation better. Frowning, she kept scanning.

A door opened for Paul to work in Troas, but he felt uneasy and went to Macedonia instead.

He ignored a God-opened door.

She dropped her Bible onto the bed and stared at the birds fighting in the branches. If Paul disregarded some doors opened by the Lord, was it wrong for her to consider opportunity as only part of the equation? Unless God commanded her, she had plenty of other factors to consider.

Mainly, Momma would regret that she didn't go. No, regret was not a strong enough word for what Momma would feel.

Papa had said he wanted the best for her. Whatever that was.

Rachel dropped her head onto her embroidered pillowslip, running her fingers across her sister's fancy stitching of two birds flying together, carrying a tied ribbon between them. How many times had she quashed a daydream about Dex's gay green eyes hovering close enough to kiss her? He'd done so only a bit ago, the pressure of his lips still buzzing on hers.

But he'd told her to go to school.

Might he have pursued her these past two years if he'd known she'd abandon college for him?

Some had questioned her parents for wasting tuition on a girl "who already knew more than a woman needed to know." A pretentious degree wouldn't extricate her from beneath their roof.

But that's exactly why Momma wanted her to pursue school. Only a man who loved her for who she truly was would bother to propose. Sound reasoning.

Rachel huffed. She had as many rationales to pass through the open door as not.

She slid her feet over the side of her bed. Would he consider marrying her before he left? He'd been writing a mail-order bride company after all, and since he'd said there was none but her, maybe she'd been wrong to assume he'd already chosen a bride. She ran her hand along the quilt's stitching.

If he didn't want to marry her immediately, she could tag along with Neil and Patricia, and they could court as long as he desired.

But what if Dex's kiss wasn't indicative of anything deep? What if it was an accident, as he claimed? Her parents would spend her tuition on another printing press the moment she crossed the border between Missouri and Kansas. If Dex didn't want to marry her now, he might not ever, no matter how many years she chased him.

She had to be more certain of his feelings.

She'd never pursued Dex, biding her time with books, mathematical equations, and Latin. Maybe the closed door she'd pined after needed to be knocked upon—or pummeled with both fists. Paul had constantly looked for a way to get to Rome. When thwarted, he kept trying. And he finally got there . . . when God sent him in chains.

All right, maybe her analogy didn't quite fit the way she wanted.

Slipping to the side of the bed, she positioned herself to pray as she had as a little girl, feet neatly tucked under her skirts, folded hands against her forehead.

Oh God, I don't want to entrap myself in a bad situation by charging pell-mell into daydreams. But You know how long I've been smitten, and You knew he'd kiss me only a day before leaving. You've known I haven't been excited about going to school as much as Momma is, that I've desired to be a wife and a mother more than anything.

Do you disapprove of mail-order brides marrying strangers? Would You look down on me for throwing myself at a man I've only dreamt loved me? Because, unless You show me in some fashion that I'm wrong in the choice I'm about to make, I'm going to forget about school and reach for my heart's desire.

Though God would only approve if her plans honored Momma.

She pushed against the mattress and steeled herself for the conversation she was about to have.

She found her mother outside on the porch, reading *The Inferno* to the accompaniment of wind chimes.

Rachel didn't bother to sit. "I've decided not to go to school."

Momma dropped her book into her lap and frowned. "I thought we'd discussed this already."

Discussed, yes. Decided? Momma had, but she hadn't—until now. "I'm going to see if Dex will marry me."

Momma puckered as if she'd suddenly found a lemon in her mouth. "Dex? Has he shown any interest in you besides these lessons?"

She wouldn't bother defending him. If Momma couldn't see his merits in the fifteen years they'd lived in the same town, she'd not convince her in a few minutes. And she didn't have that much time. "I think he has, though he hasn't been overt." Not until today. But she'd keep the kiss to herself.

"But he's going to Kansas. Your mind will go to ruin on the prairie." Momma rubbed her temples.

"No, Momma, it won't." She crossed her arms and raised her chin. Momma might have a whole slew of reasons for wanting her to attend school, but going farther west wasn't going to magically turn her mind to mush. "I could educate my children, use my analytical skills to help him choose what plants or animals to raise, maybe teach in the area's first school or keep books for Neil for some extra income."

Momma shifted in her seat, a smug look on her face. "Has Dex Stanton asked you to marry him?"

"No."

"Go with him?"

"No." She kept her head held high.

Momma shook her head. "Darling, he's had years to court you, and he's leaving tomorrow. If you weren't standing in front of me, I'd think Patricia was talking. Now, I've always told you a smooth-talking man messes with a woman's ability to think clearly, but I never thought you'd succumb." She settled back against her seat, the way she did after putting Papa in check. "You'll have plenty of time to find a good man in the city. An educated man with money. Not someone who'll drag you west and hide the gem that you are in a dirt hovel."

Rachel clasped her hands together and sighed. Had she believed Momma would answer any differently?

But she could play verbal chess too. "Even if school wouldn't make me happy, you'd want me to go?"

"You're a smart woman, Rachel, and I expect you to think with your head, not the flip flops in your stomach when a handsome boy smiles at you." Momma bobbed her head like she did when she was scheming—for the good of others, of course. "Why don't you pack a bag and take a trip to see your Aunt Val? She's entertaining enough to keep your mind off your brother and sister's departure while you wait until it's time to go to school. Even Tennessee, if you want."

So Momma figured agreeing to her choice of Tennessee over New York would distract her from Dex. Rachel couldn't help the smirk curling her lips. Momma was so easy to read. "But you believe I'm capable of making a wise decision?"

"If anyone can," she widened her eyes and tipped her head forward as if to glare the right decision into her, "it's you. You know what the right decision is."

But Dex's kiss hadn't scrambled her brains, just her heart. "And if it's not the choice you'd have me make?"

Momma picked imaginary lint from the green shawl draping

her shoulders. "Your father says all we can do is pray you'll make good decisions, not make them for you."

Rachel leaned over and kissed Momma's forehead. God bless Papa. That was as close to an agreement as she was going to get. "I'll pack, Momma."

Whether she'd go to Aunt Val's or Kansas would depend on Dex.

Did he love her as the poem he'd recited suggested, or had her longing pout lured him into an indiscretion?

She flew up the stairs faster than she had this afternoon, when she'd fled the desire to disgrace herself and kiss a man silly. However, she might do just that now if given the chance.

Dex's eyes roved over the gathering crowd as he sat on the fairground stage, intermittently twanging his Jew's harp while Jedidiah strummed a happy melody on his banjo. Why couldn't his friend play something that droned along in a minor key? The cheerfulness grated his nerves, along with the smiling faces, bubbly laughter, and giddy conversations of the nearby cluster of women arranging their blankets and baskets on the grass. The men lugging chairs and dance floor boards also seemed in high spirits despite the children playing tag getting underfoot.

Life wasn't over just because Rachel had fled from his kiss and declared she never wanted to see him again. But for the moment, it seemed so. Why couldn't the rest of the world subdue itself in an instant or two of compassion?

An auctioneer's chatter boomed from one of the tents full of people. The warm weather had brought out more people than ants, but Dex would rather have had rain.

Jedidiah poked him in the shoulder. "Why don'cha up and

do something? There's plenty of time before the music starts. Last good vittles before we hit the trail."

"No thanks." If he mingled, someone would want to talk to him, and what would he say? *Oh, you want to know how I'm doing? Well enough, I suppose, considering I'm contemplating sticking my head in the horse trough until the lack of air blacks out the feel of Rachel's lips upon mine.*

"Aw, buck up, Sunshine."

Dex scowled.

"Oh, now, that's better. And here I'd only thought a bee'd flown in your bonnet. Seems you've been chomping on scorpions too." Jedidiah sighed and went back to strumming. "At least go buy me a fritter if your sulky self insists on sucking the life out of the air I'm breathing."

Near the auctioneer's tent, Patricia's showy green hat stacked high with purple feathers bobbed above the crowd. "How about I go make sure Everett knows the meeting's been moved up?" Would it matter if he didn't bother to come back and play? His instrument wasn't necessary to keep beat or melody. Maybe he'd find himself a sore throat or a headache.

He pocketed his mouth harp and marched toward Patricia though Everett's tall, fair-haired form seemed nowhere close. Had his friend actually found a pair of scissors, snipped his ties, and wandered away from his girl for a minute?

When she spun around and caught his eye, he lost his breath as if she'd pierced his lungs with a dagger.

Not Patricia.

Rachel. Her curls were hidden under Patricia's poke bonnet, showing off her long neck, accentuating the wide neckline she'd slipped off her shoulders. The full green plaid dress was nothing extravagant, but she'd taken off the lower sleeves, letting the silk fringe at the elbows tickle her arms, milky white like the rest of her. She was exquisite.

Her eyebrow went up, and she smirked.

He tugged at his necktie, but she kept right on looking at him. Why was she smiling at him like that? She'd slammed a door in his face mere hours ago. He looked over his shoulder, but no one followed behind him.

Rachel beckoned him forward with a tilt of her head. No flecks of anger marred the mesmerizing golden eyes that drew his leaden feet forward a pace. The thumping of his heart moved him forward another step, and he wiped his damp palms on his trousers. Perhaps he hadn't ruined his chance with her after all.

"Yoo-hoo! Dexter!"

Dexter? The unfamiliar feminine call came from the road to his left. He turned to find Everett, still in work clothes, trudging along with a stocky little lady. His friend looked none too pleased about the blonde pulling on his arm. Everett bent over, and she whispered something into his ear. He nodded, and they both looked straight at him. One with a frown, the other with the brightest smile he'd ever seen.

"Dexter!" She cried again, only louder.

"I'm not Dexter," he gritted, thrusting his hands on his hips. Why hadn't Everett corrected her? He glanced toward Rachel, but her attention was on the sturdy lady in the bright yellow traveling suit—just like everybody else's in the crowd.

The blonde let go of Everett and raced unladylike toward him, her ringlets bouncing with each step. Winded, she stopped in front of him and smiled. "You're more handsome than I pictured."

"What?" The churning his gut had been doing since Rachel had slammed the door on him turned as sour as apple cider vinegar.

"Oh, don't be modest. I can see why you didn't send a picture with your letter. What girl wouldn't come running if she knew what you looked like?"

His stomach clenched. He'd only sent one letter in his life. But that didn't make sense . . . the response—

She stuck out her hand. "I know it's rather formal to shake hands with your bride, but we do have to start someplace."

His fingers curled around his belt loops. There was only one person she could be. "Miss Pratt?" Dex croaked.

Everett caught up and shrugged.

"Pleased to meet you, but you can call me Fannie." She took his hand hanging limp and clammy at his side and shook it twice.

"But I didn't . . . . I hadn't . . ."

"I apologize for not sending a telegram before I came, but I figured I'd better get here quick, seeing as you're leaving on Sunday."

"No . . . that is . . . I wasn't taking a bride with me. I just meant to start the process—"

"Oh, but I only live a day's ride away. And how's a few months of letters going to do any good when you plan on marrying a stranger anyway? Besides, it'll be easier talking to you than reading your letters, right?" She winked. "Might as well drive alongside your wagon rather than find someone to travel with later. Besides," she pointed over her shoulder with her thumb, "Mr. Cline here can tell you I brought plenty of good supplies. Practical ones too. A cook stove, dishes, barrels of salt pork, most of which I bought wholesale. My uncle's a mercantile owner."

Everett crossed his arms. "I tried to tell her she couldn't take the cook stove."

"But it's a small one, very light." She held her fingers apart, squinting at the miniscule space between them.

Everett looked to the heavens and shook his head.

Cook stove? Who cared if she wanted to take the cook stove? How was he supposed to tell her he couldn't take *her*?

"I'm sorry, but . . ."

A whisper behind him, a rustling of skirts, and an escaped giggle sent his temperature up a notch. The entire crowd had perked their ears his way—though some tried to act interested in their baskets, clothing, or the person beside them.

But even the children were quiet. Why had all these people come so blasted early?

And Rachel?

He glanced around until his gaze landed on her face. She was too far off to have heard much, but she could see. Oh yes, she could see. Her face was quite pink, as if she'd been in the sun for hours.

The woman he wanted to marry turned and walked away, hugging herself about the waist, and Miss Pratt clamped onto his arm.

"Wait!" Dex hollered, trying to disentangle himself, but Miss Pratt's slender-fingered grip was firm. "Rachel!"

Rachel looked back over her shoulder and shook her head at him, her face now ashen. "No," she mouthed.

Then Grant stepped out of nowhere with an outstretched hand. "How do, Miss Pratt? Dex hadn't told us you were coming before he left. Glad to have the chance to meet you. I'm his brother, Grant. And this here's my son, Allen, and . . ."

Dex tried to uncurl Fannie's fingers. Dagnabbit, how could such a little thing hold on so fast? When she shook his brother's hand, he wrenched himself free and darted into the crowd.

Rachel rushed toward the road, rubbing her cheek in a masked attempt to swipe away a tear. And then the crowd enveloped her, and she disappeared.

He stopped. Where were those feathers? He ran toward the road and looked east where she'd have to run to go home. But only two buggies and a wagon traveled there. Where else would she go?

Fannie jiggled his arm, and he jumped.

"I know I might be a surprise—"

"Might?" Dex sputtered.

"But you don't have to run. I'm a reasonable girl. We can work something out." She smiled so prettily that she'd have taken his breath away if he weren't so doggone sore at her for coming.

"Yes, we need to talk. Right now." He tugged on Fannie, giving her no choice but to follow. He had to put out this wildfire before it got any bigger. Five minutes and everything would be under control.

"Slow down." She pointed toward the bake sale table. "Why don't we see what they're selling? We should take one or two with us."

"Are you serious?" He stopped midstride and looked down at her, mouth agape. Had he written a second letter proposing marriage and somehow plumb forgot? Did this woman think that simply showing up gave her the right to claim him?

She fluttered her eyes. "Pretty please."

He straightened and scanned the crowd for Everett. He had to be pulling one over on him. But Everett had disappeared. Dex stared back at the little woman beside him, the weight of her arm pulling him down. Was he dreaming?

"I can cook a mean apple fritter and a rich pecan pie, but not until we get settled and set up my cook stove."

He'd had nightmares less bloodcurdling than this.

"So why not put some money toward whatever you're raising money for—"

"No." He sliced his hand through the air, and she flinched. He groaned. He wasn't going to hit her no matter how stress-relieving strangling the pretty canary might seem at the moment. "Come on." Though they'd moved away from where she'd first accosted him, a few in the crowd still eyed them. He escorted her farther down the road to a weathered stump on the outskirts of the fairgrounds. "Please have a seat, Miss Pratt."

Her sunshiny face looked a little less bright, but her smile hadn't budged.

He worked to swipe what must be a face-disfiguring scowl off his lips.

"All right, Dexter." But she didn't sit, only clasped her hands in front of her like some innocent.

"It's Dex." Why was he even arguing about his name? She could call him whatever she wanted as long as she didn't put the word *my* in front of it. "I'm very sorry you drove all the way here and purchased a wagon load of supplies, but you and I have no understanding. I was only inquiring after your advertisement. Just because a man writes to tell you a bit about his situation and ask after you doesn't mean he's promised to tie the knot."

"Oh, I realize you didn't know I was coming, but we can arrange an understanding." She sashayed toward him.

He glared at the hand she was about to put on his arm and stepped back. No, there would be no understanding. Not after he'd seen that look of despair across Rachel's face. He had a chance with her, at least he'd had one before Miss Sunshine showed up. But for some inexplicable reason, this lady was intent on ruining it. "Why are you even here?"

She let her hand drop and smoothed her bodice. "I figured since I was prepared to go, and you're looking for a wife, we could get to know each other on the trail. I don't see the harm in—"

"But I didn't ask you to come."

She clasped her hands over her stomach and looked back toward the crowd. "I realize that, but I hadn't the time to send you a letter."

"Did you think I'd read another? Having a good laugh at my misspellings isn't exactly endearing."

"I thought you might bring that up." She hung her head. "I realize now I shouldn't have done so much . . . teasing. But it was all in good fun."

"That's your idea of fun?" He had to stop her now before the pulsing vein in his forehead burst. "I'm sorry, Miss Pratt, but there is only one thing I know about your future plans: They don't include me."

Her eyes went a little too wide and her lips tightened, making the lines around her mouth pronounced, and she turned a bit . . . discolored.

Blast it, he couldn't keep ranting if she started to cry. "Are you all right?" He held out a hand, but she slapped it away as she shook her head. Her hands pressed against her stomach as she gulped a few deep breaths.

"I'm fine. I just need a little bit of something." She reached inside her hidden pocket and pulled out . . . crackers? She perched on the stump, turning her back on the fairgrounds, and nibbled.

He hated towering over her while she sat, but he sure wasn't going to bend a knee to talk to her. "Look. You're a pretty enough girl. Take your time and find someone—"

"Why won't you even consider me?" She swiped some crumbs from her mouth.

Besides her being crazier than a farmer milking a chicken? "The truth is I love someone else."

"I'm sure whoever you're corresponding with may not have ruffled your pride like I did, but we can start over, and I'm already here. With a wagon full of supplies." She offered another over-bright smile and pulled out another cracker. "You haven't had time to fall in love."

"When I wrote that letter to *The Marital News*, I'd been in love with someone for a long time. I never thought I had a chance, but I just found out I might. So if I marry anyone before I leave, it'll be her."

She closed her eyes and groaned. "This is not good. Not good at all."

He squatted down to her level. "Why don't you go home and pretend this didn't happen?"

She shook her head. "Can't."

Something pretty desperate must have sent her his way for her to show up unannounced and unable to return home. "Well then, I know a woman in town looking for a seamstress—"

"I'm not looking for work." She looked up and smiled past Dex's shoulder.

He spun to see Jedidiah, hat off, approaching with a cocked brow. "Dex?"

"Yes?" He sure hoped Miss Pratt didn't declare herself engaged to him with her next breath.

"The men were wondering if they should start the meeting without you?" Jedidiah looked toward Fannie. "If you could spare him, we'd like to get his opinion on a few things. It's the last meetin' before we head out."

"Well, of course I can spare him; he's got no claim on me." She cocked her head, all vestiges of nausea seemingly gone.

Her change in direction, however, had whipped him around so fast he might have felt sick if he'd had a design on the lady.

She smiled at Jedidiah. "You're going to Kansas?"

"Yes, ma'am."

"And are you taking your family, Mr. . . . ?"

"'Scuse me for not introducing myself. I'm Jedidiah Langston, and I've no family to speak of—not yet anyways." If Jedidiah had looked at Rachel that way, Dex would've jabbed him in the eyes.

"Well, Mr. Langston. It seems that Mr. Stanton here isn't much of a gentleman and won't help me up." She put out both hands. "Mind escorting me to the meeting? I'm going to Kansas too."

Jedidiah shot him a glance.

Dex frowned at her and scratched his chin. Letting her get away with what she'd done didn't sit well, but he didn't have time to argue if he wanted to see Rachel yet tonight. If only she would believe him about Miss Pratt. "That would suit me just fine because I can't make the meeting. Let the band know I won't be there either."

Jedidiah pulled Fannie up from her stump.

"Thank you, sir. And I know this might be terribly forward, but I'm all alone. Dare I hope you'd be willing to watch over me on the trail?" She fluttered her wide eyes. "I'm a little worried about the dangers."

Jedidiah smiled and tipped his hat before putting it back on. "Of course, it'd be my pleasure to look out for you, ma'am."

She glared at Dex for a second before turning her attention to the man at her side. "You know, it's too bad I don't have a husband, then I wouldn't have to ask such a thing. What do you think of my chances of finding a good man on this wagon train?"

Jedidiah straightened his jacket lapel. "There's more than one bachelor a-comin'."

She sighed and flashed her pretty blues. "Are they as handsome as you?"

"I don't know if I'm fit to say." He started off toward the fairground, Fannie tucked into his elbow.

"I'll just pray that God helps me find somebody honorable like you then." She rubbed her hand atop his forearm. "A man who likes pecan pie."

Jedidiah seemed to melt beneath her flattery, and Dex squirmed. He needed to find Rachel—the sooner the better—but should he warn his friend? Surely Fannie wouldn't entrap him with the promise of pastries before they left.

Dex rubbed a hand down his face and grimaced. Maybe a fellow wasn't that hard to win after all. Rachel's snickerdoodles had certainly done him in.

6

The fragrance of cinnamon and cloves wafting out of Hollenback's Bakery mingled with the unfortunate aroma of the street as Dex marched to the Olivers', leaving Jedidiah to escort Fannie Pratt wherever she wanted to go. Though one good thing had come from Miss Pratt's appearance—she'd dragged Dex to the edge of the matrimonial cliff, and it wasn't that terrifying. He wanted to jump—with Rachel. No matter that he didn't deserve her.

Now if only he could figure the woman out.

Why had she fled his kiss, then dolled herself up and come searching the fairground for him? Would she believe Fannie was insane enough to drive all the way here unasked?

And what would convince Rachel to marry him? No proposal he could dream up would be as flowery as Elizabeth Barrett Browning, and he hadn't the time to scour books of poetry again, even with Lily's help.

Turning onto Rachel's lane, he spotted Mrs. Oliver sitting on the porch bench, cradling a book in her lap. The sun wouldn't be up long enough to read an entire chapter, but then she likely could read as fast as her daughter. Frogs chirped pleasantly in the surrounding trees while a pack of them jumped around in his gut.

Swallowing against the knot in his throat, he forced himself to walk like a man in charge of himself. He tugged off his hat and held it against his leg where his mother's ring embossed his pocket. He'd run home for the slender band, but he was getting ahead of himself. He only hoped Rachel would accept letters from him while away at school.

"Good afternoon, Mrs. Oliver. I'd expected you'd be at the fairground."

She shut the book around her finger, holding her place. "I rarely attend. Mr. Oliver's always more interested in gathering news than sitting with me. Can I do something for you?"

"I've come to see Rachel."

"Sorry, but she isn't feeling well."

His doing. His stomach turned sour. The frogs hopping around his insides were likely poisonous. "I really need to talk to her."

"Now is not the time for visitors." Mrs. Oliver frowned like a bulldog. "You can talk to her tomorrow."

Tomorrow would be too late. "Is she inside?"

Mrs. Oliver stood and jammed her hands on her hips. "I'm afraid you don't understand, young man. Whatever you want to say will have to wait."

Sure, he was being pesky, but why the vicious stare? Had Rachel told her mother he'd kissed her without permission? That a mail-order bride had made a scene in front of the whole town? Had Rachel asked her mother to turn him away if he came? He rubbed his wrist against the ring in his pocket.

Lord, can I ask that Rachel at least hear me out? I always figured my reading problem was Your way of telling me she was beyond my reach. I never thought to ask You to help Rachel see the good in me. But I want that chance.

"Did you hear me, Mr. Stanton? You'll have to wait until after services." Mrs. Oliver now stood in the open doorway.

He blinked. If Rachel was hiding, he should let her know she had no reason to. "Might I borrow a piece of paper and leave her a note?"

She sighed. "If you must."

Rachel's mother disappeared into the parlor, and he paced the yard. How romantic would a proposal be with his terrible spelling? No, he wouldn't propose in a letter. But what if she avoided him at church as well? He had to write her something.

"Here you are." Mrs. Oliver returned and handed him a pencil and pad of paper, then stood, toe tapping against the floorboards. The fierce glower still contorted her face.

He sat on the porch step, his back turned so she couldn't see what he wrote, agonizing over not having a rubber. He scratched out a few words to the accompaniment of Mrs. Oliver's sighing.

Rachael: I never asked that woman you saw at the fairgrounds to come here, but more importantly Im sorrie I never told you I Love You before now. I always hav I need to talk to you. Dex

Reading it over, he couldn't find any glaring mistakes. This would have to do. He folded the note several times and handed it to Mrs. Oliver. "Please, tell Rachel I'm here."

"She'll need time to think. Why don't you go on home?"

"I'll wait for her."

"Suit yourself, but don't stay out here all night. You'll need your sleep for the morrow."

Even if Rachel would refuse him, she'd come down and say so. She was too nice to leave him out here alone.

The door to her bedroom creaked open, and Rachel subtly brushed away tears, glad she hadn't been caught sobbing. Maybe Momma would leave if she laid still enough, breathed deep enough.

"Rachel. Can you tell me what's wrong now?"

Breathe in. Breathe out.

The bed bowed in the middle, and as Momma's fingers pulled hair away from her face, another tear fell. No use pretending. "I don't want to talk about it."

"Did Dex upset you?"

Momma would tell her "I told you so" in the most long-winded way possible if she admitted he had. Rachel shrugged.

"Honey, don't waste your life weeping over a boy who isn't worthy of you."

She gritted her teeth against defending him. Why waste her breath? He'd been writing mail-order brides while wooing her with candy, poems, and kisses. How had she convinced herself his kiss meant something?

A handkerchief dropped in front of her. Rachel grabbed the lace-trimmed cotton square and wiped away the evidence of her folly. Oh, why had she told Momma she wanted to marry Dex?

Countless times, Momma had lectured about the worthlessness of a man's kiss and that wise women waited for one to pledge his life before forming any serious attachment.

Patricia had been smart enough to listen. She'd found a man intent on providing—instead of stealing kisses—and had laid aside her more charming beaus for a committed lover.

Rachel sniffled. She was supposed to be the sensible one, and here she'd left her senses for a man writing other women. And he'd pledged himself to a mail-ordered stranger who had the audacity to be beautiful. Who probably thought sewing, baking, and cleaning were the pinnacle of womanhood and most likely felt no desire to stuff her brain with parsed Latin verbs and graphed equations.

Momma was right. Romantic notions wrecked a person's ability to think and act logically.

"When you get to school, you'll forget about him." Momma's voice hummed soft and smooth, like a contented kitten. "Before you know it, you'll start to enjoy yourself. And then you'll meet a handsome man or two at a dinner party. No, better—a charity function. And you'll realize smart men of high social standing are more charming than you ever knew."

Momma laid a hand on her arm. "You don't have to settle, honey."

Rachel rolled over to see Momma's eyes. "Do you think Patricia's settling?"

Momma cupped Rachel's chin, setting her finger across her lips. "No. Despite her pretty face, Patricia can't snag the caliber of man you can. She was lucky with Everett. He'll make her a fine husband, and she'll mature on the prairie. But you don't need the grueling work of a homestead to test your mettle."

Rachel swallowed against the knot in her throat. "So do you think I was a fool to believe Dex could care for me?"

"No." She kissed Rachel's forehead. "He was a mistake." She stood, playing with something in her pocket. A sad, faraway look altered her face, careworn and old in the evening shadows. "A blunder you'll get over with in time."

"I suppose I should go to school now." Rachel wrapped her arms tight about herself.

"Don't be downhearted. By the time the fall semester starts, you'll be excited to go."

Rachel nodded slightly. She'd always had firm control on her emotions—except in regard to Dex. No matter how far her heart had led her astray today, she could rein in her feelings. Hopefully within the week. Or maybe in a month.

"I love you, Rachel. I really do. And I know college will make you happy." She picked up the copy of *The Castle of Otranto* from the bed. "But let's find you something less depressing to read." She scanned the pile of books on the bedside table. "Hmm. And without any romance in it."

Just like her life.

"Well, seems we can't have both. How about *Twice-Told Tales*?" Momma handed her the short story collection. "I think I'll go lie down and read as well. My head is beginning to ache a little."

Rachel stayed in her bed, curled in a little ball until Momma left. She then returned the book to the table and took in the disaster that was her room. Petticoats, dresses, boots, ribbons, hats, and lace draped every piece of furniture. Neil had insisted Patricia take only one trunk of personal effects, and her sister had packed and repacked for days, still unable to decide what to take and what to leave.

Perhaps sorting through her sister's things for practical outfits would keep her mind off wishing she could undo her week of blunders.

And if God granted such a fantastical wish, she'd start by refusing to tutor Dex Stanton.

Dex paced in front of the gathered wagons, the sun almost overhead. The wagon train would be leaving soon. Grant, Lily, and Allen had left ten minutes ago, but he hadn't seen any of the Olivers.

Around him, everyone scrambled to adjust any items that had shifted in the short distance they'd traveled from town. Family members staying behind either helped check loads or stood in clumps, hugging and crying with the loved ones they'd likely rarely see again.

Why hadn't Rachel at least sent him a reply saying she never wanted to see him? It wasn't as if he'd walked Miss Pratt down an aisle this morning; they'd never even been engaged.

He ran a hand through his hair, knocking off his hat. Leaning over to retrieve his Panama, he held his hand against his pocket to keep the letter he'd stayed up all night writing from falling out. If last night's note hadn't convinced her of his love, then he hadn't enough time to convince her today. But maybe the words of this new letter would weasel in and weaken the wall she'd erected—if she could read his writing.

He rubbed his sleepy eyes and slapped his cheeks. A smart woman like her shouldn't marry a man like him. But until she told him to leave her alone, he'd test out what she'd said—that a woman could ignore spelling mistakes if a man bared his soul on the page.

Another wagon passed the saloon on the edge of town, but not Neil and Patricia's. Dex's timepiece indicated they had less than an hour before the group left. Maybe he'd missed them. And where was Everett?

Spotting his friend on the other side of Jedidiah's and Fannie's wagons, Dex walked a wide circle around the pair smiling at each other like a couple of kids enjoying their first lollipops. Maybe

Fannie should marry quickly. What would a single woman do on the prairie anyhow?

As long as she kept her sights on anyone but him.

Dex hoisted himself into Everett's wagon, ducking his head under the pristine white canvas cover. "Seen Patricia and Neil yet?"

Everett's brow furrowed as he pushed a crate across the wagon bed. "No."

"Aren't you worried?"

"Nah." He used the bandanna around his neck to swipe the dampness from his hairline, then shooed a fly buzzing around his face. "Patricia is probably begging Neil to let her take one more bonnet but is waffling between a blue one or a green one. But they'll make it, even if he has to carry her and wear the other hat himself."

"Did you talk to her last night?"

"I let her talk about anything and everything. Might have sneaked in a kiss or two." Everett winked.

"I mean, did you talk about today's plans?" Dex kept his hand against his forehead to keep from punching Everett. "Her parents are coming to see them off, right?"

"I didn't ask. I said my farewells yesterday. Suppose I'll say them again if they show up." Everett cocked his head. "What do you need to see the Olivers for?"

"Do you know if Rachel's coming?" At the sound of hoof beats, Dex ducked his head outside. "Never mind, here they come." He hopped out of the wagon and strode toward Neil and Patricia. They veered to park near the edge of the gathering. No buggy followed them.

Everett appeared at his side. As soon as Neil set the brake, Everett helped Patricia down.

Dex put a hand to his brow to deflect the sun as he looked up at Neil. "Are your folks coming?"

He shook his head. "Why?"

"Your mother said they were."

Patricia tucked herself against Everett's side. "Rachel didn't feel well enough for church or the ride out here, so we said good-bye at home. Which was a good thing since Mama's been crying all morning and gave herself a headache."

"Are you all right, darling?" Everett ran his thumb along her hairline.

"I'll be fine with you."

Dex whipped off his hat and scratched his scalp. "Then I need to go back into town."

"Now, who's been preaching to us about being prepared and ready?" Everett let go of Patricia to put his hands on his hips, but she snaked her arm back around his elbow.

"It's not something I planned to do." He slammed a fist into his palm. He should have barged into the house and hollered through Rachel's barricaded door last night when he'd had the chance.

He'd rather have taken a slap in the face over silence. "Neil, a word please."

Rachel's brother hopped down and followed. "I can't think of anything you'd need from my parents."

"No, I need something from Rachel, but she's refusing to talk to me."

"That doesn't sound like her."

"I didn't think so." Dex paced a step or two, then spun and faced Neil. "Did you see the incident with Miss Pratt at the picnic?" He waved toward Jedidiah scrambling around the back of Fannie's wagon.

"No, but I heard."

"Well, Rachel saw but didn't hear."

Neil crossed his arms. "So . . . ?"

What did it matter that Neil knew his feelings before Rachel did? She was the one refusing to talk to him. "I . . . I'm in love with your sister. And I thought she felt the same for me. That is, until Miss Pratt happened. So I wrote her a note explaining the situation and your mother took it to her. But Rachel never answered. I felt sure she'd answer, if only to tell me no. So I sat outside for two hours until I had to leave to get home before dark, and I—"

Neil held up his hand to cut him off. "You gave the note to my mother?"

"Yes."

"She's intent on Rachel going to school. Rabidly so." Neil sneaked a look at his watch and stared at him for a moment. "Would you ask Rachel to sacrifice college for you?"

He wasn't worth that. "She shouldn't give up any dreams for me."

"She might, Dex. Possibly even today."

His jaw worked as he judged the look in Neil's eyes. Had Rachel talked to him? "What do you know?"

"I pay attention to my sisters." He shrugged.

"But everyone knows she's going to some fancy college out East."

"Because Ma tells anyone and everyone. But one good thing about not talking much is people forget I'm in the room, and I can study them. You're right, Rachel likes you—more than school. She would have responded to your letter." Neil frowned at him. "You told her you turned down Miss Pratt, yes?"

"Of course I did." If Neil thought Rachel liked him enough to forget schooling and leave with him today, Rachel didn't merely care for him. She must feel something more. A lot more. "But what makes you think she'd leave with me now?"

Neil held out his hand to count on his fingers. "She's always watching you. If she hears your name mentioned, she perks up. In your company, she'll migrate to wherever you are. Has for years."

"That's all?" How was he supposed to have figured out she cared for him with only those clues?

Neil smirked. "Rachel hates to fail. She won't creep out on a limb unless she's calculated the arc, the weight, the length, the odds—"

"Then how sure are you that she holds any affection for me?" She'd run from him yesterday, but then he'd shocked her with that kiss. He'd stunned himself. Had she simply left to clear her mind and decide what to do?

"She went to the fairground and sought you out, wearing one of Patricia's fancy dresses, yes?"

"Yes." And what a sight she'd been.

"Did she look at you, beckon to you, anything she's never done before?"

How could he describe what had flashed in her eyes? "Yes."

"I'd say that took her a mountain of effort, seeing how she's never done as much before."

How was he supposed to have known that? Neil would be a handy business partner if he could read other people so well.

Dex looked toward Jedidiah's wagon. "So when Miss Pratt showed up, Rachel believed she'd made an error in judgment." He turned back to Neil. "But that doesn't explain why she'd ignore my letter. I told her about Miss Pratt."

"Which means she didn't get it." Neil cleared his throat. "I love my mother, but she's manipulating Rachel into college and uses Rachel's tendency to second-guess herself."

So a dragon guarded the castle turrets. "Then how do I get around your mother?"

"Rachel's at the library now. She helps Mr. Peterson with whatever one does at libraries when they're closed."

Tremors overtook Dex as he contemplated a quick change of plans. Plans he had no time for. But he didn't have much choice—not if he wanted the woman he loved by his side.

"The group won't wait for me." What would he do with his wagon piled high with supplies for the frontier?

"What's more important, Dex?"

"Your sister of course. I just . . ." He looked between his wagon and town. Must he abandon one dream for the other?

Neil clamped onto his arm. "I'll talk to Jamison, convince him to start the group slow. If you want, Patricia can drive your team for awhile." He jabbed a finger at Dex's vehicle. "You got enough to keep my sister provided for if she comes?"

Dex's hands grew slick, and he rubbed them against his pants. Would Rachel really leave with him? Today? "We could make do."

"Then why are you still standing here?"

"The scheduled stop in Lawrence should buy me time. I'll take my wagon and catch up later." Dex shook Neil's hand and then ran to his team.

Even if Rachel cared for him as her brother suggested, would she be willing to marry him and head off to Kansas within the day?

Married. He could be married by tomorrow.

7

With a hard twist, Rachel finally turned the skeleton key in the library door's lock. A slight push opened the darkly stained oaken door, and the smell of paper and ink washed over her. Hopefully she could find some tranquility here. Though she didn't intend to do much work today, only pray and read her Bible.

Keep Neil, Patricia, and Everett safe as they start their new life. Help me figure out what to do with mine. I should have asked You long ago what You'd have me do. Please give me direction today. I know You want to give me the desires of my heart, but I should be talking that through with You. Turn my desires into Yours.

And yes, watch over Dex and his new wife too.

Opening the shades to read by sunlight, she ignored the ache the last part of her prayer created in every muscle of her body. Maybe she'd read a little, then pray until she fell asleep. Sleep should brighten her outlook, even if she had to doze upright in the little library's only upholstered chair.

She settled herself and put on the spectacles she only used

when her eyes were tired. Holding the thick Bible in her lap, she turned to where she'd left off. She hadn't the strength to search for anything, so she'd just spend time with God and hope He'd supply a verse to ease her pain. Being cut loose from the life she'd imagined for so long left her at the mercy of a fickle wind like a spent autumn leaf. She couldn't bear to live that way for long. But the further she read without receiving any balm for her soul, the more she yearned to curl up and disappear.

How long until she could think of Dex without her heart throbbing? How long until God gave her a purpose?

I give up. Can you say something to me now? Anything. Do you want me to go to school?

Knock, and the door shall be opened to you.

Doors. Opened or closed, knocked-upon or not. What did it matter?

All I wanted was for Dex to care for me. I even knocked. Granted, I didn't bother until too late. So is that what You want to teach me? Find something to knock about but don't wait so long next time?

But what should she knock for that she could have? God wouldn't condone her knocking for the love of a married man. But right now, she didn't desire anything but Dex.

Thump, thump, thump. The hair on her neck stood as the front door's shade flopped with each rap of a fist. Who thought the library would be open on Sunday?

The door flew open, and Dex slid in, breathing heavily.

Rachel's heart jumped, but she stuffed the reaction down and glanced at the ceiling. *What is this, Lord?*

"Hello." Dex's voice rumbled through her, starting her heart flopping again. Even glistening with sweat, the man looked good.

She closed her Bible and gazed out the west-facing window though she couldn't see past the buildings across the street. Why was he here? A visit from Dex certainly wouldn't alleviate her envy for Miss Pratt's position. Or rather, Mrs. Stanton's.

"Aren't you supposed to be headed to Lawrence already?"

"Yes." He stalked over and stood beside her, running a hand through his damp hair. "But I needed someone to write a letter for me, and I only trust you. The woman I love . . . was upset when she left me." He fidgeted, then quickly strode back to the door and shut it. "I figured she might hear me out if I sent her a letter."

Rachel suppressed a groan. He was asking her to win back a woman who'd left him within a day?

Father, I know I asked You to say something to me today, but I wasn't requesting torture!

She straightened in her chair and stared out the window. "If she came to you despite your spelling the first time, then you can convince her in your own hand."

"No, this has to be perfect. Every single letter."

Maybe God planned to show her through Dex's own words why she couldn't have him. A way to heal perhaps from a desire God never wanted her to have. She swallowed hard and steeled her spine. "All right." She set aside her Bible and crossed over to the librarian's desk.

"I've always admired you for giving of yourself to anyone who asks. Even when they ask more of you than they ought."

"No need to flatter." If only he knew how much this favor would pain her.

"Neil mentioned you might not be going to school. Is that so?"

She sat behind the desk, pulled a sheet of paper from the drawer, and dipped the ink pen. "I don't know. I'd enjoy going

291

to Elmira or Mary Sharp's, but . . . it isn't my dream." Sighing, she looked up at Dex who'd taken the seat across from her, but couldn't hold his intense gaze. "I'm ready when you are."

Not really. But would she ever be ready to hear this?

Dex pulled out his letter and unfolded it behind the desk where she couldn't see. On the ride in he'd decided to say this to her, to make it more meaningful. He glanced down, but he knew the words by heart—they weren't the words of a poet, but they were his own.

He cleared his throat, but the words seemed glued to his tongue. Maybe he should change some of the wording . . .

Rachel peeked at him for less than a second.

He clamped his hands between his knees, willing his heart to stop thudding against his brain and causing the sloppy roar in his ears. Neil said she'd leave with him today. If so, it didn't matter if his voice broke or he stumbled over his own words; if she loved him, she'd want to come with him no matter how badly he messed up the proposal. But what if he couldn't find a minister willing to marry them today? What were the Kansas Territory laws on matrimony?

"Are you going to be a while? I could read until you're ready."

"No, no. I just don't want to mess this up. And then I started thinking that if the woman I love answers me the way I'm hoping, I have no idea how I'll pull this off."

Did Rachel sniff?

"Well, she shouldn't expect perfection. If she didn't hold to her end of the deal and ran away, then maybe—" She grimaced. "Sorry, I shouldn't be trying to talk you out of anything. It's your life."

She propped her chin in her hand and stared at the paper. Her thick hair, usually caught up in a bun, hung loose in a tempting curtain of curls. A pair of gold rimmed glasses he'd never seen perched precariously on her nose. He wanted to slide them off and get a good look at her eyes, but then he'd get lost in them. Not good. He needed to say absolutely everything he wanted to say and make sure she heard every word.

"I'm ready now." He flattened the letter on his lap—in case he needed it—and crossed his arms atop the desk. "Tell me what you think at the end."

Her lips pressed together so tight they quivered. She shook her head but said nothing.

He took a deep breath and plowed forward. "To the woman I've only dreamed of. I figured you'd look down on me when you heard me read and saw how terribly I wrote. And yet you didn't. I've lived my whole life hiding my difficulties from everyone. Especially you. I never believed myself worthy of your beauty or intelligence. But then, in a matter of days, I realized how much of a fool I was." He waited until she caught up, hoping she'd look at him, but she didn't.

"How could I have thought you'd think poorly of me when you've done nothing but care for the people around you? You've never given up on a person. Why, most people around here believe you're a saint for not abandoning that one widow who died as bitter as ever, despite the constant vigil you kept by her deathbed."

Rachel's pen froze in the middle of the word *bitter*.

He swallowed against the tightness in his throat. She knew he was talking about her now, though she'd yet to look at him.

Leaning closer, he softened his voice. "How could a man not wish to live the rest of his life with you? Wake up to those

rich-honey eyes, run his hands through that glossy hair, appreciate the mind God gifted you with, and be ministered to by the
hands always ready to help. But when I realized I'd been wrong
and that you might care for a simpleton like me, I couldn't ask
you to exchange your dream for years of rough farming. So I
thought I'd try to woo you with my terrible handwriting, maybe
have a good home ready when you graduated, but now . . ."

He bit the inside of his cheek and waited for her to look up.
When she finally lifted her glistening lashes, he couldn't help
but smile despite the crazy question he was about to ask.

"But now that you've given up school on your own, do I have
any chance of convincing you to marry me?" He rubbed his
hands on his legs. "Um, now?"

Rachel's eyes moved back and forth as if reviewing everything
he'd said. "What about the bride you wrote to. Where's she?"

"Miss Pratt's heading west with the wagon train, but not
with me. I never asked her to come, though she must have had
reasons of her own for making it look that way."

"Would you really marry me the day you proposed?"

He leaned closer. "Could you marry a man who can't promise
he'll be able to spell your name correctly . . . well, ever?"

"If he can dictate a letter like that," she whispered, "absolutely."

He took each of her hands in his and rubbed the backs with
his thumbs. Everything in him begged to kiss her senseless, but
he had to make sure she knew what he could and couldn't offer.
"I can't promise I'll be prosperous. I can't promise you'll get to
see your parents again, or—"

Rachel placed a firm finger on his lips. "You don't have to
be perfect to make me love you. I already do."

He clasped her hands in his. "Enough to pack a trunk, hop

in my wagon, and drive all night if the moon is bright enough?" He swept a strand of hair off her rosy cheek. "But I don't know if a judge would marry us on a Sunday. If we can't get anyone until tomorrow morning, we're going to have a lot of hard riding to do."

"Harold Avery's a preacher, right?" Her eyes twinkled.

His smile grew slowly. He'd been grateful someone in the wagon train could ramble off a decent sermon while they traveled, but he hadn't considered that perk. "Right. I'm so glad you're smart."

"I'm kissable too." The flash in her eyes and the pout of her lips made him chuckle.

"Yes, very kissable."

She leaned forward, and he nearly pulled her across the desk. Her eyelids drooped, and he cupped the back of her head, her hair softer than luxurious silk. His gaze roved over the freckles he hadn't known she had, and he kissed the beauty mark near her lips before her mouth sought his. The world swirled about him, nothing but the taste of her existed. How could he ever feel worthless again if she created this much fire in his arms?

Her hands shot around his neck, and she pressed closer.

Too much fire. He broke away enough to whisper against her lips. "Save that for tonight." If his team ran half as fast as his pulse raced, they'd have no problem catching up with the wagon train by nightfall.

She hummed, eyes closed. "Much better kiss than last time."

Laughing, he supported her upper arms as he set his blushing bride back behind the desk. "And you don't even taste like butterscotch at the moment."

She opened her dreamy eyes and gave him a lazy smile. "I've waited for you for twelve years."

Twelve years? She'd loved him that long? The depth in her eyes proved her soft statement. "I truly am a fool, if that's how long you've loved me."

She shrugged and walked around the desk to him. "Fool or not, I don't want to wait another day."

"Neither do I." He held out his hand and her fingers entwined with his, spreading warmth through the rest of his body. Why had he forced himself to stop dreaming of this woman at night when she'd been dreaming of him all along?

He should have trusted God long ago with his heart's desire. "Let's ride, my love."

A LADIES OF DISTINCTION NOVELLA

GENTLEMAN
OF HER
DREAMS

JEN TURANO

1

New York, 1880

Miss Charlotte Wilson had made a decision.

She was going to marry Mr. Hamilton Beckett.

The fact she'd never actually made Mr. Beckett's acquaintance was a bit concerning, but . . . she had a plan.

She finished buttoning her gown and moved to the floor-length mirror, eyeing her reflection with a critical eye. She tilted her head and released a sigh.

She was not what anyone would call a classic beauty.

No, her hair was a nondescript brown—although it did have some lovely golden streaks running through it due to the unusual amount of time she spent in the sun. Her eyes matched her hair, her cheeks were a touch plumper than current fashion demanded, and her mouth was a tad too full.

Mr. Beckett's first wife, God rest her soul, had been a raving beauty.

She brightened when the thought came to her that although Mary Ellen Beckett had been blessed with perfect features, she'd also been cursed with a temperamental personality, and

299

perhaps Mr. Beckett was searching for a wife who wasn't causing mayhem on a regular basis.

Charlotte bit her lip.

She caused mayhem on a regular basis, not that it was intentional, but mayhem had been her constant companion ever since she was a little girl.

Deciding there was no use dwelling on that particular subject because there was absolutely nothing she could do about it, Charlotte turned from the mirror and moved to her closet, smiling when she pulled out a darling hat that would complement her outfit. She strode back to the mirror, plopped the hat on her head, and maneuvered it to a jaunty angle.

There, she didn't look too hideous.

Now all that was left to do was put her plan into action and hope for the best.

She knew she would be successful, knew it just as she'd known she'd master the feat of riding a bicycle. Not that riding a bicycle had been easy. The first time she'd attempted it she'd only traveled a mere ten feet before the fabric of her skirt got tangled in the chain and then . . . disaster descended. The bicycle came to an abrupt stop, tipped forward, and she'd catapulted over the handlebars, breaking her arm in the process.

She was all too familiar with their family doctor.

Breaking her arm hadn't dampened her determination. She'd created a gown that was more suitable to riding, coerced her friend, Penny, to stitch it up for her, as Charlotte was less than proficient with a needle and thread, and headed for her family's country house where she'd hopped on the seat, set her sights down the road, and finally, after numerous attempts, taken flight.

It had been exhilarating.

Landing Mr. Hamilton Beckett would be exhilarating.

She grinned, confident she'd be able to pull off the task of securing him as a husband because she'd made a special request in her nightly prayers a week before. She was incredibly stingy with her requests, believing God had more important things to deal with than her trivial matters, so she knew He'd grant her prayer this time.

She'd asked Him to send her the gentleman of her dreams, and He'd never failed to grant her requests before, hence the reason she was certain she'd get her man.

When she'd quite literally bounced into Mr. Beckett at a charity event the very night after she'd made her plea, she'd realized God had already answered her prayer.

Unfortunately, bouncing into a hard, unyielding male body while traveling at a somewhat rapid rate of speed, something she did rather frequently, resulted in her propelling backward, straight into a tightly knit huddle of lovely young ladies, which caused them to tumble to the ground. Shrieks were emitted, limbs flew, and by the time Charlotte was able to pull herself from the midst of tangled bodies and extend all the ladies her most abject apologies, Mr. Beckett was already moving away with one of the young ladies, weeping quite dramatically, on his arm.

Not deterred in the least that she'd been unable to secure an introduction, she'd retreated to her home where she began to devise a plan that would allow her to become known to Mr. Hamilton Beckett.

A knock on her bedroom door pulled Charlotte from her thoughts. She moved across the room and opened the door, finding Tilda, one of the downstairs maids, standing on the other side.

"Cook wanted me to tell you your picnic lunch is ready," Tilda said.

"Wonderful," Charlotte exclaimed.

"She also wanted to make certain you really needed that much food because apparently the picnic basket is remarkably heavy."

"If luck is with me today, there will be four people sitting down to dine," Charlotte said. "Two of the people are children, and since I'm not certain what children eat, I requested a wide variety of food."

Tilda tilted her head. "How old are these children?"

"Hmm . . . I have no idea, which does pose a dilemma," Charlotte admitted. "I didn't realize I'd neglected something so important, but if these children are going to be my stepchildren, I should definitely learn their ages."

"You're getting married?"

She should not have let that slip.

It wouldn't help her cause if word got out amongst the servants. They were notorious gossips, and the last thing she needed was for Mr. Beckett to hear rumors she was stalking, er . . . pursuing him.

"I have no immediate plans to marry, Tilda," she settled on saying, "but I'm not getting any younger, and I really should consider the idea. I've finally realized that I've somehow managed to become an old spinster."

"Twenty-one isn't *that* old," Tilda said.

And didn't that exactly sum up why she needed to find a husband?

She *was* a spinster and she was growing older by the second.

How she'd achieved this unpleasant state, she really couldn't say, but she couldn't ignore the facts or the idea that all of her friends, except for Miss Agatha Watson, were firmly off the shelf while she lingered there.

It was becoming downright embarrassing.

Her circumstances wouldn't have gotten nearly so dire if only some of the gentlemen she'd met over the years had possessed a zest for life. She only knew one gentleman who was as curious as she was and thrived on new experiences, but . . . he'd made it clear theirs was to be a relationship based on friendship only, so she'd tucked her longings for him deep into the recesses of her heart and never allowed herself to wonder what her life could have been like if she'd ended up with him.

And that led her back to the predicament of being a spinster, which led back to Mr. Hamilton Beckett.

He was a gentleman who fairly oozed suppressed energy, and that energy was the reason she'd decided he would suit her very well indeed.

He was handsome, possessed muscles of steel that she could attest to—seeing as how she'd careened right into them—and he owned a railroad company.

He traveled those railroads on a frequent basis, and because of that, she knew he was going to be her match.

Her thoughts were interrupted when Rose, another maid, stuck her head in the room. "Begging your pardon, Miss Wilson, but Mr. St. James has arrived. He's waiting for you in the drawing room."

Every single one of the deportment lessons she'd learned while attending Miss Godwin's Finishing School for Young Ladies flew out of her head as she hefted up her skirts, sent the maids a grin, and bolted from the room.

Henry was here.

She raced down the hallway and to the stairs, leaping down them two at a time as excitement rushed through her veins.

Henry St. James had been her very best friend since she'd been four years old. He was two years older than she was, and they'd first met when he'd come to play with her older brother, Charles. Unfortunately for Henry, Charles was a rather somber and serious boy, and Henry's mischievous nature had made the two less than compatible friends. Charles had retreated to the library in search of a good book, apparently put out at Henry for not wanting to join him. Charlotte had found Henry sitting by the side of their small fountain, his shoes abandoned as his feet dangled in the water. She'd hopped down beside him, pulled off her shoes, and they'd been fast friends every since, spending every possible second together until he'd left almost two years ago on matters concerning his family's shipping business.

It had been the longest two years of her life.

She'd missed his humor and his company.

Missed having someone around who didn't judge her antics but was more than happy to participate in them with her.

She jumped over the last remaining step and barreled down another long hallway, her anticipation increasing along with her stride.

Before she reached the drawing room, her feet got tangled in her skirts, most likely because she'd forgotten to keep them above her ankles, and the marble floor suddenly rushed up to greet her. She slid a good five feet along the slippery surface until she finally skidded into the wall, letting out a loud *humph* as the impact knocked the breath from her body.

The sound of running feet came to her and the sight of highly polished boots met her gaze. She lifted her head and felt her mouth drop open.

What had happened to Henry?

Gone was the slightly lean friend of two years before, replaced with a big, brawny gentleman with broad shoulders, a narrow waist and . . . were the arms that currently strained the confines of his shirt as he held out his hand to her really his arms?

She ignored the offered hand as she allowed herself another minute to linger on a face that was no longer thin but was now comprised of sharp cheekbones and a straight blade of a nose. Her perusal moved to his eyes, and she discovered that they somehow seemed to have deepened in color and resembled nothing less than the exact shade of the ocean right before a storm came in.

She felt rather lightheaded and realized she'd neglected to breathe.

She drew in a deep breath, released it, and then smiled as her attention settled on his hair. Here, at least, was something that was completely the same. Strands of untidy black hair stuck out at odd angles around his head, although the look had always appeared rather attractive on Henry, for some strange reason

He'd always been careless when it came to his appearance, and his hair had always been rumpled, along with his clothing, although . . . she narrowed her eyes. He was impeccably dressed at the moment, not a wrinkle to be found, and his trousers were perfectly pressed and didn't sport a single smidgen of dirt.

Who was this gentleman, and why, for heaven's sake, did her brain feel all fuzzy? And what was causing her to remain lounging on a cold, uncomfortable floor?

"I know you're active in the suffrage movement, Charlotte, but you could accept a hand up."

Good grief, Henry was still holding out his hand to her. She forced her mouth shut and took his hand, the breath leaving her once again when he hefted her to her feet as if she weighed no more than a child and then steadied her when she wobbled. Before she could get a single word out of her mouth, not that she was certain she was even capable of speech, Henry drew her into a crushing hug.

"It is wonderful to find you still the same," he said.

Charlotte wasn't quite certain that was a compliment. She eased out of his embrace, ignored the strange tingling that was coursing over her body, and lifted her chin to meet his gaze.

What she discovered there caused the small amount of air still left in her lungs to disappear in a split second.

His eyes were filled with laughter and warmth, and she hadn't realized until just this moment how much his leaving had affected her.

"I'm so glad you're home," she finally managed to say.

Henry grinned. "So I gathered from your incredibly graceful rush to get to me."

Charlotte returned his grin. "I don't know about graceful, but I *was* anxious to see you." She took his arm and pulled him into the drawing room. "I wasn't expecting this visit."

Henry walked with her over to the settee, waited until she took her seat, and then sat down next to her. "Didn't you receive my note?"

She nodded. "I did, but quite frankly, Henry, you were a little sparse with the details. All you mentioned in your note was that you would be home soon. You gave me no specific date, which was beyond annoying, although I suppose I can be charitable and forgive you for that oversight, seeing as how I'm thrilled to have you back. I've missed you quite dreadfully."

Henry picked up her hand and gave it a kiss before he dropped their entwined hands down on the settee and shifted closer to her.

They'd always held hands and sat closely to one another.

It wasn't as if it was untoward; it was natural, natural except for the fact that for some unknown reason, his touch on her hand was causing her to fidget.

She wasn't normally prone to fidgeting. Maybe she'd suffered some type of injury when she'd landed on the marble floor. Maybe she was in the throes of a fit and . . .

"What did you want to do today?"

She blinked out of her thoughts. This would never do. Henry seemed to be under the impression she was free to spend the day with him, but that certainly wouldn't work, given the fact she'd gone out of her way to learn Mr. Beckett's whereabouts for the day. She couldn't very well abandon her plan now.

Before she could think of a suitable reply, Henry leaned closer to her, his nearness causing a wave of something alarming to shoot straight through her body. "My mother told me B. Altman is having a sale on shoes. I would be more than happy to escort you there and lend you my expert advice."

She was immediately torn. She loved shoes, adored them in fact, and Henry was the only gentleman Charlotte knew who was perfectly content to accompany her shopping. His patience was endless, his tastes impeccable, and his company . . . amusing.

She'd missed shopping with Henry, but shopping wouldn't put her into close proximity with Mr. Beckett, so she pushed the longing aside and took a deep breath. Her breath caught in her throat when Henry began rubbing his thumb along her knuckles, his action causing little jolts of what felt like flames to lick up her hand.

"I would prefer going on a picnic," she said, her words tumbling out of her mouth in a rush even as she resisted the urge to tug her hand away from Henry, but really, the tingling was becoming a bit distracting.

What was wrong with her? This was Henry for heaven's sakes and . . .

"If your heart is set on a picnic, I'm more than willing to oblige you, but I must point out that it does look like rain, and I, for one, think shopping would be a better option, at least for today," Henry said.

It seemed as if she'd just inadvertently extended him an invitation to go on a picnic with her.

If her information was correct, and she was fairly certain it was, Mr. Hamilton Beckett was expected to be at Central Park today with his children, and he certainly wouldn't understand what she was doing there with another gentleman.

He might not even take notice of her, and then her plan would be for naught.

How to disinvite Henry without hurting his feelings?

An intriguing thought flashed to mind. She lifted her gaze. "Would you, by chance, happen to be acquainted with the Beckett family?"

Henry frowned. "That's an abrupt change of topic, but yes, I am acquainted with Mr. Hamilton Beckett and his brother, Mr. Zayne Beckett."

This was perfect.

He could perform an introduction.

Now all she had to do was convince him to help her, but first, she needed to reformulate the entire plan.

He could introduce her to Mr. Beckett and then . . . he could suddenly remember urgent business he needed to take care of and leave her alone with her future husband.

Fingers snapping in front of her face caused her to blink back to reality.

"What are you thinking?" Henry asked slowly. "You have a

very interesting expression on your face and one, I might add, I've seen all too often. You're scheming about something, and I have to wonder what it has to do with the Beckett family."

He knew her far too well.

She drew in a deep breath, slowly released it, and summoned up a smile. "Although shopping sounds delightful, I'm afraid I must decline because, you see . . . I have to go to Central Park today."

Henry arched a brow. "You *have* to go?"

Charlotte nodded. "It's all part of a plan."

"Heaven help us."

Charlotte grinned—she couldn't help herself. "Now, don't be like that. You love my plans."

"Charlotte, the last plan I helped you with resulted in me landing in jail."

"True, but honestly, Henry, you know poor Matilda's reputation would have suffered dreadfully if we hadn't managed to return her personal possessions to her. She most likely would have been forced to marry that cad, Mr. Blackwell, but because you managed to find her stolen undergarments in the man's house, Matilda is now happily married to Mr. Smith, and she has you to thank for it. How could I have possibly known Mr. Blackwell would arrive home early from the theater and catch us in the act?" She patted his knee. "It was very noble of you to push me out that window and take the brunt of his displeasure."

"You broke your ankle."

"You ended up with a broken nose, so it's all relative. Besides, at least I didn't end up behind bars, and my mother is still thankful for that. She believes you're a true hero come to life."

"I was less than a hero seeing as how I took a beating, left you all alone to make your way to the doctor's, and caused my parents no small amount of embarrassment over being forced to bail me out of jail."

"My latest plan shouldn't have such drastic results," Charlotte said as she got to her feet and glanced at the clock. "We're behind schedule. You did bring your horse, didn't you?"

Henry rose from the settee and nodded. "I did, along with a buggy."

"Your horse is attached to a buggy?"

"Why do I get the distinct feeling you're not pleased about that?"

Charlotte ignored his question as she tilted her head to the side and thought for a minute. "Well, no matter. I'll drive the buggy and you can ride my horse."

Henry's eyes widened. "I'm not riding Beast. He hates me."

"He doesn't hate you."

"He tried to bite off my arm."

"He's mellowed since you last saw him."

Henry took a step forward. "Why can't we both ride in my buggy? It has two perfectly good seats, so there's really no reason to take an extra horse."

"Stop being a baby. We need to take an extra horse so that my plan can succeed, which reminds me I need to send word to the livery stable to have Beast saddled instead of hooked up to my buggy." She moved to the bell pull, gave it a tug, and a mere thirty seconds later, Tilda hurried into the room. She gave the maid instructions and then turned to find Henry watching her.

"You don't need to look so worried, Henry. This is going to be a harmless jaunt."

"None of your jaunts are ever harmless."

"That's not true, and besides, if we were to run into trouble, not that I think we will, you have little reason to believe you'd suffer another beating. You've become huge in the time you've been away. Mr. Blackwell would be no match for you today."

"We're going after Mr. Blackwell?" Henry sputtered.

"Of course not. He's left the state, due to the fact he attempted to ruin another young miss, only this lady had four brothers who chased the blackguard out of New York." She walked to the door and looked over her shoulder. "We need to go fetch Beast."

Henry crossed his arms and shook his head. "Not until you tell me about this plan of yours."

"I'll tell you on the way to the livery stable. I don't want to miss my opportunity at Central Park, and time is running away from me."

Henry muttered something under his breath that she didn't quite catch, but he did join her and take her arm before they strolled down the hallway, into the kitchen to fetch the picnic basket, and out the back door. She couldn't help but smile as Cook and the other servants followed them out, all making a fuss over Henry as he asked them about their lives.

He'd always been considerate of others, especially servants.

"Why did you have Cook pack so much food?" he asked as he shifted the picnic basket's handle over his arm and took her hand in his before frowning down at her. "And why are you smiling?"

"The food is part of the plan," Charlotte said, "and I'm smiling because you're such a nice man and you didn't balk in the least at helping me, even though you have yet to learn the pesky details of what's in store for you." She squeezed his hand. "It almost feels like fate, you showing up today, because you're the only friend I have who I can trust to help me in this matter, seeing as it calls for discretion."

Henry stopped moving. "Explain."

Charlotte tugged on his hand, which prodded Henry back into motion, but she took a moment to consider her words before she delivered them. She decided the best option was to simply get it out quickly. "I'm getting married."

Henry, suddenly scowling, came to an abrupt halt, dropped the picnic basket to the ground, and let go of her hand. "What do you mean?"

"I thought it was self-explanatory," Charlotte said.

"My mother didn't mention any upcoming nuptials."

"That's because it's still a bit sketchy."

"How can a wedding be a bit sketchy?" Henry demanded.

"I'm not comfortable explaining."

"Try."

Charlotte bit her lip. "I've recently come to the conclusion that it is past time I selected a husband, and since I've had no luck obtaining one on my own, I put the matter in God's hands. He, in all His wisdom, sent me Mr. Hamilton Beckett."

Henry's eyes turned stormy. "Is that why you asked if I was acquainted with the Beckett family?"

She nodded.

"Isn't Hamilton Beckett a little old for you?"

"Of course not, he's only . . . hmm . . . you know, I'm not certain how old Mr. Beckett is, but he can't be more than thirty."

"You don't know how old your fiancé is?"

"That is the crux of my problem at the moment," Charlotte said. "He's not my fiancé quite yet."

Henry's brow disappeared beneath the shock of black hair laying across his forehead.

"In fact," Charlotte said, stalling just a minute before she made her greatest confession, "I've never officially met the man."

Her temper began to simmer when Henry released a bark

of laughter, although it was a strange type of laugh—part amused . . . part relieved.

Before she could dwell on that for a sufficient amount of time, Henry picked up the basket, took her hand back in his, and began pulling her, not toward the livery, but back toward the house.

"We're going the wrong way," she said.

"No, we're not," he countered. "We're going to take this basket back to the kitchen, and then you and I are going shopping. I'll even pay."

Charlotte's feet stopped moving. She snatched her hand out of Henry's, crossed her arms over her chest, and shook her head. "I'm going to Central Park."

Henry blew out a breath. "You just admitted you don't even know Mr. Beckett. Trust me, Charlotte, this is one plan you shouldn't see through to fruition."

She felt her jaw clench. Why was he being so obstinate? In the past, he'd always been more than willing to help her with whatever plan she was attempting. Why was he balking now?

It made absolutely no sense at all, and he didn't even know what she was planning. How could he know she shouldn't see it through to fruition? Granted, she hadn't figured out all of the particulars since he'd entered the mix, but she would do that on the way to the park—if he could be convinced to participate. She bit back a smile as she realized exactly what she needed to do to garner his cooperation.

"If you don't want to help me, Henry, that's fine," she said with a lift of her chin. "I'm perfectly capable of traveling to the park on my own, and while it would have been convenient to have you introduce me to Mr. Beckett, I assure you, I'll manage an introduction without your help."

One.

Two.

Three.

Henry released a snort, grabbed her hand, and pulled her down the walk, this time toward the livery stable.

He never had been able to refuse her anything, which was why she completely adored him and why she wasn't above appealing to his gallant nature to get her way.

"So, you're going to help me?" she asked, panting slightly when he increased his pace yet again.

"Do I have a choice?"

Oh dear . . . he sounded sulky.

That was quite unlike Henry. He rarely sulked.

Perhaps he was tired from his travels.

Perhaps she should reconsider and allow him to take her shopping. It would be the considerate thing to do, but then she wouldn't get to meet Mr. Beckett.

Henry dropped her hand and stowed the picnic basket in his buggy before he turned and, without a word, took her arm and steered her toward the stable. He paused when he reached Beast's stall, and Charlotte felt a moment of trepidation when Beast looked at Henry, rolled his eyes, and then tossed his head even as his hoof began to paw the ground.

They should definitely abandon the picnic idea and go shopping.

Before she could get that out of her mouth, Henry grabbed Beast by the reins and pulled him out of the stall, still not speaking a single word.

What in the world was the matter with him?

She hurried to catch up and stopped when Henry turned to face her once he'd reached the buggy. "Tell me again, why do we need Beast and why aren't you riding him?" he asked.

"I'm not wearing a riding habit."

"Have you given all of your riding habits away?"

Apparently he'd gone from sulky to sarcastic. She let out a breath. "I still have numerous riding habits at my disposal, but as my intention today is to meet Mr. Beckett, I wanted to look my best, and my riding habits do not show me in a flattering light. That's why I chose this gown, but it requires a bustle, and you know bustles make it extremely difficult to maintain balance—but that has nothing to do with why we need Beast. You'll need a way to get home after I become acquainted with Mr. Beckett."

"You're planning on abandoning me?"

"Not right away," Charlotte said quickly. "That would be odd, wouldn't it, if you were to introduce me and then bolt from the scene. No, I think you'll need to stay, at least for a few minutes, and then you can remember a pressing appointment and take your leave."

Henry's lips thinned into a straight line before he shook his head.

She'd forgotten he was a somewhat stubborn soul. She summoned up her sunniest smile. "Honestly, Henry, I can't very well get to know Mr. Beckett if you're hovering at my side." Her eyes widened even as the smile slid off her face. "And while I do need you to perform an introduction, how are we to arrange it so that Mr. Beckett does not come to the conclusion we're a couple?" She bit her lip. "Maybe this isn't such a wonderful plan after all. Maybe you should return home and allow me to travel to the park on my own. I'll simply have to revert back to my original plan of suffering a loose wheel on my buggy which will allow me to throw myself on Mr. Beckett's mercy, while at the same time using that to my advantage to become acquainted with him."

For some reason, Henry was once again muttering under his breath.

She arched a brow.

"I'm going with you," Henry said between gritted teeth.

Why was he being difficult? Honestly, it was not as if this was some unusual occurrence, her changing her mind. In the past, he used to accommodate her frequent flights of fancy with little more than a shrug.

She opened her mouth, but didn't have time to do more than squeak because she was suddenly hefted up into the air and then plunked down in a rather rough fashion on the buggy seat. Reins were thrust into her hand, and Henry gave her a brief nod before he stalked back to Beast's side.

Someone was obviously miffed.

She could not remember a time when Henry was at odds with her. She cleared her throat, hoping to break the strained silence. "Try to remember that Beast is a little temperamental and prefers a light hand on the reins."

Henry turned his head and rolled his eyes. "He's not a little temperamental, he's a raving lunatic of a horse, and you owe me for this, Charlotte."

She watched as Henry climbed into the saddle, unable to help but notice and admire how lithe and muscular he'd become. Her gaze drifted to his legs and then darted quickly away because it certainly wasn't acceptable to gawk at a gentleman's thighs.

"Are you going to lead the way?" Henry asked.

Charlotte felt heat take over her face. She chanced a glance at Henry and breathed a sigh of relief. Annoyance was still clearly stamped on his face, which meant he hadn't noticed her ogling him.

What would possess her to ogle Henry? She'd certainly never

done so in the past. She swallowed a grunt. That wasn't exactly the truth. There might have been a few times . . . when she'd hoped they'd be together forever, but then he'd gone and turned funny and . . .

No, she would not allow her mind to travel in that direction. She was not meant for Henry, she was meant for Mr. Hamilton Beckett, and she would do well to remember that.

She flicked the reins and the buggy set to rolling down the street, Henry pulling Beast up beside them. He was watching her somewhat speculatively, and that speculation unsettled her.

They passed the ride to Central Park in silence, and Charlotte was more than relieved when they finally reached their destination. She brought the buggy to a halt and took a moment to scan the area, smiling when her prey, or rather, Mr. Beckett, came into sight.

"I see them," she called to Henry and pointed off to the left. "He's parked over there. We need to get closer."

"It's starting to rain."

"Then I guess I should be thankful he's underneath that large tree. It's the perfect place to hold a picnic."

Charlotte edged the buggy around carriages that seemed to be making a hasty retreat from the park, thrilled to discover Mr. Beckett hadn't moved.

He *was* an adventurous soul, not intimidated in the least that it was most likely about to pour.

He would suit her well.

She pulled the buggy to a stop and turned to find Henry staring off toward Mr. Beckett. He wasn't wearing a very pleased expression, but then again, it had begun to rain harder, and water was dripping down his nose.

"All right, here's what I want you to do," Charlotte said.

"You'll ride Beast past him, call out to him, and then get off the horse. You'll have to converse with him for a minute or two, I'll leave the subject of that conversation up to you, and then, here's the best part, you'll tell him there's someone you'd like him to meet. I'll be watching for your signal, which should probably just be a wave. When I see you wave, I'll come and join you. You'll perform the introduction and after five minutes of the social pleasantries, you'll remember your appointment."

"I don't even get to eat lunch?"

Charlotte was unable to stifle a huff of annoyance. It was now raining quite diligently, and her time to attract Mr. Beckett's attention was disappearing the longer she argued with Henry. "You can take a sandwich with you. Now go and talk to him."

"Because that won't look strange, you thrusting a sandwich at me when Mr. Beckett thinks I'm going off to an appointment. It's a bit difficult to eat on the back of a bucking stallion."

Charlotte sent him a glare, which started Henry laughing and urging Beast forward. She sat back in her seat and watched as he approached Mr. Beckett, holding her breath when Henry jumped from Beast's back and shook Mr. Beckett's hand.

She realized that Henry would be calling to her soon, so she stood up and smoothed her damp skirts down, lifting her head and forcing a smile. Before she had a chance to do anything else, a loud crack of thunder split the air, and the next thing she knew, Beast was charging directly at her, causing the horse attached to the buggy to bolt forward.

Her body lurched backward and then toppled over the buggy's seat, landing with a splat into a puddle of something vile. She pulled her head from the muck, watched in disbelief as she saw Mr. Beckett driving his carriage rapidly away from her, and then turned her head ever so slightly as her gaze settled on mud-splattered boots.

"Charlotte, are you all right?"

"Why didn't Mr. Beckett come to my rescue?" she managed to ask after she spit a glob of mud out of her mouth.

"I would have to imagine he didn't see you," Henry said. "That lightning strike was too close for comfort, and he was concerned with getting his children to safety."

"Ah, he's a wonderful father."

"Anyone in their right mind would get their children to safety," Henry grumbled. "Here, take my hand."

Charlotte blinked muddy water out of her eyes and noticed that Henry was once again holding out his hand to her. She pushed out of the mud, slipped just a touch as Henry pulled her to her feet, and then peered into the distance, biting back a sigh when Mr. Beckett's carriage was nowhere in sight.

"Are you sure you're not hurt?" Henry asked.

"Only my pride," she admitted as she patted his arm, causing bits of mud to fly everywhere. "Not to worry, though. In case you were wondering, I have a backup plan."

2

Henry laughed out loud and then swallowed another laugh
when two ladies approaching him from the opposite direction
eyed him warily. He tipped his hat to them, flicked the reins to
urge his horse faster, and then grinned as the image of Charlotte as she'd looked the day before, dripping mud and looking
downright miserable, flashed through his mind.

She was more enchanting than ever.

She was also annoyingly determined—determined to proceed
with her scheme of bringing Mr. Hamilton Beckett around to
her way of thinking.

He had nothing against Hamilton; in fact, in the past he'd
enjoyed the gentleman's company. Hamilton was a fairly capital
fellow, and the ladies of New York seemed to find him pleas-
ing on the eyes and possessed of a captivating, if somewhat
brooding, nature.

To give the gentleman his due, he had every reason to brood,
as he'd been married to a shrew of a woman who'd embarrassed
him to no end before she'd died. If anyone deserved a chance at
happiness, it was Hamilton . . . but not with Charlotte.

Henry knew Charlotte belonged with him. Even though she hadn't quite realized that yet, he wasn't going to allow her to slip away without a fight.

He'd been in love with her for years.

They'd started off as friends—they'd been so young when they met—but then, somehow, through the years, his love for her changed.

It turned intense and horrible. Horrible because Charlotte didn't return his affections.

Oh, she had loved him—there'd never been a question about that—but she'd loved him as a brother or a best friend, and he'd wanted more.

The year of her debut had been sheer torture for him as he escorted her from one ball to another, forced to watch from the sidelines when gentlemen swooped to her side the moment she stepped foot across the threshold. His only solace in those days had been the single dance she always set aside just for him.

He'd cherished every step, dreamed of taking the floor with her, until one summer evening when he had arrived at her side for their dance and heard her release a sigh—a sigh that seemed to mean their dance, cherished by him, was a tiresome obligation to her.

The thought of being an obligation was abhorrent to him, and he realized he couldn't continue on with the madness of wanting her, not when the feeling wasn't returned.

He'd made the decision to leave New York and embarked on an adventure that permitted him to further his knowledge of the family shipping business, while also cementing his belief that his life's destiny was to travel the high seas as a captain. As he moved from port to port, his longing for Charlotte never abated, and his greatest hope had been that while he was away,

Charlotte would finally come to terms with her feelings for him and realize they were meant to be together.

Charlotte would love traveling around the world. Her appetite for adventure was certainly as great as his, and he'd pictured her by his side often over the past two years, the sea mist tangling her hair even as her eyes sparkled at the mere thought of what waited for them just over the horizon.

He'd tried to put his travels into his letters, wanting her to experience them even if she wasn't with him, and he'd treasured the letters she had sent back, poring over them again and again anytime he'd been fortunate enough to dock in England where her letters waited for him.

It was because of these letters he'd decided to come home.

Her letters had taken on an almost melancholy air, and he'd thought her melancholy was due to her finally realizing how much she missed his company.

He'd obviously been reading too much between the lines because Charlotte wasn't melancholy in the least; in fact, she was downright scary at the moment, with her sense of purpose and her belief God was directing her path toward Mr. Hamilton Beckett.

He was all for believing God had a hand in a person's fate, but Charlotte was apparently confusing the message she thought she'd received from above.

He was meant to be her husband.

He took a moment to send up a prayer, asking God to set Charlotte straight, and then glanced around, surprised to discover he was almost to Charlotte's house.

How was he going to convince her that her thinking was skewered and that she could have the perfect husband if only she'd open her eyes and recognize what was waiting right in front of her?

She still saw him as somewhat of a brother figure, although . . .

maybe that wasn't quite true anymore. Her eyes had lingered on him the day before, and she'd watched him with a strange expression on her face, as if she wasn't really sure who he was, and that had to be a step in the right direction.

He wanted her to see him differently, wanted her to see that he was her match, wanted her to forget they were best friends—no, that wasn't right. He wanted her to always think of him as her best friend, but he wanted to be the love of her life, and that was going to be the most difficult challenge he'd ever faced.

He would give her the entire world if it would make her happy, which explained why he was currently driving to her house, unable to refuse the recent message she'd sent him, asking him to call on her.

She hadn't bothered to add anything else in her note, which made him rather anxious. Charlotte was tricky at the best of times, and if she'd gotten something else into her head, something that involved a backup plan, he'd have to do his best to discourage her. He certainly wasn't keen on helping her, not if she wanted him to help her land Mr. Beckett.

That would be at distinct odds with what he wanted.

He brought his buggy to a stop in front of the Wilsons' Park Avenue mansion and jumped to the ground, handing the reins over to a waiting groom.

"Shall I take your buggy to the livery?" the groom asked.

Henry bit back a groan. "Am I to assume I'm not going to be in need of it in the near future?"

The groom smiled. "Miss Wilson has a wagon waiting just over there."

Henry swiveled his head and frowned. "Is that a boat on the back of the wagon?"

"Some might call it a boat," the groom said. "Miss Wilson

came home with that about a month ago. She's been patching it up." The groom grinned. "May I say you're a brave one, sir? It's not every gentleman who would take the risk."

"Risk?" Henry asked warily

The groom nodded. "I do hope you know how to swim."

"Swim?"

The groom nodded again. "That's why I told Miss Wilson I couldn't help her with this particular project. I don't swim, or I would have gone with her after her brothers, the friends of her brothers, and anyone else she asked balked at the mere thought of taking that contraption out on the water. She's right hard to say no to, isn't she?"

"That she is, although it seems there were many who did," Henry said before turning and walking up the sidewalk, determined to get to the bottom of what was obviously yet another one of Charlotte's mad schemes. "Thank you for seeing to my horse," he called over his shoulder.

The groom smiled and jumped into the seat, and Henry watched as the horse and buggy cantered away. He then set his sights on the door, shaking his head before he rapped the knocker against the wood.

She'd always been incorrigible, but instead of growing out of that particular habit, it seemed to be worsening with age, and he could only hope Charlotte hadn't gotten it into that delightful head of hers to try something dangerous.

As the groom said, she was difficult to say no to, especially since he was trying to win her favor and win her affections away from Hamilton.

Mr. Lewis, the Wilson family's devoted butler, answered the door and ushered Henry inside, sending Henry a look that appeared almost sympathetic.

"Going to the Hudson River, are you?" Mr. Lewis asked.

It seemed as if there really was some dastardly plan in the works.

"I'm not quite certain about that," Henry said slowly.

"Ah, she neglected to tell you," Mr. Lewis said. "That explains it."

"Am I to understand I've been summoned to take her boating?"

Mr. Lewis winced before he nodded. "She's been desperate to find someone to accompany her." He leaned forward and lowered his voice. "Do you know she offered me five dollars to go sailing with her?" He let out a sigh. "I must admit I was briefly tempted, seeing as how she can be somewhat persuasive, but my rheumatism doesn't do well in the wet. She understood of course. Miss Wilson is a compassionate soul, and it took me a good hour to convince her she hadn't hurt my feelings by asking me to accompany her, seeing that it brought attention to my ever-increasing fragility."

"Henry, how good of you to visit."

Henry swung his attention away from Mr. Lewis and smiled when he caught sight of Charlotte's mother, Mrs. Margaret Wilson. He stepped forward and took her hand, bringing it to his lips before he dropped it and grinned. "You're looking as wonderful as ever, Mrs. Wilson."

Mrs. Wilson beamed. "I see you've managed to get quite a bit of polish on your extended travels around the world, Henry. I've missed you, dear."

"I've missed you as well, Mrs. Wilson, but I'm not certain I got much polish on my travels. I spent most of my time in derelict ports dealing with unsavory groups of men."

Mrs. Wilson took his arm and began directing him down

the hallway. "You must tell me all about your adventures. The unsavory men sound completely riveting."

"Mother, I'm afraid Henry won't be able to tell you his stories now," Charlotte said, coming up behind them. "We're on a tight schedule."

Henry turned and felt his mouth run dry. Charlotte was wearing a gown of blue and white stripes that was nipped in at the waist, showcasing her lovely figure. Her hair was pulled to the top of her head and curls cascaded around her face, while a miniscule little scrap of fabric that he assumed was her hat perched on top of her curls, lending her a rather mischievous air.

The last thing Charlotte needed was to look more mischievous.

Before he could extend her a proper greeting, Mrs. Wilson stepped forward and sent her daughter a frown. "Why are you on a tight schedule, and exactly where are you taking poor Henry?"

Ah, Mrs. Wilson remembered the fact her daughter possessed the habit of pulling Henry, whether willing or not, into schemes that usually landed them in trouble.

"We're going sailing on the Hudson River," Charlotte said.

"You neglected to mention that in your note," he muttered.

Mrs. Wilson stiffened for a split second before a somewhat forced smile spread over her face. "I'm going to assume you dock a boat there, Henry."

"Actually, no," Henry returned.

Mrs. Wilson spun around so fast she almost made him dizzy. "Do not even tell me you've talked Henry into taking out that, for want of a better word, boat."

"It's perfectly seaworthy," Charlotte said, although her tone sounded a tad defensive.

"If you're determined to go boating today, Charlotte, we

could always take out one of my boats," Henry said. "I have several at my disposal, and I can guarantee that all of them float."

"We have to go to the river, and you stated not a moment ago that you don't dock a boat there," Charlotte said between lips that were almost completely closed.

Mrs. Wilson narrowed her eyes and began tapping her toe against the floor. "And why, pray tell, do you have to go boating on the Hudson and . . . why are you dressed like that if you're going boating? Good heavens, Charlotte, if you fell overboard, you'd sink in a split second with that huge bustle."

"Which is why I'm not planning on falling overboard," Charlotte said.

"You're avoiding my questions," Mrs. Wilson said.

Charlotte let out a huff. "Fine, if you must know, I've discovered that Mr. Hamilton Beckett has plans to sail around the bay with his children this morning, and since I've decided he's the most appropriate man for me to marry, I wanted to look my best on the chance I sail into him."

Mrs. Wilson's mouth gaped open. She finally snapped it shut, took a step closer to her daughter, and then began to sputter. "I had . . . had . . . had no idea you'd turned your attention to Mr. Beckett, and I certainly wasn't aware of the fact the two of you have been seeing each other."

"She's never met the gentleman, Mrs. Wilson," Henry said.

Mrs. Wilson closed her eyes and appeared to be counting under her breath. Henry smiled. He'd always enjoyed Mrs. Wilson, enjoyed her no-nonsense approach to life and her no-nonsense approach to her daughter, which, now that he thought about it, could actually work to his advantage.

He should have remembered Mrs. Wilson could be counted as one of his greatest allies.

She'd always adored him, always welcomed him into her home, and he'd always thought Mrs. Wilson harbored a secret hope that he and Charlotte would someday marry.

"Darling, Mr. Beckett is far too old for you, and besides, he has two small children."

Henry blinked and realized that while he'd been lost in thought, Mrs. Wilson was providing invaluable advice to Charlotte.

"I adore children," Charlotte said.

"You've never been around children for any length of time," Mrs. Wilson countered.

Charlotte tilted her head and got the mulish expression on her face that Henry knew far too well. "I see my niece and my nephews at least once a month."

Mrs. Wilson crossed her arms over her chest. "Your brothers and their wives have banned you from being alone with their children."

Charlotte caught Henry's eyes and shrugged. "It's all a complete misunderstanding."

"I don't think encouraging a six-year-old to test out your latest invention could ever be confused as a simple misunderstanding," Mrs. Wilson said with a sniff.

"Sophia needs adventure, seeing as how Charles stifles her, and how was I to know the wheels would fall off the miniature bicycle I made for her?"

"The loss of the wheels caused poor Sophia to run over her father, and that caused Charles to land in a puddle of mud, which resulted in me getting a lecture from him regarding my inability to control you," Mrs. Wilson said. "And don't even get me started on what he had to say regarding your 'special' bicycle outfit."

"Charles has always been too stuffy for his own good," Charlotte muttered. "Sophia wasn't harmed and neither was Charles. Personally, I believe Sophia was delighted over the whole affair, which just goes to prove that children adore me."

"Because they see you as one of their peers," Mrs. Wilson said with a roll of her eyes. "I do not mean to offend you, darling, but a gentleman such as Mr. Beckett, while certainly searching for a woman who would make a wonderful mother, will only consider a woman who is sophisticated and somewhat worldly."

"I can be sophisticated if I put my mind to it," Charlotte mumbled.

Mrs. Wilson arched a brow. "My dear, you know perfectly well that is not true. You've been blessed with an unusual spirit and a taste for the peculiar, and unfortunately, most gentlemen are not going to be able to appreciate that in you, including Mr. Beckett. He's far too somber, and you deserve a kindred spirit. As your mother, it is my duty to encourage you to look in a different direction." She turned and winked at Henry.

Now they were getting somewhere.

"Mother, I know you're going to find this somewhat odd, but the reason I've chosen Mr. Beckett is because I believe he's been sent to me by God."

How was a person supposed to argue with that type of reasoning?

To Henry's surprise, Mrs. Wilson nodded. "I'm sure God is directing you, darling, but you know as well as I do that God works in ways we can't understand. You might have misunderstood, which is something I do often, so I wouldn't get your heart set on Mr. Beckett just yet. God might have someone else in mind for you."

Henry watched as Mrs. Wilson sent him another wink, patted

her daughter on the cheek, and strode down the hallway, turning to pause when she reached the other end. "Do try to stay out of trouble, both of you. At your advanced ages, I would hope that shouldn't be too much to ask."

"She doesn't like Mr. Beckett," Charlotte said when Mrs. Wilson disappeared.

"She didn't say that, Charlotte. She said he wasn't for you."

"He's the most sought-after gentleman in New York City."

"But . . . you don't know him."

Charlotte released a loud sigh. "I know I don't, but if all goes according to plan, I'll meet him today."

Henry blew out a breath. "Should I even ask what part you want me to play in your little fiasco?"

"I need you to help me with the boat."

"The boat that no one believes is seaworthy?" he asked.

Charlotte gave an airy wave of her hand. "It's completely seaworthy. I've tested it out."

Henry frowned. "Where, pray tell, did you do that?"

Charlotte nibbled on her lip, the action drawing his attention. She had the most delectable lips, very plump, and he'd often wondered what it would be like to kiss them.

He shook himself as he realized Charlotte had answered his question, but since he'd been lost in his little daydream, he'd missed all the pertinent parts.

Should he ask her to repeat her answer?

No, that would only cause her to realize something was amiss, and he certainly couldn't allow her to realize that he found her lips all too enticing.

"So, you'll do it?"

"Do what?" he was forced to ask.

Charlotte released a grunt and tugged her hand out of his.

"You'll help me sail the boat over to Mr. Beckett and then introduce me to him?"

As far as danger levels went, this was remarkably mild for Charlotte, although he really didn't want to be the one to introduce her to Mr. Beckett, especially if the introduction resulted in them forming an attachment.

Uncertain what to say, he finally settled on, "You'll hardly have an opportunity to become better acquainted with the gentleman simply because we've sailed up beside him."

"That's why we're going to claim we're taking on water, and it won't really be a stretch or a lie for that matter, seeing as how my boat does have a very small, yet manageable, leak."

She'd lost her mind.

He drew in a deep breath, slowly released it, found that he was still at a loss for words, and took another breath. "We cannot take a boat out into the Hudson River knowing full well it has a leak," he managed to get out.

Charlotte turned sulky in a split second. "You said you'd help."

"No, I didn't. You assumed I'd help. I've decided not to aid you in this ridiculous plan."

There, that should put an end to the madness.

She couldn't sail the boat by herself, and since no one else would agree to go out with her, she would simply have to accept that today was not the day she was going to meet Mr. Beckett. Perhaps she would find some solace in the fact B. Altman was still running their sale on shoes.

Before he could make that suggestion, Charlotte squared her shoulders and sent him a glare. "Fine, be that way then. I'll go it alone."

"You can't sail that boat by yourself."

"I simply won't unfurl the sail," she proclaimed. "I'll row myself across the bay."

She was going to be the death of him.

"You can't row a boat across the bay," he said between clenched teeth.

"I'll never know for certain until I try."

She was the most exasperating woman he'd ever known, and yet, even though he knew her plan was at distinct odds with what he wanted, he, for some unknown reason, suddenly found himself nodding, the action causing Charlotte's scowl to immediately disappear into a lovely smile, a smile that set his heart to racing.

He really did love her. Why else would he allow her to twist him around her little finger like this?

"Come on, you'd better show me this boat of yours," he grumbled, his mind going numb when Charlotte beamed at him, took back his hand, and pulled him over to the wagon.

Trepidation rolled over him as he got his first good look at her boat.

"You call this a boat?" he asked as he dropped her hand and stepped forward, eyeing the disaster in front of him.

"Of course it's a boat. Mr. Gardner was going to toss it away, and I rescued and restored it."

Henry's gaze traveled over the length of the boat. It was slightly larger than a rowboat and had a skinny mast sticking up from the middle. "Maybe you should have let Mr. Gardner have his way."

Charlotte didn't bother to respond and instead, walked around to the front of the wagon and climbed up, turning to look at him after she sat down on the seat. "Are you coming?"

"I don't think this will float," he muttered before moving to take his place by her side. She handed him the reins, he gave them a flick, and then, much to his dismay, they were on their way to Hudson River where they were certain to meet yet another disaster.

"I used tar."

"I hope you used a lot of it," he said.

"I told you, it's perfectly seaworthy."

"You told me it leaks," Henry countered.

"All boats leak a little bit."

"No, they don't," he argued.

Charlotte let out a grunt. "Really, Henry, if I'd known you were going to be this much of a stick in the mud, I would have never requested your help. Surely you know that I wouldn't ask you to go sailing in a boat that wasn't safe? I'm not an idiot, and again, I tested the boat, in water I might add, a few days ago. It was fine." She sent him another mind-numbing smile. "Now, could we please change the subject and speak about something pleasant? You have yet to tell me anything of the adventures you wrote me about, and I've been dying to ask you so many questions."

Although he knew he should press her further regarding exactly what water she'd supposedly tested her boat on, he couldn't seem to get the words out of his mouth. She was watching him with clear delight in her eyes, and he found he couldn't refuse her request of sharing his adventures with her.

Time flew as they traveled through the city until they arrived at the bay, when Charlotte suddenly sat forward in her seat and grinned back at him. "We're here," she exclaimed, lurching against his side as the wagon hit a rut in the road, the heat from her body causing him to suck in a sharp breath. "This is so exciting."

Twenty minutes later, Henry wasn't so certain it was exciting; it was mostly terrifying. They were well away from shore and Charlotte had just unfurled the sail. To his horror, the cloth was badly frayed and ripped, although uneven stitches were trying to hold the material together. He was fairly certain Charlotte had darned the sail herself, and from what his memory recalled, she was less than handy with a needle.

"We're picking up speed now," she called.

"I don't know if that sail's up for it," he called back, his eyes widening as he watched one repaired spot slowly unravel right in front of him.

Charlotte apparently hadn't heard him, probably because her attention was settled on something in the distance. "There they are. Mr. Beckett is in that lovely sailboat right over there. Faster, Henry, full speed ahead."

Henry was trying to comply with her demands, but his attempt at tacking back and forth was met with little success, as the sail was unraveling at a rapid rate. Then, suddenly, the wind died and the boat drifted to a stop as small waves lapped against the sides of the boat.

"What are you doing?" Charlotte asked. "Why aren't we moving?"

"No wind."

Charlotte tilted her head and then smiled. "We have oars."

"There is no possible way I'm going to row you over to Mr. Beckett's boat," Henry declared. "It will take me forever, and besides, it would look somewhat odd if I simply happened to choose his boat when there are plenty of other, closer boats out here."

"We can't just sit here, and no, we're not going to accept help from any of those other boats," Charlotte grouched before she brightened. "I know . . . what if I toss the oars overboard and then we'll start yelling in Mr. Beckett's direction? He'll feel compelled to come to our rescue. Since we're wind-less and oar-less, he'll offer us a ride back to shore, and I'll finally have an opportunity to converse with him."

She was a menace.

He swallowed the snort he longed to emit, reminded himself he was trying to woo her, strange as that seemed under the circumstances, and hoped his tone, as soon as he recovered his voice, would come across as reasonable instead of annoyed. "Charlotte, you're not thinking clearly," he began. "We cannot simply toss our oars overboard. It would hardly be the prudent option as it would leave us with no way to get back to shore on the off chance Mr. Beckett, or any other boaters, didn't hear our calls, and . . ." Henry's words trailed off as he glanced down and realized the reason his foot was suddenly cold was because the boat was quickly becoming submerged. "We're taking on water."

Charlotte lifted her skirts and frowned. "So we are. How strange." Her frown deepened as she leaned forward and stuck her hand down into the water that was now completely covering their feet. "I wonder where this rather large hole came from because I assure you it wasn't here when we first set sail."

Henry could only sit there, frozen, as water began gushing upward, reminding him of the fountain in Charlotte's backyard. Sanity returned in a flash; he yanked his handkerchief out of his jacket and stuffed it into the hole, hoping it would at least staunch the flow slightly and allow him to get the boat back to land. He straightened and snatched his hat off his head, beginning to bail as quickly as he could.

Charlotte pulled the miniscule hat from her head and began

scooping water out of the boat, although the smallness of her hat didn't allow her to make much progress.

They were doomed.

The wind kicked up that moment, causing the tattered sails to billow with air, and, much to his relief and surprise, they were off. He tossed her his hat, took control of the rope, and was just getting ready to turn the boat around and head back to shore when Charlotte did something completely unexpected.

She got to her feet, splashing him with liberal amounts of water as she did so, and began waving her hands wildly over her head, smiling broadly.

"Ahoy there, we could use some assistance please."

One minute she was standing there, rocking the boat, and the next, the wind shifted and filled the sail, causing it to rip down the middle and slap soundly against Charlotte's face. She stumbled backwards, and he heard a loud, ominous crack. Before Henry could move, the floor of the boat directly beneath her feet disintegrated, and Charlotte disappeared under the murky waters of Hudson River.

3

Her concern with being fashionably attired was going to be the death of her.

As Charlotte sunk ever faster through the water, she couldn't help but recall how her mother had warned her about wearing a bustle on a boat.

Maybe she should've designed a bustle that could float.

Now there was an idea. It was too bad she wasn't going to live long enough to see that invention come to pass.

The last of her air leaked out of her lungs, and panic set in.

She was going to die.

She wasn't ready to die.

Black spots began obscuring her vision, and an image of Henry's face sprang to mind, his eyes twinkling and his lips curled with amusement.

She struggled to kick upwards, needing to see Henry one last time before she died, but the weight of her skirts forced her to abandon her efforts, the heavy fabric tangling around her legs and sending her hurtling downward.

She felt a brief glimmer of regret pass through her, regret that she'd been responsible for causing this latest disaster. She sent out a prayer, not really knowing which way was up, asking God to spare Henry's life, because this was all her fault and he didn't deserve to die because of her idiocy.

Something grabbed hold of her hair, but darkness was descending and she didn't have the strength to question what it was.

Suddenly, her head was above the surface and her mouth opened, spewing out water before she sucked air into her lungs.

"Charlotte, love, can you hear me? Are you all right? Please don't be dead, don't be dead."

She blinked water out of her eyes, felt a strong arm flip her onto her back, but then she was under water again, being sucked back into the cold abyss by the weight of her skirts. A strong arm pulled her up again, blessed air filled her lungs, and then, to her confusion, she heard what sounded like a rip. Her body immediately felt lighter just as realization set in.

"Did you just rip off my gown?" she sputtered after she spit out a mouthful of water.

"Thank God, you're alive."

She turned her head and met Henry's gaze as remorse set in.

"I'm so sorry," she whispered.

Henry smiled. "You should be—you just took ten years off my life, but you're not all to blame. I shouldn't have been so easily persuaded to help you with this madness. I knew full well that boat wasn't safe." He sobered and lifted a hand to push her hair out of her eyes. "I didn't know if I could dive fast enough to get to you. It was like someone had attached bricks to your feet."

"It was the bustle."

"Maybe we shouldn't let your mother know what happened."

Charlotte grinned. It was so like Henry to think about something like that when they were still on the edge of peril. He'd always protected her from blame, always accepted any punishment their antics caused.

He was the best friend a woman could ask for, and . . . he'd just saved her life. Suddenly, a voice coming from somewhere above her head interrupted her thoughts.

"Bring the boat around. I can get them from this side."

Before Charlotte could see who was coming to their rescue, Henry's arm was around her middle and he gave her a shove. As she rose up out of the bay, she felt her arm being clasped in someone's grip. That someone pulled her over the edge of the boat, and she fell hard to the deck, coughing up more water as she did so.

"Piper, get me a blanket."

Charlotte was flat on her back, staring up at the sky, and for some reason, she didn't seem capable of moving just yet. A shadow passed over her, and then the face of an imp appeared as small fingers reached out and poked her . . . hard.

"Are you dead?"

Charlotte opened her mouth, turned her head, and then stumbled to her knees as she crawled to the edge and let what appeared to be half the Hudson River escape her mouth.

A hand rubbed her back, and she closed her eyes for a moment, enjoying the feel of it, before she turned her head, knowing she'd find Henry by her side.

"Better?" he asked.

"I don't think I'm ever going boating again."

He laughed, continuing to rub her back as he turned and nodded at someone behind them. The next second, she felt a blanket settling over her shoulders, and Henry's arm soon followed.

There was something comforting about having a gentleman's arm draped over one's person. It signified safety and strength, and Henry had certainly proven she could find both in his arms.

That thought was rather terrifying.

He was her friend, her best friend, and she needed to remember that.

He didn't see her in a romantic way, which had become clear during her debut season. Not once had he insinuated he wanted more than their one dance per evening. No, he never sought her out, seemingly content to spend his time with other women, escorting them onto the dance floor with annoying frequency. And then, right before he'd made the decision to leave, something had changed. She could remember the exact moment it had happened. He was standing in front of her, come to claim his one dance, or fulfill his one obligation, as it appeared he viewed it. She didn't remember doing anything besides letting out a small sigh of excitement, but he seemed to have had enough of his obligation and had suddenly turned cold.

He'd left town shortly after that ill-fated ball, and she'd tried to forget that she'd longed for more with him. She'd even been somewhat successful in that regard.

Until now.

How was a lady supposed to ignore the fact that she truly cared for a gentleman—a gentleman who'd just rescued her from certain death—when all she really wanted to do was hurl herself into his arms and let him comfort her forever?

She needed to remember that she'd turned this matter over to God, and that He'd sent her Hamilton.

If she needed confirmation regarding that little matter, the next second provided it.

"Are you all right, Mr. St. James?"

Her eyes widened as she looked past Henry.

It appeared that Mr. Hamilton Beckett had come to her rescue as well. Why did her introduction to Hamilton have to come when she was leaning over the side of his boat and dressed in nothing more than her chemise and petticoats?

She suddenly longed to be back in her boat, the boat that had a large hole right in the middle of it, so she could disappear through it and not have to face the man who was going to be her husband.

"I'm fine, Mr. Beckett, thank you for asking," Henry said. "I don't know if you've ever met one of my dearest friends. This is Miss Charlotte Wilson. Charlotte, this is Mr. Hamilton Beckett."

Charlotte's heart gave an odd lurch. She hadn't been mistaken regarding Henry's feelings for her.

He did see her as only his dearest friend, not his dearest friend whom he wanted to spend the rest of his life with. Why else would he be calmly introducing her to the man he knew she'd decided to marry?

She summoned up a smile, clutched the blanket tighter around her shoulders, rose to her feet, and slowly turned, thankful when Henry reached out to steady her. Her legs felt wobbly, and she wasn't certain her wobbliness had been caused by her brush with death.

No, it most likely had been caused by her realization that she was still a little bit in love with Henry, and yet, he wasn't in love with her.

"Thank you so much for rescuing us, Mr. Beckett," she finally said. "I'm afraid Mr. St. James and I would have suffered a cruel fate if you hadn't come to our aid."

"I'm afraid your boat came to a sad demise."

Charlotte turned her head and found there was another gentleman on board, a gentleman she recognized as Hamilton's brother. She smiled. "Now I'll have to find another use for the tub of tar I still have, seeing as how I have no boat left to patch."

"And isn't that a scary thought?" Henry muttered before he grinned. "Charlotte, this is Mr. Zayne Beckett. We went to school together."

"It's a pleasure to meet you, Mr. Beckett. Whom may I thank for hoisting me out of the bay?"

"I'll take the credit for that," Zayne said before he moved closer and took her hand in his, bringing it up to his lips in a practiced move before dropping it.

The thought came to her that Hamilton had not taken her hand to his lips; in fact, he'd been perfectly pleasant but hardly what anyone would call enthusiastic regarding his introduction to her.

Maybe he wasn't meant to be hers after all.

Maybe she'd been mistaken.

And maybe she was trying to convince herself he wasn't interested because she really wanted Henry to be interested in her. But that wasn't going to happen, so she needed to remember and stick to her plan.

"Are these your children, Mr. Beckett?" she asked Hamilton before smiling down at the girl who had poked her and an angelic-looking boy who, for some reason, was making chomping noises as he glared at her.

"They are my children, Miss Wilson. May I present Miss Piper Beckett and Master Benjamin Beckett who . . ." Hamilton's voice trailed off as he narrowed his eyes, his gaze settling

342

on his son. "Don't even think about it, Ben," he said before he turned to her and sent her a smile.

He had a lovely smile. It was unfortunate it didn't seem to affect her at all. It certainly didn't give her goose bumps like Henry's smile did.

No, she wasn't going to dwell on that. She'd been so good throughout the past two years at keeping her mind away from Henry. Well, except when she wrote to him, but ever since he'd returned, she kept finding her feelings for him bubbling to the surface when she'd been sure those feelings had diminished with time.

She blinked when she realized Hamilton was speaking to her again. "We've been having a slight problem with Ben biting recently. For some reason, he bites people at random, and I'm at the end of my rope trying to deal with the matter. Would you have any suggestions, Miss Wilson?"

Charlotte looked at the little angel glaring up at her and smiled. "I used to bite when I was younger, and I think I was finally cured when Mr. St. James bit me back."

It didn't seem as if young Ben appreciated that advice because his glare turned fierce, and before she had a chance to move, his mouth was attached to her arm and his sharp little teeth sunk in.

"Just because I bit her doesn't mean you're allowed to bite her," Henry said as he pried the little darling off of her and handed him to Zayne, who took the child and walked him to the front of the boat.

Charlotte rubbed the spot where a welt was already sprouting and couldn't help but think that maybe her mother was right.

Perhaps she really wasn't good with children, which would

mean she certainly shouldn't be entertaining the thought of pursuing Mr. Beckett, especially since he came with two children who were clearly a recipe for disaster.

"Miss Wilson, I'm so sorry," Hamilton said as he lurched over to her side, the boat tilting after a strong gust of wind that seemed to come out of nowhere. "I can't imagine what you must think of my children. First, Piper pokes you to see if you're alive, and then Ben bites you."

"Not to worry, Mr. Beckett," she said, forcing a smile. "I'm sure they're just going through a rough time of it at the moment." She lowered her voice. "Losing a mother couldn't have been easy on them."

Something formidable entered Hamilton's eyes, and Charlotte realized that the subject of his deceased wife was not one he liked to discuss. She hurried to make amends. "Do forgive me, Mr. Beckett. I spoke without thinking. Perhaps it would be best to change the subject. Have you heard that there's a new theater production opening tomorrow night?"

"I rarely attend the theater."

Charlotte wasn't certain, but she thought she heard Henry laugh. She sent him a frown and returned her attention to the charming, yet seemingly difficult, Mr. Beckett. "There is also a benefit dinner tomorrow night in support of the suffrage movement. I'm certain your mother will be there. Do you have plans to attend it with her?"

"I'm afraid my evening has already been committed to attending the Watsons' dinner party," Hamilton said.

"I'm good friends with Miss Agatha Watson," Charlotte said, feeling a thread of relief run over her because she'd discovered a common interest. "Are you well acquainted with Miss Watson?"

"My mother has made certain I'm acquainted with most of the unmarried women in New York City. She seems to be under the misapprehension I'm in desperate need of a wife."

Honestly, what could she possibly say to that?

"And yet, you've never met Miss Wilson," Henry said, surprising her when he sent her a grin.

What was he up to now?

Hamilton turned his gaze on her, and while he did have lovely eyes, his gaze lacked the warmth Henry always directed at her. She swallowed a sigh of disappointment as the realization hit her that Hamilton just might not be the gentleman for her.

She was back to square one.

Maybe she was destined to be an old maid forever, but if that was the case . . . hmm . . . maybe she could devote herself to her tinkering, and then she could become known as the dear, dotty old maid who'd turned peculiar.

She bit back a snort.

That was hardly an appealing idea.

"I'm afraid I don't travel in society all that often," Hamilton said, "but I'm certain I would have requested an introduction if Miss Wilson's path and mine had crossed. Now, if you'll excuse me, I need to readjust the sail so we can get the two of you back to shore. I'm sure you're chilled, Miss Wilson, and I would hate to see you catch a cold."

As Hamilton turned and walked away, Charlotte wasn't certain, but she thought she detected stiffening in Henry's stance, which was odd, considering the boat was currently pitching back and forth, and stiffening had to be difficult to pull off under these particular circumstances.

What had Hamilton said to cause Henry's reaction?

Was it because he'd stated he would have requested an introduction or . . . was it because he'd suddenly turned charming?

Maybe Henry was jealous.

Maybe he didn't want her to pursue Hamilton.

"Are you two getting married?"

Charlotte looked down and found Piper staring up at her, her head tilted to the side, curly wisps of hair straggling around her beautiful face.

The girl's beauty reminded her that Hamilton's wife had been absolutely lovely. She swallowed a sigh, remembering that she was hardly showing to advantage at the moment. She was missing a dress, her hair had lost the majority of its pins, and, for some odd reason, her skin was tinged with blue.

Perhaps she was suffering from overexposure.

She would have to visit her doctor yet again and endure his countless questions and dire predictions that she was headed toward an early demise.

She'd heard the good doctor's predictions more than once over the years, and each time she went to see him, he always seemed surprised by the fact she was still among the living.

"Well, are you?"

She'd forgotten Piper was questioning her. Before she could formulate a suitable response, Henry spoke up.

"Miss Wilson and I are simply friends."

Hearing the words come out of his mouth caused her stomach to drop.

He really didn't see her in a romantic way.

"Then why does Miss Wilson get that sappy look in her eyes when you talk to her?"

She should invent a muzzle for children. Yes, that would be a most excellent invention, except for the part where parents would most likely balk at muzzling their little darlings. Still, it might have merit, especially for children like the too-observant child watching her so intently at the moment.

"I've never had a sappy expression on my face in my entire life," she managed to say.

"Well, not now, now you just look mad," Piper said before she spun on her little heel, turning after she'd taken only a few steps. "Don't think about marrying my daddy. Ben and I don't want another mother, and Daddy doesn't have time for girls anyways."

Charlotte decided right then and there it was time to abandon her plan in regard to Mr. Hamilton Beckett. Clearly the gentleman had plenty of other issues to deal with, and two of those issues certainly didn't seem to care for her.

Being a spinster for life was looking more appealing by the minute.

Charlotte sent Piper a nod, watching as the child sent her a glare in return. The girl spun around again and made her way to Hamilton's side.

"She's very old for her age," Henry remarked as he reached up and readjusted the blanket around her shoulders.

"I'm not sure that's a good thing," Charlotte muttered.

"What's wrong with your hands?" Henry asked, taking them into his and turning them over. "They're blue. You should have told me you're freezing."

"But I'm not," Charlotte said. "I have no idea why my hands have turned blue."

Henry looked at her for a moment and then pulled part of the blanket away from her.

"What are you doing?" she grouched. "In case you've forgotten, I'm not exactly properly dressed."

"I didn't know you knew how to blush," he said before he closed her back into the blanket and grinned. "Your neck's blue too, which leads me to believe the dye must have leaked out of your dress."

"I paid a fortune for that dress."

"Maybe next time you should have me go with you to the stores," Henry said. "You know I have a better eye for fabric."

Charlotte smiled and then sobered. "I'm sorry I talked you into taking out that boat."

Henry blew out a breath. "It's not your fault. I'm the one who captains a large freighter every day. I should have looked the boat over more carefully and realized it was unfit to sail."

He was always willing to take responsibility for everything she conned him into doing.

Why did he allow her to do that?

He was a strong-willed gentleman, and yet, with her, he gave in frequently, even when he knew there might be dire consequences.

He gave in because he knew she'd go forward with whatever plan she had in mind if he refused.

He obviously cared for her, but in a strictly platonic way.

"I'll be right back," Henry said, breaking into her thoughts. "I'm going to see if Mr. and Mr. Beckett could use some assistance. The wind's kicking up, and these sails can be tricky."

Charlotte watched as Henry moved across the sailboat, his feet steady and his gait rolling with the motion of the boat. She sometimes forgot he had lived the past two years of his life on the sea, but now, watching him, she realized he was at home on the water. At home as if he'd finally discovered where and what his life was meant to be.

A spray of water prompted her to move away from the edge,

and she looked up just in time to see the boom heading straight toward her.

"Charlotte, get down," Henry yelled.

Charlotte tried to drop, but the blanket got stuck on the railing, and before she could get a single sound out of her mouth, the boom made contact. She went flying through the air, but before she plunged overboard a second time, a strong arm grabbed her and pulled her to safety.

4

He needed to let Charlotte go.

As Henry rode in his carriage the next evening, on his way to meet Charlotte for the Watsons' dinner party, he thought about how she'd almost died twice yesterday. If he counted her fall from the buggy, it was three times in less than a week.

He'd been careless with her, careless with the one woman who mattered more to him than anyone else in the entire world because he lacked the ability to say no to her.

She deserved better; she deserved more. She needed a man who could balance her impetuous nature, and clearly he was not the gentleman for that particular job.

It had taken every ounce of strength he possessed not to grab her out of Hamilton's arms yesterday when that gentleman snagged her out of thin air and saved her from another trip into the bay. He should have been the one to rescue her, but he'd been distracted with the ropes and didn't realize Charlotte was once again in harm's way. The only thing that kept him from inserting himself between Hamilton and Charlotte was the knowledge that he obviously was not worthy of her. She deserved the opportunity to become better acquainted with Hamilton, a gentleman who had proven himself capable of keeping Charlotte safe.

He had to let her go, but first he would help her—help her in her quest to secure Hamilton. He would wait until she succeeded, and then he would leave.

He'd already informed his parents of his plan, told them he was anxious to get back on the seas and face the next order of business.

His mother hadn't believed him.

She'd arched a brow and questioned what part Charlotte played in his decision to leave so soon after he'd arrived in New York.

His mother had always been annoyingly observant, but, to give her credit, she hadn't pressed him when he relinquished relatively few details regarding Charlotte and his feelings for her. Instead, and much to his confusion, she had offered to secure him and Charlotte invitations to the Watsons' dinner party.

She was up to something, something he didn't really want to contemplate, but Hamilton would be attending the Watsons' party, so he'd agreed.

She'd gotten him the coveted invitations, told him Mrs. Watson was only too happy to extend him one. She'd also added that she'd tried to convince Mrs. Watson to place Charlotte next to Mr. Beckett, but unfortunately, Mrs. Watson seemed to have plans for Hamilton—something to do with her daughter, Agatha. For a brief moment, hope had blossomed until reality returned. He remembered his vow, and he realized obtaining Hamilton for Charlotte might be a bit trickier than he'd imagined.

Not that Henry believed Hamilton wasn't interested in

Charlotte. There had been a very male gleam in that gentleman's eye when they'd sat huddled on the deck and he'd held Charlotte close to him. Held her closer than was strictly necessary, if truth be told.

He'd felt the oddest urge to toss the bounder straight into the bay.

That would have handled the little problem sufficiently.

He'd almost done it too, until he'd looked down and found Piper watching him. There'd been something strange in the little girl's eyes, something that had appeared almost like . . . pity.

He'd been certain he was mistaken until Piper looked from him, to Charlotte, to Hamilton, and then back to him before rolling her eyes and walking off to join her brother.

It was odd to have a child roll her eyes at him.

It was odder to be the object of pity. Even his mother had seemed a bit pitying when she'd actually ruffled his hair and presented him with the invitations.

He couldn't dwell on it.

If pity was what it took to give Charlotte what she wanted, then pity he'd simply have to learn to live with.

He was going to do what was right.

He was going to get Mr. Hamilton Beckett for Charlotte.

Unfortunately, Charlotte didn't seem to be cooperating with his plan at the moment.

He'd been certain she'd be thrilled when he handed her an invitation to the Watsons' dinner party yesterday, but she'd barely glanced at it before sending him a glare.

Not understanding why she was put out with him, he'd offered to take her shopping, but even shopping hadn't improved her mood. When she'd tried on a lovely gown that would have been perfect for the dinner party, and he acknowledged that thought out loud, she'd spun on her heel, marched back to the dressing room, and, five minutes later, stalked out of the store without purchasing a single item.

It was completely out of character for her.

He was somewhat surprised that she'd allowed him to escort her tonight, seeing as everything he'd done since the boating incident seemed to annoy her.

He felt the carriage roll to a stop, and a moment later the door opened. He stepped out, taking a deep breath as he regarded Charlotte's house.

Honestly, she had nothing to be annoyed about at the moment. She was well on her way to obtaining what she'd claimed she wanted, whereas he—well, he was more disheartened and disappointed than he'd ever been in his life.

He shook off the maudlin thoughts, summoned up a smile, and strode up the walk, his smile widening when Mr. Lewis met him at the door.

"Good evening, Mr. St. James," Mr. Lewis said. "I see you survived your day of boating yesterday."

"We lost the boat."

"Good riddance, I say," Mr. Lewis said with a nod. "Miss Wilson was fortunate to have you with her. I hate to think what might have happened if she'd been by herself." He shuddered. "You know that would have occurred if you hadn't agreed to go with her."

"I shouldn't have agreed to go with her, and I should have destroyed the boat so she couldn't take it out."

"Now, sir, that isn't the way to look at the situation. Life is meant to be explored, and someone of Miss Wilson's caliber will always want to explore it to the fullest. She's lucky to have someone like you who won't stifle her spirit but allow it to fly."

353

For a moment, just a moment, his resolve faltered.

Mr. Lewis presented a compelling argument.

Charlotte was a free spirit, had always longed to fly.

Was he doing her a disservice by pushing her toward a gentleman simply because said gentleman would be a safer choice for her?

No, he couldn't allow his thoughts to travel in that direction.

She'd chosen Hamilton.

She'd never chosen him.

He needed to accept that.

"Ah, Henry, you're here. I was beginning to worry."

Henry stepped over the threshold and was surprised when Mrs. Wilson pulled him into a hug. She rarely hugged him.

She stepped back and smiled. "It's lovely that you've offered to take Charlotte to the Watsons' this evening. I do so wish I could attend the dinner, but . . . Mr. Wilson and I have other plans, so I declined our invitation two weeks ago. It never occurred to me that Charlotte would want to go, but then, two weeks ago I didn't know about her ridiculous plan to get closer to Mr. Beckett. I'm perfectly aware of the fact he'll be in attendance tonight because Cora Watson has made it known that she would find him all too acceptable for her daughter, Agatha."

"I've recently heard the exact same thing."

Mrs. Wilson smiled. "Yes, well, no matter. You and I don't need to concern ourselves with Mr. Beckett or Miss Agatha Watson. What we need to concern ourselves with is Charlotte. What do you plan to do with her?"

"I beg your pardon?"

"As you should, since it appears to me you've given up on her, which is completely ridiculous. The two of you are kindred spirits."

"I don't mean to disappoint you, Mrs. Wilson, because you know I hold you in only the highest esteem, but even though Charlotte and I are more alike than I care to admit, I've come to the conclusion I'm not good for her."

"Nonsense, you're exactly what she needs."

He'd been right; Mrs. Wilson was his greatest ally, but . . . he needed to resist her tempting words.

"Charlotte doesn't seem to really care for me at the moment."

Mrs. Wilson let out a sigh. "She's been distinctly annoyed with you ever since you returned her from that fiasco on the lake. At first I thought she was simply suffering the effects of taking in too much water, but after she got back from shopping, she took to roaming around the house, muttering under her breath, and I must admit, I've heard your name muttered more than once."

Before Henry had an opportunity to respond to that, the sound of someone stomping down the stairs caused him to turn around.

He couldn't hold back the snort that escaped through his nose.

Honestly, what was she up to now?

She was dressed in what appeared to be a gown, but the skirt of the gown was slim and . . . it seemed to be divided in two.

Good grief, she was wearing her bicycle outfit.

What would possess her to do such a thing?

She would cause a scandal.

She would ruin her good name.

"Lovely, you're exactly on time," Charlotte said as she stalked closer to him, her color high and her eyes blazing.

Right then and there, something snapped.

He folded his arms over his chest, tilted his head and then

shook it. "We're not going anywhere until you change out of that completely inappropriate frock."

If anything, Charlotte's eyes blazed hotter.

"I like this frock. It's different, and since I've been considering trying to encourage other ladies to purchase one for themselves, I've decided that tonight will be the perfect opportunity for me to solicit interest in the design." She smiled. "My friend Penny, the lady who stitched this together, thinks it's a wonderful idea."

"Well, Penny, whoever she may be, doesn't have to be seen with you tonight. I do, so you will march right back upstairs and change," Henry said.

"Forgive me, but I'm pressed for time," Mrs. Wilson said before she turned and practically bolted down the hallway, her shoulders suspiciously shaking.

Mrs. Wilson had obviously lost her mind, much like her daughter.

Henry waited until Mrs. Wilson disappeared and then switched his attention back to Charlotte. "If you're not ready within the next ten minutes, I won't escort you."

Charlotte crossed her arms over her chest much in the same manner he'd crossed his and smiled a smile that was less than amused. "I'll go by myself."

This was what always got them into trouble. She'd turn stubborn and he'd give in. He couldn't let her go by herself. She would attract entirely too much attention dressed as she was, and when Charlotte attracted attention . . . disaster normally followed.

How she'd survived during the two years he'd been gone was beyond him.

"Don't push me tonight, Charlotte," he said. "I'm in a foul mood."

"Then you should be pleased you don't have to escort me to the Watsons'," Charlotte said. "You can go home and do whatever it is you do when you're not with me."

"I relax when I'm not with you," he said between gritted teeth.

"Then go relax."

It suddenly occurred to him that she was furious about something. He had no idea what that something was, but her attitude was so out of character that he found his temper fizzling away and replaced with concern.

"Did your mother tell you that Mrs. Watson invited Mr. Beckett because she's hopeful of an alliance?" he asked.

"What?"

"Well, that's what I've heard, and I thought maybe you're out of sorts because you're acquainted with Miss Agatha Watson and don't want to compete with her over the same gentleman."

Charlotte let out a grunt that sounded a bit disgusted, turned around, and stalked away from him, swiveling her head when she reached the steps. "I'll be back. I'm going to change."

He watched as she stomped up the steps and then smiled when her heavy footsteps sounded through the ceiling as she traveled the length of the hallway.

He'd forgotten how adorable she could be when she was in a snit.

"Is she changing?"

Henry jumped and turned to find Mrs. Wilson right beside him. "She is changing," he finally admitted.

Mrs. Wilson looked absolutely delighted. "You do realize this is probably the first time she's ever not gotten her way with you. I think your plan is working."

"Mrs. Wilson . . . I don't have a plan."

Mrs. Wilson rolled her eyes and then grinned as she waltzed away. "Keep at it, my dear, you'll rule the night in the end."

He'd been right; Mrs. Wilson really *had* lost her mind.

He took a few minutes to wander around the hallway, unable to help but wonder if Charlotte was actually changing or if she was up to another one of her dastardly plans. He was just about to ring for a maid to check on her when the sound of someone descending the steps met his ears. He looked up and felt his mouth drop open once again. Charlotte had changed, much to his amazement, into the lovely gown he'd picked out for her the day before, the one she'd left behind.

"You went back to the store," he managed to say.

Charlotte shrugged. "It would have been churlish of me not to go back. I'd forgotten what impeccable taste you possess, and I absolutely adore this gown."

Henry forced his feet to move and he stepped closer to her, having the insane urge to pull her into his arms and never let her go. Resisting that urge was torture for him. Instead, he allowed his hand to move up and tuck a stray curl behind her ear. "You look wonderful. I'm sure you're going to sweep Mr. Beckett right off his feet."

Her grin disappeared. "I wish you wouldn't say that. It makes me . . . nervous."

For some reason, he knew that "nervous" wasn't what she'd been about to say, but he didn't let himself dwell on it. "You have no reason to be nervous. You'll be the most beautiful woman in attendance tonight."

Charlotte released a snort. "I'm hardly beautiful, Henry. You and I both know that, and Mr. Beckett's first wife was stunning. I can't compare to her, and I've decided I don't want to compare to her. Mr. Beckett is far from my reach, and I realize that now."

Her words caused annoyance to flash through him. "Hamilton Beckett would be lucky to receive your affections. You've always been reluctant to accept that you're a beautiful woman, something I've never understood. Do you not recall how your attention was demanded from numerous gentlemen every single time I escorted you to a society event?"

Charlotte's eyes began to shoot sparks. "Yes, I'm so sought after that I suppose I've neglected to remember all of the numerous proposals I've had to turn down from eager suitors."

Her words brought him up short. Why hadn't she elicited offers of marriage? He remembered all too well the fact that she *had* been most sought after. Before he could think about that further, she took his arm and began pushing him towards the door.

"We're running behind schedule," she said.

He blinked. There was a definite edge to her tone, as if he'd done something yet again to annoy her, but really, all he'd done was tell her she looked beautiful, and what woman would take issue with that?

"Enjoy your evening, Mr. St. James, Miss Wilson," Mr. Lewis said as he opened the door and ushered them through it.

Henry helped Charlotte into the carriage and then followed, tapping on the roof to let his driver know they were ready to proceed. Silence settled over them as the carriage began to move, and he couldn't seem to keep his gaze from Charlotte's face.

What was she thinking?

Why was she so disgruntled?

He didn't like seeing her disgruntled. He liked seeing her laughing and joking and driving him to distraction.

"I'm sorry I've been rude," she suddenly said.

He smiled. Charlotte had never been a lady who could remain

silent long. "Do you want to tell me what's gotten you in such an evil temper?"

"Do you want to tell me why you claimed to be in a foul mood?"

This conversation was certain to turn dangerous.

He had no intention of admitting to her his mood had been foul ever since he'd come to the conclusion she was not meant to be his.

He shifted on the seat and felt the small box that had been his constant companion ever since he'd returned home press against his leg.

He should have left the ring at home.

He never should have purchased it in the first place, but the gypsy woman who'd been hawking her wares had shown it to him, cautioning him against buying it. She told him the ring had been the possession of a daring princess who'd fought convention a hundred years before and taken flight to marry, not a prince, but a commoner with whom she'd fallen in love and didn't want to live without. The gypsy said the ring should only go to a woman who was wild and free and wouldn't conform to society dictates, and he'd known that such a ring was destined for Charlotte. She was the love of his life and the untamed spirit he wanted to have by his side forever.

Why he'd been lugging the ring around with him every time he'd been with Charlotte, he really couldn't say, especially since he'd decided to leave her to Hamilton and go his own way.

"What is the matter?"

He blinked out of his thoughts, stuck his hand in his pocket to readjust the box to a more comfortable position, and then froze when he noticed her gaze on his movements.

"What is that?"

For a second, just a second, he considered pulling out the

ring and presenting it to her. Sanity returned as he retrieved his empty hand and shrugged. "It's nothing."

"Oh," Charlotte said, "I thought it might be something you picked up on your travels, something unusual."

The ring was unusual all right. It would suit her perfectly.

Maybe he should just give it to her, not as an engagement ring, but as a ring to remind her of their friendship after he'd gone.

His fingers twitched as he moved them toward his pocket, but then stilled when she looked out the window and back at him.

"We're here."

Mr. Hamilton Beckett would certainly find it hard to resist Charlotte as she looked now, absolutely beautiful even with the slight trace of sadness in her eyes. Knowing that tonight would have her firmly out of his life, Henry sent her a smile and waited while the carriage rolled to a stop. He moved to the door, stepped to the ground, and turned to offer her his hand.

As they moved into the Watsons' house, the thought came to him that he hadn't bothered to inquire about the sadness lingering in her eyes.

5

Henry was an idiot.

There was absolutely no other way to describe him at the moment.

Charlotte exchanged the expected pleasantries with Mr. and Mrs. Watson at the door, absently noticed that Mrs. Watson seemed more rattled than usual. She had no time to dwell on that, however, because Mrs. Watson practically shoved her aside as her expression turned crafty and she set her sights on Henry.

"Mr. St. James, you have no idea how wonderful it is for me to see you," Mrs. Watson gushed. "I was thrilled—thrilled I tell you—to speak with your mother and learn you wanted to come to my humble gathering. Why I . . ."

Charlotte tuned out the rest of Mrs. Watson's speech as her sadness turned to temper. She'd been furious when, after going home to change out of his wet clothing, Henry had arrived at her house yesterday only to present her with a coveted invitation to the Watsons' dinner party. She couldn't believe he was so oblivious to her true feelings. He obviously was, though, considering he'd been so thrilled to admit that he'd gotten them invited to the dinner so she could continue with her plans regarding Mr. Beckett.

Maybe he'd been so keen to come this evening not to help her with her plan, but because he'd heard that Agatha, a truly beautiful and delightful lady, was in the market for a husband.

Mrs. Watson was certainly doing her best to make him aware of that fact.

"And I do apologize, Mr. St. James, but . . ." Mrs. Watson's voice lowered to a mere whisper, "I'm afraid to admit that my darling Agatha is indisposed this evening and won't be in attendance."

Charlotte's temper went from simmering to seething when, for some odd reason, Henry sent her a wink, as if he thought she'd be completely delighted by the fact Miss Agatha Watson was indisposed.

Did he think that information would please her? That she'd relish the idea her friend was obviously suffering from some type of illness? That her competition was suddenly out of the running?

She lifted her chin and stalked away, shaking off Henry's arm when he caught up with her.

"What is wrong with you?" he asked.

Oh, there was a barrage of answers she'd love to throw at him, but her pride made her keep her words to herself.

"I'm going to check my hair," she said, spinning on her heel and striding away from him, only to release a frustrated huff when he captured her arm once again.

"Your hair looks lovely."

"Wonderful," she said between gritted teeth, "then I'll check my dress. I wouldn't want Mr. Beckett to see me looking anything other than my best."

Charlotte twisted her arm out of his grasp, ignored the confusion now evident in his eyes, and set her sights on the far side of the room, hoping she'd find somewhere to be alone with her thoughts if only for a brief moment. She chanced a glance over her shoulder, and her temper flared even hotter.

Henry was already surrounded by a group of young ladies who seemed to be attempting to outdo each other as they tried to capture his attention.

She narrowed her eyes and couldn't help but notice that he still seemed to have a tiny touch of confusion on his face.

Good. She was happy he was confused, because she certainly was and had been ever since he'd pulled her from a horrible death.

He'd called her "love." She'd heard him. Granted, she'd almost been unconscious, but he'd said the word, and, she thought, meant it too. But then . . . he'd gotten strange.

He hadn't even come to check on her welfare after she'd almost been knocked out of the boat again by that dreadful sail. He seemed perfectly content to let Mr. Beckett hover over her, and while Mr. Beckett was certainly a considerate and comforting gentleman, Charlotte hadn't wanted his comfort; she'd wanted Henry's.

She'd been so sure his feelings for her had changed, but apparently she'd been wrong.

She'd misread his shortness with her regarding her plan, his soothing of her when she'd first almost drowned, and . . . the times she'd caught his lingering gaze on her.

He'd refused to allow her to travel to the Watsons' dinner garbed in her bicycle gown.

She'd thought he'd refused because he was testing her because he'd decided he wanted to keep her safe, even if only her reputation. Now, well, it seemed the more likely explanation was because he really didn't care for her, wanted to pawn her off on Mr. Beckett, and truly had been concerned she would embarrass him.

And wouldn't that have put a damper on all the attention he was now receiving from entirely too many young ladies?

"Henry's not the idiot, you are," she muttered under her breath as she reached the retiring room, stepped inside, and swallowed a groan. The room was fit to bursting with beautiful young ladies, young ladies who turned as one and set their sights on her.

"Miss Wilson," a lady by the name of Miss Sprockett exclaimed, "we were just talking about that divine Mr. St. James you brought with you." Miss Sprockett advanced. "Tell me, darling, do the two of you have an understanding, or would it be permissible for some of us to seek out his company?"

She felt her hands ball into fists, forced a smile, unclenched her fingers, and gave an airy wave. "Mr. St. James and I are strictly friends, Miss Sprockett. By all means, seek him out."

If nothing else, her words caused the room to clear in a split second. Taking the peace and quiet as an opportunity to collect her thoughts, she moved to the mirror, stuck her tongue out at her reflection, and plopped down in a delicate chair sitting off to the side of the room.

She leaned her head back against the wall and closed her eyes, turning to God for answers.

"I think I might have misunderstood, Lord," she whispered. "Mr. Beckett, while a truly wonderful gentleman, is not for me, is he?"

She opened her eyes, blinked, and then grinned.

"Agatha, what are you doing here? I thought you were indisposed."

Miss Agatha Watson slipped out from behind a curtain and returned the grin. "I've developed spots."

Charlotte tilted her head even as her grin widened. "You're perfectly fine, as you very well know, and there is not one spot to be found on your lovely face."

"Hmm, I must have experienced a miracle then," Agatha muttered. "I swear I was covered in them just a few minutes ago."

"You were probably covered in guilt," Charlotte said. "So, what's the reasoning behind your refusal to attend your mother's dinner party?"

Agatha dropped down on the matching chair right next to Charlotte's and looked around before she lowered her voice. "I don't have much time to explain, but I wanted to check on Miss Sumner, the poor woman my mother forced to take my place." She cleared her throat. "You see, Mother has decided I'm well suited for Mr. Hamilton Beckett, and I just couldn't bear it, couldn't bear being paraded around yet again as if I'm some horse up for auction." She tilted her head. "I heard your prayer, heard you mention Mr. Beckett, and I must tell you, I don't think he's your match."

"I know . . . he's not."

"Why then, if you've come to this conclusion, do you look so glum?"

"The gentleman I really desire doesn't see me in the same light. At the moment, he's outside this room, flirting with other ladies. In fact, his flirting has probably increased, seeing as how a good ten ladies darted out of here the moment I admitted that Mr. St. James and I are nothing more than friends."

Agatha eyed her for a long minute and then nodded. "I've always believed that if you want to learn the true measure of a gentleman's feelings, you need to do something to attract his attention, engage his emotions if you will. For you, well, I think a bit of tit for tat is in order."

"I have no idea what you're talking about."

"He's flirting, so give him a taste of his own medicine. You know how to flirt; I've seen you do it. Pick out a few gentlemen, smile, and see what happens."

"I bet he won't even notice."

Charlotte blinked when Agatha suddenly jumped up from her chair and dashed behind the long curtain just as the door opened and two ladies walked in, both of them nodding to Charlotte as they eyed her somewhat warily.

"Were you talking to someone just now?" one of the ladies asked.

Charlotte summoned up a smile. "I have the horrible habit of speaking to myself."

That cleared the room in less than a minute.

"Good one," Agatha said, "but it reminded me that I have to go back upstairs. Would you do me a favor? If you see Miss Eliza Sumner, a strangely dressed lady with a wonderful English accent, tell her I'm really, really sorry, and I promise to make it up to her, would you?"

"Miss Sumner is the woman your mother made take your place?"

"Unfortunately, yes. She's Lily and Grace's governess, and I'm afraid she'll never forgive me for this, but I'm hopeful that her dinner companion will . . ."

As Agatha's voice trailed off, she smiled at Charlotte and abruptly changed the subject. "Getting back to your Mr. St. James, I seem to remember the two of you being together quite often, and I must say that you might be mistaken regarding his affections. What if the two of you have suffered a grave misunderstanding, and he actually cares as much about you as you do about him?"

Charlotte was about to argue, but the door began opening, which caused Agatha to close the curtains with a snap. When the lady who'd entered finally left, Charlotte opened the curtains only to find that Agatha had made her escape through the window.

Knowing she couldn't delay the inevitable, she left the retiring room and stood on the edge of the crowd for a moment as she tried to locate Henry.

He wasn't hard to find.

No, there he was, surrounded by the beauties of New York City, a brunette on one side and a raven-haired lovely on his other.

She'd always longed to be a raven-haired lovely.

Brushing that absurd thought away, she began walking toward him, but then remembered what Agatha had said about giving him tit for tat. She straightened her spine, pasted a smile on her lips, and moved to a group of gentlemen who, surprisingly enough, were watching her approach.

"Good evening, gentlemen," she said.

"Miss Wilson, so good to see you," a gentleman by the name of Mr. Murdock said.

"You're too kind, Mr. Murdock. How is that lovely sister of yours?"

"Felicia's well, thank you for asking. She's been spending her time at the church, helping Reverend Fraser see to the needy."

"How lovely, do give her my warmest regards," Charlotte purred, unable to help but grin when Mr. Murdock blinked and then moved ever so slowly closer to her. He was just reaching out his hand as if to take her by the arm, when a different hand suddenly took a firm hold on her. She found herself yanked away from the group of gentlemen before she could get a single squeak of protest out of her mouth. Henry pulled her rapidly beside him until she finally had the presence of mind to dig in her heels and come to a stop.

"What is the matter with you?" she hissed. "Those gentlemen must think you've taken leave of your senses."

"I thought your objective was to land Mr. Beckett, not every gentleman in New York," Henry hissed right back at her.

Oh . . . dear. He was furious.

It seemed to her as if he was overreacting just a tad too much, and why would he even care if she *was* flirting since he'd just brought Hamilton Beckett back into the conversation?

She needed some time to dwell on everything, and she certainly couldn't dwell to satisfaction with Henry glaring at her. She raised her chin. "I'm going to go and find my seat."

For some odd reason, Henry smiled even as he gestured with his head. "I've already located your place card. You're sitting at the very end of the table next to those older gentlemen."

Wonderful, she would not have to suffer his unpleasant mood throughout dinner. She directed her attention to where he was staring and laughed. The two gentlemen sitting at the table were well into their seventies, and she knew perfectly well that, although Mrs. Watson had been more than happy to extend an invitation to her dinner party, it was clear she was determined in her efforts to see Agatha married, deliberately relegating the competition to the furthest end of the room. The situation didn't bother Charlotte in the least. She enjoyed the company of older gentlemen, found them interesting and full of tales, and at least this way she'd be hard-pressed to get into any of the trouble she'd certainly get into if she sat next to Henry.

Maybe she should simply admit defeat and embrace the idea of remaining a spinster forever.

A spinster enjoyed freedom once she reached a certain age, although she could experience a different type of freedom if . . .

No, she was not going to think in that direction.

"Are you all right?"

She'd forgotten Henry was still standing by her side.

"I'm fine, but I really should take my seat."

"I hate to tell you this, Charlotte, but that older woman just snatched up your place card, and . . . she's heading this way."

Charlotte's temper disappeared as the woman in question stopped by her side and sent her a grin that had mischief written all over it.

"Forgive me, dear," the woman said. "I realize we've never met before, but I was hoping you would do me just the teensiest favor. I'm Mrs. Dickerson, and I've been told you're Miss Wilson, and you see, ah, one of your dinner companions, Mr. Wallace Perry, was once very dear to me. We were the best of friends, and I always believed we would eventually marry, but alas, that was not to be. We both found different spouses, but my John passed over five years ago and his Estelle passed two years ago, and I just thought that maybe . . . Well, we're not getting any younger, don't you know?"

"The two of you were friends in your youth?" Henry asked.

"The best of friends," Mrs. Dickerson said. "I think that's what caused all the confusion in the first place." She smiled a sad sort of smile. "I loved him, you see, but thought he didn't return my affections. His sister recently admitted to me that she'd always believed I'd been the love of his life."

Charlotte felt tears sting her eyes. The story sounded all too familiar. She blinked to keep the tears at bay and nodded. "Of course you may take my place, Mrs. Dickerson, and I wish you the best of luck. May I ask where your old seat is located?"

"Ah, but of course, my dear, forgive me for not addressing that sooner. I was placed next to a Mr. Jeffrey Murdock, and I must tell you," she said with a twinkle in her eye, "he was the one who pointed you out and told me who you were sitting beside, which, quite honestly, led me to believe the gentleman has an interest, if you get my meaning?"

Charlotte watched as Henry's expression went from relaxed to stormy, but before she could comment on it, Mrs. Dickerson suddenly thrust the place card into Charlotte's hand, muttered something about Mrs. Watson, and then bustled away from them as fast as her high-heeled shoes would allow.

Charlotte soon understood why Mrs. Dickerson had made such an abrupt departure when she turned her head and found Mrs. Watson glaring back at her.

"Miss Wilson, I'm shocked. What could have possibly possessed you to rearrange my seating chart?"

Although it was tempting to place the blame on Mrs. Dickerson, Charlotte had never been one to tattle, so she took a breath and was about to deliver what she hoped was a reasonable response when Henry suddenly stepped forward and interrupted her.

"It's my doing, Mrs. Watson, and I do hope you'll forgive me."

They were back to him coming to her rescue.

Enough was enough. She was officially relegating herself to spinsterhood because she certainly didn't understand men.

"But, Mr. St. James, I don't understand," Mrs. Watson said.

"Are you insinuating that you wanted to sit next to Miss Wilson? I was under the impression the two of you were just friends, but if that is not the case, by all means, let me help you . . ." her voice trailed off as a loud crash sounded from the other side of the room.

"Oh . . . no," Mrs. Watson muttered before she hurried away without another word, the subject of the seating chart apparently forgotten.

"What happened?" Charlotte asked.

"I don't know, I can't see from here," Henry said as he took her hand and pulled her forward.

She loved holding hands with him.

She decided to enjoy the moment, realizing that it would all too quickly come to an end, because she couldn't go on like this anymore. She had to resolve matters, and if resolving matters meant running away to the country, so be it. She wasn't ashamed to run, especially if it meant leaving her dignity intact. If she had to say goodbye to Henry face to face, well, she knew she'd dissolve into hysterics, not that she was normally a hysterical type of lady, but there it was.

"Can you see anything?" she asked to distract herself from her thoughts.

Henry pulled her up beside him and smiled. "I think Mr. Hamilton Beckett's in the midst of some new crisis."

Charlotte craned her neck to see past a tall gentleman. Sure enough, Hamilton was leaning over a . . . good heavens . . . Agatha really did owe their governess if the woman now being helped into a chair was Miss Eliza Sumner. She was wearing a dress of unthinkable puce, sporting large glasses that were perched on the very bottom of her nose, and . . . well wasn't this interesting?

Mr. Beckett was giving her his undivided attention and . . . he was laughing.

She'd never seen him laugh.

"Good heavens, I've been an idiot," she muttered. "Mr. Beckett was never meant for me. I'd bet my bicycle he's meant for that lady who Agatha told me is the governess."

Before she could utter another word, Henry took a firm hold of her arm and began propelling her forward, but not to her seat. He steered her through the dining room, down the hallway, and out the door leading to the patio. Instead of stopping, he continued forward, increasing his pace with every step.

She tried to ask where they were going, but Henry was now moving at almost a run, and it took all of her concentration to keep up with him, having no desire to be dragged at his side.

Her foot slid out of her shoe, but Henry didn't seem to notice the fact she was now hobbling along beside him. A sharp stone caused her to wince and open her mouth.

"My shoe," she managed to get out.

Henry came to an abrupt halt, causing her to run into him. "What did you say?"

"I lost my shoe. It's back there."

"Why didn't you say so? Honestly, Charlotte, you could have injured your foot."

Henry dropped her arm, strode to where her shoe rested on the walk, and then returned to her side, dropping down on one knee before grabbing her foot and shoving her shoe onto it.

It would have been almost romantic if he hadn't taken that moment to look up at her and scowl.

What could she have possibly done wrong now?

Henry rose to his feet, took her by the arm, and prodded her into moving by not giving her another choice. He pulled her past the parked carriages until they reached a lovely garden on the side of the house, but before she could admire it, he yanked her further down the path until he came to a stop in another garden, this one lit by hundreds of lanterns. Tears suddenly began to blind her.

It was the perfect rendezvous spot for people in love.

"I can't do this anymore," he declared.

Charlotte blinked. Maybe she and Henry had finally reached the point where they could read minds, because she'd recently been thinking the exact same thing.

"What do you mean?" she asked.

"I tried, I really did, but it's no use. I've withheld my true feelings from you for years, and I know you don't think of me as anything other than a friend, but that's too bad. Tonight showed me that I have to be honest. There I was, surrounded by some of the most beautiful women in New York, and do you know what I was thinking?"

"That they were beautiful?" Charlotte asked.

"No," Henry said with a roll of his eyes. "I was only thinking about you, wondering what mischief you were getting into and why it was taking you so long to check your appearance. I was just about to come after you when you waltzed out into the receiving room, and what did you do? Not come to find me, no, that's not what you did. You turned into a flirt and attracted the attention of every gentleman in your vicinity."

Confusion settled over her. "But . . . you were pushing me at Mr. Beckett."

"Because you'd gotten it into your head that God wanted you to marry the man, and who was I to argue with God?"

"If you didn't hear me a few minutes ago, I've decided Mr. Beckett isn't meant for me, he never was," Charlotte admitted.

Henry's expression turned rather fierce. "Have you set your sights on someone new? Has God sent you a direct telegram filled with ideas for another plan?"

"Well, no, not a telegram, but maybe you should continue on with what you were saying," Charlotte said as the most delicious idea came to her, but she didn't want to get her hopes up until Henry finished what he had to say.

Henry looked at her for a long moment and then cleared his throat. "We've been friends for a long time, Charlotte."

Oh, dear, it was not going to be what she wanted to hear. She forced the disappointment away and lifted her chin. "You've been my best friend since I was four."

Henry muttered something under his breath and then reached out to tip her chin even higher as he caught her gaze. "I want to be more than your friend."

Right there and then, Charlotte's knees turned wobbly. "But . . . you left me, left me for almost two years."

"Self-preservation," Henry said with a nod. "I couldn't stand watching you flit from one gentleman to another or dance with partners more than once when you only reserved a single dance per evening with me."

"Because you never let me believe you cared for more," Charlotte said, unable to help the temper that was suddenly rushing through her veins. "Why didn't you ask me for more?"

"Because I didn't know you wanted more. I thought you saw me as only your friend."

"That's what I thought you saw me as, only a friend," Charlotte replied. "How could you have been so dim?"

"I was dim? What about you? You never once gave me reason to believe you saw me as something more, and then . . . there was the sigh."

Charlotte narrowed her eyes. "Are you talking about the sigh I released the very last time we danced together?"

"Of course, that's what caused me to leave. I couldn't continue on with being an obligation to you."

"You thought I sighed because I didn't care to dance with you?"

"Didn't you?"

It was fortunate she loved him because he really was an idiot.

"I sighed because I always looked forward to our dance every evening, and I was happy you'd finally come to claim it," she admitted.

"Oh."

She drew in a deep breath and slowly released it. It really appeared as if he hadn't known she'd cared about him. "Didn't you read my letters?"

Henry frowned. "Of course, numerous times, and quite frankly, I did think you sounded a bit melancholy and missed me, but then I returned to town, and the first thing you did was present me with your plan of winning over Mr. Beckett."

"You agreed to help me."

"Only because you forced me to help you, and only because I was afraid you'd get yourself into trouble if I wasn't around."

Lovely warmth spread over her. "You always have watched out for me."

Henry stared at her and then shook his head. "We're just like poor Mrs. Dickerson and her long-lost love."

Charlotte grinned. "Except that we haven't wasted quite as many years not admitting the truth to one another."

Henry moved closer to her, his gaze locked on hers. "I love you."

Her soul began to sing.

She drew in a deep breath, blinked to keep fresh tears at bay, and edged even closer to him. "I am so relieved to finally hear you say that because I love you too and will never love anyone else. I was seriously considering remaining a spinster forever if I couldn't have you."

"I don't think you'll have to worry about that any longer," Henry said before he shoved his hand into his pocket and pulled out a small box.

Charlotte could only watch in mute amazement as Henry dropped to one knee, opened the box, and extended it to her. "This ring, I've been told, belonged to a real princess. This princess was independent and a bit strong willed from the sound of things. The gypsy who sold it to me told me the ring could only go to a lady possessed of an adventurous spirit, and I can think of no other lady who is more worthy of accepting it than you, unless of course, you have no desire to marry me."

Charlotte blinked back another bout of tears, her eyes never leaving Henry's face. "Will you take me with you when you captain your boat?"

"I wouldn't consider leaving you behind. I know this might sound a little like a plea to accept my proposal, but I can show you worlds you've never imagined, and there are millions of adventures just waiting for us out there."

"I would marry you even if there were *no* adventures waiting for us because life by your side is the only adventure I need."

Henry was off his knee so quickly she barely had time to draw a breath. His ring slid over her finger and then his lips pressed against hers.

As she felt his love wash over her, she knew without a doubt that God had given her exactly what she'd requested.

He'd given her the gentleman of her dreams.

An Appalachian Blessings Novella

APPALACHIAN SERENADE

SARAH LOUDIN THOMAS

1

Delilah didn't mean to eavesdrop on her sister and brother-in-law, but when she heard her name, it was like being tugged by an invisible rope. She tiptoed down the hall.

" . . . still young enough to marry again. Why don't she find some fella to take her in?" That was Ed.

Charlotte's reply was soft. "She's not going to shack up with someone she just met, and anyway, I like having her here. Give her time. She'll find her way."

"I wouldn't mind so much if she could, you know, pay rent or some such."

"Ed Long, that's not very generous. She helps with the house-keeping and she's wonderful for Perla. A girl her age needs someone to confide in."

Delilah sighed, backed up, and closed the door to the bed-room she shared with fifteen-year-old Perla loudly enough for

381

everyone to hear. There really wasn't enough room in the little house for three adults and one teenage girl, but she hadn't had anywhere else to go when it became clear she couldn't make it on her own in Chicago. The war was ending, and men wanted their jobs back. Charlotte had talked Ed into letting her little sister join them back home in West Virginia. And now her presence was apparently causing marital discord.

Delilah marched into the room with a reasonable facsimile of a smile. "I thought I'd run the butter and eggs over to Thorntons'. Give you two a Saturday to yourselves. Maybe Perla could come with me?"

Perla came in the door with the morning's eggs and brightened. She rushed to her father's side, where he sat in an armchair, and leaned against his shoulder.

"Can I? Please?"

Ed's expression remained gruff. "I suppose so. Though I still think it's forward for your aunt to drive herself around. I suppose they do things different up there in the big city."

He shot Delilah a look that she took to mean she was a brazen woman. So be it. The family was fortunate that Ed's job as fireman for the railroad allowed them the luxury of an automobile. She'd driven fancier cars than his 1940 Plymouth, but she knew this wasn't the time to mention it. She also wasn't in the mood to remind anyone that her supposedly well-off husband had been up to his armpits in debt.

Charlotte headed for the kitchen, and Delilah followed as her sister packed three pounds of butter and five dozen eggs into a crate.

"I appreciate you making the butter-and-egg run," Charlotte said. "Every little bit helps."

"I'm glad to go. I suppose most everyone's heard I've come

home by now, and the sooner I show myself, the less they'll have to wonder about." She tucked a strand of dark hair behind her ear. "Plus, it makes me feel as though I'm contributing, since I don't have a job."

Charlotte squeezed her sister's arm and gave her a sorrowful look. Delilah hated it, but what could she do? Of course folks were going to think she was sad that her husband of fourteen years died of a massive heart attack. And she had no inclination to disabuse them of the notion. Never mind that he was . . . not what she thought when she was a foolish girl of nineteen.

Perla scampered into the kitchen with her blond curls tied back and white gloves covering her work-roughened hands. Delilah noted the gloves weren't quite as white as they could be. She pulled on her own gloves and made a mental note to show Perla how to use baking soda to whiten the fabric when they finished their errand.

Delilah slid the crate of butter and eggs into the back of the car as her niece climbed in. The soft June morning was lovely, inviting them to roll down the windows and drive slow. Delilah breathed in the scent of roses and admired the green countryside that seemed to sing to her very soul. Chicago had been exciting, but she'd missed these beautiful hills. And while the town of Wise wasn't much, she supposed she'd missed it, too. Although, goodness knows, she hadn't the least idea what she was going to do with herself around here.

They passed the schoolhouse, standing silent on this Saturday morning, then Laurel Mountain Church. Soon, they'd come to the post office and finally the store. She'd heard a filling station had been added just down the road.

"Aunt Delilah, do you think we could look at dress patterns?" Perla clasped her hands in her lap and sat up ramrod straight.

"Certainly. Is there something in particular you're looking for?"

"Oh, not really. I just . . ." Perla pinked. "I just like to imagine what I might wear . . . you know . . . one day."

Delilah smiled. She did know. It was good to dream. When she was only a little younger than Perla, her favorite Sunday school teacher had commented that Delilah would make a wonderful mother one day. She'd nurtured that dream ever since—picturing herself living in a house full of laughter and love. She glanced at her niece, so fresh and open to what life had in store. Yes, Perla should dream now, before she learned how rarely life lived up to dreams.

"We might even indulge in some peppermints or caramel creams, if they're not too expensive."

Perla smiled and leaned forward just a little, as though to hurry them to their destination. Even so, Delilah didn't drive any faster. She hadn't been to Thorntons' store since she was a teenager herself, and she wondered how people would react to her being back in town. Charlotte had explained that old man Thornton's son Robert took the store over when his father died in a hunting accident and his mother moved to South Carolina to live with her youngest son. Delilah had a vague memory of Robert, but he'd been older and she hadn't paid much attention.

She pulled up to the porch spanning the front of the store and cut the engine. Perla hopped out and scurried for the front door, but Delilah took her time, fetching out the crate of butter and eggs and looking around to take in any changes as she mounted the porch steps. Other than the shiny gas pumps just down the way, nothing much had changed since she'd been here more than a decade ago. Maybe that was a new Drink Coca-

Cola sign, and the saggy chair bottoms had been replaced, but other than that the store was much as she remembered.

Inside, Delilah squinted to help her eyes adjust from the morning sun to the dim interior. She could smell floor oil, cinnamon, and lumber. Now, that was definitely the same. She spotted Perla at a counter flipping through Butterick patterns. A man moved toward Delilah with his hands out. She wasn't certain how to react until she realized he was reaching for the crate she carried.

"Let me take that," he said in a deep baritone. "This must be from Charlotte, which would make you Charlotte's sister . . . " He turned and thumped the crate on a wooden counter, then snapped his fingers. "Delilah. I knew I'd remember. I remember the name of just about every customer who comes through that door." He took two giant steps to his right and whipped the lid off a candy jar. "And if I remember correctly, you had a fondness for caramel creams when you were a youngster." He offered Delilah a handful of candies.

She felt heat rise to her cheeks as she clasped her hands behind her back. "Oh, thank you, but I don't care for any."

The man, who Delilah realized must be Robert, winked and pushed his hand toward her. "C'mon, you know you want one."

Not certain what else to do, she plucked a candy from his hand. He grinned and rocked back on his heels. "So how you like being home again? Miss the big city?"

Delilah found it a bit disconcerting that it seemed everyone within a twenty-mile radius knew her business, but at least he wasn't offering condolences. Martin had been gone for almost six months now, and she was more than ready to move on without him.

"I'll confess I'm enjoying being back home. The city was exciting, but I missed these mountains and the smell of spring."

"Dad always said spring smelled like mud and manure, but when you run a store that caters to farmers, well, that's a good thing." Robert dumped the candies he held into his jacket pocket. "Anything in particular you need today?"

"Oh, no, not really." Delilah glanced toward Perla. "We'll just look around a bit."

She walked over to browse patterns with her niece, glancing at Robert out of the corner of her eye as she bent over the pattern book. He was greeting another customer who had just come in. Though a bit garrulous for her taste—she supposed that came with being a storekeeper—he was a handsome man. Realizing she still held the candy he'd given her, she popped it in her mouth. It tasted like childhood. Like the days when she still imagined anything was possible—a happy marriage, children, a long life filled with love and laughter.

"Why are you sighing?" Perla turned innocent blue eyes on Delilah.

"Was I sighing? I suppose I was thinking about what might have been." Delilah gave her niece a quick hug. "I always wanted a daughter just like you. Your mother is so fortunate."

"You could still have a daughter, couldn't you? If you married again?"

Delilah smiled and watched Robert ring up a sale with a flourish. "It's certainly possible. I guess I have a few years yet."

She didn't say it aloud, but she thought, *Though at thirty-four, I don't have a moment to spare.*

Robert wrapped the bit of ribbon Delilah Harding—no, it was Morrissey now—bought in brown paper and handed her the packet with his customary grin. But it took some effort.

He didn't want to smile and act the fool with the lovely woman standing across the counter. He wanted to say something . . . poetic. Instead he'd talked to her about mud and manure. And while it was more in keeping with what those who knew him would expect, he wished he could do better.

Delilah thanked him and walked out into the sunshine with her niece. The sun caught in her brown hair and shot it through with gold. If he could think such things, surely he could say them. But, of course, he wouldn't speak anyway. He'd given up any notion of wooing women a long time ago.

He'd heard Delilah's husband died a while back—hadn't thought much about it at the time. But seeing her now, seeing a graceful woman in place of the girl he remembered who seemed never to have grown into her feet, well, it gave a man ideas. He wondered how old she was. If she didn't have children after— what?—at least a decade of marriage, maybe she didn't want any. Well now, that would put things into a whole other category.

Robert whistled and began wiping down the counter and tidying the items displayed there. Yes indeedy, it might behoove him to find out a bit more about Delilah Harding Morrissey.

That evening Delilah washed the supper dishes while Charlotte dried and put them away. She tried to think of a subtle way to ask after Robert Thornton, but her sister saved her the trouble.

"Did you see that Robert has started carrying those Occident cake mixes? I can't believe anyone would resort to that. As if it is so very difficult to bake a cake."

"I didn't notice." Delilah wasn't interested in debating mixes over home cooking. "I did notice that not much has changed around the store over the past fifteen years. I would've thought Robert would want to put his own stamp on the place."

"Oh Robert." Charlotte flipped her hand in the air. "He's more interested in socializing and carrying on with everyone who steps foot through the door. Now that I think about it, I'm surprised it occurred to him to even carry a convenience food like cake mix. Maybe he's had more success with that instant coffee than folks let on."

Delilah wracked her brain to think how to steer this conversation in the direction she wanted it to go. "Maybe he needs a woman's touch." She blushed and hoped Charlotte would assume it was the heat from the dishwater. "In the store, I mean."

"Wouldn't hurt, but I know for a fact more than one woman has set her cap for him . . . and it's all come to nothing. We thought he'd marry Susanne Ross for sure, but something must have gone wrong. Last I heard she was married with four kids." She dried the last pot and draped her wet cloth over a hook beside the stove. "Gracious, Robert must be getting close to fifty by now. If no one's caught him yet, I doubt it'll happen." She wrapped an arm around her sister's waist. "Now, if it's eligible bachelors you're after, you might consider Joe Miller."

Delilah elbowed Charlotte. "I'm most certainly not interested in Joe Miller. His ears stick out past his shoulders."

Charlotte giggled and covered her mouth. Delilah risked a look at her sister and caught the giggles. They stood in the kitchen laughing like girls, and Delilah felt a bit of the pain of the past decade slide from her shoulders. Maybe she did have a future. Maybe she could find another husband—a good one—and start a family. Maybe it wasn't too late after all.

2

"Do you think there's any chance I could find a job around here?" Delilah helped her sister hang out the last of the sheets to waft in the afternoon breeze. She'd been with the family for nearly a month and was itching to do something with herself.

"A job? Why would you want a job?"

Delilah shrugged. "I'd like to be useful—to contribute to the household."

"But you do. It's so much easier—and more fun—to keep the house up when I have you to help. And Perla is really blossoming with you around. I've always thought teenage girls should have someone other than their mother to confide in."

"I do love helping around the house, and spending time with Perla makes me wish I'd been around for the first fifteen years of her life, but I still feel like I'm imposing." She picked up the empty laundry basket and braced it against her hip. "And anyway, I want to eventually have a place of my own. I can't live with you forever."

Charlotte cocked her head. "I was wondering about that but

389

hated to ask. Didn't Martin leave you with an insurance policy or something?"

Delilah tried not to clench her jaw. "He left me with little more than debt."

Charlotte ducked her head. "And memories. Surely he left you with wonderful memories."

Delilah turned and walked toward the house. "Oh, I have memories all right."

Robert hated days like this. Just when he got interested in a conversation with one customer another would vie for his attention. And before he could wait on that one, another would be tugging at his coat. He supposed it was good for business, but he didn't much enjoy it. He liked when he had time to visit with everyone who walked through the door. It was practically a community service, listening to the Talbot sisters spread gossip in the guise of neighborly concern. Or letting John Phillips drone on about his cattle. Or encouraging Frank Post to drink seven cups of coffee in a rare effort to sober up—he had hopes for that fellow yet.

But it was pretty much impossible on days like this. And days like this were becoming all too frequent. What he needed was an apprentice. Someone to stand behind the counter ringing up sales and fetching items while he did the real work of the community—listening to people and letting them know someone cared. He rang up another customer. It wasn't happening today.

He'd once harbored hopes for his nephew in South Carolina, but the boy had gone into banking, then married, and had shown no interest in his uncle's business. There were four nieces, as well, but three of them were married with families, and the youngest had become a companion for Robert's mother. They all had full lives and rarely even came to visit. No, he'd have to look elsewhere for help. He supposed what he really needed was to marry some widow with a son he could raise up like his own.

He sighed and turned his attention to Angie Talbot, who was drumming her fingers on the counter in front of him. "When will we be able to get sugar again without all this rationing business?"

"Oh, shouldn't be long now. The war is pretty much over and our boys are coming home. Sugar can't be far behind."

"Humph. Not that we have much use for sugar. Didn't have it when we were girls. Mama could do wonderful things with honey and molasses. But I've been craving a butterscotch pie and you have to have sugar to make a good meringue." She brushed imaginary dirt off the counter. "Well, fetch me some baking soda and we'll try again next week."

"Yes, ma'am." Robert wrapped the older lady's purchase and wished he had time to ask her if she used flour or cornstarch for thickening her pies. His mother always used flour, but he'd heard cornstarch made a glossier filling. Maybe another time.

A flash of color at the door caught Robert's eye. It was Delilah in a red dress that cinched in at her waist and made her look like a dew-fresh summer rose. He noticed her dark hair was caught up in a snood. He'd tried carrying those, but the local ladies seemed to think them too fancy. It looked exactly right on Delilah. He smiled and waved in welcome but couldn't go speak to her with three people wanting to be served. She moved toward the counter and stood as though waiting for him.

He nodded to Angie as she left and turned his attention to the next person in line. From the corner of his eye he saw Delilah fall into conversation with Maddie Potter. They talked and then moved over to the fabrics counter and began sifting through bolts of summer cotton. Maddie could be a challenge. She always knew exactly what she wanted but seemed incapable of communicating it to anyone else.

He finished with two customers and jumped when Maddie laid her hand on his arm. "Oh, Robert, Delilah has been most helpful. She knew just what it was I wanted. Would you cut me nine yards of that green flowered cotton? And three yards of the beige lace." She clapped her hands. "It's absolutely perfect."

Delilah stood clasping a small purse in front of herself. She shrugged at Robert's look. "It's what I would've chosen for myself."

"And that's what makes it so perfect—she understands." Maddie looked at Delilah as if she'd sprouted a halo and wings. "Thank you so much. Robert's a man. He just can't know." She drew out the word *know* and shook her head.

Robert had the notion Delilah was fighting a smile at his expense, but he chose to pretend he didn't notice. He was just glad she'd sorted out Maddie for him. He cut the fabric and rang up the purchase. There were a few other customers in the store, but they seemed content to browse. He let his shoulders slump and smiled at Delilah.

"You probably don't realize it, but figuring out what Maddie wants is something I've been trying to do for the past five years." He rubbed a hand over the back of his neck—tight as Angie Talbot's purse strings. "I don't suppose you'd want a job?"

Delilah's mouth dropped open and then she snapped it shut. Had he offended her? He had to learn to think before speaking. "Are you serious?" she asked.

"About what?" Robert looked into her velvety brown eyes and wished he'd been paying better attention. What was she asking?

"About a job? I came here to see if you knew of any jobs in the area."

"Oh, uh, yes." Had he been serious? Surely it wasn't proper for a woman not his wife to be working alongside him in the store. Or was it? He couldn't quite think why not.

"Well, I could use an extra pair of hands around here. Especially on days like this one. You know anything about running a store?"

"No, but I do know how to talk to people, and I've certainly spent plenty of time on this side of the counter." She made a graceful sweeping gesture and his eyes followed her hand the way a dog would watch a bit of steak.

"Well, I don't know as I can pay a whole lot, but if you're willing, maybe we could try it and see how it goes."

Delilah took a step forward and then pressed her purse against her stomach as though trying to restrain herself. "That would suit me just fine. When can I start?"

Robert eyed a family of seven walking through the front door. He glanced toward them and tilted his head that direction. "How about right now?"

When the store closed at six o'clock that evening, Delilah felt as tired as she had when she'd been a girl helping with the haying. But this kind of tired somehow felt more satisfying. She'd earned her keep. She'd worked hard and been a help to Robert. She'd had a job before—had lost a good job in Chicago when the soldiers started coming home—but this felt different. It wasn't only for her. It was for Robert and her sister and even Perla. And it felt good.

Robert flipped the sign on the front door to Closed and turned to smile at her. If he'd been wearing suspenders, she would have expected him to hook his thumbs under them.

"A fine day's work." He nodded and walked toward the counter. "We didn't discuss your pay."

He named an amount, and Delilah's first instinct was to say it was too much, but then again, why not take it? If Robert thought it was right, who was she to argue?

"That sounds more than fair, but you don't need to pay me every day. Why don't you pay me by the week?"

"All right, then." Robert stuck his hand out, and Delilah accepted a firm handshake. His large hand enveloped her smaller one and she was surprised by how warm it was. He held onto her hand for a tiny bit longer than he needed to and she could have sworn she saw something flare in his eyes—probably nothing.

"Can I drive you home?"

"Oh, I've got Ed's car." Delilah blanched. Ed. She'd only meant to be gone an hour or so, and she'd been gone all day.

"Everything all right?"

"Fine, fine, but I'd best be getting on home. They'll be wondering about me."

Robert opened his mouth and then closed it on another grin. He was the smilingest man she'd ever seen. "I'll be seeing you Monday?"

"You will, indeed," Delilah said brightly wondering how in the world she was going to hold down a job without a car of her own.

Ed didn't yell at Delilah or dress her down. He just glared at her and informed her she'd missed supper. He stalked into the sitting room and flipped on the radio. His rigid posture spoke volumes. Perla gave her aunt a sympathetic smile and disappeared into the room they shared. Delilah was left to explain her actions to Charlotte alone. They sat at the table and spoke in soft tones.

"I was so pleased to have a job, I didn't think. In Chicago I could ride the bus—I'd forgotten how hard it is to get around out in the country." She rubbed her temples. "And I told Robert I'd be at work on Monday, but I don't think it would be wise to ask Ed to drop me off."

Charlotte grimaced. "Well, it isn't exactly on his way. You didn't much think this through, did you?"

"I'm so used to taking care of myself. Having to consider other people . . ." Delilah feared she sounded ungrateful. "What I mean is, I'm glad to have other people in my life, but it complicates things."

Charlotte rolled her eyes toward her husband's stiff back. "It does, that."

"I suppose I could walk."

"It'd take you three hours to walk it."

"Well, if I started—"

Charlotte held up her hand. "I have an idea. Come to church with me tomorrow, and I think we can work something out." She looked toward Ed again. "In the meantime, I'd leave that man alone if I were you."

It had been on the tip of Robert's tongue to invite Delilah to have supper with him after work. Which was foolish for more reasons than one. First, what did he suppose he was going to feed her? Tinned stew? Second, it was much too forward. But he'd enjoyed having her in the store so much, and he simply hated to let her go. She had such a way with folks—like she knew what they'd come in to get even before they spoke.

He unwrapped a loaf of bread and piled cold ham on a slice. He had some hoop cheese around here somewhere. *Aha.* He added that to the sandwich and slathered on mustard from a small pot on the counter. Then he stood, holding his dinner, and staring out the window without really seeing anything.

She was a fine figure of a woman—there was no denying that. And she was charming and got along well with people. She seemed to like being in the store. Could God have finally sent him a woman who would be a helpmate in life? He'd asked for someone more than once, knowing he couldn't marry just anyone. Then there had been Susanne . . . But when things didn't work out he'd pretty well given up and moved on. Until now.

Robert bit into the sandwich and chewed like it was a job of work he needed to get done. The only question was whether she was past wanting children. He wasn't sure how old she was, but she certainly looked like she could still . . . Well, that didn't bear thinking about at the moment. Her first marriage had been childless. Had it been by choice? He had a hard time believing anyone wouldn't want children, but that was the kind of woman he needed. He took another bite and sent up a prayer. Tomorrow he'd go to church and see what he could find out.

3

Delilah very much wanted to know what plan her sister had up her sleeve, but she quelled her curiosity and kept her peace all the way to Laurel Mountain Church the next morning. She wore the blue dress Martin had complimented her on once. She'd never worn it for him again, but today she wanted to look pretty. She told herself it was nothing more than a desire to make a good impression for the sake of her sister's family.

After the service, Delilah tried to slip out the rarely used second door at the front of the church in order to avoid attention, but the ladies of Wise were not so easily dissuaded. She tolerated questions and comments from people who had known her when she was a girl as they stood in the shade of an ancient oak. She tried not to feel like folks were prying, but she wished she could just make an announcement and be done with this business. She took advantage of a moment of quiet to imagine what that announcement might sound like.

"Friends and family, thank you for your concern but let me assure you the world is a better place without Martin Morrissey in it. I'm only sad for the years I wasted on him."

Her giggle held a touch of hysteria. She clapped a gloved hand to her mouth when she realized someone was standing behind her left shoulder.

"Pleasant thoughts?" asked Robert.

Delilah blushed. If only he knew. "Oh, my imagination gets away from me every once in a while. It's nothing."

Robert's dark blue eyes crinkled and she had that impression again that he was about to hook his thumbs under a pair of suspenders. "The imagination is an entertaining companion when living, breathing people are lacking. I, however, prefer the company of people whenever possible."

"I suppose I do, too." Delilah felt pensive. "It's funny how lonesome it could get in the city. All those people and still I sometimes felt like the last person on earth."

Robert looked at her as if he knew exactly what she meant. He extended a hand, as though he was about to take her arm when Charlotte appeared tugging a young man with a red beard along with her.

"Delilah, this is Casewell Phillips. I think he might have the answer to your transportation problem."

Delilah took the young man's hand all the while wishing Charlotte wouldn't say anything in front of Robert. She didn't want him to know she didn't have any idea how she was getting to the store in the morning. A second man—leathery with a shock of dark hair—stepped over, and she saw Casewell stand up a bit straighter.

"Robert, you reckon you could open up the store this afternoon and let me get something for pink eye. That new heifer's going to infect the whole herd if I don't jump on it."

"Now, John, you know your Emily won't like us changing money of a Sunday afternoon." Robert winked at Casewell.

"Then I'll pay you tomorrow," John answered.

Robert laughed as if it were the best joke he'd heard all week. John didn't crack a smile, just stood waiting.

"Fine, fine. Let's head on over there, then." Robert nodded at the group, and Delilah thought his eyes might have lingered on hers a moment longer than the rest.

Once they departed, Casewell looked as if someone had lifted a sack of bricks from his shoulders.

"My father," he said, nodding at John's departing back.

Delilah suspected there was a story there, but was more interested in how Casewell might help her get back and forth to the store. Especially now that she could discuss the situation without Robert in attendance.

"Delilah says you can help me get around? Do you have a car I can borrow? I hate to put you out, but—"

"Not a car," Casewell said. "Did you want a car?"

"She just needs a way to get to the store and back," Charlotte said. "Tell her what you made last week."

Casewell brightened. "I do a little carpentry when I can, and I decided to try my hand at a pony cart. Turned out good, too. I'd be glad to lend it to you if you think it'd work for you."

"A . . . what?" Delilah wasn't following.

"Pony cart. It's a wooden cart with stout wheels. I wouldn't take it off the roads, but it'll get you from here to there." The young man puffed his chest out.

Delilah hated to burst his bubble. "Wouldn't I need a pony?"

"You can use Pauline." Charlotte looked downright smug.

"The donkey?" Delilah couldn't quite believe her ears.

"Sure. Ed's father used her to plow the garden, but since he got the job with the railroad, he isn't much for plowing. And while Pauline's getting old, I suspect she'd be glad for a job to do. Wouldn't take her long to haul you to the store and back."

"You want me to travel around in a wooden cart pulled by a donkey?" Delilah kept hoping it was all a joke. "What if it rains?"

Charlotte grinned. "I'd wear a raincoat and a hat, if I were you."

Heavens. Her sister was serious. "I've never driven a horse, er, donkey."

"I know Pauline—she's as gentle as they come, and pulling you in my little old cart would be a walk in the park for her," Casewell said. "I'd be proud to let you use it."

Delilah swallowed hard and looked from her sister to the earnest young man standing in the churchyard. "Well then, I guess Pauline and I will become better acquainted."

The pony cart was little more than a bench with wheels. Delilah jounced over the hard-packed dirt road with a view of Pauline's hindquarters to speed her travels. She would have sighed, but she was afraid, if she unclenched her jaw, her teeth would rattle out of her head. After what seemed like an eternity, but was little more than thirty or forty minutes, Delilah bounced to a stop in front of Thorntons' store. She stood and stretched with her hands braced in the small of her back. She glanced around and, not seeing anyone, rubbed her sore backside.

"Good morning." Robert's voice boomed through the front door.

Delilah jumped and clasped her hands in front of her, hoping he hadn't seen . . . Oh well. She had made it to work, and that was the main thing.

"Good morning. Where can I, er, accommodate Pauline?"

Robert laughed. "Is Pauline your donkey or your—" It was as though he stopped breathing for a moment. Then he inhaled sharply. "Oh, well, I'm sure you mean the donkey. I have a lean-to out back. We can stable her there."

Delilah straightened her skirt and tucked a curl of dark hair under her hat. "Thank you." Why did she have the feeling things had gotten off on the wrong foot?

Robert unhitched the donkey from the little cart. Must be Casewell Phillips's handiwork. Nicely done. He led Pauline around back, mentally berating himself along the way. He'd nearly made a fool of himself. Probably had, but thank goodness he stopped before he went too far. Fool tongue.

He situated the donkey, straightened his jacket, and headed back around to get the day started. He found Delilah already inside waiting on Emily Phillips. He stood watching through the open door for a moment. She moved about the store as if she'd been doing it for years, looked like she belonged. He felt a longing rise up in him. He didn't want to be alone anymore, wanted to have someone beside him at the store and in life. Surely God wouldn't let him feel such a longing if there wasn't a chance he—

"Robert." Robert jumped when Delilah spoke. "Emily is looking for gelatin, I didn't see any on the shelf."

He looked on the shelf, saw the vacant spot were the gelatin usually sat, and went into the back room to see if he had any more. He spotted a china trinket box that had come in the week before. He'd been meaning to set up a display of delicate items to appeal to ladies. Delilah would likely do a much better job of that. He wished he could just give her the box, but that wouldn't be appropriate. Especially not until he was sure she would, well, accept him as he was.

Grabbing the gelatin, Robert went back out and listened a moment as Delilah and Emily chatted about Casewell's woodworking, how the garden was doing, and whether they'd have an early fall. As she began ringing up the purchases, Delilah asked Emily whether she needed some soap flakes.

"Oh, my stars," Emily cried. "I forgot. How in the world did you know?"

Delilah shrugged and added the price of the flakes to the tally. "It's exactly the sort of thing I forget about, until I reach for the empty box."

Emily smiled and squeezed Delilah's hand. "Well, I'm grateful you thought of it. You know, you should come on out to the farm and have a cup of coffee with me one day—we can have a proper visit."

Delilah glided about the store the rest of the morning, waiting on customers, tidying things Robert hadn't realized needed to be tidied, and generally making his heart ache. By midafternoon, Robert was beginning to think he had made a mistake. The torture might not be worth the assistance.

Around three, a lull fell over the store. Robert saw Delilah slip a foot out of her shoe and wiggle her toes. He was a cad, keeping her on her feet all day.

"Delilah, come sit and have a cup of coffee with me." He moved to the potbellied stove and checked the pot that sat there all the time. Old. "On second thought, you sit while I make some fresh coffee."

"I can do that." She reached for the pot and Robert held it over his head.

"Nope. You've doubled my business today. The least I can do is prove that I can still make a decent cup of coffee."

Delilah looked surprised, but then she smiled and sank into one of the wooden chairs. She scooted it back, away from the warmth of the stove. "I'm not used to having a man do for me."

Robert quirked an eyebrow. "A lady as pretty as you—I'd think there'd be no shortage of men eager to serve you coffee, help you across the street, and throw their coats down over mud puddles to keep your shoes clean."

Laughter burst from Delilah as if she didn't know it was in there. "I can dream, I suppose."

Robert put the pot on the back of the stove to perk. "'But I, being poor, have only my dreams; I have spread my dreams under your feet; Tread softly because you tread on my dreams.'"

"What did you say?" Delilah cocked her head and her face softened.

"Oh, just quoting some poetry about dreams. William Butler Yeats. I think the Irish have the most wonderful way with words."

"You read poetry?"

"Now and again." Robert winked at her. "But don't tell anyone, they might start taking me seriously."

Delilah laughed again and accepted a cup of coffee. Robert didn't think of offering her some milk until he was seated and slurping at his own cup. Too late he supposed. He needed to brush up on the social niceties.

"Do you miss the city?" he asked instead.

"No, not really." She looked out the front door and the sunlight shining over the hills. "It's certainly prettier here."

"It is," he agreed, gazing at her. "Do you miss your—" he'd

almost said *husband* but caught himself—"work." It would have to do.

Delilah slanted a look at him. "Were you going to ask about Martin?"

Robert sighed and set his cup on the floor at his feet. "I was, but I don't want to pry."

She waved a graceful hand. "I don't mind. Honestly? What I miss is the idea of Martin." She sighed. "Things never turn out the way you think."

Robert leaned his elbows on his knees. "I stopped making plans a long time ago. Every time I did, seems like the good Lord changed 'em on me." He looked at the floor between his feet. "'Course, doesn't stop me from getting ideas all my own."

"I know what you mean." Delilah set her empty cup on a table. "I planned to have three or four children by now, but that hasn't happened." She leaned forward. "Do you ever wish you had someone to leave all this to one day?" She threw her arms open to encompass the entirety of the store. "It's such a wonderful legacy."

"Yes, well, children are a luxury." He stood and strode toward the back room. "Guess I'd better sort out this mess in the back. Let me know if business picks up out here."

Delilah couldn't make head nor tail of what just happened. They'd been having such a nice chat, and then Robert cut it off. Had she revealed too much? Something seemed to rub him wrong. And calling children a luxury . . . Did he think he couldn't afford to have children? It seemed to her she couldn't afford not to. Of course, she didn't get to decide. And based on Robert's reaction, she'd be looking the wrong way if she thought he might be husband and father material.

Delilah gathered their coffee cups and stacked them behind the counter. There was a sink with a pump in the back room, but she didn't want to go there at the moment. Robert had clearly tired of her company. She'd just do her job and go on home. If she wanted a husband, she might have to reconsider Joe Miller's ears.

4

Robert busied himself organizing the dusty shelves in the storage room. She clearly wanted children. He could hear it in her voice—she longed for children. That longing he'd been feeling for a wife? That's what she felt for kids. And he couldn't give that to her.

He'd been six when he contracted scarlet fever. The doctor told his mother it could affect his ability to have children one day. He'd been tested as an adult, and the doctor told him there was almost no chance he'd ever father children. And he'd accepted that. Or thought he had.

More than one woman had made it clear over the years that he would be an acceptable husband, but he'd held himself back. The kind of woman he dreamt of was the kind of woman who'd want kids. Lots of kids. A house filled with running and laughter and even tears. And now he knew Delilah was that kind of woman.

He punched his fist into his palm. Which made Delilah all the more appealing. He could hear her moving around out front and wished she would come into the back room and . . . What?

What did he want her to do? Proclaim that she would be content to remain childless? He'd never wish that for her. Not in a million years.

When Delilah stepped out the front door of the store at closing time, Pauline was already hitched to the cart, waiting to take her home. She looked around for Robert but didn't see him. She thought she should at least say good-bye, but then again, he'd surely been the one to leave the donkey and cart out front. It was the strangest combination of caring along with a clear message that he didn't want to see her.

She climbed onto the seat and lifted the reins. As she drove away, she looked back over her shoulder and could have sworn she saw Robert watching from the front window. But it was probably just wishful thinking.

Once she arrived at the house, Delilah sensed a tension between Ed and Charlotte. As soon as supper was over, Perla disappeared into their shared room. Delilah helped her sister with the dishes while Ed went into the sitting room and fiddled with the radio.

"Is everything okay?" she asked Charlotte.

"Why? Don't I seem okay?"

"Frankly, you don't. And I'm tired of trying to figure out what people are thinking, so please just tell me."

Charlotte gave her a puzzled look, then sighed. "The rail line may be closing."

"Ed's line?"

Her sister rolled her eyes. "What else?"

"When?"

Charlotte shrugged. "It's not for sure, but Ed's testy about it. He's been fireman for a while now, and he thought he might have a chance to move up to engineer before too much longer." She spoke in a whisper. "I think he's afraid if the line closes he'll lose his chance."

"What will you do?'

"Hopefully, he'll get a transfer. It could even be a good thing in the long run. Except I hate to leave the church and our friends here." Charlotte snapped the dish towel and hung it up. "Want some coffee?"

"Sure." Delilah slid into a kitchen chair and stared out the screen door at lightning bugs rising from the grass outside. "Any idea where the transfer might be?"

Charlotte laughed. "Where there's a railroad line, I imagine."

Delilah made a face. "Smarty-pants—you know what I mean."

"Maybe up north to Comstock? There are several lines up there."

"When will you find out?" Restless, Delilah popped up to fetch cups and saucers for the coffee.

"By the end of the month, I expect. Surely no later than August." Charlotte poured coffee and motioned for Delilah to follow her out onto the porch with their cups. "I hope you know you're welcome to come with us."

Charlotte sat in the swing while Delilah eased down on the top porch step and closed her eyes to better enjoy the soft breeze stirring the air. "What about a place to live?"

"The railroad company rents this house to us. If they send us somewhere else, I suppose they'll find us another one like it. Maybe it'll be bigger."

"You wouldn't need anything bigger if I stayed here." Delilah looked over her shoulder at Charlotte pushing the swing with one foot.

"Why would you stay here?"

Delilah pictured Robert's broad back as he disappeared into the storeroom, his posture screaming tension. Why, indeed?

Robert determined to behave as though he'd never had designs on Delilah. It had been foolish of him to even imagine life with a woman in it. He'd given up on that a long time ago, and just because his only employee was utterly fetching in her hat and matching pumps as she drove her donkey cart up to the porch was no reason to change now.

"Morning. You look fresh as a new calf on the first day of spring."

Delilah flushed and ducked her head. "Why, thank you, Robert. That's a . . . regionally specific compliment."

Robert laughed. She was funny, too. But then he needed to stop cataloguing her assets. He let his eyes flick to her shapely calf as she stepped out of the cart. Yes indeed, he should stop adding to the list as quick as he could.

"I've got some music boxes, china, and other geegaws back there in the storeroom. Think you could make a display out of them?"

Delilah looked like he'd offered her a box of chocolates. "Why, I'd love to."

"All right, then. I'll stow Pauline and see you inside."

She flashed him a smile and brushed past him into the store. She smelled like lavender. He made a point of not watching her walk up the steps and disappear inside. He grunted and tugged on Pauline's reins to get her to mosey on around the building. He'd thought hiring help was going to make his life easier.

Back inside, Delilah was busy arranging a small table with

the delicate items she'd rounded up from the back room. It was a pleasure to watch her.

"How's your family?" he asked, thinking it was an innocuous enough topic.

Delilah paused and then resumed her fussing. "They're fine. Have you heard anything about Wise's railroad line closing?"

Robert began stacking boxes of soap powder on a shelf. "I guess maybe I've heard something about that. Seems like it's not supposed to happen for a while, though."

Delilah shrugged. "They must have moved the timeline up. Charlotte said Ed might be transferred before too much longer."

"Transferred? Where to?" Would she go with them, he wondered?

"Maybe Comstock. Charlotte wasn't sure. And they like it here so much."

"Well now, that's a shame." Robert reached into the crate at his feet and found it empty. "Would you, ah, be going with them?"

Delilah stood back from the table and surveyed it, then moved in to shift several items ever so slightly. "I'm not sure." She flashed a look at Robert. "The only argument I have for staying is this job, and well, blood is stronger than water." She smiled. "Or dry goods, as the case may be."

He thought she was watching him out of the corner of her eye, but maybe he was imagining it. He grabbed the crate at his feet and slid it behind the front counter. "I'd surely hate to see you go."

Delilah found the feather duster and began moving about the store. "I don't really want to go, but . . . Well, maybe it'll turn out to be nothing more than a rumor."

Robert nodded and turned toward the door as the day's first

customer walked in. He felt unsettled, uneasy. Ten minutes ago he'd been thinking it might have been a mistake to hire Delilah, but now he was dreading the day she might leave. Not to mention how the closing of the railroad line would disrupt quite a few families in the area. And had the potential to impact his bottom line. He shook his head and fetched out some tobacco for Elwood Cutright. His life had become complicated beyond reason.

Every time she glanced at the little table with its display of delicate items arranged across a lace cloth, Delilah felt a surge of pleasure. It looked so nice, and several ladies had taken note. They'd even sold a little china dog to a woman who said it looked just like the cocker spaniel she'd had when she was a girl. The woman had been so happy, it felt like the biggest success Delilah'd had in a long time. And now she might have to leave it all to follow Ed and Charlotte to Comstock—or wherever.

Dinner was quiet that evening, and Delilah didn't try to liven it up like she had on previous nights. After they ate, Delilah and Charlotte started the dishes while Perla curled on the sofa with a copy of *Calling All Girls* magazine and Ed flipped on the radio, as usual.

"Ed got good news today." Charlotte poured hot water over the dishes.

"Oh?" Delilah wondered why they couldn't have talked about it over the meal. It would have been nice to have conversation while they ate their pork chops.

"Yes, they let him know if he accepts a transfer to Comstock they'll make him an engineer within six months." Charlotte's often-tense expression relaxed into a smile. "He's so pleased."

Delilah cast a glance at her brother-in-law leaning into the radio and frowning as though he didn't agree with whatever he was hearing. "I'm glad. Does that mean you're definitely moving?"

"Yes, probably in October. Certainly before Thanksgiving." She glanced at her sister. "And I hope you'll be coming with us."

"I suppose I will be," she said slowly.

Charlotte smiled and stopped washing dishes to gaze out the window. "It's good to see Ed finally getting something he wants in life."

"What do you mean?"

"Well, he's been so disappointed . . ." She scrubbed at a pan as if she were trying to wear a hole in it.

"What are you talking about?" Delilah had never supposed her sister's marriage was made in heaven, but she hadn't thought about there being disappointment—especially not on Ed's side.

Charlotte's shoulders sagged as she rinsed the pan and handed it to Delilah to dry. "I never told you . . . after Perla . . ."

"What?"

"He so wanted a son, and after Perla I wasn't able . . ." She dashed a tear from her cheek with damp fingers. "I can't have more children. That's why there's only Perla."

Delilah felt ashamed. She'd never stopped to think why her sister only had one child. She'd been gone for more than a decade with little more than superficial letters to connect her to family. And even now she was so focused on her desire to have a family of her own that she'd never thought to ask why Perla was an only child.

She wrapped an arm around her sister's shoulders. "I'm so very sorry. And mostly I'm sorry I wasn't here to see you through what must have been a terrible time."

Charlotte leaned into her sister's embrace. "It was hard, but with God's help I came to accept it." She straightened and glanced into the living room, where Ed was now kicked back in his armchair snoring. "But I don't think Ed ever did."

Delilah pondered her sister's words. "You came to accept it? Really? I want children so very much. I'm not sure I could give that dream up."

"Sometimes God gives you strength to do without because, for whatever reason, he knows it's better for you not to have your heart's desire." Charlotte carried the dishpan over to the door and dashed the water out into the yard. "Sometimes, he'll even give you peace." She looked back toward her husband again. "If you ask him."

Charlotte beckoned her sister out onto the porch to sit in the swing. "But what about you? Why didn't you and Martin have children?"

Delilah pleated the hem of her skirt between her fingers. She didn't really want to talk about it, but maybe it would do her good. "Martin didn't seem to care if we had children, and when . . ." She felt her face flush. "When nothing happened, I went to see a doctor. He said there was no reason why I shouldn't conceive." She smoothed her skirt back over her knees. "Martin refused to see a doctor. I eventually got so desperate I insisted."

"And?" Charlotte slid her arm through her sister's.

"And he struck me."

Charlotte gasped. "He never did."

"I'm afraid so. It was the only time, but it . . . changed things between us. So I gave up on having children. I never did have peace about it, though, and now, well, maybe it's because there's still time."

Charlotte squeezed Delilah's arm. "Of course there is. You're only in your thirties. I've known more than one woman in Wise who had their babies late. There've even been a few change-of-life babies." She flashed a grin. "All we need to do is find you a proper beau."

Delilah smiled weakly. Yes, that was all. She'd thought it might be Robert, but now . . . Well, maybe moving to Comstock would be a good thing. Maybe she'd meet a man there.

5

Two weeks later Robert left Delilah to manage the store on her own while he made a run to Davis for supplies. It felt like a compliment, being trusted to watch over the store on her own after such a short time. Delilah wandered the aisles, listened to the floorboards creak, and breathed in all the dry-goods smells from leather to grain to soap.

It would be lovely to know she could always come here to dust and arrange and wait on customers. She hadn't expected to fall in love with the store, but she had. Even if there was never a man in Wise for her, she was tempted to stay. She felt so very much at home, not only in the store, but also in the lovely hills she had once been only too glad to leave behind. And if she were perfectly honest with herself, she didn't think Ed much wanted her to move to Comstock.

The bell on the door jangled, and Delilah peered around a shelf to see who it was. Angie Talbot strode in and moved toward the sewing notions with great purpose, while her twin sister, Liza, drifted in her wake, looking like a child for whom a trip to the store was a rare treat. Even though the sisters had to be sixty if they were a day, Liza always had an air of youth and innocence about her.

"Can I help you ladies?"

"I need some gray thread and a packet of buttons," Angie ticked the items off on her fingers. "Plus a pound of coffee."

"Don't forget the lace, sister," Liza chimed in from where she was examining the table of delicate items Delilah had arranged.

Angie made a harrumphing sound. "I don't know why you insist on frippery. We're too old for nonsense like that."

Liza ran a finger over the skirts of a china shepherdess and smiled. "We all need a little pretty in our lives. Mother always said so."

"And Papa indulged her overmuch."

Delilah smiled at the way the sister's sniped at each other. Or maybe it was only Angie who sniped, Liza seemed more innocent in the exchange. She hurried to gather the requested items aware that Angie watched her every move like a hawk. She stepped to the cash register.

"Will that be all? Or do you need some sugar—we just got some in." Delilah bit her tongue. Now what had possessed her to ask about sugar? Angie was sure to think it was frivolous.

Angie's eyebrows shot up her forehead. "As a matter of fact I was asking Robert about sugar not long ago. For a meringue pie. I suppose he mentioned it to you."

He hadn't, but Delilah just nodded and smiled to save any lengthy explanation. She was mystified at how she so often knew what people wanted and doubted Angie would have any patience for things not easily explained.

Angie withdrew her purse from a deep pocket. "I will confess I had my doubts when I heard Robert hired a woman, but you seem to be doing a fine job."

"Thank you." Delilah felt like that was high praise, indeed.

"Where is Robert?" Liza moved toward the counter as if she were riding a cloud.

"He's picking up supplies in Davis."

Angie nodded. "He trusts you, then. That's a fine thing."

"He needs a woman in his life." Liza clasped her hands and closed her eyes. "A romance."

Delilah widened her eyes. Were they suggesting . . . ?

"Pshaw. You know very well why Robert has never married." Angie collected the packet Delilah offered and tucked her purse back into her pocket.

"But he could still have love and companionship even if he can't—"

"Hush, sister. Far be it from us to spread gossip. His mother told us in the strictest confidence before she moved to South Carolina. She wanted us to watch over her boy since he wasn't likely to marry."

Delilah realized she was holding her breath. What in the world were they talking about?

Angie leaned across the counter. "But seeing as he's your employer—"

The bell jangled again, and Delilah jumped. One of the local farmers walked through the door and tipped his hat. "Ladies."

Delilah turned back to Angie, who tugged at her gloves and nodded once. "Well, never mind. We'd best be on our way."

Liza cast a helpless look at Delilah and shrugged her shoulders. The pair passed through the front door, leaving Delilah rooted behind the counter. There was a reason Robert never married. But what could it be? Her imagination began to run wild. He didn't like women. He had some horrible disease that would cause him to die young. He'd loved someone once and it ended tragically.

"Miss?"

Delilah jumped. The farmer stood looking at her with his head cocked to the side. "You all right?"

"Yes. Yes, thank you. Can I help you with anything?"

The man began to list the items he wanted, and Delilah gathered them in a haze, adding a tin of tobacco without thinking. The man looked surprised, then shrugged, paid, and tucked the tin into the front pocket of his overalls. Delilah watched him go, thinking how much she hated mysteries.

When Robert came in the next morning he was pleased to see the store in better shape than when he'd left. Delilah was a treasure. He hated to think she'd be moving to Comstock with her family, but what could he do to entice her to stay?

He could offer to marry her, he thought, and laughed out loud. That would hardly be a good deal for her. Then again, she clearly enjoyed her job, and maybe the lure of staying on would be enough. Maybe he could promote her so she was more like a partner than an employee, although the railroad closing made that an unlikely proposition. Word was Ed and three others were headed for Comstock come the first of October, while quite a few men would lose their jobs. Without railroad workers, business might get a bit sparse.

Delilah bounced in the back door. "I got Pauline situated all by myself." She practically glowed with her accomplishment. "Those heavy grey clouds worried me when I left the house this morning, but I said a prayer and they seemed to just dissipate. Then we got here and everything was so easy today."

Robert clapped his hands. "Bully for you. That calls for a celebration!"

He took the lid off a candy jar and tossed her a caramel cream. She caught it, laughing, and popped it in her mouth. Robert's eyes lingered on her lips for a moment, but he redirected himself and cleared his throat.

"You're getting to be a fair hand at animals. Might have to expand the store to include livestock if you keep this up."

Delilah dismissed him with a wave, but he could see how her eyes danced. He wished he could step right up and dance her around the old stove that sat cold on this warm August morning. She made him glad.

"I have more good news," she said.

"Better than stabling a donkey? I can't imagine."

"Emily Phillips came by yesterday afternoon and mentioned that a timber company has approached them about selling off some land. Apparently the company is planning to come into the area. It'll mean logging jobs for the railroad men who didn't get transferred." She clasped her hands under her chin. "Isn't it wonderful? Should be good for business, too."

"That is good news. I just might have to hire you an assistant."

Delilah's laugh burbled out like a mountain stream on a hot day. "I hardly think that will be necessary, but I'm glad folks will be all right." She sobered. "Of course, if I go to Comstock with Charlotte, you'll probably need to hire someone to take my place."

Robert nearly blurted that no one could ever take her place, but caught himself. "Well, now, I supposed that's true. If you go."

Delilah twirled a bit of hair that hung loose at the nape of her neck. "I haven't decided for *certain*, but I'm leaning toward going."

Robert pushed down a feeling of desperation. "What if you had a percentage in the store?"

"A percentage? What do you mean?"

"Part owner."

Delilah looked alarmed and began to speak, but Robert held up his hand. "Let me explain. You've increased business by fifty percent or more since you came, and the store looks a great deal better than it did two months ago. You've more than earned your little bit of salary."

Delilah bit her lip. "Well, I don't know."

"Of course you don't—I've just sprung it on you. But the long and short of it is I'd . . . I'd like to keep you around. So think it over and let me know."

Delilah nodded and glanced toward the door, where the day's first customer was herding three small children inside. "I will," she said.

It was quite possibly the longest two days of Robert's life. Delilah said she'd like to talk things over with Charlotte before answering him, and he agreed. Today, Saturday, business had been nonstop with a steady stream of customers shopping, visiting, and perusing the shelves as if they were pages from *Life* magazine. It was all Robert could do to keep from shooing them all out into the dusty road to waste time elsewhere.

When closing finally rolled around, Robert hurried to flip the sign on the front door. "What a day," he said blowing out a puff of air.

"I think it was your best day since I came," Delilah said from behind the cash register.

"I guess that makes it worthwhile." He turned and looked

at her. "I didn't realize you were keeping up with the books."
He nodded. "That's good."

She pinked. "Well, I thought if I were going to take your
offer seriously, I'd better understand exactly what I'm getting
into."

"Smart," Robert said, tapping his skull. "I knew you were
one smart cookie."

"So . . . " Delilah braced her hands on the counter and looked
Robert in the eye. "About that offer."

He felt his pulse throbbing behind his ear and took a deep
breath, hoping to slow his racing heart. "Thy will be done,"
he whispered. "Yes?"

"I'm sorely tempted to accept. Charlotte pointed out that I
can always come to Comstock later if things don't work out.
And Ed might do well with a break from me."

Robert wanted to protest that any man who wanted a break
from her was a fool, but he swallowed the words. "And?" he
asked instead.

"There's only one thing that concerns me. A potential fly
in the ointment."

She looked at him as if he should know what it was. "And
that would be?"

"What if one of us gets married?"

Robert blinked twice in rapid succession. *Married?* "I don't
understand."

"If you got married, your wife might not appreciate you having a woman for a business partner." She ducked her head. "And
if I ever marry, my husband might not like me working closely
with another man. Or even working at all."

Robert scratched his head. The things women thought of.
"Well, I don't plan to marry, so I don't see that as a problem,

and if you marry I can always buy you out. We can even figure up what that might look like ahead of time."

"Why not?" she blurted.

"Why not what?" He'd been confused by women before, but he'd never felt quite this far out to sea.

"Why don't you plan to marry?" She looked directly at him again and there was a tenderness there that made his heart turn to butter. "Oh, never mind. It's none of my business. I don't think this will work. But thank you for asking." She snatched up her hat and worked to pin it to her hair as she made for the back door.

"Wait." In two long strides Robert caught up to her and grabbed her elbow.

She stopped but didn't turn toward him.

"I'll tell you why not."

She was so still he wondered if he'd frightened her, but he plunged ahead, before he could change his mind.

"I had scarlet fever when I was a boy." She turned her head, maybe so that she could catch a glimpse of his face. "The doctors told my mother it might . . . might affect my ability to have children." He stopped. Doggone, but this was an intimate sort of conversation. He was grateful the store was closed. It was no time for a customer. "Anyway, I've been to see several doctors and they all agree that there's almost no chance I'll ever . . . father a child."

He released her elbow and dropped his hand to his side. "Which means I won't ever have anyone to pass the store on to." He hung his head. He wasn't a whole man, and now she knew it. He'd never felt his shortcoming so keenly as in this moment.

Delilah turned slowly, then reached out and touched his cheek.

"And here I thought you just didn't want a woman interfering with your bachelor ways."

Robert looked up. She was smiling as if she didn't think any less of him. Maybe even admired him for admitting his defect.

"Oh, I guess I wouldn't mind a little meddling—from the right woman. You know, I wish . . ."

"What do you wish?"

Robert stepped back, breaking contact. "Oh well, my mother always said if wishes were horses, paupers would ride. I *hope* you'll stay on."

Delilah resettled her hat. "Perhaps I will. I need to think all this over a bit more. You keep giving me more information to digest."

Robert smiled. "I think that's the last of my deep, dark secrets. You take all the time you need."

6

Delilah was tempted to talk over Robert's confession with her sister, but Charlotte was already overwhelmed with everything she needed to do before they moved. Anyway, she really needed someone who wasn't invested in her decision.

Robert had insisted she take one day off besides Sundays each week and Delilah had chosen Tuesdays. Now that she found herself rattling around, getting in Charlotte's way, distracted by everything swirling around her mind, she was beginning to question that decision.

She slipped out the back door, wandered out to the little barn, and leaned on the fence where Pauline grazed. Sometimes saying things out loud helped, so she decided to go for a drive in the pony cart and talk it all out with the little donkey. She considered changing from her flowered work dress but didn't suppose she'd run into anyone who cared what she wore.

Proficient now at handling the animal and the cart, Delilah was ready to go in short order. She snapped the reins, and Pauline set out at a trot, seemingly pleased to have something to do. *We all need a purpose*, thought Delilah. Even donkeys.

Without any particular direction in mind, Delilah let Pauline choose their path, and soon they were bumping along a dirt track beside the creek that watered most of Wise. Here and there a leaf shaded from green to yellow promising that autumn wasn't far off. The sound of water cascading over rocks and the mossy coolness of the rhododendron glades soothed her spirit and invited her to linger.

Delilah clucked Pauline to a stop near a particularly enchanting spot along the creek. The water fell over a low falls into a pool surrounded by dark stones and ferns. Delilah looped the reins over a branch and slipped down to the pool. Now, here was a spot to think things through. She removed her shoes—she was a scandal without any stockings—and slipped her feet into the cold water. Heaven.

Delilah closed her eyes and tipped her head back to let a spot of sunlight filtering through the trees dazzle her eyes. Why had she ever agreed to marry Martin and leave this place? The decision had seemed a dream come true at the time.

"Oh, I beg your pardon."

Delilah snatched her feet from the water and whipped her head around. A woman stepped around a rhododendron bush and appeared shocked to find anyone here.

"I'm sorry," Delilah said. "Am I on private land?"

The woman came closer, and Delilah recognized Emily Phillips.

"Technically, I suppose you are, but that doesn't matter. I was on my way to see the Talbot sisters when I saw the cart"—she gestured toward Pauline, who seemed to be napping on her feet—"and thought it might be the one Casewell lent you."

Delilah smiled as her pulse slowed to normal. "It's good to see you, Emily. I was out rambling and this spot was too inviting to pass by."

Emily stepped closer. "I know. This is a favorite spot of mine, too. May I join you?"

"So long as you don't mind me dipping my toes back in this delicious water."

"Not only don't I mind, I'm going to join you."

Emily shed her own shoes and eased down beside Delilah on the mossy edge of the stream. Slipping her feet into the water, she closed her eyes and sighed. "Men don't always understand a woman's need to get away for a moment just to think." She opened her eyes and glanced at Delilah. "Is that what you were doing?"

"I was. I have a great deal to think about at the moment."

"Don't we all?"

Emily didn't seem inclined to press for additional information. They sat in peaceful companionship listening to birds sing and the music of water running over stones. And then a thought occurred to Delilah, and she blurted it out.

"Why is it that you only have one child?"

Emily's eyes flickered, but she didn't seem to take offense. "I don't often talk about it, but it's no secret. John and I aimed to have a houseful, but I miscarried three times before we got Casewell." She picked up a handful of pebbles and began tossing them in the water one by one. "And I had a hard time with him. Doctor put me to bed for the last three months, and he still came early. You'd hardly know it to look at the strapping fellow he is today."

She tossed the remaining pebbles into the water and brushed her hands off. "When he was born, something wasn't right with his heart. That's why he didn't go off to war—the heart defect. I'll never be glad his heart isn't perfect, but I'm thankful it kept him out of the fighting." She sighed. "After that we thought it best to stop trying."

"Are you sorry there weren't more children?"

"Oh, sometimes, but mostly I'm just grateful for what I've got." She smiled at Delilah. "And I've got more than enough. Although sometimes I wonder if I'm too protective of that boy— he might have married by now if not for my fussing." A twinkle came to her eye. "Now, are you asking because you've got a mind to raise some young'uns of your own?"

Delilah laughed and swished her feet in the water. "Am I that transparent? I've long felt like having a family was my destiny— my calling—and I'm starting to think that there might be a future for a family right here in Wise, but . . ."

"But?"

"Well, I've got the plan, but I don't have the man."

Emily laughed, too. "That is a problem. But then I suppose we do have a few eligible bachelors around here." She glanced at Delilah. "And seems to me one of them has his heart set on you."

Delilah's eyes widened. "Who in the world?"

"I've been in that store a few times since you started working there, and I've seen how Robert Thornton looks at you. Like a hound dog staring at the last piece of cornbread on the plate."

Delilah rolled her eyes and waved her hands. "Oh, he just wants me for a business partner. That's the reason I'm thinking of staying."

"Honey, he wants a partner—that's for certain. Seems to me like he'd be a fine choice, if you're so inclined."

Delilah fiddled with the hem of her skirt where water had dampened it. "Yes, but what if . . . What if children weren't in the picture for Robert?"

Emily looked serious. She crossed her arms over her chest

and cocked her head to one side. "Well, would you rather have the promise of a good man or the possibility of a child?"

Delilah considered that. Would she have been happy if she'd had children with Martin? He would likely have been a worse father than he was a husband. What if she'd subjected children to abuse at his hands?

She considered Robert. He was gentle, funny, friendly, kind, thoughtful, handsome—but there would never be children to appreciate all of that.

"Honestly, why does it have to be one or the other? Isn't the purpose of marriage to have children?"

Emily threw her head back and laughed. "Oh, Delilah, I hope you set your sights higher than that. If marriage were only about having children, I think women would have given up on the institution a long time ago." She composed herself. "Children are a blessing beyond belief, but it takes more than that to keep a man and a woman together through everything the world throws at them."

"Oh, I suppose companionship is important, too."

Emily held up her hand and began ticking off fingers. "Children, companionship, support, iron sharpening iron, and not least of all, the physical bond shared by husband and wife." She wiggled her five fingers in Delilah's direction.

"Iron sharpening iron?"

"You need a man who will challenge you, who will encourage you to be better than you are. A man who compliments you and loves on you is a good thing, but the real prize is a man who tells you when you're wrong and when you're taking the easy way out." She smiled. "Of course, it's best if he does it with love and compassion, but even so, you want a man who encourages you to be better than you are."

Delilah sat in silence. If anything, Martin had brought out the very worst in her. She'd been shrewish, bad tempered, and nagging at times. And eventually she'd become cold and withdrawn, trying to hold herself back, trying to deprive him of anything good her presence might offer. Robert, on the other hand . . .

Joining her arm with that of the older—perhaps wiser—woman beside her, Delilah felt a measure of peace settle around her, like sunbeams flickering through the leaves. She still wasn't sure what her future held, but Emily had given her a great deal to think about.

Robert felt like a cat in a roomful of rocking chairs. He couldn't settle, couldn't rest his mind. He wasn't used to feeling this way. Typically, things didn't rattle him, but waiting for Delilah to tell him if she'd stay on or move with her family was about to wear him out. They'd been working side by side all morning, waiting on customers, restocking shelves, chatting idly about the coming lumber jobs—it was about to kill him.

"How about a cup of coffee?" he asked.

"That sounds nice. I brought some chicken pie for lunch—there's more than enough to share."

"Did you make it?"

"I most certainly did not. My niece decided to try her hand at cooking, and I swear she made enough for the whole town, even though all she started with was one chicken." She gave him what he took to be a mock-stern look. "I hope you don't think this partnership is going to include cooking."

Hope surged in Robert's chest. "No, I don't see it extending that far. Although, now that you mention it, it would be a mighty fine perk."

She swatted at him with her feather duster, and he ducked before striding away to get the coffee things together. "So does that mean you're going to take me up on my offer?" He tried to sound casual but could hear the tightness in his own voice.

"You know, I think I will."

She fetched a basket from behind the front counter, lifted a covered dish, and took two plates from inside. It appeared she'd been planning on feeding him. She also took out two fresh peaches and set everything on the little table he'd placed near the stove. Some of the regulars had given him a hard time about fancying the place up, but he liked to have a spot to eat lunch with Delilah.

"Why this is a feast," he said, rubbing his hands together.

Delilah got a serious look on her face. "You work hard. Someone should be looking out for you."

"I can't think of anyone I'd rather," he said, then busied himself with the coffeepot, fearing he'd said too much.

"Robert, do you think . . ."

He turned to see why she'd trailed off. She fiddled with a napkin and seemed dissatisfied with the way things were arranged on the table.

"Do I think what?"

She snapped the napkin in the air, sat, and settled the cloth on her lap. "Do you think it would be a good idea to carry some costume jewelry along with the beauty supplies? Seems to me the ladies of this town would like a few pretty things to brighten their days now that the war is over."

Robert nodded his head. "Sounds like a fine idea. You've done so well with your powders and creams I'm inclined to think your instincts are good when it comes to what women want."

She smiled and served the chicken pie. He sat across from her and blessed the food, trying to keep his mind on his Lord rather than on what exactly it was women—this woman in particular—wanted.

7

"Where will you live?" Charlotte nestled the last piece of china that had belonged to their mother into a straw-lined crate.

"Right here." Delilah tried not to show how excited she was at the prospect of having the house all to herself. "Ed told me who to talk to at the railroad. They're hoping to sell this place to the lumber company, but in the meantime I can rent it quite reasonably."

"But what will you do for furniture? I wish we could leave some of ours, but—"

Delilah jumped in. "It's all right. Casewell Phillips has offered to make me a simple table, and Robert has a few things in the back of the store he said I'm welcome to. There's a bedstead and a few chairs that only need new bottoms." She looked around the space mentally arranging her few precious things. "I can make a rag rug for the living room and some curtains. I can do without a dresser."

"And the stove stays," Charlotte added.

Delilah rolled her eyes. "I suppose I'll have to learn to be a better cook."

"If you want to win the hearts of any men around here, you'd better. Looks don't matter half as much as the quality of your biscuits."

"Maybe that's how I'll know I've found true love—when I find a man who will eat burnt biscuits and dry pork chops."

Charlotte hugged Delilah, taking her by surprise. "I'm going to miss you so much. It seems like we just found each other again after much too long."

Delilah returned the embrace. "Comstock isn't so very far. We can see each other more often than when I was in Chicago." She grinned. "Pauline and I can make the trip together."

"Oh, that donkey. I know Ed said he was making a present of her to you, but I honestly think he's glad he won't have to cart her with us or feed her once we arrive."

"Well, whatever the reason, I'm glad she's staying." Delilah stood on tiptoe so she could see the donkey grazing beyond the fence. "I've gotten kind of attached to her."

"Perla's going to miss you, too." Charlotte sighed and slid the top of the crate into place for Ed to nail on later.

Delilah bit her lip. "Sometimes I think she's as close as I'll ever come to having a child of my own."

"Oh, don't give up yet. You might be a mother before this is all said and done."

"I'm not giving up. It's just that I'm beginning to realize that wanting a child doesn't mean God will bless me with one." She stirred the pot of beans simmering on the stove. "You wanted a houseful of children, and so did Emily Phillips, but that's not how things turned out for either one of you. Miscarrying . . ." She felt tears rise. "I can't imagine how painful that would be."

Charlotte wrapped an arm around her shoulders. "God

knows best. It doesn't always feel like it, but I'm pretty sure he does."

After a few months of having Delilah around, Robert couldn't imagine how he'd ever gotten along without her. He was even able to take an occasional day off, although he didn't really want to, because it meant a day away from her. He kept finding things he wanted her to have for the house she'd made her own once Charlotte, Ed, and Perla left for Comstock. But he was careful not to overdo it, he didn't want her to think he was trying to make decisions for her or to win her with bribes.

And he never actually went to the house. There had been some gossip at first about why Delilah hadn't left town with her family, but that eventually quieted down, and Robert felt that the two of them had settled into comfortable companionship. Of course, what he really wanted was to move their relationship into deeper waters, but he was afraid to rock the boat. Maybe he could learn to be satisfied with nothing more than what they had—friendship.

Delilah walked by deep in conversation with a customer. He watched her describe something with graceful hands, then smile and laugh. He sighed. Somehow friendship just didn't feel like enough.

The bell jangled, and Robert swiveled to see who was entering. It was a woman with several children. She had her head down so she could swipe at a wee girl's nose. When she looked up he felt as if the breath had been knocked from his chest. Susanne?

She smiled and moved toward him with her hand extended. She was older, maybe a little stouter, but still lovely. Her golden hair curled from beneath her hat and her grey-green eyes looked a shade darker than he remembered.

"Why, Robert, do you even know me?"

He jumped and stuck his hand out, almost missing hers. He recovered and grasped the gloved hand. "Susanne . . . of course I know you. You . . . look well."

She fluffed her curls with one hand and smiled, showing her dimples. Oh how he remembered those dimples.

"I'm in town visiting mother and thought I'd come do her shopping for her." She turned abruptly and grabbed little fingers reaching for one of Delilah's displays. "Rosie, stop it. I want you to meet Mr. Thornton."

The cherub had her mother's curls and dimples. She stuck a thumb in her mouth and stared at Robert.

Susanne laid a hand on each child's head in turn. "You've met Rose—she was a bit of a surprise—and this is Caleb, this is Joshua, and the oldest here is Judith. She's nine now."

The children stared at him like he was supposed to perform a trick. "Handsome children," he said at last. "And how is, uh, Herbert, isn't it?"

A shadow crossed Susanne's face. "Oh, you haven't heard, then. Children? Why don't you go exploring. Judith, keep an eye on Rosie."

Judith sighed and took the child's hand, leading her off to look at buttons and ribbon.

"Herbert . . . well, he . . . as best we know . . ." She lowered her voice. "We haven't seen him in nearly a year." She glanced around. "He could very well be dead."

Robert felt his eyebrows shoot up. "I'm sorry to hear that."

Susanne wet her lips and stuck her chin in the air. "I'm planning to file for divorce on grounds of abandonment." She lowered her eyelids. "It's a disgrace, I know, but I need to be free of him if he's not going to support us." She flicked a look at her children. Rosie was leaving smudges on the candy case, while the boys jostled each other and Judith looked bored. Delilah watched them with amusement.

Robert cleared his throat more loudly than necessary. "Well, I hope it all works out for the best." He usually had something to say, but not this time. This time he felt like a duck on ice.

Delilah glided up behind him. "Robert, do you mind if I treat these youngsters to some peppermints?"

"No, no, that's a wonderful thought." He hurried over to the counter himself and handed candies to each child. Judith hesitated a moment and then took hers, whispering "Thank you" as she did. Robert felt his heart catch. These poor kids.

"You in town long?" he asked Susanne.

"I'm not sure. Mother wants us to stay, and goodness knows we can't keep the house without . . . Well, we just can't keep it." She looked Robert in the eye, and he felt like a bug pinned to a corkboard. "I'm trying to decide if there's a future for us here."

Robert struggled to swallow and speak, but his mouth felt like sawdust. He was relieved when Delilah stepped forward.

She smiled and extended a packet wrapped in brown paper and tied with twine. "Judith gave me your list. Here's your shopping."

"Oh, thank you," Susanne said without looking away from Robert. "Can you add it to mother's tab?"

"Certainly. Is there anything else?"

"No, this will do. For now." Susanne dimpled at him again.

Robert looked at Delilah—he thought someone should, since she was standing right there. Then he remembered his manners.

"Susanne, this is Delilah—she's helping me run the store now."

"Really?" Susanne drew the word out in a way that made Robert feel as if he needed to scratch.

"Yes, she's been a wonder. Who knows? With the lumber company settling in, we may need to hire even more help."

Susanne made a noncommittal murmur and gathered her children. "It was nice seeing you, Robert—and nice to see what a success you are." She laid a hand on his arm and squeezed before turning and disappearing through the door.

"An old acquaintance?" Delilah asked.

"I suppose you could say that. She's been gone a long time, but she grew up here."

"She has lovely children."

"Yes, I suppose she does."

Robert stared at the door where Susanne had disappeared. Why did he feel as if the weather was about to change?

That evening, Delilah sat at her table eating a bowl of soup. The black-and-white cat that seemed to have adopted her washed itself in the open doorway. It wouldn't quite let her pet it but seemed content with her company. She was trying to come up with a name for the little beast.

Like Robert, she thought. He would only let her get so close. She had begun to believe he was drawn to her—that he might want something more than a business partnership. And in spite of his inability to have children, Delilah had begun to think there might be more important things in life. But she couldn't tell how he felt, in spite of what Charlotte and Emily suggested.

Before she agreed to stay, she and Robert had often shared

meals or quiet moments of companionship when the store was empty. But now it was as though he felt there had to be a measure of formality between them. Was it just for appearances? Or had his feelings changed?

And then there was the moment Susanne had walked in. The look on Robert's face expressed shock and maybe something more. Maybe a wistful, what-might-have-been look. Delilah remembered her sister saying there had once been someone named Susanne in Robert's life. Could this be the same woman?

She sighed and sopped up the last bit of soup with a piece of bread, then tossed a crust in the cat's direction. The cat stopped washing and looked at the offering as though considering whether it was worthy of her. Shaking a paw she tiptoed over to the bread and settled in to nibble at it, keeping one eye on Delilah all the while.

"Suspicious—that's what you are." She sighed and took her bowl to the sink. "And perhaps I am, too."

She turned and leaned against the sink. The cat froze, then resumed eating once it seemed clear Delilah wasn't going to come any closer.

"I'm going to call you Susanne. No, Susie." The cat flicked an ear. "And you know what else? I'm going to befriend Susanne. Her children are lovely, and everyone can use another friend." She turned around and gazed out the window. "Not least of all, me."

The next afternoon, Delilah had the perfect opportunity to begin to get to know Susanne when Emily stopped by with an invitation. "Susanne Ross—well, her last name's something else now—is in town, and I thought it would be nice to hold a quilting bee to help her get reacquainted with some of the women she used to know."

"That's a lovely idea. What can I bring?"

"Oh, we usually bring some sweets to pass, but don't feel like you have to bring anything. There'll be more than enough."

Delilah felt relieved—she hadn't had time to brush up on her cooking skills and felt certain anything she attempted would put her to shame—but when she arrived at the bee empty-handed, she realized bringing something awful would have been more forgivable. She was the only one who didn't have a dish to add to the table in the kitchen, and she was definitely getting some significant looks.

"Never mind," Liza Talbot said, patting her hand. "There's more than enough."

But the look of pity in the older woman's eyes let Delilah know she had committed a faux pas. It was as though the other women thought she was different, set apart somehow—maybe because she'd lived in the city, or maybe because she'd gone into business with Robert.

"I'm surprised to see you here," Susanne commented. "I'd have thought a businesswoman like you would be much too busy to attend a simple quilting bee."

Delilah smiled as best she could. "I like to spend time with my friends, business or no business." She looked around, trying to decide who exactly was her friend. "It must be nice for you to catch up with old friends, too."

"Yes, well, I don't get home as often as I'd like, so we do have some catching up to do. And how long has it been since you were in town?"

"Oh, well, about fifteen years."

Susanne twitched her eyebrows and looked down her nose.

"I suppose you must have been awfully busy in the big city. You don't have any children, do you? That must make things easier."

Delilah bristled. It popped into her head to say that at least she *knew* what happened to her husband, but she made an effort to swallow the words back down. "I suppose it did make things easier in terms of time, but it didn't make me wish for children any less."

She ducked away to find a seat at the quilt frame, but not before she saw a flicker of something in Susanne's eye. Was it a softening? Pity? Delilah wasn't quite as certain she wanted this woman for her friend anymore, but she was still willing to give it a shot.

As the ladies settled in to work, Susanne drifted over, and Delilah patted the spot next to her. "Sit with me, Susanne. Tell me about your little ones."

A tightness around the other woman's eyes eased as she settled into the chair with a sigh.

An hour later Delilah knew more about the four youngsters than she ever hoped to. But what she knew most of all was how badly Susanne wanted a father for them.

"The boys especially need a man they can look up to. They have their grandfather, but he'll never take a firm hand with them. They need someone to teach them . . . " She got a faraway look in her eye. "To teach them how to be men, I suppose. Herbert . . . well, he wasn't exactly a model of good behavior." She flushed. "I've said too much."

Delilah covered Susanne's hand where it rested against the quilt top. "I guess maybe I know a thing or two about falling for a man who turns out to be less gallant than you hoped."

Susanne giggled. "Gallant. Herbert never did seem that. I

just thought he was handsome." She raised her eyebrows and covered her mouth with one hand. "In the beginning."

Laughter bubbled up and Delilah leaned against her new friend's shoulder. Who would have thought? Turns out they had more in common than she anticipated.

8

The next morning the sky spit rain all the way in to work, but thankfully it didn't really open up until Pauline was safely under cover. Once inside the store, Delilah shed her raincoat and head scarf as Robert ambled over. "How was your hen party?"

"It was very nice," she said with a little extra tartness in her voice.

"Don't care for the reference to clucking?" Robert asked. "You'll never convince me there wasn't plenty of it."

Delilah flicked drops of rainwater at him, and once he got over looking surprised, he grinned. "Well, you're in a good mood today, and that's enough for me." He whistled as he opened the front door and pulled barrels and crates out under the porch roof for a sales display.

Delilah patted her hair into place and watched him work as the rain fell beyond him. It was a comfort seeing a man go about his business with such contentment as raindrops pattered on the tin roof. Delilah thought about how Martin never seemed satisfied with his lot in life, and it sounded like Susanne had run into much the same thing with Herbert. Only he decided to go out and try to find something better, abandoning his wife and four children along the way. And now Susanne would be forced to wear the stigma of being a woman scorned. Oh, the cost of the choices made.

"Robert, are you happy?"

He looked at her with eyebrows high. "Happy? I reckon so. Not much point in being otherwise."

"But don't you ever . . ." She tried to think how to put this delicately. "Don't you ever wish things had turned out differently?"

Robert put down the crate of apples he was carrying and leaned his hip against a counter. He crossed his arms and cocked his head to one side. "Are you by any chance asking if I'm mad that I can't have children?" He met her eyes. "Some days I suppose I am a little put out. But I figure God knows better than I do, and this is the life he's given me. Might as well make the most of it."

"But what if you could, say, marry someone who already had children? Wouldn't that be another way of going about it?"

Robert frowned. "I suppose so. Children are a blessing no matter who brings them into the world, but I guess I'll just have to wait and see what the good Lord has in mind." He straightened up. "Now, what's got you thinking along these lines? The weather making you gloomy?"

Delilah glanced out to see that the rain had turned into a soaking downpour. Rain generally soothed her spirit, but it made her feel pensive now. She remembered a song she used to sing to Charlotte on rainy days. "Rain, rain go away, come again another day, little Char wants to play." They'd almost believed if they sang just right the rain really would go away. She sighed. It would be wonderful to have control like that over something. It seemed she had little control over anything these days.

443

She stared out the window, and even as she did the rain slowed, then stopped. Her heart jumped. No, coincidence was all.

She turned back to Robert. "It just seems a shame that people who want children don't necessarily get them, while others have more than they know what to do with."

Pain flashed in Robert's eyes, but somehow Delilah had the feeling it was pain for her rather than him. He stepped forward, and for a moment she felt certain he was going to take her into his arms. But then the bell over the door rang, and someone made a great deal of noise shaking out an umbrella and stomping their feet.

"Thank goodness I left the children at home on such a soggy day." Susanne smiled at the pair inside the store. "I don't suppose you'd have a cup of coffee handy?"

Delilah whirled toward the stove and fussed with the pot and some thick white mugs. "Almost always," she sang out. "Come sit and have a cup."

Susanne clasped a mug in both hands, breathing in the steam. Robert stepped behind the front counter, where he focused on writing in a ledger. Susanne lowered her voice. "Did I interrupt something?"

"Why no. We were having a philosophical discussion. Robert's quite the thinker." She smiled and poured a mug for herself.

"Oh, don't I know it. I used to get so lost listening to him." She snuck a glance over her shoulder. "But when a man is as steadfast as he is, you can learn to tolerate just about anything."

Delilah wondered again if Susanne had set her cap for Robert. Their conversation at the quilting bee had made it clear she wanted a father for her children, and why not Robert? Especially if he really had been her beau once.

"Is it true that you were engaged to Robert?" As soon as the words escaped, Delilah longed to call them back. Not only was it impertinent to ask, she wasn't sure she really wanted to know the answer.

Susanne sputtered on her coffee, then dabbed at her lips with a handkerchief. "As a matter of fact, we were involved in a bit of a romance once, but it never got so far as engagement." She smirked. "Although I'm sure the ladies of the community have constructed their own story around us by now."

Delilah flushed at the thought of being caught listening to gossip. "Oh, no, it's just that someone mentioned Robert once had a girl."

Susanne waved the protestation away. "People talk." She looked sad. "And goodness knows my coming back home without a husband has given them plenty to talk about. I don't know which is worse in their books, being abandoned or getting a divorce. I think some of the old biddies would have more respect for me if I had just put up with whatever Herbert dished out."

"Is Delilah taking good care of you?" Robert asked as he walked past them on the way to the storeroom with an empty crate.

Susanne smiled over the rim of her mug and dimpled at him. "You know, she is. She really and truly is."

In bed that night Delilah tossed and turned in the house that seemed too quiet. She got up to warm a cup of milk and sat in the dark at the kitchen table, watching the stars through the window. Susie sat in a chair opposite, peering at her over the edge of the table and twitching her tail. Delilah thought the feline looked skeptical.

"Do you know what I'm thinking?" she asked. "You look like you do. And like you don't think much of the idea."

She sipped her milk and then thought to put some in a saucer for the cat. Susie watched intently and, once Delilah was reseated, hopped down to lap at the milk as if she had all the time in the world. And she probably did. No cat ever worried about having children or about being left alone in her old age. Delilah sighed and slid down in her seat—who cared about good posture?

"It would be the perfect solution," she said. Susie twitched her ears, but didn't stop drinking. "Robert must have liked her once, and if he married her he'd have children and those poor little ones would have a father. Susanne thinks Robert is a good man, so why in the world not?

"Of course, she'll have to go through with the divorce, but I think Robert is big enough to forgive that. And he's so well liked in the community, surely even the Talbot sisters will come to accept it."

Susie finished her milk and sat blinking at Delilah. She lifted a paw and began to bathe her face.

"And while I like Robert and was beginning to think there might be something between us, I don't know if he could ever think of me romantically. And that would leave me free to find a man who can give me children. Like I said, it's the perfect solution for everyone."

The cat stood and stretched, then wandered over and butted her head against Delilah's leg. Delilah was astonished. She'd been trying and trying to get the cat to come to her. She'd actually given up and accepted that Susie was simply going to do what she wanted. Now here she came. Delilah reached a tentative hand down and stroked the cat's head. Susie's purr sounded rusty, as if it hadn't been used in a long time.

"Well, at least I have you."

The cat just purred.

Robert didn't have any idea what those two females were up to, but whatever it was, it made him jumpy. Susanne seemed to be around the store as often as she was home with her children. Maybe she needed a break and her mother was finally giving it to her. And now she and Delilah were thick as thieves. He'd mostly forgiven his old flame for leaving him in the lurch—they hadn't really had a solid agreement, after all—but he hadn't quite got used to her being around again, either.

She looked up at him from where she and Delilah had dragged out every bolt of fabric in the store and fluttered her lashes. He wished he had something to do outside.

"Reckon I'll give Pauline a bait of grain," he said and hustled for the door.

"Pauline is just fine," Delilah said. "Why don't you fetch the ladder so we can get up there and clean that topmost shelf?"

Robert changed his course and dragged the ladder out from the back room. He leaned it against the shelving and stepped back, bumping into Susanne as he did so.

"Whoops, pardon me."

She laid a hand on his bicep and squeezed. "Oh, it's nothing. It's actually kind of nice to have a man to run into again."

There were those doggone dimples again. Robert flushed and extricated himself, putting the pickle barrel between him and Susanne. His thigh bumped the barrel as he scooted around, and the briny juice sloshed over onto the floor.

"I've got a rag." Susanne stooped to swipe up the liquid, giving Robert a view right down the front of her blouse that really was cut a bit low for helping Delilah around the store.

Robert looked at the ceiling and whispered a prayer. Each of these women could befuddle him individually, but together he felt completely overwhelmed.

"You ladies holler if you need anything else," he said and shot through the back room before they could stop him. He needed air.

Outside he thumped down on the back steps and cradled his head in his hands. What had his world come to? Just when he thought there might be a future for him and Delilah, Susanne showed up with a ready-made family. And if he didn't know better, he'd say she was trying to get his blood up. But was he interested?

Goodness knows she was still a handsome woman, and her fiery personality seemed to have toned down a notch. He'd been attracted to her ten years ago because she was passionate and spontaneous. She once told him that true love could conquer anything, even his inability to have children. And he'd almost believed her. Then she ran off with Herbert Millhouse, and he realized saying something and living it were two different things.

But here she was, back and perhaps wiser from her mistakes. "But she's still married," he muttered.

"She's getting a divorce."

Robert whipped around to see Delilah in the doorway behind him.

"I wanted to make sure you weren't out here spoiling that donkey." She sat down a step higher than Robert and tucked her skirt around her knees. "If you meant Susanne, she's got the paperwork for the divorce. Shouldn't be long till she's free to marry again." A stray wisp of hair blew across her cheek, but she ignored it. "I guess you cared about her once."

"I did, but that was a long time ago. We've both changed quite a bit since then."

Delilah nodded. "Change can be good." She retucked her skirt, smoothing her hands over and over the fabric. "It would certainly be one way to get that family you want."

"What would?"

"Marrying Susanne."

Robert shot to his feet. "Who said anything about getting married?"

Delilah leaned back, away from him a little. "I was just thinking out loud."

"Women. Can't you leave well enough alone?"

Delilah looked like he'd slapped her, but he stomped off to the lean-to and ignored her hurt expression. He'd resigned himself to a life alone. Then he'd begun to imagine he could have a life of companionship with Delilah. And now that very woman was trying to marry him off to an old flame with four children. He wanted a family, sure, but not just any old family that happened along. Women.

Delilah eased back inside to help Susanne finish organizing the fabrics. Susanne gave her a questioning look, but Delilah ignored it. What could she say? That Robert didn't seem nearly as interested in marriage and a family as she'd thought he would? That she'd made him mad and sent him stomping off to keep company with a donkey? She might have just made a mess of things, when all she wanted was for Robert to be happy and four children to have a good father. She slanted a look at Susanne who was preoccupied with sorting the bolts by color.

And a good man for Susanne. . . . She wanted that, too, didn't she? Wasn't that why she encouraged the other woman to spend so much time at the store? She liked her well enough, although she had to admit she wouldn't seek her out like this if she didn't have an ulterior motive.

"Where'd Robert go?" Susanne dropped into a chair, abandoning the work at hand.

"Oh, he just needed to clear his head, I suppose."

Susanne rolled her eyes. "I declare he might be too much effort."

"What do you mean?"

"I'll confess I thought he might still be interested in me, and with four children to raise up, I figured it was worth finding out. He's got a good living, and he's surely decent, even if he's not very exciting. But I'm beginning to think he might be a little too set in his bachelor ways."

Delilah picked up the bolt of fabric Susanne dropped and added it to the stack on the shelf behind her. "Maybe he just needs a little more time to get used to the idea. I mean you are still married . . . technically."

Susanne flipped a hand in the air. "There's plenty of men who wouldn't mind that."

Delilah felt shock but tried to school her expression. The bell on the door jangled, and she turned to offer assistance, but Susanne jumped to her feet.

"I'll take care of it," she said.

Delilah wasn't sure she wanted to give Susanne quite that much leeway in the store, but she bit her tongue. Susanne sashayed over to Joe Miller, who turned red, starting with those unfortunate ears.

"How can I help you today?"

"Why, ain't you Susanne Ross?"

Dimples. "I surely am, back in town after much too long away." Delilah noticed she didn't correct him with her married name. "Aren't you Joe Miller? I seem to remember your daddy owned that big farm just outside of town."

Joe puffed his chest out and explained that he ran the farm now, not to mention a pretty stand of timber the new company moving into town had been out to see. Delilah noticed that somehow Susanne, who couldn't be bothered to listen to Delilah talk about store inventory, was hanging on Joe's every word about cattle breeding and the price of raw lumber. Delilah turned back to the fabrics and did her best not to listen. Perhaps she had misjudged things all along.

9

Delilah was late. Robert tried to keep busy. No need to worry. Pauline might be sick. Or maybe Delilah overslept. There were plenty of perfectly good reasons why a woman might take her time coming in of a morning. Never mind that in the five or so months she'd been part of his life she'd never once been late.

Part of his life. She was that. And ever since she'd been so plain in speaking to him about Susanne's need for a husband he'd realized that neither Susanne nor any woman but Delilah herself would suit him. It would be her or no one. His last chance at marital bliss.

A sound outside sent him hurrying to the door. Sure enough, Delilah drove up and pulled the donkey cart to a stop. He hurried out to take the reins from her and help her down.

"Oh, Robert, I know I'm late. The Talbot sisters stopped by, and the time got away from me. I'm so very sorry."

"Don't fret. Business is slow this morning. Nothing going on here that can't wait."

He stabled Pauline, noticing there was a nip to the air, just as there should be in early October, but it occurred to him that a

452

donkey cart was going to be a rough sort of transportation once winter set in. He would have to talk to Delilah about coming up with another transportation plan before too long. He could drive out and pick her up, but something told him she'd balk at that idea. Shoot, he'd give her the use of his car and walk to the store, but she probably wouldn't like that either.

He stepped inside, meaning to tackle the subject of transportation, but Delilah seemed flustered. She drifted around the store with a sack of cornmeal in one hand and a tin whistle in the other. He walked over and took the whistle from her.

"What are you doing?"

"I was going to put this sack of meal away when I saw the whistle sitting in the wrong place, and I guess I forgot where I was headed."

Robert led her over to the stove and poured her a fresh cup of coffee. "Is there anything wrong?"

Delilah's hand shook a little as she accepted the mug and sipped the bitter brew. "I guess I didn't expect the news the Talbot sisters brought me."

"Is everything all right?" Robert shifted a chair, and Delilah sat.

"It seems . . ." She flicked a glance over Robert's face and then stared into her mug. "It seems Susanne has moved in out at the Miller place."

Robert raised his eyebrows and sat next to Delilah. "Well now, that is a piece of news."

"Angie says he's promised to marry her as soon as the divorce is final, but she saw no reason to wait to move her bunch out there. I guess it was pretty crowded at her mother's, and Joe has that big rambling farmhouse." She made a face. "The Talbot sisters felt I should know lest her bad example rub off on me, a single woman."

Robert tried to hide a smile as Delilah darted a look at him and then looked again, longer this time. "Do you mind very much?"

Robert knit his brow. "Mind? Well, it isn't one hundred percent proper, but who am I to judge? I guess what they do is between them and God."

"I mean . . . about losing Susanne to another man?"

Robert laughed, but then saw Delilah was serious and sobered. "I lost her to another man more than a decade ago. Did you suppose we'd just pick up where we left off?"

"Well, it would have given you a family."

Robert exhaled sharply through his nose. "Do you suppose that having children any which way I can is all that matters to me? If there's one thing I know after all these years, it's that you lose every time you try to outmaneuver God."

He reached over and tilted her chin up so she looked at him. "If God means for me to have children, he'll show me the way. Look what happened when Sarah talked Abraham into fathering a child by another woman. Grief. Nothing but grief. And God had a better plan all along."

Delilah touched Robert's fingers where they skimmed her chin. Tears shone in her eyes. "I'm trying to trust his plan," she said.

Robert grasped her fingers and was about to lift them to his lips when the bell rang over the door. He jumped, but Delilah was even quicker, moving away from him and halfway to the door before he could think. He turned to see Emily Phillips hand over her shopping list. He felt certain God had a plan. He just wished he knew what it was.

Delilah held the fat envelope with her address scrawled across the front. Charlotte had sent it from Comstock, and Delilah wanted to savor the anticipation of reading what she hoped would be good news from her sister. She made a pot of tea and pulled out a loaf of zucchini bread Emily had made for her. Once everything was ready, she opened the letter and smoothed the pages out on the table in front of her.

Charlotte wrote about the new house, which was indeed bigger, with a spare room that Delilah would be welcome to use. She wrote about Perla's school and how well she was doing there—how Perla had nearly taken over the cooking for the whole family and seemed to have a real knack for it. She wrote about Comstock and the kind people they'd met, about Ed's job and how he was definitely going to be promoted to engineer, which would mean a raise in pay. It was even more wonderful than Charlotte had dared hope.

Delilah broke off another piece of the moist bread and popped it in her mouth, savoring the undercurrent of cinnamon. Charlotte's description made the move sound like the best thing that had ever happened to the family.

Ah, and there was a postscript. Delilah scanned down to see a note from Perla at the bottom of the last page.

"Aunt Delilah, I think you might like to get married again one day, and my new teacher, Mr. Smathers, is wonderful. He's handsome, and his wife died two years ago. He lives with his mother, who helps take care of his little girl. I think his wife died having her. Anyway, I think you'd like him. Love, Perla."

Delilah smiled. Even her niece was playing matchmaker. Well, she knew firsthand how that sort of thing could turn out. She took her dishes to the sink and rinsed the plate and cup. That would do for supper.

She walked out into the waning light and breathed in the cool, autumn air. There was a faint scent of decaying leaves.

She closed her eyes and savored it, wishing there were someone to share moments like this with. Someone to slip outside and wrap a shawl around her shoulders as they watched the moon climb over the top of the mountains and on into the sky. Maybe even to wrap his arms around her shoulders.

She needed companionship. Maybe she should visit her sister. Just to see how the family was getting on.

Robert was more than happy to spare Delilah for four or five days. Well, not happy exactly, but he wanted her to be happy, and she certainly worked hard enough to earn a little time away to visit her family. And anyway, he needed space to think over what, exactly, he was going to do about this woman.

"Looking forward to seeing that niece of yours?" he asked as Delilah swept the already clean floorboards.

"Very much. I hate that she mostly grew up without me, and I want to be more important in her life from here on out. Who knows, maybe she can come stay with me sometime."

"I'll bet she'd enjoy that. Do you have any big plans while you're in Comstock? Shops to visit? Trains to ride?"

Delilah pinked. "Oh, nothing special. Just seeing family." She put the broom away and wiped the counter for the third time. "Maybe meeting some of Charlotte's new friends."

Robert nodded and went on about his business, but later that last phrase struck him. Delilah meeting new people. What if Ed was working with some bachelor who took a fancy to Delilah? Or what if she met a man while attending church with Charlotte? Comstock was probably lousy with men in want of a good wife. What if she met someone new?

Robert kicked the counter he stood behind while customers

browsed. He could lose a good business partner and a good woman if he didn't make a move sooner rather than later.

Delilah was on her way home when a truck pulled up beside her, and Susanne leaned out the window, waving. Delilah clucked Pauline to a stop and waited as Susanne gestured to Joe to pull over to the side of the road. She hopped out of the shiny new Ford and hurried toward the pony cart.

"Delilah, I'm so glad we ran into you." She giggled. "Well, thank goodness we didn't actually run into you in that ridiculous contraption you drive."

Delilah sighed. She didn't know what to say to this woman she'd tried to befriend and who had chosen a path Delilah didn't quite approve of.

Susanne sobered. "I've been meaning to get by the store, but Joe took me to do my shopping over in Davis—oh my, the stores are wonderful—and I haven't had an excuse to pop in since. Plus we're just so busy giving the farm a feminine touch. And the children have school, and . . . Well, you know how life can get away from you."

Delilah supposed she did, although she would have given almost anything to have the list of distractions Susanne had outlined. Well, she'd give anything except her virtue. She sighed and tried to steer her thinking back toward grace and mercy. "I do know, and while I've missed seeing you, I understand."

Susanne grabbed Delilah's hand. "I just wanted to thank you for being a good friend. I think you probably tried to steer Robert Thornton my way, and I appreciate it, but I suspect that man has other ideas."

She glanced back toward the truck, where Joe Miller was

making calf eyes at her. She twiddled her fingers at him. "Anyway, I once said something silly and romantic to Robert about love overcoming anything, and while I was just talking at the time, I wanted to tell you that deep down . . ." She laid a hand over her bosom. "I believe that to be true. At least for people who have the time and inclination to wait for love."

She squeezed Delilah's hand. "And all that time I spent watching you and Robert work side by side at the store . . . well, it makes me think you don't have to wait anymore. Now, don't get me wrong, I'd have married Robert if he'd been willing, but it probably would have been a waste when he's obviously in love with you." She smiled and started back toward the truck, turning to throw a few last words over her shoulder. "Waste not, want not, I say."

Delilah lifted her hand to wave good-bye as the couple sped on down the road. Did Susanne have any idea what she was talking about? Goodness knows Delilah admired Robert, and now that she wasn't trying to find him a ready-made family . . .

Pauline shook her head, jingling the harness.

"You're right, Pauline. I probably need a good shake. Let's get on home."

But somehow Delilah couldn't get Susanne's words out of her head. She found it so easy to help folks find just what they wanted at the store, and she'd always thought she knew just what she wanted, too—a husband who could give her a houseful of children. But now she wondered. Was she wasting a good thing? Or was she just destined to be alone?

10

"You all set for your trip this weekend?" Robert admired the way Delilah unpacked a box of sample china she'd ordered. Competent—that's what she was, supremely competent.

"I think so. Casewell will drive me to the train station in Davis, and I'm only carrying the one suitcase. I think everything's taken care of. And Emily will drop by to make sure Susie has something to eat."

"Susie?"

"My cat."

Oh. She had a cat. Why didn't he know that?

"I'd have been glad to give you a ride."

"I know." She began wiping each plate down with a soft rag. "But I hated to take you away from the store. One of these days I'll have my own car and I won't need to rely on anyone to drive me." She looked pensive. "Although I'll miss talking to Pauline as I travel around."

Robert grinned. Of course she talked to that donkey. "Speaking of a car, I was wondering what you plan to do once the snow starts flying. It can get mighty cold around here."

Delilah began wiping another plate—this one with blue forget-me-nots. "I suppose I'll dress more warmly. Maybe heat a brick to go under my feet. My grandparents went everywhere by wagon. Why shouldn't I?"

Robert scratched the back of his head. This wouldn't do. Not at all. But he had to tread carefully lest he offend her.

"Supposing someone who cared for your well-being wanted to lend you a car?" He saw a look of annoyance flash in her eyes. "Just when the weather's bad."

"Someone who cares for my well-being will leave well enough alone." She finished wiping the plate and set it down so she could put her hands on her hips. "I always thought I needed a husband and children, but I've been getting along just fine on my own since Martin died. Why does everyone suddenly think I need a man to survive?"

Robert wasn't sure what button he'd pushed, but he scrambled to find the off switch. "Who's talking about a man?"

"Susanne, Emily, Charlotte, even Perla. They all act like they know so much, but I'm a grown woman with two good eyes, and if—" She clapped a hand over her mouth.

"If what?" Robert felt as if she'd been about to say something very important. Something he wanted to hear.

She turned away from him. "If I wanted a car, I'd get it for myself."

Now that wasn't what he'd been expecting. Robert suddenly had the sense that this was his best shot. He needed to speak his piece before she went off to Comstock and found who knew what. Maybe he'd have to let her go, but he wouldn't do it without throwing his hat in the ring first.

"I think you were going to say something else."

Delilah's mouth dropped open. "What?"

"I think you were talking about something other than cars." Robert crossed his arms across his chest and stared her down.

"I . . . Well, I'm not sure what I was going to say." She picked up a china cup and flipped it over as though to read the imprint on the bottom.

"What is it that you want?" Robert held his hands out, palms up. "I mean really want?"

Tears glistened in Delilah's eyes but didn't fall. She sank onto a stool and clicked the cup in her hand into its matching saucer. "I'm not sure anymore."

Robert longed to take two steps and gather her up into his arms, but he kept his feet rooted to the spot. "Seems like you almost always know what folks want when they come in here— even when they don't know themselves."

"I do," Delilah agreed. "It's the strangest thing. It's like I can see what would please them, what would fit into their lives, like this cup fits into its saucer." She ran a finger over the delicate handle. "And I always knew what I wanted— children. When I was twelve or so, Frances Colton—my Sunday school teacher—told me I'd make a wonderful mother. I guess I treated that comment almost like a prophecy." She slowly spun the cup as though examining the pattern. "Maybe I haven't given any other future a chance."

Robert wished she'd look at him, but she kept her eyes on that fool rose-strewn cup. He took a step and reached out to still her hand. And then it seemed natural to lift her fingers in his. She let him, finally turning glistening eyes toward him. She was so lovely his breath caught, but he freed it up enough to speak.

"I don't pretend to know what your future holds. But I know what I want mine to include." He gripped her fingers a little tighter before she could pull away. "And if it's family you want, well, I may not be able to give you children, but I can give you this." With his free hand he indicated everything around them.

"The store? Robert, that's generous, but I'm not sure the store is what I want either. I—"

"Not the store." Robert tugged on her hand until she stood. "I can give you my family. I've been running this store for more years than I care to count, and in that time I've gotten to know just about everyone in Wise. Gotten to know them well."

He reached out to touch her cheek. "I can give you two spinster aunts named Liza and Angie. I can give you a little brother named Casewell. I can give you more cousins than you can count on all your fingers and toes. And as for children, I feel confident Susanne will give us the use of hers any time we'd like to borrow them. We can host sledding parties in the winter, church picnics in the summer, harvest celebrations in the fall, and just about any other kind of gathering you can think of. And best of all, God will always be Father to us all."

Delilah stood as though mesmerized, gazing into his eyes. Her tears were falling now, but she looked almost happy in spite of them. Robert caught a tear and looked at it shining on his finger.

"Delilah, this store is the heart of the community, and you . . . You're my heart. I'm not sure how it happened, but if I were to lose you, this secondhand heart I have beating in my chest might go on, but my family would never be complete." He tugged her closer and captured her empty hand in his. "I want a family, too. A family with you as its very heartbeat."

Robert held his breath and gazed at the woman he loved. It was up to her now.

Delilah couldn't quite make sense of what she was feeling. It was almost overwhelming. She'd been looking so long for that elusive something she wanted. She'd always thought it was children—the love of little hearts beating with her very own blood. A connection closer than any other. But as Robert spoke and as he drew her ever closer, she began to realize what she wanted was more. And less.

What she wanted was to belong. She thought that would happen once she was the center of a home filled with family. But as she let her gaze drift around the store, she realized she already belonged—right here at the center of a family orchestrated by God. And this family loved her. Ever since Delilah had helped her pick out fabric, Maddie had asked her opinion on every purchase. And Emily had become a dear friend. Casewell *was* like a little brother. And Liza and Angie had grown dearer to her than she could ever have imagined.

Delilah gasped, and Robert looked alarmed. "Robert . . . I have a family—with children even. Not just here, but in Comstock, too."

He smiled and twined his fingers with hers. "A big one. It'll probably get bigger yet."

The tears fell faster, but now Delilah smiled through them. She laughed aloud and flung her arms around Robert's neck. "Robert Thornton, what are you saying to me?"

He returned the embrace and then drew back far enough to see her face. "I'm saying I want you for my wife. I'm saying I want you to be smack in the middle of my vast, extended family."

Delilah couldn't contain the joy bubbling up inside her. She kissed Robert once full on the mouth. She'd wanted a husband and a family for so long—and she'd almost missed it thinking she knew just how it would look. But God knew better all along.

"You know, that's exactly what I want, too," she said.

About the Authors

Christy Award finalist and winner of the ACFW Carol Award, HOLT Medallion, and Inspirational Reader's Choice Award, bestselling author **Karen Witemeyer** writes historical romances because she believes the world needs more happily-ever-afters. She is an avid cross-stitcher and shower singer, and she bakes a mean apple cobbler. Karen makes her home in Abilene, Texas, with her husband and three children. To learn more about Karen and her books and to sign up for her free newsletter featuring special giveaways and behind-the-scenes information, please visit www.karenwitemeyer.com.

Jody Hedlund is the bestselling author of multiple novels, including *Love Unexpected*, *Captured by Love*, *Rebellious Heart*, and *The Preacher's Bride*. She holds a bachelor's degree from Taylor University and a master's degree from the University of Wisconsin, both in social work. Jody lives in Michigan with her husband and five children. Learn more at www.jodyhedlund.com.

Much to her introverted self's delight, ACFW Carol Award winner **Melissa Jagears** hardly needs to leave her home to be a homeschooling mother and novelist. She doesn't have to leave her house to be a housekeeper either, but she's doubtful she meets the minimum qualifications to claim to be one in her official bio. Her passion is to help Christian believers mature in their faith and judge rightly. Find her online at www.melissa jagears. com, Facebook, Pinterest, and Goodreads. To be certain to hear of Melissa's new releases, giveaways, bargains, and exclusive subscriber content, please subscribe to her email newsletter located on her webpage or at http://bit.ly/jagearsnewsletter.

Jen Turano, the author of seven novels, is a graduate of the University of Akron with a degree in clothing and textiles. She is a member of ACFW and lives in a suburb of Denver, Colorado. Visit her website at www.jenturano.com.

Sarah Loudin Thomas is a fundraiser for children's ministry who has also published freelance writing for *Mountain Homes Southern Style* and *Now & Then* magazines, as well as the *Asheville Citizen-Times* and *The Journey Christian Newspaper*. She holds a bachelor's degree in English from Coastal Carolina University. She and her husband reside in Asheville, North Carolina. Learn more at www.sarahloudinthomas.com.

Books by Karen Witemeyer

A Tailor-Made Bride

Head in the Clouds

To Win Her Heart

Short-Straw Bride

Stealing the Preacher

Full Steam Ahead

A Worthy Pursuit

No Other Will Do

A Cowboy Unmatched from
A Match Made in Texas: A Novella Collection

Love on the Mend: A Full Steam Ahead *Novella*

The Husband Maneuver
from *With This Ring? A Novella Collection*

Books by Jody Hedlund

The Preacher's Bride

The Doctor's Lady

Unending Devotion

A Noble Groom

Rebellious Heart

Captured by Love

BEACONS OF HOPE

Out of the Storm: A Novella

Love Unexpected

Hearts Made Whole

Undaunted Hope

Books by Melissa Jagears

Love by the Letter: A Novella

A Bride for Keeps

A Bride in Store

A Bride at Last

Engaging the Competition
from *With This Ring? A Novella Collection*

A Heart Most Certain

Books by Jen Turano

Books by Sarah Loudin Thomas

APPALACHIAN BLESSINGS

Appalachian Serenade: A Novella

Miracle in a Dry Season

Until the Harvest

A Tapestry of Secrets

More From the Authors

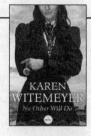

When the women's colony of Harper's Station is threatened, founder Emma Chandler is forced to admit she needs help. The only man she trusts enough to ask is Malachi Shaw, whose life she once saved. As Mal returns the favor, danger mounts—and so does the attraction between them.

No Other Will Do by Karen Witemeyer
karenwitemeyer.com

Upon her arrival in Eagle Harbor, Michigan, Tessa Taylor is dismayed to learn the town asked for a *male* teacher. Mercifully, they agree to let her stay for the winter. As Tessa throws herself into teaching, two brothers begin vying for her hand, and danger seems to haunt her steps. . . .

Undaunted Hope by Jody Hedlund
BEACONS OF HOPE #3
jodyhedlund.com

To impress the politician courting her and help her family, Lydia King is determined to obtain a donation to the Teaville Moral Society from the wealthiest man in town, Nicholas Lowe. But as complications arise, Lydia must decide where her beliefs—and heart—truly align.

A Heart Most Certain by Melissa Jagears
TEAVILLE MORAL SOCIETY
melissajagears.com

You May Also Enjoy . . .

When a fan's interest turns sinister, young actress Lucetta Plum takes refuge on a secluded estate owned by her friend's eligible yet eccentric grandson. As hijinks and hilarity ensue, and danger catches up to Lucetta, will her friends be able to protect her?

Playing the Part by Jen Turano
jenturano.com

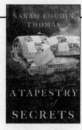

Perla Phillips has carried a secret for over sixty years. When she sees her granddaughter, Ella, struggling, Perla decides to share her story—then suffers a debilitating stroke. As Ella and her aunt look into her grandmother's past, they'll learn more than they expected about Perla, faith, and each other.

A Tapestry of Secrets by Sarah Loudin Thomas
sarahloudinthomas.com

Stella West has quit the art world and moved to Boston to solve the mysterious death of her sister, but she is in need of a well-connected ally. Fortunately, magazine owner Romulus White has been trying to hire her for years. Sparks fly when Stella and Romulus join forces, but will their investigation cost them everything?

From This Moment by Elizabeth Camden
elizabethcamden.com

◊ BETHANYHOUSE